Prai

THE INVINCIB

"A girl with unusual spunk and an inn   an
determined to forge her own destiny in Penny Haw's beautifully written novel.
In a world where women are relegated to needlepoint and parlor chairs, Aleen
sets her sights on barns and veterinary surgery. Her journey to become the
impossible is inspiring, heartwarming, and ultimately triumphant."

—Lisa Wingate, #1 *New York Times* bestselling
author of *The Book of Lost Friends*

"I loved *The Invincible Miss Cust*. The book is an important reminder of how
hard women have had to fight for the right to work and study. From Ireland to
France, I enjoyed every moment of Aleen Cust's unpredictable journey. What a
remarkable woman—and what an enthralling story!"

—Janet Skeslien Charles, *New York Times* bestselling author of *The Paris Library*

"*The Invincible Miss Cust* is an absolute delight, an exceptional, immersive work
of historical fiction set amid the beautifully detailed landscapes of Ireland and
England. Readers are sure to adore and admire Aleen Cust for her compassion
for animals as well as her courage as they follow the unpredictable twists and
turns of her enthralling story."

—Jennifer Chiaverini, *New York Times*
bestselling author of *Switchboard Soldiers*

"I loved this gripping and inspirational book! Aleen Cust's story is one of a
heroine for all ages, defying family censure and social barriers to fulfill her ambition. Her courage and independence of spirit shine through on every beautifully
written page as she faces life's triumphs and tragedies. I cheered her on every step
of the way."

—Fiona Valpy, bestselling author of *The Dressmaker's Gift*

"A skillfully told story of an extraordinary woman's grit, determination, and
devotion to her dream of becoming Great Britain's first female veterinary surgeon. Haw brings Aleen Cust to vivid life, from her aristocratic but stifled childhood to her difficult days at school to her eventual acceptance as a highly skilled
vet—all the while fighting a patriarchal system designed to thwart her every step.
Detailed and evocative, *The Invincible Miss Cust* is an engrossing read."

—Shana Abé, *New York Times* bestselling author of *The Second Mrs. Astor*

"A vivid, compelling story of a daring and determined woman. Emotionally rich and bringing light to an incredible life and legacy, you won't want to miss this inspiring novel of England's first female veterinary surgeon."

—Audrey Blake, *USA Today* bestselling author of *The Girl in His Shadow*

"An amazing story! *The Invincible Miss Cust* introduces readers to Aleen Cust, Britain and Ireland's first female veterinary surgeon, and we are better for the acquaintance. Haw's descriptive prose and deft characterizations lead us through Cust's remarkable life, setbacks, and triumphs, and leave us in awe of her perseverance, determination, and loyalty."

—Katherine Reay, bestselling author of
The London House and *The Printed Letter Bookshop*

"A gripping story of one woman's unrelenting quest to treat and care for our four-legged friends. Readers will be rooting for Aleen as she comes up against and triumphs over a mountain of obstacles. A must-read for all animal lovers."

—Renée Rosen, *USA Today* bestselling author of *The Social Graces*

"*The Invincible Miss Cust* is the gripping true story of a young woman who dreams of becoming a veterinary surgeon. Aleen Cust is a determined free spirit whose love for animals surpasses the challenges and hardships faced by a woman pursuing a profession in the 1890s, a time when women were rarely allowed to dream of an education or a career. Readers of James Herriot will find this a delightful, inspiring read."

—Julia Bryan Thomas, author of *For Those Who Are Lost*

"This work of historical fiction is a powerful portrait of an inspiring woman whose stubborn determination and passion for her calling drove her to defy her family's wishes, stand up to the sexist norms of society, and take the reins of her own life no matter the cost. Bravo!"

—Samantha Greene Woodruff, author of *The Lobotomist's Wife*

"Penny Haw takes us deep into the heart and choices of Aleen Cust, who defied convention to become Britain's first woman veterinary surgeon. A vivid, beautifully written, and compelling novel."

—Louisa Treger, author of *Madwoman* and *The Dragon Lady*

"A fascinating true story of a woman determined to become a veterinarian in the late 1800s. Aleen Cust is everything I love in a heroine: fiery, determined, confident, and smart. No matter what life threw at her, Aleen continued to pursue her passion. We could all learn a thing or two from Aleen Cust."

—Martha Conway, award-winning author of *The Physician's Daughter*

THE INVINCIBLE MISS CUST

a novel

— PENNY HAW —

sourcebooks
landmark

Published by Sourcebooks Landmark, an imprint of Sourcebooks
P.O. Box 4410, Naperville, Illinois 60567-4410
(630) 961-3900
sourcebooks.com

Library of Congress Cataloging-in-Publication Data

Names: Haw, Penny, author.
Title: The invincible Miss Cust : a novel / Penny Haw.
Description: Naperville, Illinois : Sourcebooks Landmark, [2022] | Includes
    bibliographical references.
Identifiers: LCCN 2022006668 (print) | LCCN 2022006669 (ebook) | (trade paperback) | (epub)
Subjects: LCSH: Cust, Aleen, 1868-1937--Fiction. | LCGFT: Biographical
    fiction.
Classification: LCC PR9369.4.H385 I58 2022 (print) | LCC PR9369.4.H385
    (ebook) | DDC 823/.92--dc23/eng/20220322
LC record available at https://lccn.loc.gov/2022006668
LC ebook record available at https://lccn.loc.gov/2022006669

Printed and bound in Canada.
MBP 10 9 8 7 6 5 4 3 2 1

For Sebastiaan,
who taught me more than anyone.

CHAPTER 1

1874
Tipperary, Ireland

BEFORE I DISCOVERED THAT THERE WAS MORE TO ASPIRE TO, I DREAMED of becoming a jockey. Not just any jockey, mind you. I wanted to be Harry Custance, who, in 1874, won the Epsom Derby for the third time. Because the English jockey had also ridden winners in the 1000 Guineas Stakes, Ascot Gold Cup, and St. Leger Stakes, Custance's fame had reached as far as the Premier County—that is, Tipperary in Ireland—where I, a horse-loving, adventure-seeking six-year-old girl, lived with my family.

"Let's race from here to Ram's Field," I urged as my brothers and I turned toward home on a ride one afternoon. "The winner shall be addressed as Harry Custance by the others for the rest of the day."

Orlando and Leo glanced at Charles, whose Thoroughbred, Pebbles, had the tall, lean look and nervy disposition of a racehorse. My strawberry-roan Welsh pony, Taffy, was several hands shorter than the other horses, and while I was only slightly shorter than my brothers when standing alongside them, I was younger than Charles, Orlando, and Leo by four, three, and two years, respectively. Being younger did not temper my self-assurance. In fact, it spurred my competitiveness.

Charles stretched his neck to peer over the dense hedge ahead of us. "Over both gates and fields?"

"Yes. The horse that lands on the other side of the wall first is the winner," I said, straightening my reins.

Orlando blinked in surprise, and Leo stared at Charles, his mouth ajar like that of a landed fish. They too, I saw, expected Charles to oppose the idea of me racing them. It would have been typical of our oldest sibling to bow to our parents' decree that "competitive little girls are terribly unladylike." However, the probability of victory, it emerged, was too tempting—even for the most compliant of the Cust family.

We lined up, our horses tossing their heads and stamping their hooves into the soft turf as they sensed our excitement.

"Ready?" said Charles from his high horse. Three heads nodded.

"Go!" he shouted.

Taffy was as eager to beat my brothers as I was. She took off like a grouse from the heather. I crouched low against her neck, my hands high on her mane. While his horse's head was level with my saddle for the first few yards, Leo soon fell back. I knew I would beat him. He had a poor sense of how to pace a horse and lacked the true will to win. Charles and Orlando, though, were quickly ahead. Taffy's legs might have moved faster, but her stride was shorter.

As I looked up, I saw the muscles in Pebbles's thighs flex as she launched over the first gate. Orlando's gray took off seconds later. Taffy did not hesitate at the obstacle, and as we landed on the other side, I saw mud spattering from the hooves ahead. I had not anticipated the wet patch, however small, on the hallowed fields of Tipperary.

I leaned to the left, steering my pony away from the sludge that had slowed Orlando and allowed Charles to extend his lead. Despite having to change her line, Taffy did not reduce her speed and made good headway across the dry ground. As we neared the second gate, we were neck and neck with Orlando.

"Faster!" I shouted, laughing as Taffy responded to my voice by lowering her head and lengthening her stride. How game she was.

Orlando and his horse were taken by surprise. A fraction's hesitation on their part allowed Taffy and me to vault the second gate ahead of them.

"Hey!" cried Orlando, the surprise in his voice tinged with amusement. I laughed louder.

Charles and Pebbles were not quite halfway across the final field. The wall was in sight, but because of the unexpected earlier encounter with the mud, or because of the angle she took over the second gate, or maybe because Charles was complacent and not paying attention, Pebbles was not following the most direct route to the finish. There was time and space for Taffy and me to arrive ahead.

"Faster, Taffy, faster," I whispered now, lying low against her neck again, imagining that Charles would be less likely to spot his mistake if my face was hidden.

The pony responded with vigor. She was powerful, fit, and determined. By the time Charles realized that Pebbles was not galloping directly toward the gap in the wall, we were alongside them. I steered Taffy to the right, swerving in front of Charles so close that Pebbles took fright and faltered, allowing us to leap ahead over the wall.

As I pulled up, victorious, and watched my older brothers on their larger horses jump the stones into Ram's Field, I had never felt taller. Charles pointed Pebbles toward the gate leading out of the paddock and rode away. Orlando stopped alongside me, shaking his head. We laughed as we followed our brother to the road. Laughing with Orlando was easy and frequent.

"You veered into my path before the wall," said Charles as, a little later, we rode down the lane toward Cordangan Manor, our horses still breathing hard.

"*I* am Harry Custance," I replied, smiling at him.

"It was unsporting," he continued in a tone that reminded me of our father's.

There was, in fact, much of Papa about Charles, with his furrowed brow, rare smile, and a posture as stiff as that of a startled cat, but Charles also had our mother's deep sense of decorum. *Manners maketh man. Do not draw attention to oneself for fear of being at odds with one's place in society. Being polite is more important than being right.* Just thinking about the restraint required to yield to such demands made me weary.

I stretched forward and rubbed Taffy's sodden neck. The whiff of damp leather and sweat was a smell of happiness. My heart swelled with affection and pride. What a pony she was.

"That is how racing works," I said. "Every horse should be run to the best of her ability in the interests of the race."

Charles did not reply, and for a while, we rode quietly. The pastures around us were, Orlando had told me, part of the Golden Vein of Ireland, named as such not only because it was beautiful but also because it was the finest dairy farming land in the country. Certainly, the cows in the region were sleek, their udders plump, and their milk rich and creamy, but I wondered about the horses. Was Taffy not the finest pony in the land? Was that also because she was fed in the pastures of the Golden Vein of Ireland? I looked over the hedges toward the green hills that created soft waves against the sky and tried to stop smiling. It was difficult.

Orlando spoke as we turned into the yard. "Perhaps we should not say anything to Papa."

"Why not?" I asked, joy still governing my thoughts and clouding reason.

"He will chastise you for being unladylike."

"For racing you? Or beating you?"

"Both."

"And for gloating," said Charles.

It was true. Our parents would be displeased by my behavior. It was bad enough that I went riding with the boys. Mama wanted me to stay indoors and practice my manners, deportment, needlework, and music. I tried to please her, but an hour in the drawing room was interminable.

Moreover, the boy-girl divergence made no sense to me. I was as able and energetic as my brothers. More so even. Had I not just beaten them? Why should my life be different? Sitting in the house, pushing and pulling a needle and thread through cloth, or playing scales (I had never progressed further) on the pianoforte bored me. I would tug at my collar, stare through the window, and see our Newfoundland dog, Goliath, gazing back at me, his dark eyes pleading for adventure.

Nanny told me that Goliath had been at my side from the moment I was taken from my mother, cleaned, swaddled, and placed in my crib. He was, she said, the reason I learned to walk so young. I clutched his shaggy neck and, pillowing my face in his black fur, pulled myself up, and toddled alongside him. We had been walking side by side ever since.

I glanced at Orlando. He gave a small smile and shrugged. His eyes, with their remarkably long, thick lashes, were apologetic. I knew Orlando felt sorry about robbing me of my bragging rights, but he disliked discord more.

"Perhaps if I tell Papa, he will allow me to come hunting with you," I said, pouting now.

"He will not. He will be incensed. Anyway, you are too young. Papa says girls can only hunt when they are twelve," said Charles, staring straight ahead.

It felt as if he had won the race after all.

As I dismounted and handed Taffy's reins to the groom, I looked around for Goliath. Although he was old and gray-muzzled, the dog never failed to greet me when I returned to the manor. The groom pointed to a stable.

"He's in there, miss," he said. "Been there for hours, whimpering quietly about his old bones."

Goliath created a large, shaggy mound in the hay. Curled up, facing the wall, he was no longer crying but did not stir when I called his name. He briefly opened his eyes as I knelt beside him and ran my hand across his back.

"What's wrong, boy? Come. Let's go."

He did not move, not even his tail.

I ran to the house and found my mother at her writing desk in the drawing room.

"We have to call the doctor. Goliath is ill."

She looked up and sighed. "I beg your pardon, young lady? Would you like to try that again without barging into the room as if pursued by wolves?"

"But Mama, please. He won't get up. There is something terribly wrong with him."

"The dog is old, Aleen. You understand, do you not? He is old and his time has come."

My mouth was dry, and my stomach felt hollow, as if I had not eaten all day. I swallowed. "But he was fine this morning. I know he is old, but I don't think that is why he is unwell now. Please, can I call the doctor, Mama? I'll ride to Tipperary town myself and ask him to come. Perhaps he can do something."

She stood and walked toward me, glancing at my mud-spattered riding habit. My mother was, as ever, immaculate. Her small, sleek frame was clad in an olive-green dress with vertical seams and tucks that molded the fabric snugly to her waist before blossoming into a bustle below. The black buttons that formed a tight line down the center of her bodice were as shiny as the dark coil of hair that rested on the back of her neck. I pushed a wayward red curl from my face and hid my hands, still in my grubby riding gloves, behind my back.

"You are not going anywhere except upstairs to wash and dress for dinner," she said.

"But there is something wrong with him. Perhaps he has eaten poison, and if we—"

"The doctor will not attend to a dog. Do not be foolish, Aleen. You are six years old. You must learn to be gracious and accept that Goliath is a very old dog. Let him go without a fuss."

I stared at her, overcome by helplessness. It would not do to argue with my mother. It would be impudent, no matter how unreasonable she was being. I felt hot with frustration. How was it possible that nothing could be done for Goliath? He was part of the family. He was my friend. I understood that he was old and that old animals, like old people, died, but it made no sense to me that he would be fine one day and dying the next. What if he had swallowed something that made him ill? Or been stung by an insect and could be treated? Why would my mother not even try to help him? How could she be so heartless? I ran from the room.

That night, I took a blanket from my bed, crept out of the house, and went to the stables. Goliath lay exactly where he had been hours earlier. I curved my body around his and pulled the blanket over us.

I woke up in my bed the next morning.

"We've buried him, miss," said the groom as I tugged at the stable door. "I'm sorry."

My sobbing had subsided by the time Orlando found me beneath the trees at the river. It was one of my favorite places at Cordangan. Goliath and I had spent many happy afternoons weaving between the alders and crossing the river back and forth wherever the boulders allowed. Today, though, I sat on a rock, watching the water as it ran quick and clear over and around the mossy river stones, curling into graceful eddies where the pools were deeper.

Although it was not quite spring, the light green fuzz of the trees' leaves—which, but for the color, reminded me of the fine fur on kittens' ears—held the promise of it. It was, however, cold in the shade, and I was too miserable to move into the sunshine. It seemed fitting that I should be punished by the chill. How was it possible that I had slept, allowed myself to be carried to my bed, as Goliath took his final breath? I should have been awake to comfort him. I was not only cold but empty too, as if someone had forgotten to stoke the fire that usually burned within me.

Orlando stood on the riverbank watching me for a moment, his eyes glassy.

"Mama says you are to come to the house for lessons. Mr. Walsh is here," he said eventually.

I stood and made my way up the path. Orlando held out a hand to help me. I ignored it, pushed past him, and marched ahead through the meadow.

My parents were standing near the entrance of the manor, my father's horse, Hero, waiting for him to mount. I kept my head down and made my way to the front door.

"Aleen," said my mother, "come here."

I approached, eyes down. I did not trust myself to look at her. My anger at her for not allowing me to seek help for Goliath simmered close to the surface once more.

"Your father has something to tell you," she said.

I shuffled my feet.

"Look at me, daughter," he commanded. I lifted my eyes and stared at my father's narrow, drawn face. He always looked tired, as if the effort of living was too much. I wondered how it was that he did not seem happy, given the many hours he spent riding Hero across the county in his role as a land agent.

"The groundsman at Ormond Castle's Labrador Retriever has a litter of pups. I have sent word that we would like a male as soon as they are weaned."

I wanted to shout in disgust, *"A new puppy? After you ignored Goliath when he needed your help? Do you really believe that is all it will take to forget my friend and forgive you?"*

I wanted to yell at them. Instead, I nodded.

"Aleen," prompted my mother, her voice low.

"Thank you, Papa." I bobbed a curtsy, turned, and ran inside before they saw my tears.

By the time I arrived upstairs in the school room, I was dry-eyed once more. Mr. Walsh ushered me in and closed the door. The boys were already seated. Orlando glanced at me with a small smile. The others paid me no attention.

Despite their resolve to make a lady out of me, my parents bent the rules when it came to my education. Unlike other girls of my age and class, I did not have a governess. Instead, I shared with my brothers Charles, Orlando, Leo, and our younger brother, Percy, their tutor, Mr. Walsh. My mother said it was a practical and temporary thing. Until "good governesses" were available in Ireland, Mr. Walsh would include me in his lessons. I did not complain. Even then, I may have been aware that it was unlikely a governess would explain the theories of Darwin to me or encourage my interest in the natural sciences like Mr. Walsh did, even if only by default as he taught the boys. A governess would have replaced Darwin, numbers, and Latin with more lessons in needlework, deportment, manners, and music. When I remembered to say my prayers at night, I asked God to keep the "good governesses" in England.

That day, though, I was less engaged by Mr. Walsh's lessons than usual. The physiology of the earthworm made me think of Goliath's big body encased in damp soil, and I could not concentrate.

"Are you unwell, Aleen?" asked the tutor. "You are very quiet today."

"I am fine. Thank you, Mr. Walsh."

"Goliath died," said Percy, who, at just four years old, was barely able to sit still during lessons, let alone comprehend anything that was taught.

"He was old. It was his time," said Charles, as ever an echo of our parents.

"I'm sorry," said Mr. Walsh.

I wondered how it was that the groom and tutor could express their sympathies while no one in my family found a way to do it.

"Aleen wanted to call the doctor," said Percy.

Charles and Leo sniggered.

"If our grandmother was here, she might have known what to do," said Orlando.

Mr. Walsh frowned. "Is that so? What do you think she would have done?"

"I am not sure exactly," said my brother, glancing at me as if he hoped I would add something, "but she wrote a book about taking care of cats."

Charles and Leo laughed again, and although I am quite sure he had no idea what the others found funny, Percy laughed even louder.

Orlando was right. My father's mother, Lady Mary Cust, might have known what to do to help Goliath. She was, for a time, in royal service as a woman of the bedchamber to Queen Victoria's mother, the Duchess of Kent and Strathearn. That, however, was not her passion. Grandmama was an exceptional horsewoman and fond of other creatures too. She studied and wrote about the breeding habits of chameleons, and hers was the first Saint Bernard dog brought to England from Switzerland. When she traveled from her home at Leasowe Castle in Cheshire, her carriage was always flanked by two magnificently athletic Dalmatians. The dogs were her protection against highwaymen.

Among the items Grandmama carried with her on her travels was a shagreen case containing various ivory-handled apparatuses, including a knife, scalpel, file, scraper, small hammer, and large needle.

"She needs the tools to deal with the highwaymen once the dogs have tackled them to the ground," said my father, without any indication that he might be joking, when Orlando had inquired about the instruments on a visit to Leasowe.

Grandmama had laughed and said that they were for her to treat her horses should anything happen to them during their travels.

My favorite paragraphs in her book *The Cat: Its History and Diseases* introduced the section on the treatment of ailing cats. I admired the stern tone Grandmama took to admonish fair-weather animal lovers: that is, those who fawn over their animals when the creatures are healthy but are unwilling or too squeamish to administer to them when they are unwell. The paragraphs went as follows:

> Having now written as much as is interesting upon the history of cats from the authority of several learned authors, interspersed with my own remarks and observations respecting them, I shall proceed to write upon the management of them, and their treatment under disease, which I have found the most efficacious (believing no one has yet done so) a study in which I have ever taken interest and pleasure—the trying to alleviate, by the best means in my power, the sufferings of every creature formed by the Almighty hand that made all.
>
> Permit me to remark that no person with any proper feeling will pamper their favourites with unnecessary luxuries (that should be better bestowed), and over-lavish them with caresses, whilst they are in health and beauty, merely because they contribute to their own vanity and amusement; and then discard them from their affection and even presence when they have the misfortune to be ill and suffering;* and because the offices of cleanliness, in which they are in health so strictly careful, and can no longer perform for themselves, are obliged to be performed for them, and are naturally not agreeable. Agreeable they certainly are not, for all animals are fretful, and even cross, when suffering or old; and a degree of quiet courage and resolution is requisite to administer to their necessities. But I have always found that I have been repaid for my trouble and annoyances by the gratitude and increased attachment of my patients of every kind, from the largest to the smallest animals. And, after all, I have only done my duty as a Christian, for is it not written, "The righteous man is merciful to his beast"? He "who tempers the wind to the shorn

lamb" meant not His creatures to be ill-used or neglected by man, for whose use they were created.

　　* Would I do so by thee?

Indeed, Grandmama was particularly fond of cats. Her Persian, Jewel, traveled with her on her annual summer sojourn to her villa in Madeira in a basket secured by five padlocks.

"Perhaps you should write to your grandmother and ask what she might have done for Goliath, Aleen," said Mr. Walsh, once he had shushed my brothers.

I opened my mouth to say that it was too late, but then I thought about the puppy my father had spoken of earlier and nodded. The idea of replacing Goliath had angered me when my father mentioned it. That he and my mother imagined I would forget my old friend at the mere mention of his replacement was insulting. Now, though, I realized that the puppy would need me. I would write to my grandmother. That way I could take better care of my next dog when he grew old.

CHAPTER 2

⌖

1878
Tipperary, Ireland

FOUR YEARS LATER, CHARLES, ORLANDO, LEO, PERCY, AND I WERE STILL being tutored by Mr. Walsh at Cordangan Manor. It was not necessarily because God had answered my prayers or that my mother did not intend to ever find me a governess. However, when she gave birth to our sister, Ursula, Mama decided she might as well wait until the baby was old enough to also require a governess, at which time she would find someone suitable for us both. Moreover, with Charles now fourteen years old, which was the maximum age boys could become junior midshipmen, and due to join the Royal Navy soon, Mr. Walsh would have a smaller class. So my unconventional education continued.

It was possible that Mr. Walsh was poorly that day. Or perhaps I had snuck away from the schoolroom to visit the horses. I do not recall how I came to be at the stables, but it was while I watched the farrier working on Hero's hooves that I was finally informed enough to make the decision that would define my future.

I sat across the yard from them while Ned, the big Retriever, lay his head in my lap. On the far side, the other horses looked over their stable doors.

While I could see and hear the men clearly, neither the smith nor the groom was aware of my presence. If they had been, the Irishmen would probably not have spoken of my father.

"So your man has more trouble, I hear," said the farrier, his forehead resting against Hero's dappled gray shoulder.

"No more than any other Protestant, I'd say," replied the groom.

"What happened with the nun then?"

The groom made no attempt to disguise the sneer in his voice. "She was laid to rest without England's blessing."

"The cheek of it," said the farrier. "I'm surprised she was not unearthed and an apology demanded."

"Oh, believe me, His Lordship did worse."

It was not the first time I had heard about the incident involving the nun. Papa had bellowed his account of it to Mama in the hallway the day before.

My father, Sir Leopold Cust, had been Mr. Smith-Barry's land agent in Ireland for six years prior to bringing my mother, Lady Isabel, to Cordangan after they were married in 1863. They had lived comfortably in the manor ever since, but Papa's task, he regularly argued, was not one for the lily-livered. The Irish, particularly the farming folk, were "obstinate and unreasonable," he fumed. That Mr. Smith-Barry's estate charged farmers one penny for every firkin they sold at the Butter Market was not a law written by Papa but simply one that he was required to administer. Then, when the priest buried a nun at a convent on Mr. Smith-Barry's land without seeking Papa's permission, it was not *Papa* who made it unlawful, but it was his job to ensure that the rules were obeyed.

"But, Leopold," said my mother, "was it not provocative to have placed your boot upon the poor woman's grave?"

My father was incensed. "Did you not hear me, Isabel? The man challenged me! What would you have me do? Bow to his defiance? You know how men of the cloth like to portray themselves as invincible and yet also victims. He is an insurgent trying to save face," he roared.

Indeed, I knew the story about my father and the nun, and so I did not pay much attention to the groom's take on it. I was, at that age, naive and largely oblivious to the discord between landowners and tenants in Ireland. I was certainly unaware of how the tension multiplied where the factions were also distinguished by nationality and religion. None of the discussion about my father made an impression on me that morning. It was what the two men discussed *after* the nun story that struck me.

"What happened to young Mr. Kelly then? Is he blacksmithing out of the county nowadays?" asked the groom.

"The lad's up and studying to be a veter…" The farrier paused and closed his eyes. The words, it was clear, were unfamiliar to him. "He's studying to be a veterinary surgeon across in London."

"A veter…a horse doctor, then?"

"That's right. More of an animal doctor though."

"Why'd he want to do that?"

"Said he wants to learn to do more than shoe horses. There's more money in it too, I suspect."

"What'll he do then? Tend to cattle and sheep too?"

"Aye. It's getting to be big business."

"Will he be learning about injured limbs, calving, and foaling? And lambing, no doubt?"

"Aye," said the farrier, taking his nippers to a hoof.

"Will he treat the worms, do you think?"

"Oh aye, the worms will be big business, that's for sure."

An animal doctor? Taking care of horses, cattle, and sheep. Caring for injured limbs and helping with calving, foaling, and lambing. And treating worms. I stroked Ned, aware of a pulsing in my ears. I wanted to know more, but the men were quiet as the farrier tapped Hero's hoof. After a while, I stood up and walked to them.

"What's the name of an animal doctor? The words you used," I asked.

The men looked at me in surprise. It did not occur to me then, but it is possible they were concerned that I had overheard them gossiping about my father and that their indiscretion could be exposed.

"Miss Cust…erm…what are you doing here?" asked the groom.

The farrier stood upright and wiped his grimy hands on his apron. "Good morning, miss." His smile made his eyes crinkle. He looked kind. It made me happy for the horses. He closed his eyes again, concentrating on the words. "An animal doctor is a veterinary surgeon. A veterinary surgeon."

I repeated the words in my head several times. I would, I thought, write them down when I got to the school room and check the spelling with Mr. Walsh.

"Why did you want to know, miss?" asked the farrier.

I knew why but was not ready to say it out loud. Perhaps, I anticipated the response. Even if the smith and groom were too polite to laugh, their inevitable amusement was not something I risked rousing.

"I like to know things," I said.

I walked away, Ned at my heels. As I passed the other horses, I paused to rub their muzzles.

"Hello, my beauties," I whispered, one hand on a horse's nose and the other on Ned's smooth head. "Do not worry. I'll find a way. I will tend to you if you are injured or unwell. No one will say to me, 'Ah, they are just animals.' Or 'He's old; his time has come.' I will find a way."

I imagined how many horses I would meet when I became a veterinary surgeon. I looked into the paddock where our three black dairy cows grazed and pictured all the long-lashed, wide-eyed calves I would help bring into the world. It did not matter that I was not sure exactly what else I might be called upon to do to animals as a veterinary surgeon. The idea of being with them and knowing how to help them made me skip through the grass toward the river.

Thus, it was decided. I would work as a veterinary surgeon every day, except on holidays, when I would be a rough rider training two-year-old horses and on hunt days, when I would be the whipper-in or the master of the Foxhounds. I had it all worked out, and it made me happy.

I thought about the shagreen case of instruments my grandmother had bequeathed to me when she died the year before. She and I had exchanged a few letters about how best to take care of dogs after I had written to her about Goliath, and although my mother insisted she take care of the case until I came of age, it was my most prized possession.

Later, at lunch, I was surprised to see Charles in the dining room. He had ridden out with Papa on Mr. Smith-Barry business after breakfast, which usually meant they would be gone until evening. Papa, it emerged, was not feeling well. His knee was swollen and sore, and he suffered shortness of breath, even while mounted. He was resting upstairs and the doctor had been summoned.

Without Papa at the lunch table, my mother, having sent the nursemaid upstairs with Ursula, was in command of the conversation. She and Charles spoke more freely than they would have done had Papa been present.

"It might be wise to delay your leaving," said Mama.

Charles looked at his plate as he answered her. "No. Papa and I agreed that his discomfort should not be cause to change my plans. It would not be an appropriate start to a naval career."

"Surely, the admiralty would understand. Your father might write on your behalf."

"No. Anyway, it would not make any difference if I were here. I am not able to take on Papa's duties on the estate. Already, there is much dissent. It would not be proper."

My mother raised her hand, indicating that Charles should say no more. It was one thing to talk about the Royal Navy, but she would not discuss the affairs of the Smith-Barry estate while Orlando, Leo, Percy, and I were within hearing shot. We finished our meal in silence.

My father did not recover. He took to his bed on the very day that I decided I would become a veterinary surgeon and did not leave it alive. Perhaps it was a sign of the road ahead, but even if I had thought of it at the time, I would not have paid the omen any heed.

Mama gave Charles the task of telling his siblings. She might have reasoned that if he was old enough to join the navy, he was man enough to convey the news of our father's death.

Orlando, Leo, Percy, and I stood in a semicircle around Charles in the nursery, silenced by his blunt words. "Papa is dead."

Eventually, Orlando spoke, his voice quivering. "But...but...are you certain?"

"Of course I am certain. Why would I say such a thing if it were not true?"

"But we did not say goodbye," said Percy with a tiny stamp of his foot.

We were quiet again. We had not said goodbye. Mama had told us that the doctor said Papa should not be disturbed, so we had kept away. We were prohibited from going into our parents' bedchamber at all times unless sent for. I had not thought of going to Papa. Why would I?

Orlando sniffed. I glanced at him and saw several fat teardrops trickling down his cheeks. I looked away, unsettled by my brother's tears.

"We must not be dramatic," said Charles, his voice tinier now. "Mama has enough trouble on her hands as it is."

I walked to the window and looked out toward the stables.

"Can we go riding?" I asked.

There was no reply. I turned and saw that Charles and Orlando had left the room. Leo and Percy were sitting on the floor, where they were quietly piling wooden blocks on top of one another.

Although the doctor had trotted out a long list of problems that contributed to Papa's death, the locals believed it was retribution from God. My father had placed his foot on a nun's grave, and he had paid the price. On March 9, 1878, *The Tipperary Free Press* reported his death as follows:

> On Sunday evening last, Sir Leopold Cust died of a combination of diseases, and, strange to say, immediately after his death became known, the Tipperary Brass Band turned out and paraded the streets, playing airs of rejoiceful character. The hills around blazed with bonfires, and there was quite a demonstration of an extraordinary character because of the event. It is understood that the deceased was very unpopular in the capacity of agent to A. H. Smith-Barry, esq., which was the cause of this demonstration. The Tipperary Board of Guardians, today, refused to adjourn, as proposed by Captain G.M. Dawson, D.L. Very severe comments were made on the deceased gentleman's character as a land agent.

Naturally, I was not privy to the arrangements, but given the speed with which we left Ireland following Papa's death, it seems my mother might have arranged the family's return to England before he died. In all likelihood, my father's friend Major Shallcross Fitzherbert Widdrington, who became my guardian on Papa's death, had a hand in it. Papa's corpse was hastened from Cordangan to Cork by carriage and then shipped to England. We followed shortly thereafter.

At the time, I was baffled by the event of Papa's death and our hasty retreat. Years later, when I learned about the establishment of the Irish National Land League, formed little over a year and a half after my father's death, and the ensuing Land War against the power of landlords, our rapid departure made sense. It was not just that my father had stood on a Catholic nun's grave; the Irish hated him for that and everything he stood for.

Uncertain about what was expected of me, how I should behave, or what I should say following my father's death, I looked away to avoid the pity I recognized in the eyes of people around me. Perhaps if I had succumbed to more of Mama's lessons on protocol and gentility, I would have been better prepared. My stomach churned with an emotion that felt similar to that which I had felt when Goliath was ill and my mother would not let me call the doctor. Was it anger? Frustration? Hopelessness? Grief? I was not sure.

Something I was sure of was that my father had died before I properly knew him. I was already ten, but he and I had not spent much time together. My most treasured memory of Papa was when he finally acquiesced to my badgering and allowed me to join him and my brothers on the hunt. Even then, though, his assent was unenthusiastic, and I knew that he agreed only because he disliked my pestering rather than because he wanted me there.

Despite Charles's and Mama's disapproving glares, I cried as I climbed into the carriage at the manor for the last time. Cordangan was the only home I knew. I understood that my family was English, but Tipperary was where I was born and where I had learned to walk, ride, and talk. It was as if as I had ridden Taffy through the forests and over the fields of the Golden Vein of Ireland, I had made my mark on the land. I felt that part of me would forever ride or run through the pastures with Goliath or Ned at my side, fish for brown trout in the River Ara, and lie in the grass watching badgers forage on the hillside. I could not picture myself anywhere else.

We drove away, leaving Ned standing on the front stairs with the servants. He watched me go, his tail slowly moving side to side as if warming up
to wag properly should his wish be realized. It was not to be. The Retriever,
my mother had told me earlier, belonged to the estate and was not ours to
take.

"That's not so!" I had cried. "He's mine! Papa got him for me from
Ormand Castle when Goliath died. You cannot have forgotten that."

"Your father paid for him with Smith-Barry money. He belongs to
Cordangan."

"But Mama—"

"You can get another dog in England."

I stared at her. Why did she not understand?

"I do not want another dog. Ned—"

"That is my final word on this, Aleen," she said as she walked away.

I was shaken, and as I had nestled his head in my arms to say goodbye, I
apologized to Ned. If I had known sooner, we could have run away together.
I put a tuft of his fur and strands of Taffy's mane alongside the tiny clump of
Goliath's fur in the heart-shaped gold locket my aunt had given me, having
long since removed her dull locks from it.

I do not recall much about the trip to Sansaw Hall in Shropshire, where
we were to stay with my mother's sister, Aunt Charlotte, for a while. I do,
however, remember feeling aggrieved anew when I learned that although
my brothers would attend my father's funeral at the church in the nearby
village of Leaton, I would have to stay at home with my baby sister and her
nursemaid. I had hoped that being at his funeral would clarify exactly how I
felt about being fatherless.

"But Mama," I protested, "why should my brothers attend and not I?
Percy is younger than me."

She adjusted her black lace veil with a gloved hand and said, "Because
you are a girl, and there are, as you will continue to discover in this life, many
things that girls cannot do."

"But, Mama, I can. I am able—"

"It is not only about one's abilities, Aleen." Her voice had risen. "There
are things that are neither appropriate nor acceptable for girls to do. This is

one of those things. If you want to make a successful place for yourself in polite society, you need to accept this. The sooner you learn that this is how the world is, the easier your life will be. Now, do stop being difficult and go upstairs."

CHAPTER 3

⟨⁓⟩

1878
Shropshire, England

I DID NOT GO UPSTAIRS. IN A FUTILE ACT OF DEFIANCE, I FLED THROUGH THE front door and into the garden. My mother did not come after me, and I watched from behind a tangle of pink roses as a pair of glistening black horses pulled the carriage away.

The party had barely left when it began drizzling. Dragging my feet through the grass—as if ruining my shoes would improve my mood—I made my way to the gazebo at the far end of the garden. I plonked myself down on a bench and, clenching and unclenching my fists, thought about why being excluded from the funeral made me so angry.

There was nothing about attending church that appealed to me. I was typically bored of the sermon within minutes, disliked the melancholy nature of most hymns, and found the pews cold and uncomfortable. I resented the hours we were obliged to spend there every Sunday morning, particularly when the sun was shining. I wanted to be outdoors riding, walking, or fishing. Even when the weather was not good, I could think of several things I would rather do. Not that I was brave enough to risk the wrath that would inevitably be unleashed in Mama by revealing my aversion. Like my brothers, I endured our ecclesiastical rituals silently and neutral-faced.

Neither was I—I do not think—cross about missing the opportunity to commemorate my father's life. My feelings about his death and those triggered by having to leave Ireland and my animals remained intertwined. I could not separate one from the other.

The primary source of my anger, I concluded, was that I was prohibited from attending the event simply because I was a girl. My mother's rules about what my brothers could do versus what I was permitted made no sense—no matter what she said, how often she repeated it, and despite her insisting that it was "the way of polite society." That I could not do certain things or go to particular places and events because I was not a boy was unacceptable to me. Where was the justification? There was no evidence to suggest I was inferior. I could list my arguments against discrimination quicker than a sparrow could take flight: I was a better scholar than my brothers, bar perhaps Charles, who had the advantage of many more years of education; I was physically stronger than Leo and Percy in all instances; and I was the best rider by far.

It infuriated me that all of this meant nothing simply because I was born female. It further incensed me that my lot in life should be to learn how to best serve the egos and interests of males.

I flicked my plait over my shoulder. Would I rather be a boy? No. I was not asking for that. All I wanted was the option of going to the places, doing the things, and having the experiences and opportunities that my brothers had. It made no sense that I did not have those options.

That was why I was angry.

The sight of Aunt Charlotte's chestnut-and-tan Spaniel, Ruby, scampering through the rain distracted me. I sat on the floor and, ignoring her muddy paws, pulled her onto my lap and stroked her silky ears. A cold wave of shame washed over me as I thought of Ned. I was certain my mother could have found a way to bring him to England with us if she had wanted to. Indeed, I was angry about that too.

"Why are people so fickle?" I said, resting my chin on Ruby's head. "We do not deserve your loyalty."

I wondered who would ride Taffy with me gone. Would another family move into Cordangan Manor? What if they did not like dogs? What would happen to Ned? What if they neglected Taffy and the other horses? Those were the thoughts that trotted through my brain. Papa was dead. There was nothing I could do for him, but the animals were alive and relied on us for their well-being. I should have done something for them.

Ruby stared at me, her melted chocolate eyes droopy with adoration, despite having only met me a few days earlier.

"I will make up for leaving them behind, I promise," I said.

The Spaniel alerted me to the funeral party's return when she jumped out of my arms and ran toward the house. I stayed where I was, bored, cold, and hungry but determined to provoke my mother. She was unlikely to be worried about me, but if my behavior at least annoyed and embarrassed her, it would have to do.

I expected Mama to send a servant or Orlando to summon me. The girl who walked across the wet grass toward me, graceful and measured in a voluminous black dress, was a stranger. I stood up and straightened my skirts.

"Hello, Aleen," she said, giving me a small smile as she climbed the stairs to the gazebo. "I am Dorothy Widdrington."

"Hello," I replied, annoyed by Mother's ruse to lure me to the house. How could I complain to a stranger about how unfair and unkind Mama was?

Major Widdrington had spoken of his daughter Dorothy and her younger siblings Ida, Gerard, and Bertram. Dorothy, three years older than me, was the oldest. I had overheard the major tell Mama that until the death of his Aunt Dorothy, after whom she was named, his daughter had been called Dolly. Her quiet and thoughtful nature was, he had said, more suited to her proper name, and the nickname fell away. He had not mentioned how beautiful she was.

"I am sorry about your father," she said.

I nodded, staring at her dark hair, which was as glossy as the wide, black ribbon that held it from her face.

"Did my mother send you to fetch me?"

"No. I could not bear to be inside. All the words spoken that say so little wear me out. I saw you here when I got out of the carriage."

She placed her hands on the rails that enclosed the gazebo and looked down toward the little stream that trickled through the trees at the bottom of the garden.

"Are there any fish in there?"

Her question took me by surprise. She did not look like a girl who might be interested in fish.

"I have not seen any, but we have only been here for a few days, and Mama will not allow… Do you…do you fish?"

"It is one of my favorite things."

"Oh."

"Do you?"

"Yes. Aside from riding, there is nothing I like more. At home…at Cordangan in Ireland, where we live—lived—we fished in the River Ara all the time. For brown trout."

"My father says he will invite your family to Newton Hall when things settle. Will you come?"

"Is that where you live? In Northumberland?"

"Yes. We could fish and ride. Our house is not far from the beach. We sometimes ride there. Do you hunt?"

I stared at her. It did not seem possible that a day that had begun so badly could have delivered such a wonderful surprise. It had even stopped raining.

The crunching of gravel made us look toward the house. A boy, younger than me, ran across the drive and onto the lawn toward us, Ruby bounding at his feet.

"Ah, my youngest brother, Bertram. We call him Bertie," said Dorothy, raising her fine eyebrows in his direction. "He sniffs me out wherever I am. I believe he might be part Foxhound."

I gave a small laugh, the first in ages, and watched him approach. Bertie had the same dark-brown hair as Dorothy, except that his was denser and so straight that it stood over his broad forehead like the edges of a thatched roof. His complexion was fair, but his cheeks were as rosy as a rooster's comb.

"His redeeming characteristics are that he is a great hunter of worms and not a chatterbox like Ida and Gerard, which make him an excellent fishing companion."

Bertie paused at the bottom of the stairs and ascended slowly, glancing at me shyly as I crouched to pat Ruby.

"Bertie, this is Aleen," said Dorothy. "She's going to teach us how to catch brown trout."

He looked at me, eyes wide. "Here?"

"No, silly," said his sister, ruffling Bertie's hair, "when she comes to Newton Hall to stay with us."

"Will you come with us when we leave tomorrow?" he asked.

I looked at Dorothy. She seemed to know more about my life than I did.

"No. But hopefully, soon," she said, smiling at me.

I hoped so too.

That night, as I made my way down the passage toward my bedroom, Orlando called to me from the doorway of his room.

"You did not miss anything…really," he said in his quiet way.

"What do you mean?"

"At Papa's funeral."

I shrugged.

Orlando walked toward me, tightening the chord of his scarlet dressing gown. My brother was always perfectly groomed, even when about to go to bed. That and his long eyelashes were the only things I could discern that he had inherited from our mother.

"I heard you ask Mama if you could come."

"So?"

"I just wanted to tell you that nothing happened there that would have made you feel any different."

"Oh."

I wondered what he thought I had hoped to achieve by being at the funeral. Orlando was the kindest and most sensitive of my brothers, but I could not imagine that even he knew how it was to be excluded simply because I was a girl.

"The coffin was closed. We could not see him.".

I caught my breath. It had not occurred to me that it would have been possible to *see* my father. Was it an option? I had never been to a funeral. Neither did I want to see his or any other corpse. I had seen dead horses, cattle, and sheep. They were stiff, bloated, and cold. Their eyes were cloudy, and there was no sense of what they were like in life. It did not matter if they were skittish, fearful, playful, or anything else when they were alive. Dead, they were all the same: empty, nothing. I understood that much about death. My father would be no different.

Orlando went on. "The church was cold. No one cried. The minister was dull and went on for hours. He started up again in the cemetery. When he finally finished and we got into the carriage to come home, Mama said it was good that it was over and that she felt a sense of finality. Percy seemed baffled, but Charles and Leo agreed. I did not but said nothing. All I felt was relief that we could leave. I do not feel any different about Papa than I did this morning."

I remained silent.

He sighed. "Well, I just wanted to tell you…in case you thought it might have made a difference to have been there."

I nodded and walked away. I should have thanked him but did not trust myself to speak.

CHAPTER 4

❦

1881
Northumberland, England

ALTHOUGH AUNT CHARLOTTE ARGUED THAT TWO YEARS' BEREAVEMENT FOR widows and a year for children mourning their parents was acceptable, my mother decided we required three years to grieve Papa. Finally, in the summer of 1881, our aunt cajoled her into rejoining high society in time for the London Season.

"Really, Charlotte, do you think it is appropriate for me to discard my mourning gown and immediately throw myself into the dizzy series of balls, dinners, garden parties, and exhibitions that come with the Season in the city?" asked Mama.

"If you are serious about upholding the Cust name and want to ensure suitable matches for your children in the years to come, yes," said Aunt Charlotte, without missing a beat. "I would say that you dare not wait any longer, Isabel."

My mother needed no further persuasion. She bundled Percy and Ursula, who she felt were too young to accompany us, into a carriage bound for London with her, and at last, Orlando, Leo, and I traveled to Northumberland to visit the Widdringtons. Charles was, by then, faithfully installed in the Royal Navy.

Major Widdrington and Dorothy met us at the station in a carriage drawn by a perfectly matched pair of bay Clydesdales with white markings. I walked around the horses as our bags were loaded into the carriage, admiring their uniformity and staring up at their massive proportions. They were, I estimated, more than nineteen hands tall and probably, if what I had learned from the grooms in Ireland was anything to go by, weighed around one hundred and forty stones each. However, there was something about their soft brown eyes, white socks, feathered hooves, and almost identical wide blazes running pink over their noses that assured me they were gentle souls.

"They're full sisters," said Dorothy, reaching up to place a hand on each of their muzzles. "Just a year between them."

"Did the major—your father—breed them?"

"No. He bought them in Scotland. I went with him and saw the sire and dam."

I felt a twinge of two-pronged envy. How lucky she was to have a father who took her on trips with him and to have been to a Clydesdale stud.

"We have two riding options for you at Newton Hall, Aleen," said Major Widdrington, gesturing toward the carriage door with a gloved hand. His ginger beard was longer than I recalled but still army neat. "Arion is a calm, reliable hack who will do whatever you ask of her, while Stanford is faster but can be temperamental."

"She will choose Stanford," said Orlando, climbing into the carriage behind me.

Neither he nor Leo was that enthusiastic about riding, but Orlando knew how much I had missed it. My mother insisted that it was inappropriate for us to ride while we were with my aunt. The period of mourning, she said, should be a time of quiet reflection. I argued that I was at my most thoughtful when I was on a horse, but she raised her eyes heavenward and walked away without bothering to respond. I had given up counting the months since I had last settled into a saddle.

The thought of galloping across the fields again made me twitch with joy. Orlando was right; I would choose Stanford. Unpredictable horses were exciting. I loved the idea that they might suddenly decide not to obey their riders. Sometimes, people needed to be reminded about how powerful horses were. A little rebellion from them also confirmed that their spirit had not been broken. A horse without spirit might as well be a machine. Indeed, as much as I enjoyed a horse's quick response to my instructions and urging, I liked the idea of the animals thinking for themselves and, at least occasionally, making up their own minds about whether to do something—or not. Those were the kind of horses I understood and most respected. I was eager to meet Stanford.

The carriage from Chathill Station covered about five miles of coastal countryside to Newton Hall. I stared out the window, picturing myself galloping into the distance. With its rolling dunes and mudflats, this section of Northumberland was very different from Tipperary and Shropshire. The wind carried with it the smell of the ocean and buffeted the fine grass and swaths of unfamiliar pink, yellow, and purple flowers that blanketed the earth.

"It's beautiful," said Orlando, leaning over me to look out.

"You have come at a good time," said the major. "Many of the wildflowers here are found nowhere else in the world and are at their prettiest now."

I glanced at him, surprised by his talk of flowers. It was not a subject my father would have addressed. In fact, I did not recall Papa's having ever acknowledged the existence of a blossom, let alone its loveliness. Orlando, the romantic of the family, had told me how gentlemen expressed their interest, amorous or otherwise, in ladies by presenting them with flowers and that the type and color they chose conveyed a specific message. I did not, however, realize that gentlemen might also admire flowers simply because they were pretty. Then, I wondered why they should not. Were men not also human beings? Wasn't the notion that males and females had more in common than they had dissimilarities the very argument I had increasingly put to Mama over the years? Wondering what else my eyes might be opened to in Northumberland, I stole another look at my guardian.

That he was impeccably dressed in a long morning coat, light-colored trousers, and a double-breasted waistcoat was unremarkable. Thus was the uniform of gentlemen of the day. But I had never seen shoes as shiny as those he wore, nor a top hat—now on his lap—as smoothly brushed. As his image and deportment demonstrated, Major Widdrington, who had been High

Sheriff of Northumberland some years previously, was a gentleman of high standing. I knew that because my mother repeated it regularly. Of course, she would not have permitted my brothers and me to visit his family if it had not been so—even if my father had appointed him my guardian. I had also overheard it said when he visited us in Ireland that the major was an exceptional huntsman. I wondered if he would permit me to join him and Dorothy on a hunt. I was about to ask when the carriage slowed and turned.

Several rows of hollyhocks, tall and robust, lined both sides of the drive like pink and purple guards during a royal procession. Behind them, vast beds of yellow daffodils bowed their heads as if in deference to us. I looked at the major, half expecting him to salute the flowers.

He looked at me and gave a small smile. "As I said, it is a good time to visit Northumberland."

For a moment, the two-story house that appeared beyond the avenue of hollyhocks reminded me of Cordangan. It was of a similar size, shape, and pale color. But when the carriage stopped, I saw that Newton Hall was built of ashlar blocks made of sandstone, which created a light pink hue. The limestone bricks used for our Irish home were dull and gray. In contrast, Newton Hall seemed to glow. Perhaps, rather than the sandstone, it was the reflection of the spring garden that created the effect. Either way, there was something welcoming about the Widdrington home, including the smile on Bertie's face as he ran down the stairs to greet us. His mother followed. She smiled too, and I saw it was from Lady Cecilia Widdrington—known as "Lady Widdrington" despite her insistence that she was the wife of a major and not a lord—that Dorothy had inherited her oval face and glossy hair.

Thus began the first of what would become countless happy visits to Newton Hall for me over the years. Northumberland exceeded my hopes for hacks, hunts, and other horsey endeavors. "Major Fitz," as Lady Widdrington insisted we call him, did not hesitate to say yes when Dorothy asked him if I could join them on the next hunt. He knew, she told me, that I had already hunted in Ireland, where the hunts were believed to be unrulier and much more taxing than English meets.

"My friend the late Sir Leopold Cust's daughter Aleen," I overheard him say to another horseman over the excited yapping of the hounds as we prepared to ride out. "Keep an eye on her. She is just thirteen, but you are unlikely to have ridden with such an accomplished young horsewoman before."

I felt my face grow warm and looked away, trying to pretend that I had not heard him, but Dorothy caught my eye. Hers twinkled.

"He's not exaggerating," she said.

Stanford tossed his head and pawed at the cobblestones. He was as eager to get going as the hounds were. I leaned forward and patted his neck. The insides of my gloves were damp with perspiration.

"Patience, boy. We will be on our way soon…I hope," I whispered.

I had ridden the sleek bay several times at Newton Hall and knew that Stanford was as keen to please as he was highly strung. Accustomed to being ridden in large groups, he would be unlikely to embarrass me by bolting past the other horses during the hunt. As a guest at the meet and a junior, I would be expected to ride near the back of the first flight. If I wanted to hunt regularly with the Widdringtons (and, of course, I did), it was crucial to show that I understood and respected the etiquette and rules. I resolved that Stanford and I would be on our best behavior.

At last, with more riders assembled in one place than I had ever seen before, we set off down a long, narrow lane, the hounds creating a tail-wagging, head-bobbing pack ahead of the huntsman as the rest of us followed. Stanford snorted his approval and settled into a smooth trot. I took a deep breath. It was still early, but already, the air was warm. I glanced at Dorothy as she urged her horse alongside Stanford.

"Kicker," she said, nodding at a large chestnut with a tell-tale red ribbon tied to her dock and edging us around the horse. "I can never work out whether I am excited or terrified at the start of a hunt."

I knew what she meant. My heart was thumping in time to the clip-clop of the horses' hooves.

"I am excited," I said. "But also a little terrified. I think that is how it is meant to be, is it not?"

"If you say so," laughed Dorothy.

We veered off the road and into a meadow, our horses pricking their ears and jangling their bridles as they felt the grass beneath their hooves. A change in pace was imminent.

"Hold hard," called the master, lifting a hand in a commanding manner befitting the role of the man in charge of all matters at the hunt.

As we waited, the huntsman, who was responsible for controlling the pack of dogs and his assistant, the whipper-in, took off, hooves thundering and hounds singing, across the wide field toward a grove of trees in the distance. As I watched the two horses rise and propel themselves over a dense, green hedge, I instinctively shifted in my saddle, imagining Stanford was clearing the obstacle alongside them. The horse responded by curving his neck, flinging his nose forward, and pulling the reins out of my hands. With his head free, he executed a tidy half rear. I squeezed my legs together, and clenching the second pommel of the saddle for support, I lurched and snatched up the leather straps to restrain him. I grunted loudly with the effort; even with the top pommel to support one leg and the second one curved to secure my lower leg, it was not easy to retain my balance in a sidesaddle position.

I thought of how fleetingly excited I had been when—with Mama having insisted that at, the age of seven and for the sake of modesty, I was too old to ride astride—Papa had presented me with my first sidesaddle. It had taken a short ride down the lane on Taffy for me to realize that rather than acknowledging my progress as a rider, the new saddle simply represented another disadvantage of being a girl. Even so, I had no choice but to master it. I was pleased for having done so now as, in a final expression of excitement, Stanford took several steps to the side, bumping into another horse.

A flash of red caught my eye. It was the chestnut kicker. She flattened her ears, drew her lips tightly across her teeth, and swung her rear toward us. I wrenched the reins short and jerked Stanford to the left. He moved quickly, just enough to be out of range of her flying hooves.

With my horse calm again, I turned to face the portly man on the chestnut. His eyes, as round as his face, were clouded with confusion. He was not, it seemed, sure what had happened.

"I beg your pardon," I said, hoping the moment had not ruined my chances of being invited to other meets in Northumberland.

"Oh no, miss. My apologies to you," he stammered. "This one is temperamental. Terribly so."

"Well saved, Miss Cust," said the master, before urging his horse after the hounds. "Onwards!"

We rode for about four hours, by which time our shadows were short. It was an unseasonably warm day, and the sun's rays were shimmering hot across the earth. The hounds found and lost the quarry's scent three or four times, leading us across several meadows and plowed fields, and back and forth through the woodland multiple times. We plunged through rivers and over walls, fences, and gates. Two people fell when one of their horses slid down a bank, pushing the other into the river. Though drenched, spluttering, and red-faced, both riders remounted and rode on.

Stanford more than redeemed himself after the incident with the chestnut. He never faltered, and he responded eagerly to my every instruction. Even so, I was relieved when, with the hounds at a loss again, the master called to hold hard once more and said it was time to ride back to the village. The horses were lathered with sweat; the dogs, ducking into the shade whenever they could; and we riders, puce with exertion and overheating in our largely black riding habit. There was no fox to show for the morning, but we had had a magnificent run.

Dorothy fell in alongside me again. "So? Is an English hunt that different from an Irish one?"

I had forgotten about that notion: that hunting in England was much more subdued and cautious than it was in Ireland.

"I think they are equally thrilling," I replied.

"Perhaps whoever warned you of that was thinking of hunting further south. Around London maybe," she said. "You and Stanford are an excellent match."

"He is wonderful. Though I loved her dearly and she was braver than most, Taffy was not nearly as comfortable."

"Shorter legs, you said?"

"Much shorter," I replied, feeling a tug of betrayal about preferring Stanford to my old pony.

As I glanced at my friend, I saw one of the hounds standing alone near a hedge, head and tail hanging low. The rest of the pack was far ahead. I pulled up Stanford. Dorothy stopped, following my gaze.

"He does not look well," I said.

"No. Is it the heat?"

"Probably," I replied, recalling a story my grandmother had told me about one of her Dalmatians collapsing from heat exhaustion. "I will go to him. You ride ahead and let the whipper-in know."

Dorothy cantered away and I rode to the dog. He was now lying down, his chest heaving, tongue lolling, and eyes open. He did not move when I knelt alongside him and stroked his head.

"Poor boy," I said. "We overdid it. We should have watched you more carefully."

I fanned him with my hat. He needed water immediately. If I remembered my grandmother's story correctly, it would not be enough to get him to drink; we would need to submerge and cool him down as quickly as possible. I stood up and looked around but there were no signs of water close by. How could I get him to the river we had crossed earlier? Although he was one of the smaller hounds in the pack, he was too large for me to carry any distance on my own. I was wondering how I might sling him over Stanford when I saw Dorothy riding toward me.

"My father rode on to tell the whipper-in. Is he all right?"

"No. We need to get him to some water. He is completely limp."

"There is a soggy ditch ahead," she said, dismounting and tying her horse up alongside Stanford.

Dorothy and I carried the lifeless dog across the field to the ditch, which contained a shallow puddle of muddy water.

"We need to put him in it," I said, "and cover him with as much water as possible."

Once we had laid him in the wet patch, I removed my gloves and began digging to increase the space around him. The earth was saturated, and the pool swelled. Dorothy did the same, and we were soon able to scoop water over the dog. I carefully wet his nose and mouth, hoping he would begin drinking. My friend poured handfuls of water over his body.

"Why is he not moving? Trying to drink?" she asked, her brow furrowed. "Is it too late?"

"I hope not," I said. "You fan him while I splash."

Dorothy waved her hat over the dog as I doused him. After several minutes, his tongue moved, and he licked his lips. I opened his mouth and poured water into it. He opened his eyes, looked at me, and swallowed.

The dog had lifted his head, shifted onto his chest, and was lapping water when we heard a horse approaching. It was the whipper-in.

"I hope he will not be angry," I whispered.

"Angry? You saved the animal, Aleen," said Dorothy. "How did you know what to do?"

"*We* saved him. My grandmother told me how she treated one of her dogs that could not keep up with the carriage in the heat. But," I said as I glanced at the man pulling up his horse nearby. "Papa told me it is forbidden to do anything with a hunting hound without the whipper-in's permission."

"I think there are exceptions, and that this is one."

She was right. The whipper-in was pleased.

"Thank goodness you spotted him," he said. "He is one of the strike hounds—too young, though, to know how to pace himself. We should have kept a better eye on him."

I glanced at Dorothy, not sure what to say.

"My friend saw him and knew exactly how to revive him," she said.

The man bent over the dog and nodded. "You did well, miss. Very well indeed."

"I do not think he is up to walking home though," I said, stroking the dog's wet head.

"No. The huntsman said he would arrange a cart for him. I will wait here if you young ladies would like to ride back and, um, clean yourselves up."

Dorothy and I looked at one another. Our clothes were wet and muddy, and our hands and faces smeared with dirt. We began giggling. The whipper-in laughed too. The dog looked at us, his tail weakly slapping the water.

It was not only Dorothy and Major Fitz who made my brothers and me feel welcome at Newton Hall. Gerard and Ida created a lively foursome with Orlando and Leo, with Ida leading their games in the playroom and garden.

Occasionally, she herded the boys, and they joined Dorothy and me on outings to the beach with the major's whippets, Samson and Delilah, and Lady Widdrington's Pekingese, Pepper.

Bertie, as Dorothy had indicated he would, trailed his oldest sister like a faithful puppy. My worries that he might be a nuisance or be jealous of my friendship with his sister came to naught. Bertie, I discovered, was incapable of being either annoyed or annoying. He was extraordinarily reasonable and considerate, particularly for a boy so young, and perhaps because he was so much in her thrall, he listened closely to everything Dorothy said and never argued with her.

"Aleen and I are going to ride to Brunton Burn today. We are thinking of it as an exploratory outing. We want to find the best fishing spots and work out how long it takes us to get there and back. Next time we go, you can come too," she explained to Bertie one day.

"Don't forget to look around for good worm hunting places too," he said as he waved us goodbye from the front stairs.

We had only been at Newton Hall for a few days when I realized how happy I was. For the first time, I believed it was possible to experience the joy I had known at Cordangan elsewhere. It did not occur to me at the time to feel guilty about not missing my mother. It was freeing not to have her disapproving eyes following me as I walked into or out of a room. Before long, I stopped wondering whether I was talking too loudly, walking too fast, laughing too frequently, or spending too much time outdoors.

Then, there was Lady Widdrington. On the face of it, Dorothy's mother was every bit the lady my mother was. She was stylish and popular, with teams of friends and extended family who regularly attended dinner and garden parties at Newton Hall. Lady Widdrington oversaw two households (the family also kept a house in Kensington, London) without displaying any of the jaw clenching, eye rolling, and chest heaving we were accustomed to at Cordangan Manor and which accessorized most of my mother's interactions with her servants wherever else she went. That is not to say Lady Widdrington was demure. She wasn't, not even in the company of men. Although she was fourteen years younger than her husband, she seldom deferred to him when there were decisions to be made or information to be shared.

When she was not entertaining or visiting friends, she was reading. The large table in the library at Newton Hall was permanently covered with newspapers, which she read from cover to cover and discussed at length whenever opportunity allowed. Indeed, Dorothy's mother was the most opinionated and insatiably curious woman I knew. She encouraged the same in her children, but although they largely obliged, adding their opinions and sometimes even opposing hers, only Ida ever challenged their mother for the position of most ardent orator in the room. Even that happened infrequently.

Orlando, Leo, and I were unaccustomed to the notion of dinner conversation when we arrived at Newton Hall. It was startling in itself that Major and Lady Widdrington sat down to dinner with their children every night unless they had other adult company. My brothers and I were used to eating before our parents, and even then, the dinner table was not considered a place of social discourse. We were excused as soon as the slowest eater among us (Percy) had cleaned his plate.

At Newton Hall, dinner discussions, led by Lady Widdrington, went on long after our plates were cleared. She urged everyone to have their say and, within a few days of our arrival, was even able to elicit a few words from Leo.

"Sophia Jex-Blake is a medical physician. Britain's first lady doctor. She has rooms in Edinburgh. She is remarkable. It is extraordinary what she has endured to get this far. She is among the modern young women who prove to the world that women are stronger than anyone realizes," she said one evening, when the subject under discussion was the questionable quality of journalism.

"She and six other women students were pelted with mud while they were training," said Ida, probably noting the blank expressions on three Cust faces.

Lady Widdrington continued. "Yet, journalists write about the allegedly uninhibited, unladylike way she allows her hands to swing while she walks on the village green on the weekend. Why? Surely, the way she walks is of no consequence and says nothing about her character or her abilities as a physician."

She paused and looked around the table. "What say you, Leo? Do you think the way a lady, a doctor to boot, moves her arms is a matter that requires public scrutiny and reportage?"

Orlando and I looked at Leo, expecting him to blush and shake his head, but he didn't. Instead, he said, "If she swings her arms while she is walking, it might mean that she is energetic."

Lady Widdrington raised her eyebrows, inviting him to continue, but my brother had said his lot.

Bertie helped him make a point. "It is good to be energetic; energetic people get things done. Is that not what you told me, Dorothy?"

I cannot recall how the rest of the conversation went. Not only was I taken aback by the fact that Leo had spoken in company, but I was also distracted by the notion of a woman having become a doctor. I thought about how scandalized my mother would be by the information.

Thrilled to have unlimited access to horses, I spent many hours at the Newton Hall stables. It was there one morning that I came across Major Fitz talking to a stranger as they examined the major's chestnut hunter's legs. Apollo had begun limping when Dorothy, Major Fitz, and I rode home after the hunt and had not improved during the days that followed.

Major Fitz looked up, beckoned to me, and introduced the man as Mr. Abbot, a veterinary surgeon. He instructed the groom to lead Apollo across the yard, and we watched the usually graceful horse list clumsily. As they turned and walked back toward us, Mr. Abbot stepped forward and crouched to watch the horse from the front.

I recalled a similar scene in Ireland involving my father, a farrier, and Charles's horse, Pebbles.

"The pain is low on his off fore," I said, looking at Apollo's front right leg.

The veterinary surgeon turned to look at me. For a moment, I thought I might have spoken out of turn and insulted him, but he nodded. "Yes, I believe so. How low, though, would you say, Miss Cust?"

I had seen Apollo balancing on the tip of his fore hoof on the off side as he stood earlier. "Somewhere below his fetlock joint," I said, with less certainty now.

"Hmm. How do you arrive at that conclusion?" asked the major.

I looked at Mr. Abbot. He was smiling.

"Because of the way he dips his head as he steps on his near side and then lifts it in pain as the off side hoof touches the ground," I said.

"But what makes you think it is low on the leg?" asked Mr. Abbot.

"Well, um, yes… I am less sure of that," I conceded, "but it seems from the timing of his limp that it is somewhere below the fetlock. Also, the ground was particularly dry and hard on the hunt last week. Some of the landings were rock hard. I think he might have hurt it on impact."

Mr. Abbot pursed his lips. "Have you seen this in a horse before?"

"A horse in Ireland—my brother's—had a similar injury. We had to rest her for more than a month."

I remembered how angry I had been with Charles when he refused to dismount and lead Pebbles home when she began limping during a ride.

"Major Widdrington, I believe that my expertise is redundant at Newton Hall. You have a young expert of your own," said the veterinary surgeon. He was still smiling, but I felt no sting at his teasing.

"I see that," said the major.

Mr. Abbot bent forward and ran his hand down Apollo's leg. When he applied pressure above his hoof, the horse lifted his foot. "If only it were possible for women to become veterinary surgeons," he said.

"If only," came a quiet voice from behind us. It was Dorothy, who had come to find me.

As we left Mr. Abbot, Major Fitz, and the groom discussing Apollo's treatment and walked toward the house, I glanced at my friend. "Do you imagine that it might be possible for women to become veterinary surgeons one day?" I asked.

"I don't know. You heard my mother talk about the woman doctor in Edinburgh. Perhaps it is."

"My mother, on the other hand, believes that it is vulgar and unlady-like for girls to want to do anything beyond learning how to be a wife and mother."

"Yet, she has educated you in many subjects I do not know."

"By accident really. It was convenient for me to share my brothers' tutor. I do not think that my mother considered the consequences. Not yet anyway."

Dorothy chuckled. "My mother said yours will take on the role of woman of the bedchamber to Queen Victoria soon. Did you know that?"

"Yes. My grandmother was also woman of the bedchamber."

"Does your mother not consider *that* as something of an occupation?"

"Good heavens, no," I replied, mimicking Mama. "Being in service in the royal household is not an occupation; it's an honor."

We laughed.

"Do you want to work, Aleen?"

"Yes. Don't you?"

"Well, I would like to have a purpose beyond running a home and bearing children. To be frank, I am not really sure I want a husband."

"Oh?"

She clenched her hands. "Please do not repeat that. I could not bear the ensuing discussion. It is just…well… I would rather do something else with my life."

"Me too. Though, I wonder how I will ever manage it. My mother is solidly opposed to the idea. So is Charles. One of their arguments is that working creates the perception that one *needs* to earn a living, which makes working crude and low."

"Unless you are a man, and your occupation involves managing other people's lives."

Was Dorothy referring to my father's work as a land agent in Tipperary or that of hers as High Sheriff? I did not ask. The image of my father standing with one foot propped before him on the freshly mounded earth of a grave flicked through my brain like the wings of a crow past a window.

"But what if the work is of a service nature?" I asked. "Why should it be unseemly for a woman to want to help others? The world? Animals? What do you want to do?"

Dorothy frowned. "That is the problem; I have no idea. What about you? You want to become a veterinary surgeon, I suppose?"

I sighed. "It is my greatest dream."

She stopped and looked at me.

"To become a veterinary surgeon," I said, in case it was not clear to her.

"Really?"

"Yes."

"Then you should make it come true."

CHAPTER 5

1883
Cheshire, England

ALONG WITH THE CUST BARONETCY THAT HE INHERITED FROM OUR FATHER, my brother Charles—that is, Sir Charles Leopold Cust, the Third Baronet of Cust—came into possession of our grandparents' home, Leasowe Castle, on the Wirral peninsula in Cheshire.

Built by the Earl of Derby in the 1500s, the castle was separated from a long beach by less than a hundred yards of low dunes, which, in the evening light, looked like the rounded backs and heads of a hundred crouching cats. By 1883, Charles, whose naval career kept him largely ocean-bound, and my mother had agreed that his brothers and sisters would settle at Leasowe with Mama, who used it as her base for the fortnight every month that she was not occupied by Her Majesty. In London, she had rooms in Onslow Square, Kensington, where my siblings and I also resided when in the city.

I was no longer dogless by then. As we had prepared to leave Shropshire, my aunt insisted I assume ownership of Ruby. The Spaniel had, after all, trailed me all day and slept at the foot of my bed every night for almost as long as we had been guests at my aunt's home. These facts notwithstanding,

Aunt Charlotte reasoned that I should take Ruby to Leasowe with me because "You are the only one she permits to clean and dry her ears."

I was not fooled by my aunt's reasoning. It reminded me about what my grandmother had written in her book about caring for cats, in particular, the section regarding people who "over-lavish" animals with attention when they are healthy and beautiful but discard them when they are ill and suffering. I could have argued that it was not so much that Ruby *permitted* me to attend to her ears but rather that I alone cared enough to do it and was not squeamish about the job.

The Spaniel and I settled in quickly at Leasowe. There were beaches to explore, horses to ride, and endless inland paths to discover. We had not been there long when I overheard the head groom, Samuel, bemoan his workload given how much training was required for the group of two-year-old Thoroughbreds bred at the castle. The timing was good; Mama was in London. I leapt out of bed at first light the next day and ran to the stables. If he was surprised by my appearance, Samuel said nothing as we led the horses outside. From then on, whenever Mama was absent, I worked alongside him with the youngsters.

"If I may say, Miss Cust, you're a natural," said Samuel one day as we returned from a satisfying ride, me on Caesar, the most excitable of the two-year-olds with minimal drama. "I've never seen a horse respond so quickly to training."

His comment pleased me, but although the rough riding demanded stamina, strength, and sometimes courage, I learned that there was no mystery to training horses. It was simply a case of patiently getting to know each animal and understanding what approach they responded to best. For example, Caesar was tightly wound, and his nerves needed constant soothing. Every step of his training, whether it was getting him used to the feel of the saddle or teaching him to heed instructions, required first mollifying him. A low voice worked well, as did long, firm strokes of my hand beneath his mane. As soon as he was calm and reassured, Caesar thought clearly and responded well. When his nerves were lulled, he was intelligent, willing, and agile. His stablemate Amber responded to a different approach. She was quiet and gentle but slow to learn. I had to repeat everything again and again, day after day, until the filly took it in. Once she knew it, it stayed, and she became a reliable, responsive ride. They were different characters, each agreeable and eager to please in their own way.

It was not just that I learned more about horses from Samuel during that time. The horses themselves taught me to listen, watch and get to know them. I discovered that understanding animals required more than love; it demanded patience and the willingness to observe and take cues from them. As I trained the horses, they trained me. I could not have been happier.

One day, on a walk with Orlando, who was home from boarding school, my brother pointed across the ocean beyond where Ruby mock-charged the tiny waves that brushed the shore like frothy sheets of lace.

"Did you know that if you swam in that direction for long enough, you would arrive in Dublin?" he asked.

I looked over the water, which, as the sun set, looked like smelted gold. I could not picture myself getting far.

"I shall build a boat and sail across, and then take a carriage to Tipperary to visit Ned and Taffy," I said.

"You might be disappointed if you count the years."

He was right. Ned would have been nine, and Taffy, older. While it was possible the dog and horse were still alive, they might not have been. I recalled Goliath's last hours and hoped that Ned had someone who loved him even when he grew old, slow, cloudy-eyed, and smelly. I did not want to think about what might have happened to Taffy in her old age.

Although Ursula had a governess at Leasowe, I continued my lessons with Percy and his tutor until Percy, too, left for boarding school. I won the right to do so by reasoning with my mother that because I was so far ahead of my sister—she was nine years my junior—it would benefit Ursula to have the full attention of a governess. It helped, I think, that Ursula was content to learn to sew, play music, draw, and make polite conversation, and that Mama suspected that my presence during my sister's tutelage might be disruptive. In addition, my mother was usually too weary to argue when she came home from her royal duties. There were times, though, that she felt my transgressions absolutely warranted it.

During one of my visits to Newton Hall, I learned from Lady

Widdrington of anatomist Henry Gray's book, *Anatomy: Descriptive and Surgical, Anatomy of the Human Body*. The book, she told me, for who else would be as shrewd to do so, featured detailed illustrations of the entire makeup of the human body by Henry Vandyke Carter. I longed to see a copy and, for a while, fantasized about creating a similar book featuring the anatomy of different animals.

As such, I began collecting the blanched bones and teeth of creatures that I found on the beaches and in the dunes near Leasowe. I kept them under my bed in an old wooden toolbox. Whenever I found something new to add, I would slide the box out, sit on the floor, and examine my collection to see if I could identify similarities or work out where the bones might fit in relation to one another.

I am not sure who alerted my mother to the existence of the box, but there was nothing uncertain about the distress it caused her. I was summoned to the drawing room one afternoon where I found her standing, hands on hips, with my box open on the table before her. Ursula sat in the corner, pretending to embroider.

"What, pray tell, daughter," said my mother, breathing like an old pony on a winter's morning as she jabbed a hand toward the box, "is the meaning of this? Do I need to explain how unsettling it is to find a skeleton beneath one's daughter's bed?"

"It is not a skeleton," I said, peering into the box to confirm my collection was still intact. "It is simply a collection of miscellaneous bones and a few teeth."

"For what purpose, Aleen? Why would you collect pieces of dead creatures? It is repulsive. Are you…are you…is there something…?"

Her jaws were clenched, and she was unable to complete the question. Ursula sniggered. I decided it was time to reveal my plan. I was fifteen. In three years, I would be presented at court. If eighteen was old enough to be married, it was old enough to begin working toward my dream. I needed to prepare my family. The bones on the table presented the ideal opportunity.

"I want to train as a veterinary surgeon. I am collecting bones to help understand animal anatomy. They are instructive, educational."

My mother stared at me. Had she stopped breathing? Ursula gave up the pretense of needlework and fixed me with her eyes too. The only sound was the click-click-click of hedging shears from beneath the window outside.

"What?" said Mama eventually.

"A veterinary surgeon. An animal doctor."

Her shoulders slumped. "A childish fantasy," she said, her mouth twisted in a sneer as she shoved the box away from her. "You are too old for such silliness. You must stop it before you embarrass yourself any further."

"It is not a fantasy, Mama. It is what I want. It is what I plan to do."

"It *is* a fantasy, because it is impossible. You know that."

"Women are becoming physicians. Why is it impossible for them to become veterinary surgeons?"

"Women physicians? Doctors?" she said, holding on to the edge of the table as if to keep herself upright. I wondered how it was that I could train horses but had no idea how to pacify my mother.

"It is appalling. Unacceptable. You know what Her Majesty thinks about such women. My daughter will not be one of them! I forbid it, Aleen. I will hear no more about it."

"But why, Mama? You know how—"

"No more!" she shouted. This time she gave no sign of trying to restrain herself. The clicking of the hedging shears stopped.

"I do not want to upset you, Mama, but—"

"Then get out!"

We locked eyes across the table. She was breathing heavily again. The gardener began clipping once more. I reached out to take my box.

"Leave it!" she growled.

I saw neither the box nor its contents again.

There was no more discussion on the subject until months later when Dorothy visited Leasowe on her way back to Northumberland after her first London Season. Whereas many eighteen-year-old women might have twittered with excitement and gossip after being presented to the Queen and having experienced a summer of dinner parties, balls, breakfasts, and concerts, Dorothy was subdued. The only events that she told me about in any detail were the Derby and the Ascot.

"I have never seen such a splendid lineup of horses," she said as we strolled to the beach the afternoon she arrived. "They were shinier, leaner, and stronger than any I have ever seen. I wished you were there to admire them with me."

"Me too, but... well, there were plenty of other people with you, surely?"

"Yes. Hundreds. All poring over one another's outfits, discussing who had the finest milliner, and giggling when a man tipped his hat in their direction. They might as well have been at another ball."

"Oh dear. Was there nothing enjoyable about the Season, aside from the racehorses?"

"Well, I had some pleasant rides in Hyde Park and watched the birds in Kensington Gardens."

I glanced at her. She was thinner and paler than when I had last seen her at Newton Hall earlier in the year. I wondered what others had made of her in London. Because she was beautiful, educated, intelligent, and a Widdrington, Dorothy's reserve would no doubt have taken some by surprise. They might even have mistaken it for aloofness and imagined her cold, but I knew otherwise. Dorothy preferred the outdoors to drawing rooms and would rather wade chest deep in water and cast a salmon line or sit in the woods and watch the birds than dally and gossip at tea parties. She was ill-disposed to large gatherings and disliked talking for the sake of talking. The only time Dorothy became truly engaged in conversation was when the topic entertained books, the writing of Wordsworth, fly-fishing, ornithology, horses, or science.

"Perhaps when it is your turn in a few years, you will find it satisfying, Aleen, but I did not."

"I am sorry."

"It was tiresome wearing my hair pinned up all the time and being laced into a corset every day. The introductions. They were endless, and there was seldom time to be alone to read or think. The talking...oh, how the constant chatter exhausted me. I had not realized before what peace and freedom being a girl in the country afforded me," she said.

"Did you not meet anyone you liked?"

She glanced at me with a smile. "You sound like my mother. She despairs. Fortunately for her, Ida will love London and make up for my disappointing Season."

We stood and looked across the sea while Ruby dug a hole in the sand at my feet. Leasowe delivered another magnificent sunset. A walk to the beach to watch the sun touch the clouds with pink and orange and draw a golden pathway to the horizon was something of a mandatory undertaking for visitors. It seldom disappointed.

"It is wonderful to be away from the city," said Dorothy. "If I had my way, I would never return."

"Why should you?"

She ignored my question. "Do you remember I told you that I did not like the idea of being married?"

I nodded.

"The Season confirmed it for me. I will not do it. Marriage is nothing but matching women with the right backgrounds to men with the right backgrounds. Or women with healthy dowries to men whose wealth is threatened. Or wealthy men to women whose families' worth has shrunk. I want none of it."

"Did you tell your parents?"

"Not yet, but I will."

We did not move, even though the sun was almost gone, taking with it its warmth and colorful palette. Dorothy's tone was listless. I was sorry she had not arrived earlier so that we could have gone for a ride. Being on a horse always cheered me up, and I could not imagine it being any different for anyone else.

I wished I knew what to say about marriage that might lift her spirits. I pictured myself with a husband one day. I had not given much thought to having children or running a home, but I liked the idea of sharing my life with someone who enjoyed the things I did and who understood and supported me even if others thought my choices in life were unusual. I would like to be with someone who looked at me the way Major Fitz looked at Lady Widdrington, even when she grew excited about something she had read in the newspaper and raised her voice at the dinner table.

"What will you do?" I asked as we walked back toward the castle.

"I have asked Miss Herbert to find out how soon I can go to a hospital to train as a nurse," she said, referring to her former governess, who had become a friend.

"A nurse?" I repeated, thinking, of course, of Florence Nightingale who had just months before received the Royal Red Cross. I wished my mother would listen to me long enough for me to put Miss Nightingale forward as an example of a well-bred woman who worked and was not rejected by society for doing so.

"Yes, I cannot continue living with my parents indefinitely. Being a nurse is one of the few things open to me."

"I think you will make an excellent nurse."

As we approached the front door of the castle, I pictured Mama standing over my box of bones. "I told my mother that I want to become a veterinary surgeon."

Dorothy grasped my wrist. "My goodness! How did she respond?"

"As you can probably imagine, she was appalled. Did not speak or even look at me for days afterward and continues to be curt."

"You have time to win her over."

"I wonder if it will ever be possible. Charles castigated me too when he was last home. Mama wrote to him. He said I should not toy with our mother's health or risk others' hearing about my ridiculous notions. He and Mama, he said, are custodians of the Cust name, and I should not undo their efforts to maintain its proud history."

I did not mention that Charles had also forbidden me to help Samuel with the horses, which, I suspected, Ursula had informed him about.

"I believe Percy has joined the royal household as Her Majesty's Page of Honor. That will surely help uphold the family pedigree," said my friend.

"Indeed," I said, wondering, if one day, my achievements might be seen in the same light.

CHAPTER 6

⚜

1885
Cheshire, England

WITHIN TWO YEARS OF DOROTHY'S INSISTING THAT MARRIAGE WAS NOT FOR her and Percy's ratifying the Custs' royal connections by taking on the task of keeping Her Majesty's robes from trailing the ground at official events, my friend was engaged and my youngest brother dead.

My mother's vacant gaze mirrored the family's shock at Percy's death. It did not seem possible, but we were even less prepared for it than we had been for my father's demise. Fourteen-year-old Percy was at boarding school at Wellington College, where he attended classes between performing his duties as Her Majesty's Page of Honor, when he fell ill. He was tucked into an infirmary bed but within four days—before word of his illness reached my mother's ears—had died. Mama, once again swathed in black, was momentarily comforted when a representative of Buckingham Palace attended the funeral at Bidston near Leasowe Castle and placed a wreath from Her Majesty on Percy's grave. Then she took to her bed in the castle, refusing to see anyone but Charles and Ursula for more than a fortnight.

It was Orlando who told me that I had inherited £958 from Percy's estate, our youngest brother's inheritance having been divided up among my other brothers, sister, mother, and me.

"Will it be available to me? I mean, separate from my inheritance from Papa?" I asked.

"It will be added to that from Papa," said Orlando.

In other words, the money from Percy would mean nothing to me until I reached the age of twenty-one, and even then, it could be meaningless. If I was married at that age, my inheritance—that from Percy and my father—would become part of my dowry, and my husband would take ownership of it. If I was not married when I turned twenty-one and was released from the guardianship of Major Fitz and my mother, I would still not have free access to the money. In terms of my father's will, the patriarch of the Cust family—that is, Charles—would decide how much and when my inheritance would be apportioned to me. Essentially, he would allocate me the living allowance that he deemed adequate. I would have no financial sovereignty.

"Are you anxious for it? Percy's inheritance, I mean," said Orlando. "What do you need money for? You are only seventeen."

"To study."

"To study? Really? What do you plan to study?"

"I want to train as a veterinary surgeon."

He pursed his lips. "Still? Charles told me about the bones, but that was years ago. You are still set on the idea?"

"Why would I have changed my mind?"

"Perhaps, because you can see now how difficult…impossible…it will be for you. Mama and Charles will never let you attend university. Even if they did, do you understand what would be in store for you? And to work as a veterinary surgeon? Be reasonable, Aleen."

I looked away. Orlando was the only sibling I thought might understand my dream. Now, I feared even *that* was too much to hope for.

He went on. "You must know what difficulties women face when they insist on being educated. I have heard of men, fathers, and husbands who have had their daughters and wives committed to mental asylums because they want to go to university. I—"

"You think Charles and Mama would have me locked up?"

"No. No. I mean, I do not think so. They would certainly not want to attract attention to the family name by initiating unnecessary drama, but you know how they are. I do not know what they would do. But it is not just the family, Aleen. You would be ostracized by society. Not to mention taunted at college. Why would you put yourself through that?"

"Because I want to do something with my life, even if it involves work, struggle. I want to help animals."

"Our grandmother helped animals. You could be like her. You already are," he said.

"No. It is different. I want to work. I want to be a veterinary surgeon."

"Is it possible, even, for a woman to do the work required by a veterinary surgeon? I mean—"

"Women are stronger than anyone realizes," I replied, echoing Lady Widdrington. "I want to work with animals, for animals. It is that simple."

Orlando took my hands in his. I was not mistaken; he was nothing like the rest of us. We were not an affectionate family. We did not express our attachments or our emotions. We did not cry easily or laugh together frequently. The Custs typically kept stiff upper lips or left the room before the tiniest of trembling was spied. Orlando, though, was a different species. He gave in to his emotions and was affectionate, and most surprisingly, he was not ashamed of it.

"I know you do, my dear sister," he said. "I know your love for animals. Everyone does. You understand and handle horses and dogs and all other creatures as if born to take care of them. There is nothing stopping you from having packs of dogs, herds of horses and cattle, flocks of sheep, and whatever else you want when you are married and have a home of your own. You can breed them, train them, ride them, and care for them all day long. They will be the most fortunate animals in the kingdom. But you cannot turn your love for animals into a profession and work as a veterinary surgeon. It is not appropriate and would be too difficult to even attempt. For you. For all of us. The Cust family would not survive it."

His dark eyes reminded me of Ruby's when she thought it was time for another walk to the beach. A walk would not satisfy Orlando; he wanted me to agree for the sake of peace. I could not.

"You do not understand," I said, pulling my hands from his. "You are free to live your life the way you want. You wanted to leave and make a life for yourself in Ellesmere, and so you did. Nobody frowns upon you, Charles, or Leo because you are unmarried and doing things that involve neither your family nor the creation of a new one. You have no idea what it is to want to do something with your life and yet be forbidden simply because of your gender."

"No, I do not. And I wish it were not so, Aleen, but I do not make the rules."

"No. But other men do. And women like Mama and Her Majesty do nothing to change things. That is why I, and other women who want to take different paths, have to take on the battle."

"Battle?" His voice rose. There were few things that upset Orlando more than confrontation. Even talk of it made him pull at his collar as if he were being strangled. "There must be another way."

"If you find one, let me know."

Little over nine months later, we shelved our mourning faces to celebrate Dorothy's nuptials in Northumberland.

The gardens of Newton Hall had never been as immaculate, which was no small feat; the wedding had been brought forward a few months to accommodate the campaign of the groom, Edward Grey, as he led the Berwick-upon-Tweed division of the Liberals. The gardeners were still at work when Dorothy and I rode toward the stables the afternoon before the wedding. The hedges were table-flat, and the maze, as meticulously groomed as a pony on show day. Scattered across the estate like cushions in autumnal shades of yellow and orange, several beds of chrysanthemums grew tall and bold. The flowerpots that lined the entrance were ablaze with golden-yellow black-eyed Susans.

We had ridden to Embleton Bay and raced one another across the hard sand, laughing into the wind as our horses threw themselves into the challenge and thundered neck and neck to where the shore met the road. Uncertain when we might next have the chance to ride together, we had done the same the previous day.

"I do not know why they bother," said Dorothy, glancing at a young man clearing a path. "They will have to rake again tomorrow morning. That is what happens when you have a wedding in October."

Leaves from the trees bordering the carriageway fluttered onto the lawn while the remaining foliage, buffeted by the sea breeze, flapped on the branches like netted fish. The air was cool, but with the low sun tinting the clouds a muted version of the orange leaves and bright flowers, autumn was modestly beautiful.

This time tomorrow, I thought, Dorothy would be married.

When she had written that she was engaged to Edward, whom she'd met hunting the previous winter, I'd had to read the letter twice for the news to register. Once it had sunk in, I felt unsettled. I worried that marriage would uproot Dorothy from my world and replant her in another one. Edward, it seemed, was set for a life in politics. Would that not mean they would have to settle in London and that our meetings and enjoyment of the countryside would be no more? Responding to my letter asking as much, Dorothy insisted otherwise.

"Edward and I have agreed that our relationship is based on the shared interests of rod and line, hunting, walking, and ornithology, all of which are undertaken in the countryside. As such, I will, as far as possible, remain at his family estate Fallodon Hall, which is a lovely ride from Newton Hall when he is working in London. You will always be welcome there," she had written.

The groom took our horses, and after admiring the neatly braided manes of the pair that would pull the bridal carriage, we walked toward the house. That was when Bertie, almost a teenager now, appeared. He continued to worship Dorothy and accompanied her and me whenever he could. Ida insisted it was because Bertie was smitten with me.

"What nonsense," I'd told her. "He is five years younger than I am. He idolizes his big sister and likes being with us because we are more adventurous than you and Gerard—and we like fishing."

"Josephine was six years older than Napoleon," said Ida, with a showy wink.

"You are being silly. Stop it," said Dorothy.

Now, as he walked alongside his sister, Bertie's cheeks were flushed; he looked every bit the excited youngster he was.

"Did you see the carriage, Dorothy? It is so shiny, you could check your teeth in it."

Dorothy nodded.

"Are you excited?"

"Of course. Do I not look it?"

"Frankly, no. You look the same as you did yesterday after you had also ridden with Aleen."

"Oh? And how is that?"

"Sunburned and windswept."

Dorothy chuckled and reached up to ruffle Bertie's hair. When had he grown so tall?

Smiling, the three of us entered Newton Hall to find Major Fitz and Lady Widdrington drinking tea in the library with my mother, who had arrived from London while we were out. I had not seen her for several weeks and was pleased to see that the color had returned to her face after having drained away with the news of Percy's death.

"Hello, Mama," I said, bending to touch her cheek with mine.

"Aleen," she said, turning away slightly. "You look so well that I shall forgive you the whiff of horse you carry with you."

It was like my mother to temper her rare praise of me with rebuff. I ignored it and accepted a cup of tea.

"Ah, Isabel," said the major, smiling at her, "there will be plenty of time tomorrow for the young horsewomen to spruce up."

"I have no doubt that Dorothy will be the most beautiful bride," Mama said, turning her attention to my friend. "What a handsome couple you and Edward make, Dorothy."

I glanced at Dorothy, who detested comments on her good looks but who was also gracious, and she smiled at my mother.

"Did you travel with Charles, Mama?" I asked.

"She did," came a deep voice behind me. I turned to see Charles, tall and lean, standing in the doorway. My oldest brother, who had worked his way up the ranks of the Royal Navy to the position of sub-lieutenant by then, had arranged leave specifically to attend Dorothy's wedding. I wondered if he would do the same when my time came.

"It seems that it was just yesterday that we sat in this very room discussing how you might train to become a nurse," said Charles, after he had greeted Dorothy. "Instead, tomorrow, you will become the wife of, from what I hear, a consummate young politician."

Dorothy laughed quietly. "I had no idea at the time."

"That brings to mind an article I read," said Lady Widdrington. "Dr. Jex-Blake is to open a school of medicine for women in Edinburgh next year."

"To train nurses?" asked the major.

"No, Fitz. She's a physician. She will train other women to become doctors." Lady Widdrington frowned at her husband. Then she turned to address the room at large. "It occurred to me that Dorothy might have trained to become a doctor rather than a nurse. If she had not met Edward, that is."

Charles and my mother exchanged glances.

Dorothy smiled and shook her head. "I do not believe that I have what it takes to be a doctor. What about it, Aleen? You are much smarter and infinitely more capable than I," she said, her eyes twinkling as she looked at me.

"Good heavens, no!" said my mother. "Do not put such ideas in her head."

I interjected. "Well, I do not think that I—"

Mama held up her hand. "Please, Aleen, this is neither the time nor the place."

"I did not—"

Charles cut me off this time. "Your parents tell me you will move with Edward to Fallodon Hall, Dorothy," he said. "Will you go there immediately after the wedding?"

"Yes. Tomorrow."

"Did you know that the Irish woman Sophie Bryant has a Doctor of Science degree, Isabel?" said Lady Widdrington. "She has a paper published by the London Mathematical Society."

My mother glanced down. "No, I did not," she replied. Then, she turned to Dorothy. "Will you—"

But Lady Widdrington was not swayed. "Does Her Majesty keep up with the progress of educated women and the work of the suffragists?"

Mama was rescued by the appearance of Major Fitz's butler, who spoke quietly in his ear. The major stood up.

"Excuse me. Winborne informs me that Samson has taken a turn. I shall go and take a look at him."

"I shall come with you," I said, not looking at my mother as I followed him out of the room.

The whippet, trembling and groaning, was curled up in a corner of the kitchen. He barely acknowledged me when I crouched down and placed my hand on his spine. I lifted his eyelids. The dog's pupils were tiny.

"How long has he been like this?" asked the major.

Winborne glanced at the footman who stood near the door, twisting his cap in his hands.

"I noticed him and the bitch nosing about near the waste barrow less than an hour ago," said the man. "He seemed fine then."

"Where is Delilah?" asked Major Fitz as he squatted next to me and peered at the dog.

"Outside. Seems fine," said the footman.

"Was there old food or perhaps bones in the barrow?" I asked him.

"Aye, Miss Cust," he said. "I don't know about bones, but it was due to be dumped."

Major Fitz called for the cook, who confirmed that the barrow contained the remnants of a deboned chicken, which had been cooked several days earlier and discarded because it stank.

"No bones then? You are certain of that?" asked the major.

"The bones were gone days ago, Major, and the rest of the waste was soft matter, vegetable cuttings and the like. I can't imagine what might've stuck," said the cook.

"I do not think that is the problem," I said. "He's been poisoned by the rotten meat. We should purge him."

Four pairs of eyes looked at me. No one offered an opinion or advice. Samson groaned. I stroked his head, trying to imagine what would induce me to be sick.

"Do you have any mustard prepared?" I asked the cook.

She did, and within a few minutes, I had forced Samson's jaws open and placed a full spoon of the pungent yellow paste at the back of his tongue. The footman held him upright, and I supported his head while the dog retched into a bucket clutched by Winborne. The butler wrinkled his nose in disgust and looked at the major, as if asking to be rescued. Major Fitz looked away. Samson's mustard-colored bile was dotted with foul-smelling, half-chewed bits of white meat and some other miscellaneous debris. He heaved until his stomach was empty. I asked for a bowl of water, and the dog took a few half-hearted laps from it before lying down once more.

"Is he going to be all right?"

It was Bertie. I had not realized he was in the room.

I shrugged. "I hope so. Look how he is stretching out. It seems that the pain has eased."

Major Fitz nodded and smiled at me. "Do you prescribe anything else, doctor?"

"Keep the water near him. Encourage him to drink every half hour or so. Offer him a little bland food in a few hours."

"How did you know what to do, Aleen?" asked Bertie as we made our way down the passage.

"I imagined what might make me feel better if I had eaten something bad and what would make me vomit."

Bertie pulled a face. "So dogs are just like us?"

"No. They are not," I said. "Maybe in some ways, but in other ways, animals are completely different from humans. What I did with Samson was a guess. That is why it is important to study such matters."

It was getting dark when Dorothy and I, out of our riding habits, and bathed and dressed in gowns for the evening meal, took a short stroll around the garden with Samson, Delilah, and Pepper at our heels. Although he declined his mate's urging to chase and be chased, the male whippet had largely recovered. Winborne informed me that he had even eaten a little supper.

"Bertie was so full of admiration for you this afternoon that it made me wonder if Ida is not right," said Dorothy.

I laughed. "You see! That is why I simply have to become a veterinary surgeon. I shall gather admirers."

"You will gather them regardless of what you do."

"If I have just one admirer who looks at me the way Edward looks at you and the way your father looks at your mother, I will be satisfied," I said.

"I hope I will not disappoint him," said Dorothy quietly.

"Of course you will not. Why would you even think that?"

She shook her head, gave a tiny smile and, clearly not wanting to pursue the topic, changed tack. "I am afraid my mother upset yours earlier with her talk of the suffragists."

"Did the conversation continue after I left?"

"It did not evolve into a conversation but rather a monologue as Mother recited some rather radical thoughts on education and equality for women that she had read in the paper. Your mother did not add to the topic."

"No."

"I sympathize with her."

"With my mother?"

"Yes. Even if she were to support the suffragist cause, she is not free to admit it. She is essentially bound by the beliefs of Her Majesty."

"Do you think so? As I understand it, Her Majesty's own daughters support the idea of improving the lives of women. Princess Louise has met with suffragists, and Princess Helena has publicly admired the work of Florence Nightingale."

"My mother has informed you well," said Dorothy.

"Yes."

"But it is different. Her Majesty's relationship with her daughters is different from her relationship with your mother. Your mother is not empowered to express her opinion to Her Majesty like the princesses are. Mothers and daughters have a unique bond."

"Or no bond at all," I said.

CHAPTER 7

❦

1886
London, England

IF MY MOTHER WAS DISAPPOINTED THAT THE PRINCESS OF WALES, PRINCESS Alexandra, stood in for Her Majesty when I was presented at court the year I turned eighteen, she hid it well. It was possible that Mama was relieved not to have to worry about what Her Majesty might make of Lady Cust's unusually tall daughter with her unruly red hair and inquiring gaze. Or it could have had something to do with how glamorous the petite princess was that evening in her cream-colored dress and train, which were embroidered with colorful flowers and finished with a lilac satin border.

"I have never seen her looking more splendid," whispered Mama, her eyes on the diamond tiara, feathers, and veil perched expertly upon Her Royal Highness's head. "Do you see how she resembles a woman in her twenties although she is nearly forty? That is why it is so important to stay out of the sun."

It was true; the princess's complexion was as smooth and creamy as her outfit, and her shoulders and arms as delicate as those of a child. I pulled at the neck of my own gown, suddenly aware of how I towered over the people around me. My mother glanced at me.

"Do stop fidgeting, Aleen. You will upset your outfit."

I thought about how I might talk to Princess Alexandra about hunting. She was an expert horsewoman and continued to hunt even after Her Majesty had implored her to stop. The princess and I might have something in common. However, as the proceedings got under way, I saw that any conversation with her would be impossible.

As I looked across the many rows of debutantes, amassed as we were in yard upon yard of glowing satin and frothy lace, veils and feathers, I thought about what Dorothy had said about the London Season. She was right. It was like a pony show, where our chaperones—by and large, our mothers—were our breeders, eyeing out the competition while several young women looked like they might kick or bite if anyone came too close.

At my mother's insistence, I had practiced the act of kissing Her Royal Highness's hand while simultaneously undertaking a full-court curtsy several times a day for weeks before we headed to London. Finally, although Mama declared eleven-year-old Ursula infinitely more elegant than I at the feat, she conceded that I would probably manage it on the day. That did not stop my heart from speeding up when my name was called.

Judging each step carefully to avoid becoming entangled in my gown, I walked across the room. When I reached the designated spot in front of the princess, I lowered myself as my mother had taught me, bending my knee so that it was just above the floor. Staying in position, I leaned forward to kiss her hand. For a moment, I felt my weight shift and my legs tremble. Holding my breath, I pictured myself toppling face forward into her cream-colored lap. I panicked, and instead of the press-your-lips-on-the-back-of-the-hand move I had learned, I kissed the air, rose, and backed away. Princess Alexandra gave no indication of having noticed my transgression and held her hand out to the next debutante.

"Well done," said my mother when I reached her side. She had not seen the air kiss or my trembling torso, but I noticed that her chest, like mine, was heaving. She too had been holding her breath.

Dorothy was also right about riding in Hyde Park being the best thing about the London Season. I was fortunate that Major Fitz was in town to act as my chaperone on rides down Rotten Row and Ladies' Mile, and I enjoyed getting out of the house and seeing so many splendid horses on the bridle paths. Bertie accompanied us once or twice.

"How was the ball?" he asked as we rode between the trees the morning after I had been presented at court. It was a warm summer, but the leaves were dense and paths shady. We had risen early to avoid the crowds, and in some places, it was almost possible to imagine we were not in the city.

"Exhausting, but more so for my mother than for me."

"Because she had to fight off all your suitors?"

"Because she had to wrestle me into yet another ball gown."

Bertie laughed. "I remember Dorothy complaining in similar terms when Mother and Father presented her, and yet, two years later, she was married."

His voice, I noticed, had deepened and his shoulders were much broader. Every time I saw him, Bertie seemed to resemble his father more. Although the major's hair was pale ginger and curly while his son's was dark and straight, they had the same wide foreheads and noses that could have been carved by a Grecian sculptor. It would not be long before Bertie was taller than me. Indeed, he was no longer a child, which was just as well; Bertie would join the army the following year.

Major Fitz pulled up his horse and looked over his shoulder at us. "Speaking of Dorothy, we are to meet Edward at Stanhope Gate. Shall we canter?"

I had not seen Dorothy's husband since their wedding. A month after she became Lady Grey, Edward had, at the age of twenty-three, become the youngest member of parliament in the House of Commons. Although that meant he spent a great deal of time in London, Edward kept his word; Dorothy stayed at Fallodon Hall, and he returned to her when work allowed. My friend's letters gave no indication that the regular separation affected her enjoyment of marriage. If anything, it made her fonder of her husband.

"We have so much to talk about and fit in when he is home," she had written. *"I have converted him into an ornithologist, which means we are outdoors practically all weekend. I could not wish for more."*

Edward was waiting at the gate astride an elegant, dappled gray mare who stomped her hooves impatiently as we approached. We set off toward the Serpentine River, me riding between Edward and Major Fitz, and Bertie alongside his father. Dorothy's husband—a lean, angular man, whose large, hooked nose somehow added to, rather than detracted from, his good looks—ran through a little small talk and then turned to me.

"I mentioned a visit I undertook on a trip to Edinburgh to Dorothy the other day, and she said you might like to hear about it and the interesting man involved," said Edward.

"Oh?"

Edward explained that he had been invited to tour the New Veterinary College in Edinburgh by its principal, who was eager to promote it. The man, who had the whimsical name of William Williams, was a Welsh farrier turned veterinary surgeon and had previously been principal of Dick's Veterinary College in Edinburgh.

"He's very involved in the profession and is also a former president of the RCVS," he said.

"What's that?" I asked.

"The Royal College of Veterinary Surgeons. It oversees the training of veterinary surgeons," said Edward, leaning forward in his saddle so that Major Fitz could also hear him above the clip-clopping of our horses' hooves. "The college is an impressive, progressive place. Williams most certainly had the ways, means, and foresight to build what is surely the most modern school of its kind. He has included all manner of specially designed equipment and facilities. There are stables, laboratories, operating theaters, classrooms, and testing and treating equipment. I could not work out exactly what some of the machinery was for, but I was intrigued and impressed by the obvious specialization."

"Have you visited other veterinary colleges?" I asked, envying Edward for the first time. I had no idea politics might open such interesting doors.

"Only the Royal Veterinary College here in London. It is much older and, unless I missed something, did not seem half as well equipped as Williams's school."

We rode without speaking for a moment as I pictured the place. I wondered if Edward might have reason to go back to Edinburgh and visit

Principal Williams and, if so, whether there might be a chance I could accompany him. Was that why Dorothy had imagined I might be interested in hearing about the visit? I was about to ask when the major spoke.

"Did you see any students? At the college in Edinburgh?" he asked.

Edward nodded. "Yes. They were there."

"No women?"

"No."

I looked at Major Fitz, expecting him to go on. Why had he asked? Was he making a point? Putting to rest any ideas I might have about attending the college? What was Edward's point? Why had he told me about the college? What had Dorothy said to him? I wished that Lady Widdrington were there. She had recently told me about a French doctor who had taken a course at a veterinary school in Lyon, France, and set up a practice in Paris. Lady Widdrington would not have hesitated to question Edward and the major. I tried to imagine what she might ask.

Major Fitz continued, "You say the college is progressive, Edward. Does that mean that Principal Williams is himself progressive? Is it not possible—"

We were interrupted by the appearance of a pair of riders who were acquaintances of Major Fitz, stopping for introductions and obligatory chitchat about the Season. After the father and daughter had ridden on, our conversation took another tack, and before I had a chance to get back to Principal Williams and his college, Edward said he had a meeting, bade us farewell, and trotted away up Rotten Row. I watched him go with the empty sense of having heard all but the punch line of a joke.

"We should make our way back to Kensington," said the major. "I have to be at the club for lunch."

"You asked Edward about the students at the veterinary college, Major."

"Yes."

"Do you think that if the principal is as progressive as Edward seems to think that he might consider taking women students?"

Major Fitz frowned. I wondered if he regretted having broached the subject. "I know it is something you dream about, Aleen, but I am reluctant to get involved. Your mother and Charles are *so* set against your seeking further education, let alone training as a veterinary surgeon. It is not my place."

"But you are my guardian. You could—"

"Yes, but alas, we are not family. If it were simply a case of offering you advice and guidance, it might be different. But to be involved in financing your training… I am sorry, Aleen, but I cannot in good faith take that on—no matter how much you, Dorothy, and Cecilia urge me to."

"I understand," I said, wanting to plead my case.

The major rode on. Behind him, Bertie reached over and gave my hand a quick, firm squeeze.

"He really wants to help you," whispered the boy. "Be patient."

It was as if he had clasped my heart.

I was still thinking about the veterinary college in Edinburgh that evening when my mother came into my bedchamber before we were due to leave for another dinner party. She pushed her fingers between the laces of my corset, tightened them, and cast her eye over the gown she had instructed the maid to lay out for me.

"Edward rode with us this morning," I said, knowing that that would please her. The Cust family's association with the increasingly popular member of parliament was something she noted whenever the opportunity arose—and sometimes even when it did not.

"How kind of him. He is well, I hope?"

"Yes. He recently returned from Edinburgh, where he visited a veterinary college."

My mother stiffened. How quickly I had ruined things for her.

"He spoke very highly of the college. I thought I might ask him if it might be possible for me to visit it—perhaps with him, next time he travels north."

She folded her arms and looked out the window.

"I could ask Dorothy to come too. 'The Viscount and Viscountess Grey of Fallodon accompany Miss Aleen Cust on a visit to the New Veterinary College in Edinburgh.' Does that not sound like a pleasing news headline? Is there anything wrong with the idea?"

Mama turned and glared at me. "You are not a child anymore, Aleen.

Why do I have to repeat myself? It is time to let go of your silly fantasy. It is not amusing, only embarrassing."

"It is not a fantasy. The reason I have talked about it for so long is because it is something I desperately want to do. I wish to become a veterinary surgeon."

"But it is not possible! You know how Her Majesty feels about women who seek equality with men. It is unseemly and shameful that you should even consider the prospect."

"Why? More and more women are becoming physicians, and Miss Buss and Miss Beale are reforming education for girls."

"Physicians," she snorted. "What about those doctors who say that if women study too much, it inhibits their ability to have children? Who will marry you then? Hmm?"

"There is no evidence of that, Mama. It does not make sense. Learning takes place in the brain, not in the womb."

I thought about how she had absent-mindedly permitted me to study with my brothers. It had not only exposed me to the work of Darwin, Huxley, and others, but also allowed me to prove to myself that I was of equal, if not better, intellect to the boys. However, I knew it would serve no purpose to tell her so.

"Were Miss Nightingale's endeavors unseemly and shameful?" I asked.

With neither Charles nor Orlando present to prevent the discussion going further, my mother felt obliged to respond. "Florence Nightingale? Yes, she certainly had little regard for what is expected of ladies in polite society."

"But not everything is about polite society. There are other—"

"Did you know that one of your grandfather's relatives was an acquaintance of William Nightingale? William's thinking was apparently widely influenced by his time on the Continent. It was he who educated Florence and her sister."

"Was that a bad thing?"

She looked out of the window again and said in a tone of resignation, "If you are so set on a profession, Aleen, let it be nursing. At least *that* has some semblance of respectability since Miss Nightingale's efforts."

I had never, not even when Dorothy expressed an interest in it, considered taking up nursing. However, it was the first time my mother had indicated she might support my doing anything other than finding a husband, and because I relied on her and Charles to finance my ambitions, I could not let the opportunity pass me by. I wondered too, if like the doctor in Paris, I might use what I learned about taking care of people to treat animals.

"I shall make inquiries tomorrow," I said.

"Be discreet. Please do not discuss this with anyone," she said, sighing and leaving the room without looking at me.

CHAPTER 8

❦

1888
London, England

Nursing was not for me. I knew this within hours of scurrying behind the matron down the long, cold hallways and crisscrossing countless wards in London Hospital with the exasperated boom of a doctor's voice in my ears, but I did not freely admit to it for some weeks. The satisfaction my surrender would give my mother compelled me to hang on. Though that was not all I feared. There was no doubt that Mama and Charles would be even less inclined to allow me to study to be a veterinary surgeon if I quickly gave up the one thing I had been permitted to try. I had trapped myself in a corner.

It was only when, almost a month into my nursing training in 1888, Orlando came to London for a weekend that I revealed how miserable I was. I managed to get him away from Mama and Ursula by convincing him to accompany me and Ruby, gray-muzzled and stiff-jointed by then, on a walk in Kensington Gardens. I had not, I discovered, been as successful at concealing my discontentment as I imagined.

"What is troubling you, dear sister?" he asked, tucking my arm beneath his as we stepped into the street.

"What makes you think I am troubled?"

"Mama says you are simply quiet because working at the hospital tires you, but I know better; you are invigorated by activity. It would take more than a long day on your feet to silence you. So?"

"I loathe it." It was difficult but also liberating to say the words.

"The training? The work?"

"They are one and the same. Mostly, I dislike the hospital, where I am closeted inside all day. I feel entombed, not only by the place but also this city. Separated from the countryside by layer after layer of walls."

"I can see how that would displease you," he said quietly.

"Then, there is the constant, anxious shouting of instructions by doctors, which unnerves everyone and turns many of the matrons and senior nurses into tyrants."

"Is that not simply because you are still in training? Surely, it will change."

"No. That is how it is in hospitals. One is either commanded or a commander."

"But what of the work? The nursing? Are there no rewards in that?"

I had thought about that, hoping that helping the ill and the injured would make up for being closeted indoors and shouted at all day. It did not.

"There have been moments when I have found satisfaction in helping patients, but even then, it is not enough," I said.

We had arrived at the gardens. Ruby managed a short trot through the gate ahead of us before she stopped in the shade, panting heavily. The Spaniel had found it as difficult as I had to adjust to life in the city where visits outside were rare and regulated. Typically, the moment she felt the bare earth or grass beneath her paws, she sprang to life, forgetting for a moment that she was almost twelve years old. She had been bothered by spells of coughing, which I imagined were caused by the smog that hung low across London. I crouched to stroke her.

"Take it slowly, old girl," I said as I rose and walked on with her at my heels. In the distance, I saw a group of riders canter away, dust rising behind them. I had not ridden for weeks and ached to be on a horse again.

Orlando asked what I planned to do. I explained my fears and implored him not to mention a word of what I had said to anyone.

"The only thing keeping me going is the idea that I might be able to use what I learn at the hospital to become a veterinary surgeon," I said. "If I can continue there for at least a year, it will not seem that I gave up easily, and perhaps Mama and Charles will allow me to use some of my inheritance to go to veterinary college—if I can find one to take me."

He emitted a small snort and shook his head. "So *that* is why you signed up at the hospital. I wondered."

"It was the only thing Mama would concede to."

"There is a great difference between emulating Florence Nightingale in a London hospital and treating horses, cows, and sheep in the countryside. Aside from the fact that no women have trained as veterinary surgeons, the work is vastly different. Even if you work as a nurse for five or ten years, I cannot imagine our mother agreeing to your becoming a veterinary surgeon."

I sighed. "What else am I to do?"

"I don't know, but living in the city, trying to be a nurse, and hating every minute of it is not the answer. I have never seen you as thin, pale, and pinched."

"Pinched?"

He reached out and squeezed my wrist between his thumb and forefinger. "Pinched, yes."

We walked without talking for a moment. When I glanced behind to check on Ruby, she was nowhere to be seen. I called but still there was no sign of her. We turned and retraced our steps.

I found her sprawled beneath a bench. Her body was limp and her breathing shallow. Orlando did not object when I asked him to remove his coat so that we could lay it down, roll her onto it, and carry her home. She opened her eyes a couple of times as we walked and lifted her tail once in a weak, apologetic wag but was otherwise still in her tweed hammock.

Without mentioning my intentions to anyone, I did not return to the hospital on Monday. Instead, I went to the Royal Veterinary College in Camden Town, where I intercepted a student after following him up the stairs and into the three-story, redbrick building. He was agitated by my attention, possibly, I suspected, because he was late for class. I pretended not to notice his impatience as I quickly described Ruby's symptoms.

"What would you advise?" I asked.

He rolled his eyes. "Our training is serious and does not concern pets, miss. We work with large animals."

"But surely you—"

"However, it would seem to me that your old dog has heart failure."

It was what I had feared. "Is there anything I can do for her?"

He shrugged. "Keep her quiet and warm and try to get her to eat and drink. She should get some light exercise so that she remains mobile. What else can one do with anything or anyone at such an advanced age?"

I watched as the man hurried away and disappeared into a room. The building was quiet, presumably because lessons were under way. I looked down the long passage, which was lined on either side by a series of closed doors. The floor was shiny and the walls bare, but I felt none of the stifling oppression I experienced at the hospital. Just imagining what discussions took place beneath that roof made it different. There were no clues to what I might learn there, but I longed to follow the man into a classroom and find out.

I heard footsteps and turned. A short, stout man with gray whiskers and a large book under his arm peered at me through oval spectacles.

"Can I help you, miss?" he asked.

Yes, I wanted to say, you can point me to where I can sign up to train as a veterinary surgeon. Instead, I tried to smile. "No. Thank you."

Ruby was lying where I had left her when I arrived home. She lifted her head and wagged her tail once, twice. I encouraged her to eat some chicken, and she drank from the saucer I held out to her. I was pleased that she was no longer coughing and left her sleeping.

"Aleen! Thank goodness," said my mother as I walked past the drawing room.

I halted, confused. I had not expected her home from the palace until later.

She looked at me and said, "Did the hospital send you away?"

"No, I—"

"You *cannot* go back there!"

"What? I don't understand. What has happened, Mama?"

My mother paced the room, wringing her hands as she recounted the story she had been told by other members of Her Majesty's staff. The mutilated corpses of several women had been discovered in Whitechapel in recent months. Police believed the murders were the work of a serial killer who remained at large.

"You cannot return to the hospital," she said. "It is at the very center of the monster's hunting grounds. I forbid you to go back."

I was speechless, not only because of the gruesome account of the murders but also because of the reprieve my mother had unintentionally given me. She mistook my silence for imminent rebuttal.

"It is out of the question; you cannot go back," she repeated.

"Yes, Mama. I see that."

She looked at me, head tilted. "Good. Good. Come to think of it, how is it you have heard nothing of this at the hospital? In Whitechapel? Is this the first you have heard about the murders?"

"It is," I replied, wondering if I had missed something because of my preoccupation with the awfulness of being at the hospital. "Perhaps such news travels faster to the palace than it does closer to home."

"Then I am glad of it. We will not risk having the Cust name flushed through the gutters of London."

It had not occurred to me that my mother might place my safety above the reputation of the family. As such, her comment neither shocked nor hurt me. Or perhaps, it was easier to ignore when carried by a wave of relief.

Barred from the hospital and silently grateful for having been saved from nursing—albeit by the despicable deeds of someone who was soon referred to as Jack the Ripper—I could find no reason to linger in London. Within a few weeks, Ruby and I left the city to enjoy the country pleasures of Northumberland with Dorothy and her family.

CHAPTER 9

❧

1893
Northumberland, England

IT WAS FIVE YEARS LATER WHEN I FIRST IMAGINED THAT I MIGHT SERIOUSLY have to let go of my dream of becoming a veterinary surgeon. Up until then, I had hung on to the belief that I would somehow win over Charles and my mother. With the number of women training as physicians growing, and with Miss Buss and Miss Beale having educated more and more girls, I had hoped Her Majesty's attitude toward the role of women in the world would adapt. An adjustment in her opinion would almost certainly effect change in my mother. I sensed, too, from the occasional sympathetic glance he gave me, that Charles would not stand in my way if our mother capitulated. Alas, the stimulus I required to help change my mother's mind never came.

I was riding Major Fitz's light-footed young hunter, Juno, from Newton Hall to Fallodon to visit Dorothy when admitting defeat occurred to me. Why then, I cannot say. Perhaps it was that the previous morning, I had been told about the establishment of a registrar of farriers by the smithy who shoed the major's horses. He mentioned that the Royal College of Veterinary Surgeons was among the parties behind the development. It saddened me to think that the Royal College was progressive enough to look for ways of improving the work and lives of farriers but that neither I nor any other woman might ever benefit from its foresight. I longed to be on the inside of such professionalism.

The notion of giving up my dream could also have had something to do with having recently celebrated my twenty-fifth birthday. Most women my age were married and producing offspring. Others bore the weighty disappointment of their families as they were threatened with futures of spinsterhood. I had spent the years raising and caring for my animals. It was not that I did not imagine one day experiencing matrimony and bearing children. The aspirations did not, however, dominate my thoughts. I had no desire to live a life that could be sustained by being idle and ignorant, which seemed to me what many women of my standing settled for in marriage. If that meant putting my other interests ahead of finding a husband and making a home, then so be it. Even at twenty-five, when I recognized that I might never become a veterinary surgeon, I remained firm in this resolve. If I could not be further educated, I would do something else involving animals that would give me purpose.

Ruby had outlived the heart condition that showed itself in Kensington Gardens by several years. As if making up for what I was unable to do for Goliath, Taffy, and Ned, I cared for her like a hen clucking over her chick. I learned from a physician that dandelion root reduced fluid build-up around the heart so that it could pump more effectively and thus treated Ruby with a little each day. The Spaniel's meals, bland and unvarying small portions of chicken and bread, coupled with two short walks a day, kept her dark eyes and silky coat shiny and her tail wagging—until one morning, it wagged no more. She died sleeping on the carpet next to my bed in Leasowe Castle. It took me several months to stop expecting to see her at my heels, but my mourning for Ruby was tempered by the many years of happy companionship we had shared and by my being able to care for her to the end. It helped me, too, that Ruby was not an only dog when she died.

Prompted by my mother—who, I suspect, was not so much enchanted by Her Majesty's collection of Pomeranians (she had thirty at one point) as she was eager to participate in her sovereign's passion—I decided to purchase a breeding pair of the fluffy, fox-faced dogs.

The Queen, Mama said, was intent on breeding tiny versions of the animals, which had already been miniaturized from the Spitz-type sled dogs of northeastern Europe. Six royal Pomeranians were entered into the 1891 Crufts Dog Show. No one was surprised when one of the palace favorites, Winsor Marco, won first place in the Pomeranian category.

"She wants to reduce the breed's size to seven pounds," said my mother. "You should get a breeding pair, Aleen. You argue you want to do something useful with animals. This is your opportunity."

Helping Her Majesty reduce the size of the Pomeranian was not what convinced me to take a closer look at the dogs. Instead, I was encouraged by the unusual notion of my mother encouraging me to do something with animals. The breed's perky, self-assured demeanor, expressed by their straight-legged strutting, husky yap, peaked ears, and voluminous soft coats, won me over within a few minutes of meeting one.

So it was that I first purchased a male Pomeranian called Nugget from a breeder in Birmingham and then a bitch, Honey, from an estate near Manchester. I then began building my reputation as a serious breeder, exhibitor, and expert on Pomeranians from Leasowe. It was the one thing I had done with my life that pleased my mother. Our conversations—few as they were—became dominated by Pomeranian-related questions from the Queen.

"Her Majesty wants to know what you think about the role of diet in reducing the size of your dogs."

"How much exercise is your pair getting? Her Majesty thinks it is important to keep them active without building unnecessary muscle. Do you agree? How much exercise is enough?"

"Do you think stripping their coats improves growth and glossiness? Her Majesty wants your opinion."

For once, my mother and I were connected, if only through my and the Queen's interest in Pomeranians. It was not much, but I was grateful for not disappointing Mama for once. I even felt a little smug at having something to discuss with my mother that excluded Ursula. I did not, however, realize how tenuous the connection was until I again raised the topic of studying to be a veterinary surgeon.

"Her Majesty wants you to measure your dogs so that she can compare their dimensions to those of hers," said my mother, when she returned to Leasowe from Buckingham Palace one weekend.

"I shall do so," I replied. "You know, Mama, I think I could be more helpful to Her Majesty if I knew more about the anatomy of Pomeranians."

My mother looked at me, her mouth in a line as straight as a set of carriage tracks across a flat field.

"If you and Charles were to permit me to train as a veterinary surgeon, I could learn how to help Her Majesty breed the lines she desires. It would please her I am sure, and I could—"

"It would repel her," she said, her jaw clenched.

"But Mama, surely—"

"Her Majesty has a veterinary surgeon. *He* provides everything that is required."

"Imagine, though, a veterinary surgeon who is also an expert on Pomeranians. Her Majesty could—"

"Stop it, Aleen. It will never happen."

The helplessness of the situation made me resentful. I stared at her, tempted to say that she would receive no more information from me about Pomeranians to convey to Her Majesty for as long as I was forbidden from pursuing my dream. I caught Ursula's eye across the room. She did not try to hide the smirk on her face.

Perhaps, I thought as Juno clip-clopped over a gray stone bridge, I should discuss the notion of giving up my dream once and for all with Dorothy. Her opinions almost always calmed and reassured me. She could tell me about her thoughts on whether I should devote myself entirely to breeding dogs and horses. I knew it would please my family, but that did not stop the thought from saddening me. I urged Juno into a canter, imagining as we passed through the woods with the soft Northumberland hills in the background how it would be to let go of the dream I had held on to for so long. With the trees behind us and the road becoming flat and smooth ahead, I leaned forward and pressed her to gallop, as if going faster might leave the bitter thought behind.

Dorothy was waiting for me outside the large front door at Fallodon. I assumed she had been alerted to my arrival by the clatter of Juno's hooves on the drive. We had not seen one another for several months. Edward had recently been appointed Under-Secretary of State at the Foreign Office, and the couple had spent several months in the country in Hampshire so that he had easier access to London.

I dismounted, and she took me by surprise by embracing me. It was only when she stepped back and took my hand to lead me into the house that I noticed her red-rimmed eyes.

"Is something wrong?" I asked. Dorothy avoided touching people, even those she cared for. Even if her eyes had not been red, the embrace and hand-holding would have startled me.

"Come," she replied, climbing the stairs. "Tea is laid out in the drawing room. Edward arrived a few hours ago. He is waiting for us there."

I saw from Edward's tight smile that something was most certainly amiss. "What is it?" I demanded.

Edward had learned, minutes before boarding the train that morning, that Orlando had died the previous day shortly after being diagnosed with meningitis. I sat down, shock taking the strength from my legs.

Orlando. Warm, kind, and thoughtful Orlando. The only one of my siblings who truly listened when I spoke of my ambitions and allowed me to declare my frustrations. The brother with whom I laughed…the one I loved and loved me in return. He was only three years older than I was and yet, his life was over. How cruel it was. No more walks on the beach at Leasowe with him. No more jesting in the drawing room. Who would keep the peace at the dinner table? Who would acknowledge that my complaints about the injustice of life were valid?

I do not remember much about the next few days. Dorothy accompanied me to Leasowe where my mother, Ursula, Charles, and Leo were waiting, silent and stony-faced. Whether they had exhausted conversation about Orlando before I arrived or had chosen to deal with his death with the kind of silent stoicism that prevailed among the Custs, I cannot say. I suspect it was the latter.

My mother's eyes were empty, just as they had been when Papa and

Percy had died. I wanted to convey to her how sorry I was for her grief. She had lost a husband and two sons within fifteen years, and although she was not yet sixty years old, she looked much older.

"Mama," I said, approaching her when we arrived, my arms open, "I am so—"

She turned from my embrace. "Yes, Aleen, I know."

My mother's coldness hurt, though I wished it did not. Fortunately, Dorothy was there. It helped to have her with me. We walked on the beach, where she listened as I spoke freely about Orlando and my anger at his death. She handed me her handkerchief when I cried. Dorothy knew how fond I was of my brother and that I believed that he was my only ally in the family.

Days later, Major Fitz—he and Lady Widdrington had come to Leasowe for the funeral—assembled my mother and siblings in the dining room. It was only then that I realized just how much of an ally Orlando had truly been.

"Your beloved son, Isabel," said the major, giving my mother a tiny nod before glancing at the rest of us, "and your brother entrusted me with his last will and testament, which he wrote and signed some three years back."

He held up a one-page letter. The room was quiet.

"I shall read it to you," said the major. So he did; the room grew quieter still.

Unsurprisingly, Orlando ensured that we all inherited from his estate. What was unexpected was that he stipulated that a portion of his wealth be paid to me independently of my inheritance from Papa and Percy, and that I should have full and immediate access to do with it as I pleased.

"May I see it?" I asked when Major Fitz reached the end of the document.

He handed the paper to me. It was exactly as I had understood the major's reading of it.

Charles took it from me, rolling his eyes in my mother's direction once he had read it. I could think of nothing to say. It was astounding. In death, Orlando had stood up for me in the most daring and forceful way possible. My peace-loving brother had provided me with the means of training to become a veterinary surgeon—if I could find a place that would take me. As the rest of the family trailed silently from the room, I sat speechless with love and gratitude. Major Fitz sat next to me.

"Did you know about this?" I asked eventually.

"Not until this morning."

"It is so unlike Orlando. So risky. He must have known how this would upset Mama and Charles," I said.

"He cared for you."

"He did not anticipate dying young enough for me to use it to study."

Major Fitz stared at me. Clearly, he was unsure of how to respond. I started to laugh, quietly at first. He chuckled. The grief, anxiety, and fatigue that had amassed within me since I learned of Orlando's death seemed to bubble to the surface. I continued laughing until I realized that I was also crying. I placed my head in my hands and sobbed. As Dorothy had days before, the major handed me a handkerchief and sat without talking until I was done.

At last, I sat up. "I am going to inquire about studying as a veterinary surgeon."

"I know," he replied. "You might begin your inquiries in Scotland."

"Scotland?"

"Do you remember the college Edward told us about when we were riding with him in Hyde Park years ago?"

"Yes, of course."

"I visited some months ago and met the principal. Remember the man with the memorable name of William Williams?"

"Yes, indeed. You met him?"

Major Fitz glanced away. "I did not want to upset your mother by saying anything at the time or getting your hopes up, but now, with this…" He gestured toward Orlando's will, which lay on the table. How remarkable that such an ordinary-looking sheet of paper could hold such powerful promise of change.

"You spoke to Principal Williams about me…about a woman enrolling at his college?"

He nodded. "He said that you would be required to obtain a certificate of education with credits in specific subjects from the University of

Edinburgh before commencing the veterinary course but that it should be possible for you to do that within a year."

I grasped the arm of the chair as if I might fall off if I did not.

"But...I..." My head swam. I did not know what to say. "Are there other women students there?"

"A few at the university but not at the New Veterinary College. You would be the first."

"But Principal Williams will support my application?"

"Yes, indeed. We have providence to thank for that," he said. "At least, in part."

Major Fitz reminded me about what Edward had told us: that Principal Williams had established his own veterinary college after having run a different one, also in Edinburgh, for several years.

"As you can imagine, there is keen rivalry between the two colleges," said the major. "But I sense that Principal Williams is steering a more progressive organization and would consider it a victory to be able to claim to have trained the first woman veterinary surgeon."

"That is providence," I replied, still giddy.

"He did, however, allude to how difficult it might be, given that you would be the sole woman at the college. He inquired at length about your character. I explained that you had been raised with three older brothers and that you are one of the most determined people I know. Not to mention, a proficient horsewoman and successful dog breeder."

I gave a small laugh. "Thank you, Major. I am indebted to you."

"Not at all. If I had not been able to help, you would have found another way," he said. "I will, if you agree to it, write to Principal Williams and request another meeting—to introduce you."

I nodded, aware of my heart thundering in my chest.

"Will you tell your mother and Charles?"

"Yes. There is nothing to suggest that they might change their minds, but I continue to hope. I do not want to alienate the few members of my family that remain, but now that Orlando has provided means, I will do this with or without their blessing."

My instinct was correct. If anything, Mama and Charles were even more opposed to the idea of me going to university and working than they had ever been. After bidding Dorothy and her parents farewell the next day, I told my mother and brother that I would begin investigating training as a veterinary surgeon. Mama turned her back. Charles glared at me.

"After everything Mama has gone through, you are going to add *this* to her worries?" he said, his upper lip curling in a snarl.

"I do not want to be the cause of any worry. I simply want to realize my dream of becoming a veterinary surgeon. It has been my ambition for as long as I recall."

"That is the problem," said seventeen-year-old Ursula, appearing suddenly behind me. "If you were a proper lady, you would not be *ambitious*."

She spat the word, as if it was poisonous.

"I am a lady, a lady who aspires to do something worthwhile with her life. I cannot understand why that upsets you all so."

My mother swung around. Her dark eyes flashed. "Because it is embarrassing. Gravely so! You will bring great shame on the family if you go ahead with this, Aleen. I am not sure how I will hold my head up in company. What will Her Majesty think?"

"And I am due to come out next year," said my sister. "Are you so selfish that you cannot see what your stubbornness might do to *my* future?"

I thought of several responses to Ursula's charge. Did it not apply both ways? Was she not also selfish to deny me my desires? Was my happiness not as important as hers?

The collar of my dress, high and scratchy, seemed tighter. I gave it a tug as I opened my mouth to speak. "Why is your—"

I stopped myself.

Charles made a valid point about our mother's woes. Her grief was fresh, and her position in the deeply conventional royal household made her particularly sensitive to anything Her Majesty might consider improper. Part of me wished that I could brush off my family's disapproval like a horse might disperse a fly with her tail, but I could not. Despite their censure and conformist ways, I was proud of being a Cust and yearned for them to feel the same about me.

"Actually, there is no reason to worry," said Charles, addressing Mama. "None of the colleges or universities will accept her. They will not entertain this madness. Women are not permitted to study to become veterinary surgeons. It is ludicrous to imagine a woman working with animals. Her appeals will come to naught. We should ignore her threats."

Ursula sniggered and stared at me, as if daring me to refute his statement. I could have told them about Professor Williams and the New Veterinary College but thought better of it. What if they contacted the college and the principal had second thoughts? I called Nugget and Honey and, with the two prancing gaily at my heels, walked to the beach.

CHAPTER 10

❧

1896
Cheshire, England

IT WAS EASY NOT TO REVEAL MY PLANS TO MY FAMILY AFTER THAT. CHARLES returned to his nautical life and my mother to hers mollifying Her Majesty. Ursula and Leo, whose sojourns at Leasowe sometimes coincided with mine, more or less ignored me.

Over the next few months, Major Fitz wrote a letter of introduction and intent to Principal Williams, which I followed with a dispatch of my own. Once I had established which university subjects I needed to study to obtain what he called the certificate of education necessary to enroll at the veterinary college, I mailed my application to the University of Edinburgh. When I received confirmation of registration from the institution, I wrote as much to Principal Williams. He replied immediately, inviting me to meet him and tour the veterinary college as soon as I arrived in Scotland to begin university.

I stood in front of the fire in the drawing room in the castle in Leasowe and stared at the letter for several minutes after reading it. It did not, despite my fears, disappear. It was real. Finally, in 1896, I would begin working toward becoming a veterinary surgeon.

"Thank you, Orlando," I said to the empty room. Nugget heard and trotted to me. I knelt and hugged him.

As agreed upon with the Widdringtons, I would travel to Northumberland and leave him and Honey at Fallodon with Dorothy. Major Fitz would accompany me to Edinburgh to introduce me to Principal Williams before leaving me to settle in the city. After a year at the university, I would begin training at the New Veterinary College. Three years later, I could begin work as a veterinary surgeon.

I wondered briefly whether my father had ever imagined that his friend would go to such lengths to support me. The major's guardianship might have officially expired when I turned twenty-one, but his support never waned. Of course, my father could not have predicted as much. Why would he? Papa would not have entertained thoughts of his daughter pursuing the kind of unorthodox life that would require such patronage.

The sky was gray and the wind cold, but I wanted to be outdoors. I sent word to the stables to saddle Caesar. I would celebrate my imminent new life by riding across the beaches and fields of Cheshire. Perhaps the sound of pounding hooves and crashing waves would help drive reality home. It would also be an opportunity for me to say goodbye to the Leasowe countryside. Who knew when I might return south?

Dorothy met me at the station when I arrived in Northumberland the following week. Nugget and Honey bounced around the carriage like lambs with grass beneath their hooves for the first time. They were elated to be free of the crate they had been confined to on the train.

"How was your mother when you left?" asked Dorothy, trying to calm Nugget by stroking his back as he sat on her lap.

"The same." I did not meet her eye.

"What do you mean?"

"I have not told anyone about Edinburgh. I will write once I have settled there."

She frowned. "Oh dear. I suppose procrastination is one way of approaching the matter."

"I told her I was coming to Northumberland and was not sure when I would return. I do not believe she gave my leaving much thought. She is accustomed to my being here for months at a time."

"Yes, but you will not be here."

"I know. I am a coward. I should have told her, but I—"

"You are not a coward. You are the bravest, most resilient, independent woman I know. You will find a way of appeasing your mother and Charles soon. I am sure of that." She paused. "I worry more about how it will be for you in Edinburgh."

"As a student you mean?"

"Yes."

"The university has accepted women for several years. The Edinburgh Seven cleared the way for me."

"Yes, but you know how difficult the men made it for them, and what a trial it remains for women students to this day. Then, when your year at the university is complete, you will be the first woman at the veterinary college. Will the men there be ready for you?"

"They will have to be."

"You will not take on a masculine disguise and become the veterinary surgeon version of James Barry?"

I laughed, thinking it a joke, but Dorothy's expression was earnest.

"No, I will not," I said. "I am considering using just my initials. A pseudonym might also provide some cover. Or ambiguity, at least. But I cannot imagine dressing as a man. James Barry was slight. I have the full form of a woman. Can you imagine me successfully hiding this shape?"

Dorothy glanced at me and shook her head. I sensed that there was more that she wanted to say.

"What is it?" I asked.

She looked down at Nugget, who was finally sitting quietly on her lap.

"Dorothy, tell me."

There was no reply, so I continued. "I thought assuming a pseudonym might also comfort my family. If I do not use the Cust name, they might be less concerned about others learning of my endeavors, thus causing them the embarrassment they so dread."

"Edward told me of a man who had his daughter admitted to a mental asylum, claiming symptoms of insanity because she demanded an education and wanted to attend university."

I recalled Orlando's accounts of similar incidents. If my brother believed I would manage it, who was I to fear what might lie ahead?

"That will not happen. Neither my mother nor Charles is cruel."

"I know that," she said quietly, "but—"

"They might disown me, but they will not risk drawing attention to the family by doing anything drastic. I am sure of that."

"They will not disown you, Aleen. Surely not? You are family. In time, they will accept your decision. Be proud even."

I shrugged. "It is what I hope too, but if they cannot bear it and Mama, my brothers, and Ursula turn their backs on me, I have the Widdrington family on my side, including my friends, Viscount and Viscountess Grey of Fallodon, do I not?"

Finally, Dorothy smiled. She reassured me that I could, as ever, count on her support and asked what pseudonym I would use. Who I would be if not Aleen Isabel Cust?

"I thought I would go by A. I. Cust," I said. "The initials do not give anything away. However, Cust is an unusual name, and the few Custs who exist are almost certainly kin."

"The advantage of using a variation of your actual name is that you cannot be accused of being deceitful."

"If it makes life easier and is more acceptable to my mother, I am happy to risk it. I do not think using only my initials will be enough, though. Your suggestion of a variation of Cust is a good one."

"How about A. I. Custard?" she asked, her eyes twinkling. "You are fond of custard, so it should not be difficult to remember."

We laughed, and then it came to me. "I know! I shall be A. I. Custance. What a perfectly appropriate name for a veterinary student."

"Custance? Like the jockey?"

"Yes."

Although Harry Custance had retired from racing by then, he regularly joined the Quorn Hunt in Leicestershire and the Cottesmore Hunt in

Rutland, which was where I had had occasion to be introduced to him when I went to a meet at the invitation of one of Major Widdrington's friends a few years earlier. Mr. Custance had laughed and blushed when I told him how my brothers and I had raced our horses across the fields in Tipperary years before for the honor of being addressed as Harry Custance for the day.

"That is a most excellent idea," said Dorothy. "What man who knows anything about anything would not be overjoyed to have Miss Custance treat his horses?"

"A. I. Custance, Member of the Royal College of Veterinary Surgeons, please, my lady."

The first thing I noticed when Major Fitz and I stepped out of the carriage at Forty-one Elm Row in Leith Walk, Edinburgh, was the stone sculpture of a horse standing between a dog and a cow, the latter two lying with their legs folded beneath them and their heads raised. Set on a corbel to the left of the entrance of an expansive, two-story building, the statue marking the New Veterinary College made me think about how nondescript the institution's equivalent in London was. I thought too about how disinclined the student I had met there had been to provide advice on treating Ruby, as if *that* was not the duty of a veterinary surgeon. The memory made me even happier to be in Scotland than I was. I imagined how I might one day be approached at college by a stranger looking for advice and how I would not brush them off with an arrogant few words.

The main entrance led into a hallway that was enclosed at the back by a pair of windowed doors. I looked through them onto a series of adjoining buildings that formed the rectangular shape of the college out back. In the center, the open courtyard was paved, save for a strip of gravel that ran down the middle for about fifty yards.

My scrutiny was interrupted by a young man who escorted us into the principal's office, where he asked us to wait. I walked to the bay window, which offered an even more commanding view of the courtyard. A group of men followed as a bay-and-white Clydesdale was led onto the gravel path. They stood as the horse was walked and then trotted up and down before them. After a few laps, the horse was brought to a halt and a man, presumably a teacher, stepped forward, handed his top hat to someone, and lifted one of the horse's giant, feathery front hooves. The men gathered around and peered closer. Were they investigating an injury? A new technique of shoeing? The horse looked at me. Although he was too far away for me to be sure, it seemed we made eye contact. I wondered why none of the men seemed to be watching the horse's face, noting what his eyes might say. They were possibly missing clues about whatever it was they were investigating. I would have suggested it if I could and was impatient to be among them, wishing it was not necessary for me to study at the university for a year.

"Why are you sighing?" asked the major.

I turned from the window. "Now that I am here, I am even more eager to begin. It has taken so long."

"But you are here, and in just a year you will be here every day."

"Yes, but still I—"

The door opened and a trim man in a dark suit with neat gray hair and a matching mustache walked in.

"Major Widdrington, it is good to see you again," he said.

The men shook hands, and when the major introduced me, the principal presented his hand to shake mine. I was pleased to do so but could not help briefly imagining my mother's displeasure. She believed that if a lady was to relegate herself to shaking a hand, it should only occur if she initiated it. I did not agree. The handshake seemed respectful and professional. It was a social leveler. In this instance, I fantasized it might mean that one day Professor Williams and I would be peers.

"I am sure I do not have to warn you that your presence here will ruffle feathers," he said, after we had discussed the subjects and standards I would need to achieve at the university before starting at veterinary college.

"No, you do not," I replied.

"My colleagues and I will do what we can to prepare the other students for your arrival, but I am afraid I cannot guarantee that they will not make it difficult for you as the only woman in the college."

"I understand," I said. "I expect that I will be accustomed to it after being at the university."

"Perhaps, but as you know, there have been women there for some years now. Dr. Jex-Blake and her peers broke the ground for you there; you will be the first here." Professor Williams's eyes glimmered behind his spectacles, and he tugged his waistcoat toward his trousers as he stood up. "The first woman in the empire to train as a veterinary surgeon in fact."

"I hope I shall be the first of many," I replied.

"Is there any clarity yet on the Royal College of Veterinary Surgeons' stance on women training for the profession?" asked Major Fitz as we made our way to the door.

Professor Williams shook his head. "The RCVS is not a body that moves unless it is compelled to do so, and even then, it does not embrace change swiftly."

"But you are confident that it will not take measures to prevent Aleen's education?"

There was a pause. It was as though the principal was conducting a final assessment of how firm my resolve to become a veterinary surgeon was.

He looked at me and sighed. "Forbearance may be necessary. However, I am hopeful that by the time Miss Cust is enrolled as a student here, things will have changed—not only for the RCVS but for women's education and vocation at large."

He gave a small smile. "You indicated in your letters that you did not want to wait until that time, and I assume, because you are here, you are still firm on that. Are you absolutely sure you want to go ahead with your training with the official sanction from the Royal College still pending?"

"I am," I replied. "I do not want to wait another day. It has been too long already."

Major Fitz and I had lunch at the Waverley Hotel before he accompanied me to my lodgings, which I had arranged with the help of one of Lady Widdrington's Scottish friends. She was aware of how far Orlando's bequest would have to stretch to cover my student years. Even so, I was unprepared for what that really meant.

I had calculated that I would have to get by on six shillings and sixpence a week while I studied. What I only realized when I saw it was that that would mean living in a modest terrace house with a privy in the backyard. The only consolation was that the house was within walking distance from both the university and the college—essential since, for the first time in my life, I had neither a carriage nor a horse.

My landlady, the widow Mrs. Logan, opened the door almost immediately when I knocked. She filled the doorway sideways but had to raise her head to look at me.

"Aye, Miss Cust, I take it?" she said in a strong, no-nonsense voice.

"Mrs. Logan? I am pleased to make your acquaintance."

She nodded to the major, who tipped his hat from where he waited alongside the carriage.

The attic room, with its low ceiling and wrought-iron bed, chair, desk, and cupboard, was smaller than the pantry at Newton Hall. A single window looked out onto a gray wall across the street. I glanced around for a fireplace. There was none.

"It's a typical student room," said Mrs. Logan from the doorway behind me. The chamber was too small to accommodate us both.

"Yes. Thank you," I replied, summoning a smile.

When I came out, Major Fitz was standing on the same spot, stroking his beard as he was inclined to do when he was anxious.

"Well?" he said, daring to glance up at the narrow house. "Will it do?"

"It will."

"Good. Good." He placed his silk top hat on his head. "Remember, Newton Hall is only eighty-five miles away. When your studies allow, you should come home."

I felt my throat thicken. His invitation was kind, and that he spoke of Newton Hall as if it were home to me meant more than he could imagine.

"Thank you, Major Fitz."

He touched the brim of his hat and turned to climb into the carriage. As he placed his foot on the stair, he paused and turned back to me.

"Do not delay writing to your mother, Aleen."

I wrote to her little over a month later.

Dear Mama,

I trust that you, my brothers, and sister are in good health, and that all is well in London and at Leasowe?

You will see from the address above that I presently reside in Edinburgh. I will almost certainly spend most of my time here for the next four years and look forward to receiving correspondence from you at this address until I advise otherwise.

I have, with the assistance of Major and Lady Widdrington, found lodgings, which will suffice while I study toward becoming a veterinary surgeon. At my request, the major accompanied me from Newton Hall to Edinburgh to introduce me to Professor William Williams, who is the principal of the New Veterinary College. I will start my training there next year when I have completed studying the necessary subjects at the University of Edinburgh this year. The course work I am undertaking at the university is similar to that studied by medical students in their first year and includes chemistry, biology, histology, and pathology. The university has been open to women medical students for some years, which means that I am not the only woman in my class.

For so long you have opposed my ambition to become a veterinary surgeon, but now that I am engaged in the training to become one, I hope you will accept my decision. It would mean a great deal to me to have your support. I hope too that you will appreciate my sincere attempts to ensure that my plans do not cause you any shame or discomfort. I am studying as far away from London as possible, and by using a pseudonym wherever I can, I hope to protect you from the embarrassment that you dread.

I hope you will have time to write to me soon and let me know that you are reconciled with my decision. Please convey my best wishes to my brothers and sister.

Your loving daughter,
Aleen

Weeks became months, but I received no word from my family as I adjusted to life in Scotland. There was a great deal of adapting to do. A new city to navigate with no old friends to lean on. A small, student existence to endure. Interesting but sometimes difficult things to learn. Mrs. Logan was an easygoing landlady, but because I could afford just one hot meal a day, I only saw her briefly in the evenings when we ate together before I headed back upstairs to study. With no fire, my room was bitterly cold, and often, when I finished working and wanted to sleep, I went out into a quiet backstreet and ran back and forth a few times to warm up before climbing into bed.

My studying paid off and my results were good, but I was lonely. For the first time in my life, I was without a dog for company. Dorothy wrote telling me that Nugget and Honey had settled well at Fallodon.

"They are energetic ramblers for such little dogs and have learned to lie still while Edward and I are birding," she wrote.

I glanced around my room. I pined for the dogs but realized how fortunate it was that they did not have to live in my tiny room in Edinburgh.

On the weekends in particular, I missed spending time with the horses and being able to gallop across the countryside. I tried to fill my yearning by greeting the animals I saw on the streets, ignoring the curious glances of their people. My attempts to befriend a feral cat who lived nearby extended no further than getting her to take a piece of chicken from my hand. I could not afford to share much more of my food, so we remained distant acquaintances.

My days were varied and busy, and my thoughts dominated by my studies. Even so, I woke every morning hoping that it would be the day I would hear from my mother. It would be comforting to know that she sometimes thought about me. Occasionally, before I fell asleep, I fantasized that she and my siblings missed me. However, with no letter appearing, I had begun to believe mine had not reached my mother in London, when I found an envelope addressed in Charles's hand on my desk one afternoon. I tore it open. Had something happened to my mother that he had written and not her?

Dear Aleen,

Mother received your letter while I was at sea, but I cannot say that her distress had eased when she showed it to me on my return months later. That should come as no surprise to you. The tone of your letter shows that you anticipated her anguish, as does the fact that you did not have the decency to let us know your plans before you left for Edinburgh. Yet, knowing the anguish you would cause, you went ahead anyway.

What is also deeply upsetting is that you would take advantage of Major Widdrington's kind patronage to support your endeavors to be educated. I have written to him to apologize on your behalf.

We have not mentioned your selfish undertaking to anyone outside the family but are concerned that news will reach ears that matter in due course. Mother is deeply concerned about what Her Majesty might think should she come to hear of it. If you are unaware or have conveniently forgotten her stance regarding the enfranchisement of women, Her Majesty has made clear her opinion and it bears repeating here. Mother noted it, word for word, from Her Majesty's papers as follows: "Were women to 'unsex' themselves by claiming equality with men, they would become the most hateful, heathen and disgusting of beings and would surely perish without male protection."

Your letter implies that we should be grateful that you have taken to educate yourself in Edinburgh rather than in London as if Scotland is in another world. Similarly, you suggest that we take comfort that you are using pseudonyms as if your duplicity will not add to our disgrace when your undertakings become public. We are not comforted in any way.

It falls to me, your oldest brother and protector of our mother, to insist that you immediately give up this foolishness and return to London before we suffer further shame. It would be a pity to have to cut off our association, but if that is what is required to defend the Cust name and the honor of our mother in court, it

may become the only option if you are unwilling to be sensible and
return to London.

Yours sincerely,
Charles

I read the letter three times. With every reading, I hoped it would reveal a part of my oldest brother that I had dreamed would emerge with time. I wanted to see in Charles someone who was principled but fair, who recognized my ambitions as he did his own and was proud that I wanted to do something useful with my life. There was, however, no sign of that version of him. The only Charles I saw was the deeply loyal son, naval officer, and Third Baronet Cust of Leasowe Castle. The letter writer was not a brother in the sense that Orlando had been but a man who placed queen, country, and title above sister. A brother who wrote of family as if I were an outsider. If there had been a fireplace in my bedroom, I would have thrown the letter into the flames and tried to forget I had ever read it, but there was no fire—and anyway, Charles's words were imprinted in my heart.

CHAPTER 11

❦

1896
Edinburgh, Scotland

Although Sophia Jex-Blake and the six other female medical students—who, when they arrived to sit their exams, were pelted with mud and insults by pugnacious male students during the Surgeons' Hall Riots of 1870—had, if not paved, at least cleared the way for women to study at the University of Edinburgh, my gender was still a novelty on campus by 1896. It did not help that, despite the institution's professing to welcome us, the attitude of the staff seemed to indicate the opposite. We were barely tolerated, and although I set my sights firmly on receiving an education and turned a blind eye to all else, moving around campus was not always easy.

For the most part, I ignored the stares and jeers that my skirts elicited as I made my way across the courtyards, down the passages, and into the classrooms of the university. I thought that, given my experience with my brothers, I would be unaffected by being one of only a few women among many men, but I soon saw that surviving student life was nothing like standing up to the injustices of being the sister of four brothers. Even when they were not patently abusive, the men at college were aloof and prickly.

"Do you know where Professor McDonald's extra anatomy lesson is taking place?" I asked a fellow student during my first week at the college.

"If you believe you are clever enough to be here, you should be able to work that out for yourself," he replied, his nostrils flaring like those of a frustrated bull.

I wanted to say that his argument was nonsense but thought better of it. I censored myself by recalling Professor Williams's warning. It would, he had said, be worse at veterinary college. I was determined to train myself against responding to the gibes by focusing on the work and my plans to become a veterinary surgeon instead. I imagined it was like schooling a skittish yearling in that the hard work, consistency, and resilience put in during the early stages would pay off in the long term. It was a pity though, I thought, that many men were not as amenable, intuitive, or sensible as horses.

Occasionally, I responded by fixing my hecklers with a cold stare, but I always moved away as quickly as I could. One afternoon, though, following several demanding classes and a test that had kept me studying well into the night, ire got the better of me.

As I made my way out the gates at Surgeons' Hall onto Nicolson Street, aware of my stomach grumbling—I had foregone lunch to do some last-minute reading before the test—I noticed two men leaning against a wall, their eyes on me. I walked by, looking directly ahead.

"How do you keep going?" one of them called out loudly. "Learning by day and opening your legs by night?"

The other snorted.

I felt a ripple of tension scuttle across my shoulders like a crab on a beach. My face grew warm. As if maneuvered by a puppeteer, I turned and marched toward the men, rising to my full height. Their smiles disappeared as I stood over them, so close I could smell the ale on their breaths.

"I beg your pardon," I said. "I did not hear you. What did you say?"

The larger of the two straightened and leaned toward me. The top of his head was in line with my nose. It was not unusual for me to be taller than others, but these two were especially short.

"You have no business here," he said, his mustache waggling with each word and spittle collecting in one corner of his mouth. I felt a flash of regret about having approached them, but it was too late to pretend I was not provoked.

"My business is the same as yours: to be educated."

"Women do not require education. You have neither the brains nor the civility for it. You repulsive, bluestocking types have no respect for polite society or your place in it. Go back to your streetwalking. You are—"

"Come, Rupert. Let us not—" said his friend, placing a hand on his elbow. Rupert shook it off.

"You are a disgrace," he continued, stepping closer so that his chest heaved against the bodice of my dress. I wanted to move but did not want to give him the pleasure of sensing my alarm.

I pushed my shoulders back. "You know nothing about me and my place in *polite* society. How dare you—"

"How dare I? How dare I?" He was shouting now. "Who are you, you... you giant woman? You do not belong at university. It's unnatural, unlady-like." He lifted his arm, his fist clenched. "You are a—"

"Rupert!" His friend grabbed at the man's arm, but again he twisted out of reach, continuing to stare at me, breathing hot, stale hop fumes up my nostrils. He raised his fist again. This time, I stepped back. He followed.

"You are nothing but a towering strumpet masquerading as a—"

"Step away from her. Now!"

The shout—the voice was unexpected, yet not unfamiliar—was accompanied by the thumping of feet approaching quickly. I turned to see the black trousers and red coat of a broad-shouldered soldier running toward us. His short hair was dark and dense, and his cheeks as rosy as a robin's breast. It was Bertie.

He thrust himself between Rupert and me and, grabbing my tormentor's wrists, shoved him hard. The man's head smacked back against the wall. Once. Twice. Three times. His friend grabbed Bertie's shoulders and tried in vain to pull him away. Rupert's head pounded into the stone once more.

"Bertie, stop!" I yelled.

He froze and the three men stared at me. Rupert's eyes glimmered with loathing, but as they slid sideways to focus on Bertie, I saw fear too.

"Are you finished?" said Bertie, giving Rupert another, slightly less violent push.

"Let me go," he sneered.

The other man walked away. Bertie pulled Rupert from the wall and shoved him after his friend. He swung around as if contemplating challenging Bertie but changed his mind.

"Bah!" he said, spitting on the ground before following his friend.

Bertie and I stared at one another silently for a moment. He had become a man in the years since I had seen him. A tall, striking man. Why it surprised me, I do not know. He was, after all, twenty-three years old. Then his face broke into a wide, unaffected smile, his eyes crinkling at the edges, and with the grin, my best friend's little brother was back.

"What are you doing here?" I asked.

He raised his hands. "I am a soldier. I go where I am commanded."

"Of course, but—"

"We are here for two nights with high command on some official business. I thought I would take you out to tea. Or, you know, rescue you from a pair of hoodlums."

We laughed, but then Bertie grew serious.

"What was going on, Aleen? Is that typical? Dorothy told me it was not easy for you, but this? Is it normal?"

I tried to reassure him, saying it was not, and that I had exacerbated the situation by challenging Rupert, which was not my usual way.

Bertie widened his eyes. "You do not *usually* respond to their scorn?"

"No, I do not."

"I cannot imagine you letting it go…if I think of the debates around the dinner table at Newton Hall."

"The people of Newton Hall are reasonable. It is different here. If I am to get ahead, I must choose my battles with care. Mostly, I choose to avoid them. I should have today. You arrived at an inopportune moment."

"I wish I was always here to protect you."

It was the kind of thing I would have expected Bertie to have said to Dorothy if she had been in my situation. I was touched and smiled at him. The red of his cheeks spread across and down his neck and he glanced away.

"Can I take you to tea? I have to be back at my barracks in two hours," he said.

Bertie and I would not have stepped out in London alone together. Decorum prohibited it. In Edinburgh though, where we were strangers to most and likely to be mistaken for brother and sister, I was untroubled by being seen with him in the tearoom at Jenners Department Store. We shared a pot of tea and plates of delicate sandwiches and petits fours in the bustling restaurant room with its ornate Jacobean ceiling and miniature Ionic columns. I did not mention to Bertie that it was the finest food I had eaten since I had lunched with his father at the Waverley Hotel. He might, however, have guessed it, given my appetite.

He asked me about my studies, listening without interrupting as I explained that I had initially been intimidated by the material but was coping well. I told him about Mrs. Logan, her modest home, and how I ran through the streets to warm up before going to bed. I meant to amuse him, but he frowned.

"You cannot afford lodgings with a fireplace? Surely, Charles would not allow that."

"You must know about his and my mother's attitude toward my studying," I replied, reluctant to spoil an enjoyable afternoon by talking about my family.

He sighed. "I did not realize it was that severe. Can you not accept a loan? From my father? Dorothy? Me?"

"I am fine, Bertie. Thank you for offering, but as I told your father and Dorothy, no thank you. My lodgings are, indeed, a great deal less comfortable than Newton Hall or Leasowe or even—and you know how I dislike London—the apartment in Kensington, but I want to do this on my own. It is the only way I will earn the approval and respect of my family."

"But—"

"Tell me about the army. Is it all you imagined it would be?"

Bertie, I knew, was serious about his career as a soldier. It had always been understood he would follow Major Fitz's footsteps: join the army and apply himself conscientiously to rise through the ranks. That day, however, in the tearoom at Jenners, he was determined to entertain me, and his accounts of army life were anything but serious. As we laughed our way through two pots of tea, it occurred to me how comfortable I was with Bertie and how long it had been since I had enjoyed the easy company of a man. It reminded me of being with Orlando, and I felt a pang of sadness.

"Is something wrong?" asked Bertie.

"No. Go on, please."

"You seemed pensive suddenly."

"I was thinking about Orlando and just that, well, it is lovely to sit here and chat with someone who is like a brother to me. A kind, funny, and interesting brother."

He frowned. "Brother?"

"Well, you are my best friend's brother, which makes you something of a brother to me." I chuckled.

Bertie gave a small smile but did not meet my eye. I had, it seemed, embarrassed him. "We should get going," he said.

As we left the tearoom, I noticed several young women looking at Bertie from beneath their eyelashes. I glanced at him, seeing him as they might. A fine-looking man, indeed.

Later that evening, I lingered a little longer than usual at the table with Mrs. Logan. After several days of hard work, I felt I deserved a break from my books. I told my landlady that I had had tea at Jenners.

"Treating yourself?" she asked.

"No. My guardian's son, Bertram Widdrington, is in town briefly. He is with the British Infantry."

"He's a-courting then, this soldier?" she said.

"Oh, no. His older sister is my best friend. He is several years younger than me. He is like a brother to me too. A caring one."

"My husband was younger than me."

"Oh?"

Although she and I discussed several things, we had not reconnoitered the realms of our personal lives. We spoke of the weather, the (sometimes dubious) quality of the meat she included in her stews, the aches in her knees, and the noisiness of the neighborhood. She never asked about my family—although it was possible that she knew about my circumstances from Lady Widdrington's friend. It suited me not to talk about how my family had rejected me or explain why I was addressed as A. I. Custance on some of the envelopes delivered to the house. I knew she was widowed, but Mrs. Logan had not previously mentioned her late husband. My dismissal of Bertie as a suitor because of his youth, however, oiled her tongue.

"It was one of the things that set his family against me," she said, "that I was older."

"Oh?"

"I will tell you this much, Miss Cust. It did not matter to Alfred and me. Not that I was almost ten years older or that his family cut us off."

"Cut you off? Entirely?"

"Aye. Came to his funeral, though. 'Too late now,' I told them."

"I am sorry."

She brushed a few stray hairs from her face and straightened her bun. "Och, don't be sorry. If I had my life over, I'd do it no differently. The years I had with him, though too few, were the best of my life. Don't let anyone tell you who is right or wrong for you, Miss Cust. Only you know your heart."

Heart? I had not imagined Mrs. Logan a romantic. She recognized the incredulity on my face.

"Aye, heart. It surprised me too. I was raised a practical girl. No time for flights of fancy in my family. But then I met Alfred. It made no sense... except it did. Only he and I knew that."

"What about your family?"

"Do you see them around?"

I shook my head.

"No. They laughed when I introduced them to Alfred, and I left."

"But now?"

"My parents are long dead, and I have no call to know my brothers. It is possible to outgrow family, you know."

Was it? Part of me wanted to believe Mrs. Logan, but I could not imagine never seeing my mother and siblings again. I might have tried to disguise it for their benefit, but I was a Cust. If not, who was I? Perhaps finding a partner and creating a new family would help.

"I hope I meet someone who makes me as happy as Mr. Logan obviously made you," I said.

Her eyes glistened. "I hope you do too, Miss Cust. Aye, I do."

CHAPTER 12

❧

1897
Edinburgh, Scotland

FOR THE MOST PART, I WAS ABLE TO NUDGE GLOOMY THOUGHTS ABOUT MY family to the far corners of my mind where I strove to ignore them. I channeled all my attention into my studies and pored over my books. In 1897, after a year at university, I received the certificate of education that I needed to register as a student at the New Veterinary College. Finally, I was truly on my way to becoming a veterinary surgeon.

However, as thrilled as I was to make my way to Forty-one Elm Row, not everything changed, and indeed, as they had at the university, my skirts and long, red hair continued to draw attention.

"Are you lost, love?" jeered a short, muscular man with a boyish face when I made my way to class on the first day. "The teahouse is on the other side of the street."

"Do you think she knows what we are here for, Toby?" asked his friend, who I later discovered was nicknamed Piggers, despite—or perhaps because of—his bony frame.

I am here for the animals. What about you? I thought.

"Are you aware what veterinary surgeons do?" said Toby, flexing a bicep as if that might clarify the matter for me. "You are tall. I shall give you that, but no woman is strong enough to wrestle a bullock with colic. Or a horse with a twisted knee. Or pull a calf or a foal."

Lady Widdrington's words appeared in my thoughts: *Women are stronger than anyone realizes.* But these words, too, I kept to myself.

Other students limited their displeasure about my presence by fixing me with cold glares, which seemed to imply that I tainted the profession.

One man always muttered as he passed me in the hallway, eyes lowered as if seeing me was too much to bear, "It is ridiculous. Bloody ridiculous."

As had been my tack the previous year, I ignored the gibes. Things could have been worse. During protests against women wanting to take degrees at the University of Cambridge, hundreds of men had recently gathered in the town north of London. The event culminated in the mutilation of an effigy of a woman on a bicycle, which they hung from the window of a shop. The news infuriated me, but I kept my emotions to myself. I did not want to have to fight. I simply wanted to become a veterinary surgeon.

When, after one of my first sessions in the dissecting room, I found a cow's eyeball in my satchel, I took it out and set it alongside the inkwell on my desk as if it might keep watch over me. The room sagged with disappointment at my response.

During the second week, Professor Williams stopped me as I was leaving late one afternoon.

"Ah, Miss Cust, the first to arrive and the last to leave," he said.

He was right. I was there every morning well before classes began. It gave me time to visit the animals, ill or injured, who were housed in the college stables and stalls while they were being treated. Calling on them filled some of the emptiness I experienced from not having my own animals around. In the afternoons, I often worked late in the library, which was more spacious and warmer than my bedroom at Mrs. Logan's.

"Dare I ask how you are finding things?" he asked.

I glanced around. I did not want the others to think that the principal was granting me special attention. The hallway was empty.

"Good, thank you, Professor. No. Excellent, in fact. I am where I want to be, and I shall not allow anyone or anything to make me wish otherwise." He smiled. "You might look at it this way: if you can survive this lot, you will be fully equipped to handle the most belligerent of beasts."

"I have every intention of not only surviving but thriving."

He chuckled, waved, and walked into his office.

It would be unfair to say that all the men training alongside me at college were hostile. A few even dared to befriend me.

Frederick Taylor was a tall, sandy-haired young man from Oxford, whose family was shocked—his father was a tailor—when he told them he wanted to be a veterinary surgeon.

"They are town folk and somewhat afraid of animals," he explained, having introduced himself. "Neither my father nor mother has ever ridden. Our milk is delivered by the farmer and meat purchased cut and wrapped. I am not sure how, at a young age, I came to be fascinated and fond of four-legged creatures. Even so, my parents were taken aback when I told them I wanted to be an animal doctor. I would imagine yours were surprised by your choice too?"

"Indeed."

My monosyllabic reply did not dissuade Mr. Taylor. He accompanied me to classes, sat next to me, and took his lunch with me in the tearoom, which, providing cheap and adequate meals, was conveniently located at the back of the college. However, when he tried to help me lift an ox leg during a lesson, I asked him not to. Later, as we walked across the courtyard, I felt compelled to explain.

"I hope you do not think me rude, Mr. Taylor, but please do not offer to help me. If you do so, it confirms what the others think: that I am not strong enough for this job."

"Of course," he replied. "I should have realized that. My apologies. I will not do it again."

"Thank you."

"But if you *do* need help, I hope you will ask me for it."

"Thank you, Mr. Taylor. I will."

"Will you call me Fred?"

"And I am Aleen. Without an *i*."

He did not miss a beat. "Without an eye? But it seemed you had an extra one in class the other day."

It was good to have a friend at college. It helped that Fred was an excellent cricketer—sporting prowess counted for a great deal among veterinary surgeon trainees—and my classmates held him in high esteem. His presence at my side deterred the sneering. That is not to say, however, that my mettle was not still occasionally put to the test.

One day, once the teacher had gone and as I gathered my things to leave the dissecting room, I saw Toby close the door and lock it. It was the end of the final class of the day, and I was eager to leave for the library and to go through the notes I had made during the typically messy session. There was a strange hush in the room.

Fred, catching my eye from a few yards away, jerked his head toward a corner. I pointed toward the door. He shook his head and again gestured to the corner. What was going on? Was I being set up? Why lock the door? I looked around for clues. That's when I realized why Fred insisted I move; I was plum in the middle of the pitch. I hurried to the corner.

Across the way, Piggers posed like a batsman in front of a chair, holding an ox forelimb and scapula we had dissected and examined earlier. On the opposite side of the room—behind the very spot I had just abandoned—Toby gathered a pile of fascia; that is, the membranous coverings of the muscles we had torn away to reveal the structure beneath it. He was the bowler, and pieces of fascia, the balls. The other students—the fieldsmen—moved into position around the room.

"Psst, psst!"

I looked at Fred. He gestured that I should put my books on the floor. I grimaced but obeyed.

Toby walked backward until he reached the wall. He glanced at the blob of fascia in his hand and performed a slow, theatrical bowling motion, which culminated in his arm windmilling above his head and dispatching the tissue across the room.

Piggers stepped forward and swung the bone, which connected with the fascia with a solid splat. An arm shot out over a desk and caught it, but not before a spray of watery blood spewed across its path. There was a cheer.

"Good shot, Piggers!"

"Come on, Spreull! Look lively!"

"Well caught, Dobson!"

Toby ambled back to the pile of fascia, selected a piece, lined up, and bowled again. Piggers walloped it across the room. This time, nobody caught the blob of membrane. It slapped into the wall, where it was momentarily suspended before sliding down, leaving a bloody trail in its wake.

The game continued, faster and noisier with every delivery. The men applauded and laughed. The room was a mess. I looked around, pitying the janitor who would have to clean up. I noticed Fred staring intently at me once more. He gave his head a small nod toward the batsman. I needed to pay attention apparently.

I looked at Piggers as he swung the bone again, calling as he did, "For you in the midfield, Miss Custance!"

What I had not noticed was that sinewy fascia had, in this instance, been replaced with a particularly bloody piece of liver. It hurtled toward me in a soggy mass, spurting gore as it flew. The ball games I had played with my brothers prepared me well, and as I lifted my arm, opened my hand, and caught the meat, the men roared their approval. I suppressed a scowl as I looked at the smashed organ dripping in my hand and the mess it had made of my skirt.

Fred beamed.

Referred to as "muscle fights," the pitching and hitting of the remains of dissected animals was officially prohibited at the college. However, the bois-terous, blood-spattered event was something of a rite of passage for first-year students. Thankfully, once a class had engaged in the game a couple of times, muscle fights lost their appeal, and dissecting classes took place without any post-lesson sport. I was pleased. However, just because I had proven myself able in the midfield did not exempt me from demonstrating my abilities in other disciplines.

One morning, while investigating hoof rot in a pony with my class in attendance, Professor Williams called for a volunteer to lift the animal's infected front leg. I stepped forward, ran my hand down the limb, gently lifted the mare's hoof, and bent her leg to reveal the underside. Professor Williams pointed to the infected area around the underside of the hoof, called the frog, and described how it should be cleaned and treated.

As the teacher crouched down and ran his finger around the toe area, I felt the pony shift and lean against me. Thinking she might have lost her balance, I pushed back, hoping to right her. She did not move away. In fact, it felt that she was leaning further into me. I pushed back but still, the pony did not straighten herself. She was not a large horse but heavy nonetheless. I felt my face grow warm with exertion and moved my feet apart to bolster my position. It made no sense that she should lean against me, but I did not want to interrupt Professor Williams or appear weak. Then, I heard the quiet shuffling of shoes. I looked under the horse and saw that four of my fellow students were standing on the other side of her, pushing her onto me.

I emitted an unladylike snort of laughter. Professor Williams looked at me in surprise. He raised his head slightly and saw the men on the other side of the pony. They moved away, the horse stood straight, and I took a deep breath of relief. The principal shook his head and spent a few moments explaining preventive measures for hoof rot before stepping back.

"That will do, Miss Custance," he said, deftly using my assumed name for the sake of the other students.

As I placed the pony's hoof down, I felt the sweat trickle between my shoulders, and as I straightened my back, my muscles burned.

"I wanted to warn you, but I could not catch your eye," said Fred later. "I thought you were going to buckle."

"So did I. Thank goodness the pony was no heavier."

"Thank goodness you have a sense of humor."

After that, bar an incident involving a seething mass of tapeworms, which I almost scooped onto my fork as I tucked into what I believed to be an innocuous plate of bangers and mash at lunch one day, the tomfoolery stopped. Perhaps it was my stoicism or good humor. It might also have been because I achieved the highest marks in most subjects and was well on my way to winning the best first-year student award. Exactly what put a stop to the pranking, I was not sure. What I was sure of was that each week, my classmates increasingly ignored my gender. They addressed and treated me as they did one another. For the first time, others were beginning to realize, as I had long since known: I was where I belonged.

Unfortunately, as I discovered when Professor Williams sent for me one morning, my optimism was premature.

The Royal College of Veterinary Surgeons had a committee dedicated to ratifying students' certificates of education and organizing professional examinations in London, Glasgow, and Edinburgh. It had come to the attention of this committee that a New Veterinary College student, that is, A. I. Custance, was a woman. The revelation, explained the principal, had sparked a debate about whether I was eligible to write the twice-annual professional Royal College examinations. Without writing and passing these examinations, it would not matter if I graduated from the New Veterinary College; I would be prohibited from officially practicing as a veterinary surgeon.

It was worse than any taunting I had been subjected to.

"Of course, while we have not advertised it, neither have we had to defend your gender until now," said Professor Williams. "I have no idea how it came to be known and put up for discussion at this time, but it has."

I felt light-headed and leaned against his desk. During my first weeks at college, I had feared the RCVS might dispute my enrollment and that I would have to fight to stay. However, as the months had passed and I settled in, I stopped worrying. Despite the initial resistance from my classmates, there had been no formal objections, and I'd begun feeling secure. It had not occurred to me the Royal College would turn a blind eye to my attendance but block me from writing their crucial examinations. Was the organization saying I could train but never practice? Did the committee believe I would give up and go away without creating a fuss? How cruel it seemed.

I wondered why it had happened now. My name had been on the list since I registered at the college at the beginning of the academic year. Why had my gender only been discovered now? There was little over a month to go before I was due to sit my first RCVS examination. Why wait so long to challenge my rights to the profession? Did the fact that the head office of the Royal College was in London have anything to do with it? Could my mother or Charles have taken the matter up with someone there to thwart my plans? These, however, were not questions Professor Williams could answer.

"What does it mean? What will the committee do?" I asked instead.

"No one is certain at present. I explained to them that you've proven yourself competent enough to attend the college, and there is no doubt that you qualify to sit the examinations. I reiterated that like all students here, you provided the stipulated requirements for admission that affirm you are eligible to study and, therefore, to sit the exams. They insisted on seeing your certificate again. I presented it."

"Clearly, they were not satisfied."

Professor Williams removed his spectacles and cleaned them with his handkerchief. "The committee has referred the matter to a solicitor."

"A solicitor?"

"I am afraid so. They will send me a copy of his report when it is done."

"So?"

"Until then, we…you shall continue as usual."

"I should prepare for the examination?"

He nodded. "Indeed. Who knows how long the solicitor will take with his report, particularly with Christmas upon us? Besides, this does not affect your college studies and examinations. As such, you should continue as before."

Christmas. I had looked forward to spending it at Newton Hall with the Widdringtons. To seeing Dorothy, Nugget, and Honey. To riding, even if it snowed. Would I still enjoy it with this news hanging over me?

The principal rubbed his glasses vigorously. "I argued, and I will put it in writing for Mr. Thatcher—he is the RCVS's solicitor—that since women are now admitted to medical schools, veterinary colleges should make a quick and independent judgment in your favor. *That*, I know, will rustle a few feathers. The Royal College hates the idea of the medical field showing them up."

Professor Williams's wily approach pleased me. It was widely alleged that the medical profession enjoyed a more esteemed reputation with the public than the veterinary profession. Even matters concerning animal diseases, where veterinary surgeons' wisdom of comparative pathology was without doubt superior, failed to impress those outside of the profession. Despite the comparable complexity of the subject matter, physicians were infinitely more revered than veterinary surgeons. We joked about it, but it stung. This time, however, where it might provoke the Royal College to be more progressive, it could work in my favor.

"What if the solicitor finds against me?"

He replaced his spectacles and peered out of the window into the court-yard. "We will fight it. I did not encourage you to begin your training with the idea of allowing it to be brought to a halt by outdated thinking, Miss Cust. Neither am I going to keep the administrative challenges from you. I believe it is important that you know what is going on in all instances. This is your life after all. But I do not want you to worry unnecessarily about it. You have the makings of an excellent veterinary surgeon. That should be your focus. Let me deal with the committees, councils, and solicitors."

As comforting as it was to once again hear that the principal was on my side, as he had been from the moment Major Fitz first spoke to him about my ambitions, I did not feel entirely at ease when I left his office. What if Professor Williams was unable to convince the committee? Would he risk his college's association with the RCVS to flout their ruling? For one student? It seemed unlikely.

"Something amiss, Aleen? You are looking peaky," said Fred as we walked into the tearoom later. "Did you miss breakfast again?"

I shook my head, ordered a pot of tea, and sat at a table by the window. The sky was low and threatening. I hoped it would not rain and make it impossible to go for my run to warm up before bed later.

"But that is ridiculous," said Fred, after I'd told him what I had learned that morning. "Surely, they were aware that you were a woman when you enrolled months ago. I mean, aside from using a different name, you have not done anything to hide it. Why was the objection raised so late? And so soon before the examination?"

"The chairman of the examination committee said he was not aware until recently that A. I. Custance was a woman. Given that there were no questions on the registration forms that required me to specify my gender, it was, they might argue, not obvious."

Fred chewed quietly, his eyes on mine. He swallowed and dabbed his mouth with a serviette. "You are saying that they did not know then because they did not ask," he said. "How did they come to know now though? Did an inspector visit Edinburgh?"

"No. It is unclear how and when they came to know and why they have chosen to respond now. It does not really matter, does it?"

"Do you think that they might have known earlier in the year?"

"I do not know," I replied, suddenly weary.

"Is it possible that one of Professor Williams's rivals objected? Someone from Dick's?"

That was not something that had occurred to me. The professor had been principal of Dick's Veterinary College for several years before he left to establish his own school. Competition for the best teachers and the most students was fierce in the early years, but now, from all accounts, the rivalry had eased.

"I doubt it. I think Professor Williams would be canny enough to know that."

"You are probably right," said Fred. "However, were—"

"It does not really matter how they found out. What difference does it make? In fact, there is no point discussing it any further."

I did not want to think more about who might be behind the development and was certainly not going to mention my suspicions.

"But if—"

"Let us talk about something else," I said. "Did you see the boar with the abscess behind his ear brought in today? I do hope we will be able to see it being lanced at some stage."

CHAPTER 13

❦

1897
Northumberland, England

THERE WAS NO WORD FROM THE SOLICITOR BEFORE THE COLLEGE CLOSED
for Christmas and Hogmanay. As I packed my trunk for Newton Hall, I
told myself it was good news and that with a typically slow start to the new
year, both the college and RCVS examinations would come and go before
Professor Williams heard any more on the subject. Even so, I spent the time
on the train from Edinburgh to Northumberland refining and adding to my
list of points to argue should the solicitor find against me.

"It is ludicrous," said Lady Widdrington after I had described my uncertain future as we sat in front of the fire in the drawing room later. "Regressive
and unjust. And why now? After you received a certificate of education from
the university, have been at the college for several months, and are preparing
for the examinations? It is not only preposterous but also reeks of incompetence. Is there anything you can do, Fitz?"

The major rubbed his beard. "Would it help to hire a solicitor for you,
Aleen?"

"Professor Williams says not. Certainly not at present," I said, regret-
ting I had raised the subject so early in my visit. It was good to be with my

friends, not to mention good to feel warm for a change. The air was thick with the resinous scent of the fir tree, which, resplendent with Christmas baubles and ribbons, took up an entire corner of the room. We should have been clinking glasses, laughing, and embracing a festive spirit, not trying to analyze the obscure motivations of the Royal College.

Dorothy and Edward had arrived from Fallodon Hall with Nugget and Honey shortly before me. While both dogs greeted me with excited skips and yelps, only Nugget was moved enough by my presence to sit at my feet. I tried not to feel hurt by Honey's indifference.

"The dogs look exceedingly well, Dorothy," I said, rubbing Nugget's ears. "Honey looks ready for her first litter. She will be three soon. I think we should let nature take its course at her next estrus. Do you agree?"

Dorothy glanced at the floor to where Honey lay, her head raised as she surveyed the room. She was elegant and alert and, at that moment, looked like a fluffy miniature version of the Lion of Knidos.

"You are going to trust *me* with her breeding?" said my friend.

"Of course. What choice do I have? That is what we agreed, is it not?"

"I was teasing. It will be my pleasure, but you are going to have to get back here for the kennel show in the spring. I could probably manage Honey—she's a natural show-off—but I have no confidence with Nugget in the ring."

"I have already mailed the entry," I said, hoping that I would be able to make it—but not because I had been barred from college by then.

Edward turned his back to the fire to look at me. "Will Her Majesty show her dogs? I ask only to establish what you will be up against."

We laughed. The Queen's Pomeranians continued to win every competition their handlers entered. The unspoken understanding was that second place to a dog from the palace was as good as first. For a moment, I pictured Nugget with a red rosette (second to Her Majesty's entrant, of course) attached to his collar, and thought about how the achievement and news of Honey's puppies might give me cause to write to Mama again. She would surely want to discuss her daughter's Pomeranian breeding successes with her Queen. She might even be pleased enough with me to write back. Lady Widdrington could have been reading my mind.

"Speaking of Her Majesty, have you heard from your mother recently, Aleen?" she asked.

Major Fitz and Dorothy stared at her, their eyes hooded and reproachful, but the question did not offend me. I had written to Dorothy to tell her about Charles's letter, knowing that she would relay the information to her parents. There was nothing unusual about Lady Widdrington's candor. In fact, her familiarity was one of things that made me feel at home at Newton Hall.

"No. There has been no word from any of my family since, well, you know, they threatened to renounce me," I said. "I guess it was not an idle threat. I wrote to both Mama and Charles, explaining that I had not changed my mind and that I hoped they would reconsider their stance. Neither replied."

The room was quiet but for the crackling of the fire. It occurred to me again that even as it gave me relief to talk about the wretchedness of being cast aside by my family, my presence was not adding any merriment to Christmas. Major Fitz broke the silence.

"I called on Isabel and Ursula in Kensington a few weeks ago," he said. "I thought they might join us for Christmas."

Edward added a log to the flames. A window rattled, and I saw that it had begun raining again. Or was it sleet?

"She said they planned to go to Leasowe. That Charles and Leo would be home," continued the major.

"Did she look well? My mother?" I wondered whether anyone else in the room might suspect that Mama and Charles had a hand in the RCVS's sudden interest in my education. If so, I hoped that they would not give voice to their suspicions. I felt sufficiently ashamed of my own mistrust and did not want the added burden of my friends' embarrassment.

"She did."

He rubbed his chin again.

"You told her that I would be here?"

The major gave a short nod. "I wish there was more I could do, but she has only recently begun receiving me again after she discovered that I accompanied you to Edinburgh."

"I am sorry."

"There is no reason to be. I do not regret it. What I do regret is that Isabel and Charles are so set against your plans and that I am unable to change that and cannot intervene. I regret it not only because I owe it to your father as your former guardian but also because I know how much more difficult it makes life for you."

I swallowed but was saved from having to voice a response when Winborne tapped at the door and declared lunch ready.

While the weather remained cold and windy, the holidays improved. Dorothy and I found a few dry hours and, swathed in scarves, gloves, and hats, walked toward the beach with the dogs the afternoon before Christmas. Light snow had fallen earlier, a smattering of which lay on the roadside. Excited to be outside, Nugget, Honey, and the major's young black Labrador Retriever, Coal, chased one another down the muddy road, their paws leaving dark prints when they strayed off the track and into the snow.

Dorothy and I chatted easily. Though our lives had taken different paths and I no longer had time to do the things we both loved, there was no distance between us. Dorothy told me about how she and Edward had built a cottage in the Ichen Valley in Hampshire.

"I have never been happier than I am there," she said. "There is no place more beautiful and peaceful. The cottage—it is a tiny tin place—is sheltered by tall lime trees, and the garden leads into a meadow that ends at the water. The trees, reeds, and indeed every other bit of foliage are alive with birds. Edward built a bench in the bushes so that we can hide there and watch them. You must visit us next summer."

"Do you not feel lonely?" I asked, thinking of how I missed the liveliness of Newton Hall when I was in Edinburgh, particularly over the weekends. "Do you stay alone when Edward has to go to London?"

"Of course I do. Why would I be lonely? When he goes, I commune with nature, leaving the doors and windows open. Once, on a particularly warm night, I made a bed on the lawn and slept there with Honey and Nugget curled at my legs." Her eyes were bright and her skin glowed.

"I can see it brings you great joy," I said.

"Oh yes, it does. I am not at all a good London wife, but I know I am a good cottage wife."

"Cottage wife?"

She was quiet for a moment, as if arranging her thoughts.

"You must know, Aleen...have guessed perhaps, that Edward and I are not... well, we are not a typical couple."

I did not know what she meant. "Because you are so often apart? You do not accompany him to London events?" I ventured.

"No. Well, in part. I suppose." She looked straight ahead and kept walking. "We do not...we have a platonic marriage."

"Platonic? You mean—"

"Yes. That is what I mean."

"Oh."

"I wanted it that way. After the honeymoon. Edward agreed."

"Oh."

It should not have surprised me. It was not that Dorothy was prudish or cold, but she disliked being touched and touching others. She had an aversion to shaking hands and to having her hands and cheeks kissed. She detested dancing, which not only involved hand-holding but also meant having partners place their hands on other bits of her body. She had told me more than once when we were girls that she did not picture herself being married. So indeed, that she was more physically aloof than other wives might be was not remarkable. However, the mutual affection between Dorothy and Edward was obvious. There was never a moment when they were together that it seemed they were dissatisfied with one another. They were a striking young couple who never ran out of conversation or laughter and shared an interest in birds, nature, and books. It was hard to imagine that there was no passion between them in the bedchamber.

"What about—"

"We will not have children. We have agreed on that too."

That was unconventional. As the heir of Fallodon, Edward would, I assumed, be expected to produce offspring. It made me realize how little one knew about what others, even one's closest friends, wanted or expected from life and how pointless it was to speculate. I had learned a great deal about sexual reproduction in class at university and college, for which I was grateful. The extent of my knowledge on the subject as conferred upon me by my mother was that it was necessary, not only to produce children but also to curtail a husband's visits to prostitutes. I understood enough to know it was another thing that men demanded and felt entitled to. Was Edward different?

"That is good. Good that you agreed on it, I mean," I said, unable to think of a smarter comment.

"I wanted you to know because, well, you are my dearest friend and discreet, and if there was ever talk about our marriage, I want you to know the truth about it. Now, you know that I am happy, that our arrangement was my idea and agreed to by Edward. In fact, it was you who gave me the courage to tell him what I wanted."

"Me?"

"Yes. You are so brave about getting what you want, living the life you want. When I realized that I neither wanted to be with Edward in that way again nor wanted to have children, it was your example that gave me the courage to tell him."

"Oh," I replied, wondering if Edward would remain cordial toward me if he knew my role in his sexless marriage.

"For that, I am grateful. I am living the life I want, like you are. Like you *will* when those old-fashioned men of the Royal College are outvoted. We shall live the lives we want and deserve."

"I hope so," I said.

Dorothy smiled. "It will work out in your favor, Aleen. You are my muse, and I know you will achieve your dream. Because of you, I am a good and happy cottage wife in every way that my husband knows me to be a good wife."

It is possible that we might have spoken more about what it meant to be "a cottage wife," but I was not sure how to proceed without embarrassing Dorothy or being naive or disparaging. As it was, we stopped talking to watch a tall man stride down the lane toward us, his long coat billowing behind him. He lifted an arm and waved, his broad face breaking into a smile, which nudged his rosy cheeks upward. It was Bertie.

The dogs ran to greet him. He paused to pat them and walked to us, with Nugget, Honey, and Coal trotting at his heels. It reminded me of when we had met as children, when he ran toward Dorothy and me in the garden in Shropshire with Ruby. I had not known then how the sight of Bertie would come to please me through the years. I felt warm for the first time since we had left the house.

"No one told me you were coming," I said as he stood before us.

Dorothy chuckled. "We wanted to surprise you."

"What surprises *me* is that you did not ask if I would be here," said her brother.

"It did not occur to me that the army would allow you home for Christmas. Who is looking after the kingdom? Are we safe while Her Majesty's forces make merry around the tree?"

Lady Widdrington had invited several other people to Newton Hall for Christmas Eve, and contrary to how tiresome I had found it during my London Season years previously, I took pleasure in dressing for the evening. It had been a long time since there had been occasion to titivate. Lady Widdrington's maid, Pattison, brushed, trimmed, and assembled my hair on top of my head, securing it with a gold hair broach my grandmother had given me. I donned my favorite gown, one in a pale blue hue, which, thanks to my meager meals in Edinburgh, slipped easily over my hips as Pattison helped me into it.

"It is too loose?" I asked, examining myself in the mirror.

"Oh no, Miss Cust," she said, looking over my shoulder. "If you don't mind me saying so, you look splendid. The gown sets off the red in your hair, and you seem to glow."

"Thank you," I replied, rather pleased myself.

When Nugget and I went downstairs, Bertie and Major Fitz, in their pressed, glossy, and handsome formal evening attire, were drinking eggnog in front of the fire. They turned as they heard us at the door. Bertie, who was about to take a sip of his drink, froze, his glass tilted toward his mouth. Then, he blinked and took a long swig. I wondered if he too had spotted my glow. Or perhaps his reaction was simply because he was more accustomed to seeing me in riding habit or day wear.

"Bertie was just telling me how he stopped you roughing up a pair of hooligans at university last year, Aleen," said the major, handing me a warm glass of the creamy liquid. "You have been circumspect with some of the details of life in Edinburgh, I fear."

I squinted at Bertie. "*I fear* your son exaggerates, Major."

"Are you saying you were not harassed?"

"It was an isolated incident exacerbated by my not ignoring the baiting as I typically did."

"So, nothing isolated about it at all then?" said Bertie quietly, his eyes on mine over the rim of his glass.

"And at veterinary college? Are you baited there? Do you still need a soldier at your side?" asked Major Fitz.

I laughed. "Not at all. There was a little, well, agitating during the first weeks, but the instigators quickly grew bored. My classmates are mostly congenial and—"

"She has a fellow student at her side nowadays," said Dorothy as she and Edward walked into the room with Honey following.

I had told her earlier about Fred, how he had tried to help me during the first weeks and how we had become friends. It had not occurred to me that he might come under scrutiny by the Widdringtons. I was suddenly aware of Bertie's eyes on me.

"I do not need his protection. Mr. Taylor is simply a friend," I said, feeling the blood spread across my chest. I grew warmer, although I could think of no reason to blush. I glanced at Bertie. He looked away.

"Mr. Taylor? Do we know this Mr. Taylor?" asked the major.

I was not unhappy when Winborne interrupted to announce the arrival of Lady Widdrington's friends Mr. and Mrs. Edward Ford and their daughter, Enid. Bertie put his glass down and glided across the room to welcome them. I did not know the family, but he, I saw, did and was animated by their arrival. I watched as he shook Mr. Ford's hand, kissed Mrs. Ford's hand, and bowed theatrically at Enid before placing his lips on her hand too. The young woman, whose cheeks were as colorful as Bertie's and whose dark eyes were accentuated by thick, black lashes and brows, giggled prettily.

"Mr. Ford is a famous sculptor from London," whispered Dorothy. "Bertie rather filled his daughter's dance card at court a few years ago."

I tried to look away but failed. "He appears taken by her."

"I think the Fords and the Widdringtons are taken by the match."

"Match? Surely, Bertie is not—"

Dorothy looked at me. "He is no longer a little boy, Aleen."

"Of course not, but he has only just begun his military career…"

She shrugged as I allowed the sentence to trail off, incomplete, wondering why the sight of my friend's younger brother smiling at another woman should hold my attention. I wondered, too, why it felt necessary to me, urgent even, to reassure Bertie that Fred was a friend, a colleague, and most certainly *not* a suitor.

CHAPTER 14

❧

1897
Northumberland, England

THE OPPORTUNITY TO TALK TO BERTIE ABOUT FRED OR INDEED ANYTHING else that Christmas did not arise. That evening, we were seated at opposite ends of the long table. Not far enough, though, to spare me an unfettered view across the holly-and-pinecone centerpiece of him and Enid enraptured in constant conversation. What subject matter could sustain such entertainment? Much later, when I bade the other women good night and went to bed, the men were still in the major's study drinking port, smoking, and doing whatever else it was gentlemen did behind closed doors.

It seemed I had not been asleep for long when I was awoken by Nugget barking—at Pattison.

"Miss Cust, Miss Cust," she said, prodding my shoulder as she leaned over me. "Wake up, Miss Cust."

I sat up and looked around. She had opened the curtains, and although it was not properly light outside, I saw that it was morning.

"I am sorry to wake you so early, Miss Cust, but Major Widdrington bade me to do so. You are wanted at the stables."

"The stables?"

"Yes. One of the horses is down. That's all I know. The major said to ask you to make haste."

I pushed the blankets aside and placed my feet on the cold floor. Pattison gathered some clothing and helped me dress.

"Happy Christmas," she called as Nugget and I left the room.

Major Fitz, Winborne, the head groom, Watts, and a young stable hand called Peter stood at the door of one of the stables.

"It's Phantom," said the major. "He's down and cannot get up."

The men stepped aside so I could look over the half door. The gray gelding, one of a matching pair who drew the Widdrington's carriage, lay on his side. His eyes were open and his breathing labored, but no more than I would have expected of an animal of his size who was lying down. He was more or less in the middle of the stable and thus, not cast—that is, lying too close to the wall to get up. He could have stood, if he was able or wanted to do so.

"Did you see him go down? Fall?" I asked, looking at Watts and Peter.

"No, miss. He was like this when I arrived this morning," said the boy. "I shouted, tried to urge him to his feet, but he didn't move. I even went in, thinking I might drive him up."

"Did he try? Make any attempt? Was he groaning?"

Peter shook his head.

"What do you think it is?" asked Major Fitz. "I mean, look at him. He is strong. Only four. In the prime of his life. What would make him collapse in his stable?"

"Has he ever gone down before? That you have noticed?" I asked.

Watts and Peter looked at each other and replied together, "No."

I opened the lower section of the door. The horse did not move. "Do you often see him lying down? Noticed any wobbling perhaps?"

The men shook their heads.

"I've seen him rolling in the paddock on warmer days. Particularly when he and Ghost have had a sweaty run with the carriage," said Watts. "No more than that. And you, Peter?"

"No more than that," echoed the stable hand.

"And no sign of the head staggers? When wearing blinkers perhaps?" I

asked, recalling a discussion at veterinary college about whether horses wearing open bridles ever suffered head staggers, which is a condition during
which a horse's head and neck tremble, or whether the disorder was limited
to those in blinkers.

Peter and Watts shook their heads once more.

"He was standing last night?"

Peter nodded. "Yes. He was looking over his door when I left as it got
dark."

"Could it be colic?" asked the major.

"It is unlikely. He is not showing typical signs of discomfort."

I told Peter to fetch a head collar.

"Put it on," I said, when he returned. "You go in too, Watts. I need you
and Peter to make sure he does not stand while I examine him."

Winborne and Watts shared another look, and it occurred to me how
unusual it was for the men to take instruction from a woman. I caught the
major's eye. He gave me a small smile.

"Go on then," I said, looking pointedly at Watts.

Phantom did not move when, with the groom and stable hand at his
head, I walked slowly around him, looking for any obvious injury or awkwardly positioned bones. I saw nothing untoward. I asked Winborne for
his pocket watch, crouched down, and placed my fingers on the inside of
Phantom's jawline to feel his pulse. It was not unduly elevated. I looked at his
gums and his eyes, paying particular attention to the nictitating membrane.
The coloring was normal. In fact, there were no obvious abnormalities.

Was the horse's problem neurological? Surely, it would have shown
earlier with signs of stumbling. Also he did not look anxious, as would be
typical of a horse in distress. Though watching me closely, Phantom seemed
neither unnerved nor confused. He was responsive, alert, and yet lying down
and making no attempt to stand. Had he somehow injured himself in the
stable? There was no evidence of his having slipped, though it was possible
he was lying on the marks.

"Bring me a whip," I said. The men looked at one another as if for
approval.

"Well?" I asked.

Peter hastened to the tack room, returning with a carriage whip. I took it and ran the rounded end of the stick along the horse's spine. His skin twitched, indicating that all was well with his nerves in that area. I lifted his tail. It was not limp, which showed his spinal cord was probably fine. I touched his anus with the stick. It puckered.

"It is odd," I said, glancing at the men, whose faces expressed varying degrees of curiosity, astonishment, and perhaps—particularly in Winborne's case—aversion. "His reflexes are good. Normal. He is alert and apparently not in pain. If he has a neurological or musculoskeletal disorder, it is not obvious."

"I thought you were going to whip him to his feet for a moment," said Major Fitz.

"No. Although if I thought that that would get him up, it would be preferable to leaving him lying here. As you probably know, the prognosis is not good for a horse who lies prone for any length of time."

"Might we try to pull him up?" asked Watts.

"Yes, in a moment. Can you bring me some feed? Something you know he particularly likes."

Peter returned with a bucket of oats. I offered Phantom a handful. His whiskers prickled and his rubbery lips chomped and twisted against my skin as he ate the grain, sniffing my hand for more when it was gone. He was hungry, attentive, and calm. I was baffled.

We tried pulling, pushing, and prodding the horse to his feet to no avail. We even rolled him over, in case, for whatever reason, he felt he could rise from the other side. Phantom looked amused by our efforts but made no attempt to stand. We stood back, breathing heavily from our attempts.

"We will have to hoist him. Perhaps once he is up, he will remember how to stand and I can examine him more thoroughly," I said, going on to describe the materials we needed to make a sling: a large piece of canvas, some metal pulleys, several long chains, ropes, and bolts.

It took us a while to assemble the contraption. The hood of the gig we used as the canvas was the perfect size since the carriage was designed for a single horse to pull and thus not too big or small. We managed to get the material underneath Phantom, looped the ropes over the rafters, and, with a man in each corner of the stable, eased the horse onto his hooves. Although he had been remarkably calm throughout the morning, I expected Phantom to panic as we pulled. He did not. He was passive, worryingly so, and when his legs straightened beneath him, he did not put his weight on them. Instead, they hung limply below him. I walked around him, running my hands over his body and limbs, scrutinizing every inch of the animal for signs of injury and irregularities. I found nothing. I massaged his legs, pulling them straight. Still, he did not extend them or support himself as normal.

"Let him down a little, slowly," I instructed.

The men released the ropes, inch by inch. As the sling sank, so too did the horse. Like a slack-stringed puppet, Phantom made no attempt to support his weight and would have lain down again if I had not told the men to stop.

"Shall we bolt the ropes to the walls to hold him up?" asked the major when they had pulled the horse upright again.

"Yes, but not yet. I do not want him to rest his full weight in the sling. It will put too much pressure on his system. We need to also prop him up from underneath and support him on either side with something soft. Do you have empty feed sacks?"

"Yes. Plenty," said Watts.

"Good. We will need many—filled as tightly as possible with straw."

It was midday before Major Fitz and I walked to the house together, leaving Phantom secure in the sling, cushioned below and on all sides by straw. I had massaged his legs again and Peter fed and watered him. The horse seemed comfortable and oddly satisfied.

"Will you send for the veterinary surgeon?" I asked.

"Would you advise me to do so?"

"He might see something that I do not."

"What might that be?"

I glanced at him. "If I knew, I would not wonder if another set of eyes, qualified ones, might not be called for."

"The animal is eating and drinking and, thanks to you, not risking damage by putting undue pressure on any parts of his body. What else could anyone do?"

"Nothing that I am aware of."

"What else would you advise?"

"Watch for any changes. Release the sling slightly in the morning and afternoon. Keep massaging his legs and try to get him to stand on his own."

"Then that is what we will do." We walked into the house and Major Fitz shrugged off his coat.

"Well done, Aleen. Let's get cleaned up and have a sherry before lunch. It is Christmas after all."

Christmas? Of course. I had forgotten. My stomach rumbled, reminding me I had not eaten that morning before going to the stables.

Once I had washed and dressed, I found Lady Widdrington, Dorothy, Edward, and the major in the drawing room. We spoke briefly about Phantom, Major Fitz entertaining us with his version of how I had "taken control and ordered the men around most admirably."

"Congratulations, Aleen," said Lady Widdrington. "I am certain that one of the keys to success as a woman veterinary surgeon is the ability to get men to do things for you. Did you not say that one of the Royal College's arguments against women in the profession is that they do not have the muscle for the job? Who needs muscle when your minions have plenty of it and you can command them to do your bidding?"

We laughed, and I made a mental note to add a modified version of Lady Widdrington's argument to my list of points to put forward to the RCVS if necessary. She was right. The ability to effectively manage and instruct other people while working with animals was essential to any veterinary surgeon, man or woman, and I knew I had an aptitude for it.

"Where are the others?" I asked, catching sight of Winborne leading the footmen as they carried the first course toward the dining room.

"The Fords had to leave urgently after breakfast," said Lady Widdrington. "Their son is unwell, and Mrs. Ford was suddenly anxious to get back to London."

"And Bertie?"

"He had to leave this afternoon anyway and decided he might as well share the carriage to the station with them."

I pictured Bertie and Enid together in the coach, chatting and laughing as they had the night before. It was unlikely that they would have noticed that Phantom had been replaced by another horse to draw their carriage. The thought of them engaged in friendly conversation annoyed me, and I tried to persuade myself they would have run out of things to talk about by now.

I spent hours with Phantom the next week. Peter and I massaged his legs, and every day, he was able to support his weight for a little longer. By the time I was due to leave Newton Hall for Edinburgh after New Year, Peter was leading Phantom around the yard twice a day. The horse looked fully recovered, but because I still did not know what had caused his malaise, I instructed the stable hand to continue exercising him only lightly and to watch for any instability. I was pleased that he had recovered, but it bothered me that I did not understand why Phantom had collapsed.

"Watts mentioned Phantom's mysterious lying down to the farrier yesterday," said Major Fitz as he and Lady Widdrington gathered in the hallway to bid me farewell. "He had never heard of such behavior and took another look at his hooves. He is as confounded as you are."

"I shall consult Professor Williams and write to let you know what he says."

"Please do."

Dorothy and Edward, who were on their way back to Fallodon Hall, took me to the station. I held Nugget's little face in my hands and kissed the top of his head as I said my goodbyes. Honey sat on Dorothy's lap and looked across the carriage at me with her pretty brown eyes.

"I shall see you all in spring."

Dorothy stroked Honey's head. "Perhaps this one will have a belly full of pups by then," she said.

I opened my notebook on the train and read what I had written on the way to Newton Hall two weeks earlier, adding Lady Widdrington's point about my ability to elicit help where necessary. On a new page, I sketched what I imagined might be the ideal horse sling. I added straps that would secure the fabric around the horse's rump and chest. I also noted the value of an additional pulley system that could be attached to another horse to help pull should there not be enough people available to do the job.

As I gazed out of the window and watched the wintery landscape flash by, I thought about being back at college and discussing my experience with Phantom with my teachers and fellow students. Despite not having diagnosed what caused the problem, I was proud to have been able to successfully treat him. It occurred to me that, while I had enjoyed the warmth and comfort of being at Newton Hall with my friends, I had no regrets about leaving and returning to my studies. I wanted to learn as much as I could and not to have to wonder, as I had after we hoisted Phantom to his feet, whether I had missed anything. There was nowhere else I would rather be heading than back to the New Veterinary College.

CHAPTER 15

⚜

1898
Edinburgh, Scotland

FOR THE FIRST FEW WEEKS OF THE NEW YEAR, IT SEEMED MY WISH THAT THE Royal College's solicitor would draw out his investigations indefinitely might come true. Professor Williams believed it possible too. It was not unusual, he said, for bureaucratic matters regarding the governing body to be protracted. I quietly fantasized that, better still, Mr. Thatcher would advise his clients to let me sit their examinations and continue my studies and that, sheepish about their prejudice, the Royal College would say nothing, hoping the matter would disappear like dandelion seeds in the wind. Others might be angered by the anxiety it had caused, but I would be happy to let it go.

As such, with neither Professor Williams nor I having heard anything further from my detractors, I not only endured the icy Edinburgh winter at my desk late each night and sat the college examinations with Fred, Toby, Dobson, Spreull, Piggers, and our other classmates but also came top of the class in most subjects. In fact, my results in zoology were better than any others had ever attained in the subject at the New Veterinary College. The year could not have begun on a better note.

"Is that a good idea, Aleen? Being the top student, I mean," said Fred as we took tea together after receiving our results.

I smiled at him. I could not stop smiling. His expression, however, was serious.

"What do you mean?" I asked.

"The results will no doubt be seen by one of the Royal College committees. You are hoping that they will ignore you, forget about you. What are the chances of that if your name appears at the top of the list and you win all the awards at the college? Will that not remind them or draw further attention to your presence here?"

I stared at him, no longer smiling. Fred's words took me back to Ireland, to the day I raced Taffy and beat my brothers for the first time. My mouth felt as furry as the underside of an old saddle. Even though I was no longer a girl and had just excelled in my college examinations, nothing had changed. Still, I could not celebrate my successes. Still, it was necessary to censor my ambitions, modulate my achievements.

Just as Orlando had cautioned me at Cordangan Manor not to mention my win to my parents that day, Fred was suggesting I keep quiet about my results. Orlando was right. Was Fred? The stakes were higher now. When I was a girl pretending to be the jockey Harry Custance, I risked provoking the ire of my parents. Now, as A. I. Custance, I risked having my dream shut down. Could evidence of my proficiency perhaps have the opposite effect and convince the RCVS that women could become excellent veterinary surgeons?

We finished our tea in silence. I left Fred in the tearoom and went to see Professor Williams, to whom I recounted my friend's concerns.

"Is there a chance, the smallest even, that the Royal College might see my results as reason to let women into the profession? It makes sense, does it not? Shows that I am, and therefore other women are, capable of learning. Of excelling in their professional examinations. Of becoming veterinary surgeons," I said, eager for the principal to dismiss Fred's argument.

Alas, he did not.

"Yes, it makes sense, but I have my doubts that the governing body will see it that way. There are too many conservatives on the council. They are unlikely to relinquish their long-held dogmas because a woman student shows her aptitude for the profession. I am sorry, but I am afraid Mr. Taylor is not the only one who is concerned."

"You are too?"

He nodded. "It is likely that noting your results—as the committee surely will if we submit them as they are—will increase their appetite for debate and possibly even raise the number of objectors. It is my experience that some men are threatened by intelligent women, women who are easily educated."

"But *that* and my results should strengthen my case."

"Yes, they should. And they would in a just world. In a reasonable world. It vexes me to admit to it, but Mr. Taylor is probably right."

"What are you saying, professor?"

He did not meet my eye. "My advice is that we should do what is necessary to let sleeping dogs lie, as painful as that might be, Miss Cust."

So it was that my marks were adjusted before the college's results could be seen by the RCVS. The records showed that I neither ranked at the top of the class in any subjects nor won an award. The notion was that my name would be buried somewhere in the middle of the list of results from the New Veterinary College.

It was to no avail.

We never ascertained whether my muted college examination results had any bearing on the committee's decision, but despite the solicitor's report remaining unavailable, because of my gender, it seemed the Royal College would continue to prohibit me from sitting its examinations.

Spring was approaching, and it was just becoming possible for me to go to bed without my nightly warm-up run when Professor Williams eventually received the letter from the RCVS outlining Mr. Thatcher's findings. As I walked through the park to college that morning, I noticed early displays of primroses and daffodils beneath the trees with their fresh, fuzzy green leaves. I would travel to Northumberland to show Nugget and Honey in a month or so and check whether the bitch was in pup yet. Perhaps I would be there long enough to go hunting with Major Fitz and fishing with Dorothy. I would make time to check on Phantom.

Professor Williams had been unable to emphatically diagnose what might have caused the gelding to suddenly lie down and not stand on his own, but he suspected a neurological disorder. He prescribed a series of tests that might be done on the horse. I had written to the major and suggested that he give the list to his veterinary surgeon. He replied that Phantom was well and back at work and that, unless anything changed, he would wait for me to do the tests. The thought of Major Fitz's faith in me and the idea of soon seeing my friends and dogs, and going hunting, fishing, and riding among the wildflowers of Northumberland, buoyed my spirits.

The principal was waiting for me when I arrived at college that morning. He led the way into his office and handed me the document. The solicitor's findings and suggestions took up one page and the Royal College's directives another three. I read the pages twice. They contained many words but made only a few points.

Quoting a large section of the Veterinary Surgeons Charter of 1844, the solicitor wrote that he could find no rational reason why I should not be admitted to veterinary college—aside from the fact that no woman had been educated there before. His proposal after all this time? That the Royal College take the matter up with its lawyers.

The outcome of the discussion with the council was detailed on the other pages. The views varied from reluctant resignation about the inevitability of women becoming veterinary surgeons to absolute outrage. Only one participant in the discussion was in clear favor of women being admitted. He was silenced by another who, among other things, argued that it was out of the question entirely that women could become veterinary surgeons and that "no true womanly nature would tolerate such an idea."

"What does that mean?" I asked Professor Williams.

He shrugged.

The objector went on. *"Nor is a woman physically fit or would it be decent for her to castrate, fire, calve, foal, or many other jobs that a busy veterinary surgeon is constantly doing. There is a delicacy over such matters, proper that it should be."*

Another member—strangely, the ones with the strongest opinions chose to remain anonymous—was quoted as follows: *"The medical schools may open their doors, but let us pray to the gods for strength to keep ours closed. Is it not galling enough to have to meet, and hear of, men in the profession who are not gentlemen without having added to the number of ungentlemanly vets an equal number of 'ungentlemanly women'? 'Some men can sometimes be gentlemen, but no woman can' is an apparently absurd remark made by an eminent novelist when speaking of the new woman. There is also to be considered the second and more selfish reason—that of the overcrowding of an already overcrowded profession."*

"'An ungentlemanly woman?' Is that what I am?" I asked.

Professor Williams shrugged and gave his head a small shake.

"Is he correct? Is the profession overcrowded?"

"Only for those vets who are unsure of their skills," he replied.

I placed the pages on his desk. "So the minutes will be published in the *Veterinary Record,* and we must wait for the response? What then?"

"The final verdict will be published once the Royal College has heard from its professional members."

"So, my fate remains undecided?"

"The RCVS is undecided, yes. But your fate is up to you."

"How so? It seems they are determined to stop me."

"And yet, here you are. You have the support of this college. Nothing has changed in that regard."

"I continue as before?"

"Yes. That would be my recommendation. You continue. Only from now on, we will not adjust your results for any reason."

"But what if they decide against allowing women to qualify? Be certified? Will they not penalize you? The college?"

Professor Williams scoffed. "And risk losing the fees they receive from me every year? Not to mention the reputational damage they might incur. No, Miss Cust. You should not worry about me or the college. This profession will progress. Women will become veterinary surgeons, starting with you. And my college will have the proud legacy of not only training the best veterinary surgeons but also training the best who happen to be women. You should not worry about me, only about yourself and the work ahead of you to become an excellent veterinary surgeon."

Not for the first time, I thought about how lucky I was to have been introduced to Professor Williams. If it had not been for Edward's visit to the New Veterinary College years before, followed by Major Fitz's call and introduction, I was not sure what I would have done. For that, I was grateful. For all the stubborn bigotry that so many men demonstrated, there were those, few as they were, who were equally determined to allow women to be more than wives and mothers. I recognized that and resolved not to forget it, even during those moments when I felt frustrated and helpless.

A month later, Professor Williams summoned me to his office again and, without saying a word, handed me a copy of the new edition of the *Veterinary Record*. The Royal College published its opinion under the headline "Ladies as Veterinary Surgeons." I sat to read it.

> A lady student has qualified for her first professional examination, but the council hesitate to take the step of admitting her. They are supported by the following counsel's opinion: Although the word "student" is applicable to both sexes, I am afraid the intention is manifest everywhere in the Act of qualifying only men. Having regard to this fact, and the fact that in the case of the medical profession it was deemed necessary to pass a special Act, viz., 39 and 40 Vict., C.41, to enable women to become registered practitioners, I think the case is too doubtful to justify the council to take the important step of admitting women without the authority of a court of law. I should, therefore, advise the council to refuse to admit the lady, and invite her to *mandamus* them. This refusal should be framed in such a way as to raise the point of law and exclude any possibility of discretion.

"Mandamus?" I said, massaging the back of my neck.

"It means that it is your responsibility to take the professional body to court and to show the judge why you should be admitted."

"I need a solicitor after all?"

"I am afraid so. Someone from London."

"London? Are the Scottish courts not able to make a ruling on such an issue?"

"Mr. Thatcher insists such a trial take place in London, in the Queen's Bench Division. Perhaps because most of the members of the committees involved are located there or maybe because it is where the solicitor lives, and he dislikes traveling."

My head ached. Even if I found the money to pay a solicitor, I could not stand before a judge in London, where court reporters would almost certainly write about the case. The publicity would not only humiliate my mother and possibly damage her position in court, but it would also ruin any chance I had of reconciliation with her and my siblings.

"Are you all right, Miss Cust?"

"No. I mean, yes." I looked up and tried to smile. Even that hurt. "I am sorry. I am feeling a little unwell. It…it is all a bit much."

"Do not get up. I shall bring you some water. Or would you prefer something stronger?"

"Water will do. Thank you."

I sat with my head in my hands and, as Professor Williams left the room, was unable to stop my tears. He closed the door behind him, and grateful for his tact, I indulged myself and sobbed.

Up until that point, I had somehow managed to convince myself the RCVS would eventually yield and allow me to write their examinations, thus officially admitting me and any other women who might want to train as veterinary surgeons to the profession. It was not in my nature to be pessimistic. I would never have gone against my family's wishes and taken such drastic steps if I had doubted that I would be able to see it through. For years, I had watched what women had done in education and in the medical profession—as nurses and, more recently, physicians—and had believed their successes would pave the way for mine. No matter how many times I heard the argument about women not being physically strong enough to work with animals, I told myself that it would not hold up indefinitely. Women were excellent handlers of animals, great and small. I had proved that at veterinary college and Newton Hall already. I had demonstrated I could do everything the male students could do. If I did not have the muscle for a job, I improvised and found a different way of getting it done. Not everything relied on physical strength.

What would it take to convince the men of the RCVS of my abilities? I briefly thought about suggesting to Professor Williams that he invite them to Edinburgh, where they could watch me at work in a stable of horses or a field full of cattle. But even if it was possible, they would not come. Instead, the committee—or was it the council—wanted me to pay money I did not have to appoint a solicitor to represent me in a courtroom I dared not enter to defend a dream they could not imagine being denied. It was hopeless, and I felt defeated.

Professor Williams returned, followed by a woman from the tearoom carrying a tray with a glass of water, a pot of tea, and two cups. I managed a smile.

"This calls for tea and a strategy," he said.

"A strategy?"

"Have you met my son? Owen?"

"Yes. Last semester, when he visited to teach us about rinderpest."

The principal's son, Professor Owen Williams, had followed his father into veterinary surgery and was making a name for himself as an academic, with the idea, I had heard said, of one day succeeding his father as head of the New Veterinary College.

"You might not know that Owen is on several RCVS committees. He is also an advocate for admitting women to the profession."

"I am pleased that he stands with you on that."

"In fact, he not only stands with me on the matter but proposes we do more."

"More?"

"Yes. Owen and I have decided to appoint our own solicitor to sue the Royal College for refusing to examine a qualifying candidate. The New Veterinary College will also claim damages from the professional body for the costs incurred by us and the student, who not only spent a year at the University of Edinburgh to earn a certificate of education but has also studied here for several months—where she has more than proven herself qualified to pursue a career as a veterinary surgeon."

He handed me a cup of tea. I stared at it, momentarily confused.

"Do you take sugar, Miss Cust?" he asked, presenting the sugar bowl.

I said nothing as I added two spoonfuls to my tea and stirred it.

"Drink up. You look pale."

I placed the cup on his desk.

"You are going to sue the RCVS on my behalf? But why?"

"For the exact reasons I have set out. The Royal College is mandated to represent the profitable and effective business of its colleges. By refusing to allow an exceptional student, in whom we have already invested several months of training, the council is doing the contrary. We will sue the RCVS in a court in Edinburgh."

"In Edinburgh?"

"Yes. We are taking the initiative in this regard, and we shall decide where the case should be heard."

"But a solicitor? A hearing? It will prove expensive for you. For the college."

"If we win—and we believe we will—the RCVS will be compelled to pay our legal fees."

I reached for my tea and drank. Whether it was the sugar or the idea of Professor Williams and his son going into battle for me, I do not know, but my tears were gone, and the will to fight for my dream was once more alive within me.

CHAPTER 16

❦

1898
Northumberland, England

THOUGHTS OF COURTS AND MEN, MOST OF WHOM WOULD BE STRANGERS,
arguing about my future were temporarily set aside when I traveled to
Northumberland a few weeks later to stay at Fallodon with Dorothy and put
the Pomeranians through their paces at The Kennel Club show.

Nugget and Honey had never looked better, with the latter some weeks
into her first pregnancy. Although she seemed unusually apprehensive and
was more affectionate than normal, Honey displayed none of the fatigue or
decreased appetite typical of bitches during their first trimester. Washed and
brushed by the servants at Fallodon, the dogs' coats were as soft and fluffy
as duckling down, their eyes alert and shiny, and their expressions—mouths
slightly open, tongue a little exposed, and lips stretched toward the back of
their snouts—ever smiling in the happy Pomeranian way. How could the
judges not be charmed?

The show was held indoors in a spacious agricultural hall, which was
fortuitous, given the drizzly, gray day that greeted us as we carried the dogs
from the carriage. The weather did nothing, though, to discourage the
crowds. In addition to the queues of dog owners waiting to register their

arrival, throngs of spectators, dressed as if for a day at the races, drifted about oohing and aahing at the miscellany of breeds present.

"Good gracious," whispered Dorothy as she looked around and hugged Honey to her bosom as if someone might snatch her. "I had heard that these events were fashionable, but I had no idea that they drew so much interest."

I felt a jolt of guilt for dragging my friend away from the peace and quiet she so enjoyed. "Me neither. I hope the day will not be too onerous for you."

"Look at all the dogs. The shapes and sizes. How could I not be distracted by them?"

Our arrival was noted by the organizers, and we were given the numbers of the stalls in which Nugget and Honey should be placed for the first round of judging. If they were among the finalists, we would be called upon to parade them in the ring before the chief judges.

"Should we have a look around?" asked Dorothy, after we had placed the dogs in the cages and closed the doors. Nugget stared at us through the metal bars, annoyed by the indignity of being shut up like a canary. Honey pranced on the spot, licking her lips anxiously. They were in adjacent stalls, which would give them some comfort. I put my fingers through the bars and scratched their noses, explaining they would only be there for a while and should be on their best behavior for the judges.

"They will be all right. Let us have a look at what they are up against and perhaps find a cup of tea," said Dorothy.

I had never seen as many different dogs in one place. They ranged from leggy Russian Wolfhounds with their long snouts and curved spines so tall they reached the armpits of their owners, to slobbering and snorting Bulldogs with their muscly chests and thighs, to tiny Yorkshire Terriers with nervy eyes and bows on their ears. There were also plenty of Pekingese, a favorite among highly adorned young women, who giggled as they tucked the little dogs under their arms and carried them about as if the animals had been bred without legs. Two rows of stalls were filled with hunting dogs, who lay quietly, accustomed to the cages and indifferent to the yapping around them.

The most impressive, though, were the Saint Bernards occupying several enormous cages on the far side of the hall, where they sat or lay with the eyes of bored old men and observed the people who milled by. They reminded me of my grandmother and how she was the first Englishwoman to have owned such a dog. I turned to say as much to Dorothy but saw that she had been delayed by an acquaintance. As I walked on, my head still turned, I collided with a man who was staring into one of the Saint Bernard stalls.

"I beg your pardon," I said, looking up. He turned.

"Oh, no, I am—Aleen!"

It was Charles.

We stared at one another, silent for a moment. The last time I had seen him was after Orlando's funeral. His face was tanned and the skin around his eyes lined. It was the countenance of a man who spent most of his days staring across the sea, squinting against the reflection of the sun on the water. He was otherwise the same tall, lean man I remembered.

"What are you doing here?" I asked.

He tipped his head toward the Saint Bernard. "Wondering what would possess our grandmother to import such a hound."

Of course, we were thinking the same. We had the same grandmother, the same history. We were family.

"And you?" he asked. "You have given up on Scotland then? Too much—"

"Charles!" Dorothy's voice cut him off as she appeared at my side. "Good gracious. What a surprise."

My mind churned. Was he going to say, "Too much trouble from the RCVS?" Would that confirm my family was somehow influencing the council's move to prevent me from registering to practice as a veterinary surgeon?

I stewed, but my brother's face lit up. He did not disguise his pleasure at unexpectedly encountering Dorothy. He bowed to her, smiling widely, but he did not kiss her hand. How gallant of him to remember her aversion to being touched. I stood back and watched as they conversed like long-separated friends.

"Aleen and I were on our way to the tearoom. Do join us, Charles." She looked at us. "Please," she added, as much to me as to him.

I followed them out of the hall, down a long passage, and into the restaurant. We found an empty table against the wall and sat down. Dorothy pulled the pin from her hat, removed it, and placed it on her lap. Charles's eyes flicked over her hair for a moment.

"What brings you to Northumberland? To the show?" she asked.

"I had a meeting at the port in Blyth and decided to stay on in the county for a few days to visit a friend and his wife. She is thinking of breeding Yorkshire Terriers, so he and I accompanied her here to meet breeders. I said I would wander around to allow them to talk business. Are you breeding, Dorothy?"

"We are here to show Nugget and Honey."

Charles frowned.

"Aleen's Pomeranians. Did you not know them?"

"They were very young when Orlando died," I said, looking at my hands. "Mama wanted me to help Her Majesty's drive to reduce the size of the breed."

"Of course," he said.

A waiter arrived to take our order. He had no sooner left when Dorothy excused herself, leaving me and my brother alone, staring at the table. Eventually, I broke the silence.

"How is Mama?"

"She is well, considering… Have you given up? Studying, I mean."

I held his eyes. "No. I am here for a few days to show the dogs, and then I will return to Edinburgh. As I explained in my letters, I have no intention of giving up."

Charles took a deep breath and exhaled, looking away. Why was he unable to look me in the eye? I willed him to say something that might reveal his part in the Royal College's efforts to deter me. Or better still, to confirm that my family would never do such a thing.

"Nothing has changed then. Not for you or for our mother," he said.

"But *you* could change things, Charles."

"How so?"

"Mama will listen to you. Even if Her Majesty wants to deny women education and equity, her daughters are progressive. If you, as the next generation, were to encourage Mama to see that things are changing, she would listen to you. After all, you are the Cust patriarch."

"I am not against the education of women."

"You are not? Well, then—"

"What I *am* against is women trying to take on men's work, men's professions."

"Veterinary surgery is not only suited to men. It is not true that women cannot do it. I have—"

Charles leaned across the table and said in a low voice, "Even if you enlist the help of stable hands, farmers, dairy men, it is indecent for a woman to castrate, foal, or calve an animal. It is improper, Aleen, and nothing you say or do—or learn—will make it anything else."

I repeated the words in my head, "…indecent for a woman to castrate, foal, or calve." Those were the exact words one of the objectors had written in the *Veterinary Record*. One of the anonymous objectors. I felt the hairs at the base of my skull rise and the blood rush between my ears.

"Did you write to the *Record*?" I asked, struggling to keep my voice down.

"The *Record*?"

"The *Veterinary Record*. It is a professional journal." I was struggling to breathe.

He shrugged. "I have no idea what you are talking about. What would I have to do with a veterinary journal? I am a naval officer for goodness' sake."

I looked across the tearoom where others laughed and chatted easily. Was it possible that any of them were siblings?

"I was at the top of my class, you know, in our recent examinations," I said.

"Of course you were, Aleen. Winning was always most important to you. Even at the expense of everyone else's discomfort."

I thought about my classmates. Any discomfort that they had experienced initially by my presence at college had disappeared. Unless they hid it well. None of them showed disquiet about my achieving better results than them in the exams. They had grown accustomed to my ambition and achievements by then. I did not bother trying to explain that to Charles.

"It is not about winning," I said instead. "It is about becoming a veterinary surgeon, working with animals, and doing what I have always wanted to do. It is about living a full life. Doing something useful. That makes my life worthwhile."

"I understand," he said, taking me by surprise.

"What? You do? Well, yes, of course. Your career in the navy is similar," I jabbered, excited by the idea that Charles might finally take my side. My hope was misplaced.

"The difference is your ambition is at the expense of your family's reputation; mine is not. It is not so much that you are ambitious but rather that you are the most selfish person I know. I am ashamed of you, Aleen. Our mother is ashamed of you. Orlando would be ashamed of you."

I snatched up a fork from the table and clenched it in my fist. "How dare you, Charles! Orlando made special provision for me in his will. He *wanted* me to follow my dream. He would not be ashamed of me. Quite the contrary. Of that, I am certain."

"He pitied you. He did not expect to die while you were still young enough to find a college mutinous enough to accept you."

I stood up. "Tell Dorothy I shall see her in the hall," I said, turning and making my way to the door. As I reached it, I realized that I was still clutching the fork. Breathing like a racehorse pulled up after the finish line, I swung around and flung the silverware across the room at my brother. I marched away, the image of a room full of wide eyes, including those of Charles, imprinted in my mind.

Dorothy found me in the Beagle aisle later.

"I'm sorry," I said, unable to meet her eyes. "It was rude of me to leave, but I could not stay. I hoped he might listen, agree to talk to our mother, but nothing has changed."

"Apparently, you nearly impaled a waiter with a flying fork."

"Oh, I should apologize. I could not contain myself. If it is any consolation, I would have known how to suture the wound."

She covered her mouth with her fingers as her shoulders shook with laughter.

"I should be ashamed. My behavior only confirms what my family believes me to be...a wild, ambitious, selfish, and unladylike creature."

"Charles was upset, but perhaps not entirely for the reasons you think," said Dorothy, giggling now under control.

"Oh?"

"He misses you."

I gave a small, disbelieving laugh.

"He says the family is incomplete without Orlando, Percy, and you," she said.

"He said that?"

"He did."

"Then why does he not try to understand me? Support me?"

"Because, above everything else, he is your mother's son."

"So indeed, nothing has changed."

"There is more," said my friend. "Charles is to be appointed equerry to Her Majesty's grandson the Duke of York."

My heart sank. Following the death of his older brother, Prince Albert, six years previously, Charles's friend George, the Duke of York, was the second in line to the throne, after his father. Charles's appointment as his equerry sealed my family's association with the royal court and my fate as the outcast daughter.

Dorothy looked at me. I shrugged. What was there to say?

"Shall we go and see if Nugget and Honey have been judged?" I asked.

They had. What is more, both were invited into the ring, where Nugget was named second best male Pomeranian on show and Honey won first place as the best bitch. The results would allow me to increase the price of their puppies, which might be a way of contributing to Professor Williams and his son's legal costs. By the time we left the hall, five people had asked me to reserve puppies for them.

A short while later, Dorothy and I sat in the carriage and watched the light and mist flick by through the trees on the way back to Fallodon.

"Did you see Charles again, after the tearoom, I mean?" I asked.

"No. I suspect he left immediately. Why do you ask?"

"I thought if he saw how well Nugget and Honey did at the show, he might offer that as consolation to our mother."

"I shall ask Father to drop it into the conversation the next time he sees her," she said, stroking Honey, who was curled up on the seat alongside her.

We laughed. Nugget looked down his nose at us, still bristling with the indignity of having been caged in an agricultural hall and perhaps also a little miffed that his rosette was red while his mate had won blue.

CHAPTER 17

⌣⌣

1898
Edinburgh, Scotland

PROFESSOR WILLIAMS ASSURED ME HE AND HIS SON HAD APPOINTED
Edinburgh's finest legal team to present their case at the Court of Session.
We agreed that because the legal action had been brought about against the
Royal College by the New Veterinary College, it would be imprudent for me
to attend court that day.

"Let us keep the fox away from the hens as we demand his right to dinner,"
joked the principal. I tried to think of a better metaphor, but my wit forsook me.

As such, I attended classes as normal that dark, gray June day in 1898
when the judge heard the case. I was as distracted as a pony in a show ring
with a swarm of bees buzzing about his ears. Even a lesson on the potential
complications during gestation in cows, as important as it was, could not
hold my attention.

"You can borrow mine," said Fred as he followed me from the classroom.

"What?"

"My notes. You did not write much this morning."

"Thank you. No. I do not know why I bothered to come today. My head
is filled with thoughts about what might be going on in Parliament House."

"Of course it is."

I did not have to wait long to find out what had happened. Professor Williams was back at the college by lunchtime. My heart sank when I recognized the crease in his brow and the agitated way he was cleaning his spectacles.

"I anticipated obscurity from the Royal College's lawyers but not this," he said, gesturing to a chair as I walked into his office.

I remained standing. "What happened?"

"The judge declared our action null and void."

"What?"

"Yes. Mr. Thatcher argued that the Royal College has no domicile in Scotland."

It took me a moment to consider what that meant.

"How is that possible? Three RCVS colleges are *in* Scotland. If anything, the RCVS has greater domicile in Scotland than in England."

The principal sighed. "He told the court that the organization is in London. Said it has its primary offices there. The judge agreed, saying that Scottish courts have no jurisdiction over the matter and that we should bring fresh action in the English courts."

I sat down heavily. "At great expense. In London."

He nodded. Slumped behind his desk, Professor Williams looked as defeated as I felt. He took his spectacles off again, rubbed the bridge of his nose, and then, having replaced his eyeglasses, he shuffled through a small pile of letters, extracted a page, and handed it to me. It was a letter from the RCVS, informing its members of a meeting due to take place later in the year. I read it and looked up.

"What am I to make of this?"

"Look at the addresses at the top of the page."

The pre-printed stationery featured four addresses: the Royal Veterinary College in London, Dick's Veterinary College in Edinburgh, the Glasgow Veterinary College, and Professor Williams's own New Veterinary College. The details were printed in the same font in one neat line across the top of the page. There was nothing distinguishing one address from the other, nothing to suggest any hierarchy. The RCVS colleges, one in England and three in Scotland, were, as depicted by the organization's own stationery, on par.

"This was not shown in court?" I asked, holding up the page.

He shook his head. "It should have been. Alas, it only occurred to me now."

He took the letter from me, stood up, and walked toward the window that overlooked the courtyard. It seemed like decades ago since I had looked out the same window as I waited to be introduced to the principal by Major Fitz. What had I thought then? I could not have imagined the current scenario.

"We could appeal," he said, turning to look at me.

"And spend more time and money? If they can do this, who is to say what they might come up with next?" I asked.

Professor Williams removed his glasses again and rubbed his eyes, saying nothing.

"You say it is not my case to fight, principal, but we both know that is not true. You established a college to teach veterinary surgery, not to keep solicitors in new coats. You should let this go. I will investigate taking it up in my personal capacity. If it is to be fairly debated in court, let it be led by the one who wants that most: me. Let us put the fox in the hen house."

He sighed. "That will be expensive and will require going to hearings in London. Is that what you want?"

"No, but there is no other choice. Is there?"

He shrugged and shook his head.

"I will discuss it with Major Widdrington," I continued. "He is well connected and knows the courts better than anyone."

"On one condition, Miss Cust: do not suspend your studies here. Not for a single day and no matter what happens. Even if the RCVS refuses to ratify your examination results, continue at the college. The Royal College cannot stop you from writing our examinations and us from marking them. You will continue to train as a veterinary surgeon and emerge an excellent one. Let us not allow this trickery to prevent you from doing that, even if they will not ratify your qualifications."

My throat felt thick. I swallowed deeply, tried to smile, and left to attend my next class.

I wrote to Major Fitz that night. He replied saying he would travel to Edinburgh so that we could discuss the matter in detail. As I waited for him to arrive, I strengthened my resolve to study and not become distracted by thoughts of taking on the Royal College. Professor Williams assured me that the organization had no authority over the day-to-day activities of the college and that there was no need for me to worry about them trying to prohibit me from writing the college examinations and graduating. That did not, however, prevent me from worrying about how it would be possible to find work as a veterinary surgeon if, by the end of my third year, I was still unable to officially sit any of the RCVS examinations. Without those examinations and a certified diploma from the Royal College, no one would employ me, and I would be unable to legitimately open my own practice.

"You are getting ahead of yourself, Aleen," said Fred, when I voiced my concerns one morning after tossing and turning all night. "We are two years away from finishing the course; things will have changed by then. Look at how many more women are becoming physicians. Look at what Mrs. Fawcett is doing. You read the papers, do you not? She is determined to achieve equity for women through legislative change. It will *have* to happen. It is implausible to think that the RCVS will forever be able to obstruct you from entering the profession."

He was right. Millicent Fawcett—whose sister Mrs. Elizabeth Anderson was Britain's first woman doctor—was the leader of the National Union of Women's Suffrage Societies. According to newspaper reports, while she was unambiguous about her support for women's suffrage, Mrs. Fawcett took a moderate position politically. It was said she believed that a militant approach soured people's opinion of feminists and harmed women's chances of fair representation in government and society.

As frustrated as I was by how prejudiced the world was against women, it was not fair to ignore the fact that without the assistance of men, namely Orlando, Major Fitz, and Professor Williams, I would not be training as a veterinary surgeon. It was one of the reasons I favored peaceful change and therefore admired Mrs. Fawcett's approach. If I were to ever reconcile with my family without giving up my ambition to become a veterinary surgeon, it would require the least bellicose path. I wanted change, impartiality, and the ability to work as a veterinary surgeon, but I also wanted peace and congeniality. Moreover, I wanted to feel like part of my family again. The Widdringtons' supporting me long after the major's official guardianship had expired was something I would forever be grateful for. However, despite how cold and uncompromising my family had been toward me, I longed to be accepted by them and for them to be proud of my accomplishments.

While Mrs. Fawcett was working to achieve equity for women through legislation, it was not the route Major Fitz proposed for me. By the time we met in the lounge of his hotel, the major had already consulted several legal men. While only some of them were eager to represent me, all agreed that, fought in my individual capacity, the lawsuit brought against the Royal College would result in immense court fees.

"You know that I am willing to lend you the money—and yes, I know that you will not take it," said Major Fitz. "But even if neither of those points was true, the solicitors concur that the RCVS has deep pockets and that it will fight the case in the House of Lords, which, unless you have changed your mind, is the one place in the world I believe that you would most like to avoid."

I looked away across the room, wondering if it was possible to feel ashamed of one's shame. "I have not changed my mind."

"Then I am sorry, Aleen, but it is my considered opinion that you should not fight the Royal College in court."

I was not surprised, but it did not stop a wave of hopelessness from washing over me.

"It is kind of you to have come all this way to tell me that there is nothing I can do," I said.

"But it is not over, Aleen. I came here to ensure that you understand that." He leaned forward. "You wrote that Professor Williams wants you to continue to study and complete the course. Do that. Write the college examinations. Excel at them. Graduate. Even if you are not permitted to sit the RCVS examinations, that will not change the fact that you will be appropriately trained. Continue to take your education as seriously as you have. There are many women and pro-feminists fighting for similar causes. Go on, Aleen, in the hope that by the time you finish, you will be permitted to sit the Royal College examination and become a registered veterinary surgeon."

"Yes. That is what I am encouraged to do by the professor, my friends, and now you. Thank you, Major. I appreciate it, but what if nothing changes? What if, after all that, I cannot practice?"

"You will work as a veterinary surgeon. Of that, I am convinced. You already do." He smiled. "You will help me treat my horses the way you treated Phantom. Save dogs, the way you saved Samson and that hound on the hunt when you were just a girl. For goodness' sake, Aleen. You are a veterinary surgeon. You always have been one."

"No one will employ me, Major Fitz. It is forbidden without being registered with the RCVS. I will not be able to open a legitimate practice. I will not be able to make a living from my services. It will all be for naught. My family will be delighted."

His mouth twitched. "I do not think that is true, and I am convinced that things will change—soon. But even if they do not, you have come too far to give up. You have not allowed the naysayers to inhibit you yet. Why would you allow them to do so now? Do not give up."

The major was right. I had already risked so much, and having spent more than a year at the college, I was more convinced than ever that I belonged in the profession. Regardless of the hurdles ahead, I would not shift my focus. I would forge on and become a veterinary surgeon.

CHAPTER 18

❧

1900
Northumberland, England

I ONLY SAW HONEY'S SECOND LITTER OF FOUR PUPPIES ONCE BEFORE THEY left Fallodon Hall for their new homes. They were already almost a month old when I was able to escape Edinburgh for a weekend visit.

"I do not recall Honey, Nugget, or any of the first litter being so round," I said as Dorothy and I sat on the lawn with the fluffy bundles tumbling over one another like balls of cotton in the breeze. Honey, fed up with their sharp teeth tugging at her teats, was eager to wean them. She did not give us a second glance as, noting that her brood was distracted, she trotted to the far end of the garden where Nugget was nosing about in a bed of tall, pink gladioli.

"They are the most adorable creatures," said Dorothy, picking up a particularly energetic male and handing him to me. "Their effect on everyone who meets them is a source of great amusement. Even Edward and my father crawled around the grass playing with them last week. If Honey produced one hundred, we would still not have enough for all the buyers."

"One hundred—just imagine," I replied, rolling the pup on his back and gently wrestling him with my hand.

"Did I tell you that Bertie will take one of the females to the Fords? Remember them? My mother's friend the sculptor and his family?"

"Yes. I remember them, but no, you did not say."

I had not seen Bertie since he left Newton Hall with Enid and her parents. Dorothy had not said anything up until now that gave me reason to suspect that their friendship might have evolved.

"When will Bertie fetch the pup?" I asked.

"Next week. I told him you would be here this weekend, but he was unable to leave earlier."

"Is he in London often? I mean, that is where he will deliver the pup to the Fords, is it not?"

Dorothy saw through my faux nonchalance. "No, I do not think Bertie sees much of Miss Ford. Father offered to take the pup, but when we realized that Bertie would be in London earlier, we decided it would be more suitable if he took it."

"Please thank him for me. I am sorry that I have not seen him for so long."

"You and Bertie should write. At least you would stay in touch without having to interrogate me about each other. I will give you his address before you leave."

"Yes. Of course. Thank you."

In fact, Lady Widdrington had sent me Bertie's address several months previously. It was not that I did not think about him and mean to write, but I did not have time in Edinburgh. My correspondence was limited to that of Dorothy and her parents. I also made a point of writing to my mother, Charles, Ursula, and Leo every Christmas and on their birthdays. I wanted them to know that despite their determination to ignore me, I had not forsaken them. My letters were brief but cheerful. I asked after their health, inevitably mentioned the Edinburgh weather, included a short, innocuous line about my studies, and ended with my best wishes. Every letter and postcard included my address in Scotland. Perhaps, one day, one of them would be moved enough to reply.

"You are certain you are not going to breed from Honey again for another two years then?" asked Dorothy. I wondered, as I often did, how it was that my friend knew exactly when to change the subject and what to say.

"Yes. There are some studies on the recovery time between mating and pregnancy in mammals, and I believe she needs a break now. I am sorry to disappoint everyone who wants a pup, but it will not be healthy for her to get pregnant again for a while."

Indeed, the demand for Pomeranian puppies was great. My mother had done me a favor by suggesting I breed them. Helped by their popularity at court, they were the dogs du jour and among the most expensive. When, about a year and a half previously, Dorothy had written to say the first litter of pups had been fetched by their new owners and that she would send me the money, I had told her to keep a portion of each sale to cover the costs of taking care of the dogs at Fallodon. She ignored me and sent the full amount, for which I was grateful. My living conditions in Edinburgh remained spartan. Now, with my final year of college under way, I was even more thankful for the money, particularly with the inevitable additional costs I would incur during the month I was due to be in Dundee.

One of the conditions of training at the New Veterinary College was that students would spend the final summer of the course working alongside a qualified veterinary surgeon. Nothing had changed for me since I had accepted that I would not take legal action against the Royal College. I continued my studies and excelled in all the college tests and examinations. Every morning, I woke up and hoped that this would be the day something would shift to force the RCVS's hand. Every day, one closer to graduating, my faith dwindled. As such, I was heartened when Professor Williams told me that his friend Mr. Andrew Spreull had agreed to take me on as an assistant at his veterinary practice in Dundee in July.

"His son, also Andrew—I think of him as Young Mr. Spreull—is in your class. You know him, I suppose?" asked the principal.

I did. I knew the younger Andrew as my closest rival in several subjects and as a middle-weight boxing champion. He was a quiet, hardworking Scotsman with a remarkably firm and calm hand. He, it seemed certain, had "the lucky hand." I admired him but had not known that he had the advantage of having a veterinary surgeon for a father.

"Will Young Mr. Spreull be there too, working alongside his father, I mean, when I am in Dundee?"

"No. You will go alone. Young Mr. Spreull will be in Ireland."

"Ireland?" How fortunate he was. Not only was he the son of a veterinary surgeon, but he was also going to the land of Taffy and Ned.

"Young Mr. Spreull is going to work with Mr. Willie Byrne of County Roscommon, where he will experience how different it is to work for a rural practice compared to one like his father's in town."

"How lucky he is to be going to the country," I murmured.

The principal stared at me over his spectacles. I felt myself redden.

"Forgive me, Professor Williams. That sounded ungrateful, which I am not. It is just that, well, I forgot myself for a moment and felt envious of Young Mr. Spreull being in the country, particularly in Ireland. I have fond memories of riding my horse and running with my dog in Tipperary as a girl. My apologies if it seemed ungracious."

He held up a hand. "Say no more, Miss Cust. You will learn a great deal in Dundee—though I certainly could also picture you helping Irish farmers with their animals."

"Has he practiced for long? Mr. Byrne, I mean."

"Not at all. He only qualified in recent years, in London, where he has the record for completing the course and passing the examinations in the shortest time possible. He is something of a vanguard veterinary surgeon, who has almost as great a following in his profession in his country as he has as a nationalist."

"Nationalist?"

"He is the president of the Athleague branch of the United Irish League."

I recalled my father's fury as he berated my mother when she dared to question the wisdom of his placing his boot on the Irish nun's grave. I had not understood what it meant at the time and why the farmers of Tipperary had celebrated my father's death. Did I fully grasp their sentiments now? Perhaps Dundee was the better choice for me after all.

In fact, working with Mr. Spreull was a highlight of my veterinary training, and the month I spent in Dundee was memorable for several reasons.

Mrs. Spreull insisted rather than find lodgings elsewhere, I move into the family home in Magdalen Green in the West End. It was a large, sumptuously furnished house, and Mr. and Mrs. Spreull were welcoming and kind. Any concerns I might have had about staying in my teacher's home disappeared when I discovered how much Mr. Spreull loved his work and the opportunity to talk about it.

"Oh, Mr. Spreull," said his wife, the first evening I was there. "Give the young lady a moment. I do not believe she wants to hear about the innards of an ox at tea."

"No, Mrs. Spreull, quite the contrary," I interjected. "I am happy to hear it. If it does not upset you, of course."

She gave her husband a sideways glance. "My dear, I married a veterinary surgeon. It is who he has always been. And then there's the small matter of our sons being in the business of doctoring animals too. If hearing about it at breakfast, lunch, and dinner upset me, I would have been gone a long time ago."

Mr. Spreull laughed and patted his wife's hand. His chin was shaven, but he wore a luxurious mustache that practically hid his mouth and ended in neat twirls at the base of each cheek. He dabbed his lips with his serviette and went on to explain how he had cleaned and replaced the animal's organs, sewed up the incision, and returned to the farm two days later to see the ox grazing in a field.

"It is all about cleanliness, Miss Cust," he said. "If one can keep the bleeding down, and the organs and wounds clean, healing will almost certainly take place."

As much as I had learned at college over the previous two and a half years, I arguably picked up more during the one month I worked alongside Mr. Spreull in Dundee.

We left the house at first light for the practice, where ill and injured in-patients were kept in adjoining stables. The first hours of the day were spent examining, treating, and feeding the animals in the infirmary, replacing dressings, undertaking procedures, and carrying out euthanasia where it was deemed necessary. Mr. Spreull's second business, the forge, where he employed a blacksmith and two farriers, also required attention.

Appointments for farrier services were made at the practice, and either Mr. Spreull or I examined all the horses who were brought for shoeing before their hooves were attended to.

"My father was a farrier," he explained. "I learned as much about horses while helping him as I did from the professors at college. There is no better way to learn this business than by working with animals every day."

At nine o'clock, the first telegrams requesting our attention around town or in the nearby countryside were delivered by the boy from the post office. How our days unfolded from there on depended on the nature of the calls and the demands at the practice.

As the days went by, I grasped the full meaning of Mr. Spreull's assertion about there being no better way of learning than by doing the job. While reading and attending lectures were useful, working in a busy veterinary practice opened my eyes to the true nature of the profession. I realized that it was crucial not only that I trust my instinct and education but also that I was as pragmatic as I was creative. At times, I despaired at how little I knew. Mr. Spreull assured me my doubts were natural.

"Get accustomed to it, Miss Cust. I have been doing this for decades, and almost every day, I am confronted by something new that makes me feel adrift. The truth is we know so little. There is no time, though, to panic or bemoan the fact. If you are going to succeed, you must learn how to be decisive and practical, and you need to move quickly. I can see you can do it, but it only matters that *you* see it and act upon it."

Mr. Spreull also taught me how to manage the business of a practice, teaching me the importance of keeping a meticulous ledger and a detailed diary, carefully balancing income and expenses, and managing medicine stocks.

Most importantly perhaps, Mr. Spreull showed me the most effective way to communicate with people. He demonstrated how to keep conversations with clients concise when we were busy without being rude. I watched him and learned how to reassure people about their animals without guaranteeing the outcome and how to placate them when things were bad. I learned how to manage time and prioritize cases.

Professor Williams was right about the experience of a town practice being invaluable. The pace and busyness that came with being in town pleased me. The cases were many and varied, and the days flew by, leaving me tired but satisfied. Even so, one of the things I enjoyed most about the job in Dundee was riding one of Mr. Spreull's horses out of town to visit clients in the country.

During my first week there, I made calls with Mr. Spreull. We rode down the cobbled streets of Dundee and onto the country roads side by side. When the paths were clear and the fields wide, I longed to gallop, but with Mr. Spreull at my side, I never urged my horse faster than a canter, during which he kept up an endless stream of conversation. Mr. Spreull was an accomplished rider but not, it seemed initially, inclined toward speed and cross-country adventure.

Mr. Spreull's clients made no attempts to disguise their surprise when I rode into their yards alongside him.

"Your daughter then, Mr. Spreull?"

"Out for a social ride, are you, Mr. Spreull?"

"The lass lost her way, then?"

He responded to each with the same firm introduction. "This is Miss Cust, trainee veterinary surgeon. She is here for the animals and will be working alongside me today. In fact, she will do the work, while I observe."

The first two farmers we visited together tipped their hats in my direction and were congenial if only, it seemed to me, for Mr. Spreull's sake. The third, Mr. Andrews, however, gave me a disbelieving glance and then ignored me, even as I sank my arm into his cow, turned her calf, pulled the young bull free of his mother, and placed him in front of her to clean. All the while, Mr. Spreull leaned against a fence, nodding and clicking his tongue.

"Well done," he said as we left the barn. "Mr. Andrews, will you bring Miss Cust some clean water to wash with, please?"

Mr. Andrews dropped the bucket at my feet, water splashing my already wet skirts. I glanced at Mr. Spreull. He narrowed his eyes but said nothing until we had ridden some distance from the farmyard.

"You are going to have to behave more like a veterinary surgeon and less like an English aristocrat if you are to succeed in this business, Miss Cust."

I thought I had misheard him. "English aristocrat?"

"Yes. Well, of course, I know that is what you are, but it is unlikely to work in your favor in this business."

"What do you mean, Mr. Spreull?"

"Mr. Andrews was disrespectful. He glared at me while you did the work and pulled his calf—which you did extremely well, I might add. He wanted me to stop you. I ignored him, but you should not have."

"What should I have said? Done?"

"That is not for me but for *you* to decide. This is a proud and honorable profession, Miss Cust. Veterinary surgeons are respected, as they should be. Regardless of their gender." He looked at me, his eyebrows low and his gaze stern. "I am not proposing you respond with equal rudeness, but you need to work out how to convince clients you are as capable as I know you are. If you do not, they will not believe it."

I saw his point, but not entirely. "How was my behavior that of an English aristocrat?"

"You pretended you did not notice his snub. You politely ignored it. He responded by practically throwing a bucket of water at you. What if I had not been there and you had needed Mr. Andrews to help you do something? It is crucial, Miss Cust, that our clients listen to us and do our bidding. You need to be more forceful. Assert your confidence. Do not expect deference. You will not always get it. Insist on it."

As we rode back to town, I thought about what Mr. Spreull had said. I had, over the years, won the respect of my classmates. It took time, but seeing me as they did every day, they were eventually won over. It was going to be more difficult among clients, who only saw me occasionally. I would have to work out how to quickly gain their respect.

I watched Mr. Spreull with his clients over the following days. I saw how friendly yet consistently firm he was with them. There was no doubt he was the professional. He was trained to take care of their animals, and he demanded their respect. He asked questions and listened carefully to the replies, but he was always absolutely in charge.

On my way back to Mr. Spreull's rooms after helping one of his farriers clean up a hoof one morning, I encountered the boy from the post office on his way to deliver a telegram to the practice. I took it from him and read as I walked. It was from Mr. Andrews.

I found Mr. Spreull in the stables examining a horse who had been injured after the cart it was pulling had been overloaded. I held the paper up to him.

"It is from Mr. Andrews. I shall go, shall I?" I asked. "I am finished with the farrier."

He held my gaze. "I think you should."

The ride to Mr. Andrews's farm was much quicker than it had been the previous week with Mr. Spreull. I took a shortcut over a field that included a low fence and two ditches, and opened Mr. Spreull's horse up across the dry marsh. If the animal was surprised by the adventure, he did not let on. I wondered if the veterinary surgeon moderated his riding to set an example for me.

Mr. Andrews did not greet me when I rode into the yard. Instead, he pursed his lips and looked beyond me for Mr. Spreull.

"Just me today, Mr. Andrews," I said, dismounting.

He grunted but did not move.

"Another cow, I take it?"

His nostrils flared. I tied up the horse and walked to the shed. Sure enough, there was the cow. She had given birth and lay in the center of the stall, her calf curled up in the corner. The stench gave it away. The placenta had not all been expelled by the cow and was putrid.

"When did she calve?" I asked, hearing Mr. Andrews's boots shuffle in the straw behind me.

"Where is Mr. Spreull?" he asked.

"He is in town with another client. When did she calve, Mr. Andrews?"

"Three, four days ago."

"Is she allowing the calf to suckle?"

He shook his head. That was not a good sign and suggested she also had mastitis, which meant her udder was infected and too painful for her to allow the calf to suck. Before I could consider treating that, though, I would have to remove the rotting placenta and do an internal examination. It was going to be a messy job.

"She needs cleansing," I said. "We will have to get her on her feet so that I can have a proper look and get to it."

Mr. Andrews stared at me, his mouth twisted with disapproval. I placed my bag at my feet and rolled up my sleeves.

"First, you need to fetch a head collar and a large bucket of warm water," I said, my eyes on his. "Right now, Mr. Andrews, if we are to save her."

He sighed and turned to go.

"Oh, and Mr. Andrews?"

He looked back at me, his mouth soft and sullen.

"Take care not to trip and wet my skirts again when you return," I said. He blinked several times before walking away quickly.

It was not only the foulest job I had undertaken but also the trickiest and most unpleasant. The fetid smell of dead tissue settled in my nostrils where I knew it would stay for days. My clothing too would long reek of the job, no matter how careful I was. It did not matter. This was the work of a veterinary surgeon. What mattered was not *my* discomfort but the comfort of the animal. Knowing I could help her felt good.

"Come, girl," I said, stroking her rump. "Let us sort you out."

After I had removed as much of the placenta that I could, I washed her vulva and the surrounding area. Then, I soaped and rinsed my hands and arms thoroughly. I caught Mr. Andrews's eye as I slowly pushed my hand into the cow. He looked away.

With my arm sunk deep, I pictured the diagrams I had studied at college, visualizing the twists and folds I might encounter ahead of the pelvic cavity. Just beyond the end of the canal, I touched something hard and round. I felt around.

"Blazes!" I gasped.

Mr. Andrews stared at me.

"There is another calf in here," I added, hoping it would explain my cussing.

Indeed, the cow had not only retained part of her placenta but had also been pregnant with twins, one of whom was still inside—dead. I closed my eyes and leaned against the cow, gathering my thoughts. The stench filled my nose, and I fought the urge to gag. For a moment, I regretted having come alone and contemplated riding back to town to call Mr. Spreull. I imagined the smirk on Mr. Andrews's face and pushed the idea aside. He and I would remove the calf and save the cow.

The calf's forelegs were curled up beneath it. With great effort, I managed to push the head back, pull both forelegs forward, and straighten the head. There was no way, though, despite the good positioning, I would be able to pull it out alone. I turned to the farmer, aware of the beads of perspiration trickling down my face.

"We need two ropes," I said. "And more hot water. Two buckets full. And soap."

I washed again and rummaged in my bag for a bottle of liquid paraffin, placing the waxy substance within reach. Having made slip knots with each rope, I pushed my arm back into the cow to locate the forelegs once more. I placed nooses above the carpal joints one at a time, going as high as possible to help ensure that I could remove the entire body all at once. I asked Mr. Andrews to hold the end of the first bit of rope, while I secured the second and handed it to him while I lubricated the area with paraffin. Once that was done, I took hold of the rope on my side once more.

"We must pull one at a time in a gentle walking-type motion," I said. "I shall count, with me beginning on one and you following. Gently now."

The cow, restrained after we had tied the head collar to a pole, grunted and moaned.

"Sorry, girl," I said. "Just a while longer. Slowly, Mr. Andrews. Little by little. There is no rush and we do not want to hurt her unnecessarily."

"Aye," he said.

We look our time and finally, with a groan of relief from the cow, removed the dead calf. I was exhausted, sweating, and filthy. Mr. Andrews took the carcass away and returned with a fresh bucket of water that I had not requested. He placed it carefully at my feet.

"Thank you," I said, bending to wash. "You might need to feed the calf separately for a bit and keep an eye on them both. Hopefully, she will let it drink in a while,"

"Aye," he said, stroking the cow's nose. He untied her. "Would you like a cup of tea, Miss Cust? Before you ride back to town?"

"I would. Thank you, Mr. Andrews."

Mrs. Andrews, a small, bashful-looking woman, suggested we go to the parlor for tea, but I deferred and said given the state of us, I was happy to take it in the kitchen.

There was an awkward silence as she handed me a cup.

"So you're working with Mr. Spreull, Mr. Andrews tells me," she said.

"Only for a few more weeks. I am still at college."

"You know an awful lot for a student," muttered Mr. Andrews into his tea.

The weeks flew by in Dundee. I saw that a veterinary practice in town involved endless work with horses; no one wanted their transport to be out of action. I was also surprised by how many dogs were brought to the practice. I commented on it to Mr. Spreull.

"When I began in this business, the only dogs I ever saw were working hounds. Sheep farmers, whose dogs work harder than anyone on their farms, understand the value of healthy dogs. When something happens to them, it is as awful for a farmer as it is for a stagecoach driver when one of his horses is ill or injured. When a working dog stops working, sheep farming is impossible. Aye, those dogs see the veterinary surgeon. Nowadays, though, people—particularly wealthier city folk—bring their pet dogs in when they are unwell too," he said.

"I notice that many of them are well bred. Do you think it is because people know the value of pedigree dogs?" I asked.

"It could be a reason, though many of my clients are not breeders. They are simply dog lovers. It is a growing business for veterinary surgeons, establishing practices to work with smaller animals—not that it is that new, mind you."

He reached into a shelf and handed me a book. *The Management and Diseases of the Dog* by John Woodroffe Hill. I leafed through it.

"I believe he is authoring one on cats at the moment too," said Mr. Spreull.

We were quiet for several minutes as I paged through the book. Mr. Spreull seemed deep in thought. Eventually, he spoke again.

"Would it interest you, Miss Cust, to specialize in smaller animals, perhaps set up a practice in a town? Like Dundee?"

I chuckled. He was surely teasing. "In opposition to you, Mr. Spreull?"

"No. Goodness gracious, no. I should hope not. I was thinking we could add a new room."

"Are you serious?"

"Yes. A canine practice for the dog fanciers. You must have noticed how many dogs there are in Dundee. Mr. Henry Gray—I've always wondered whether he is related to the late anatomist Henry Gray—has opened a rather elegant infirmary for horses and dogs in London. Kensington, I believe."

Kensington? I was distracted for a moment and wondered whether my mother and Ursula knew Mr. Gray. Was it possible they might think about me if ever they passed by his rooms?

"Well? What do you think, Miss Cust? Would it be something you might consider?"

I gave my head a small shake to shift my attention back to Mr. Spreull. On one hand, I could not have hoped for a greater compliment. That he considered me a worthy colleague was deeply flattering. However, I wondered if, even after watching me work for a month, he doubted my abilities with horses and cattle. Surely, I had proven myself capable?

"An elegant infirmary for dogs? No, Mr. Spreull, I cannot picture myself specializing in canines, as much as I like them. I would rather work with horses, cattle, and sheep—and working dogs, of course. I would like to live and work in the country."

I almost mentioned how I hoped being in the countryside would make it easier for me to ride and hunt when I was not working, but having seen how hard Mr. Spreull worked, I sensed that it might seem fanciful.

"Well, if you change your mind, Miss Cust, I would be glad to discuss it."

"Thank you, Mr. Spreull. I do not think I will change my mind, but I am honored by your confidence in me."

"You will make a fine veterinary surgeon. The only trainee I know who is as good, I am bound to say, is my son."

I laughed and felt silly about questioning the motive behind his offer. "I wonder what *he* would say if I told him of your proposal?"

"He would try to convince you to accept it, I believe."

It was not the only time the idea I might work with dogs was proposed while I was in Dundee. When time allowed, I walked on Magdalen Green, which overlooked the River Tay, the Tay Rail Bridge, and the peninsula of Fife. The wide green strip of grass was a prime dog-walking area, and I encountered breeds aplenty. I greeted the animals and, in many cases, struck up conversations with their owners. When they discovered I was an assistant to Mr. Spreull, they typically asked, "You take care of the small animals then, do you?"

"I take care of whatever animals need my help," I replied. "Occasionally, they are as small as dogs."

Watching the dogs of Dundee revived my longing for Nugget and Honey. I reassured myself it would be but a few months before I finished in Edinburgh. While I did not know where I would be the following year, I hoped it would be somewhere suitable for the Pomeranians too. Ideally, it would be a place with stables, so I could get a horse. Somewhere in the country where I could ride and hunt whenever I had time.

A few days before I bade Mr. and Mrs. Spreull farewell, I received a letter from Lady Widdrington that renewed my hope the Royal College would finally be moved to allow me to write their examinations so I could become a registered veterinary surgeon. Lady Widdrington wrote:

> The timing could not be more fortuitous for you, dear Aleen. Mrs. Fawcett's National Union of Women's Suffrage Societies (though I do wish they had a catchier name) is finding more and more support, not only among working-class women but also among my friends and educated women. She is, it seems, set on campaigning for the legal profession to be opened to women. If that happens, the stubborn men of the RCVS will have the rug pulled from beneath them.
>
> The good news does not end there. Mrs. Fawcett's efforts are supported by Mrs. Emmeline Pankhurst, who, I am told, is prepared to take a more militant stand than Mrs. Fawcett. So, my dear, if one does not succeed and fight for your rights to be registered to practice, the other will. It is just a matter of time!

As such, I left Dundee with more spring in my step than a highly bred Hackney, buoyed by the confidence of Mr. Spreull's endorsement and hopeful that Mrs. Fawcett and Mrs. Pankhurst would soon dispatch with the Royal College's resistance.

CHAPTER 19

❧

1900
Edinburgh, Scotland

"IT IS JUST A MATTER OF TIME," LADY WIDDRINGTON HAD WRITTEN. SHE WAS not wrong. I, however, was wrong for hoping that Mrs. Fawcett, Mrs. Pankhurst, and other brave suffragettes would win the battle for me by the time I graduated from the New Veterinary College in 1900 and was ready to write the final RCVS examination that would allow me to officially practice as a veterinary surgeon.

How entitled I was. Having long since given up the fight myself, I had attended every lecture, demonstration, test, and examination at college in the hope that, somewhere in the world, groups of hardworking, passionate, and courageous women would do the difficult work and overturn the injustice that prevented me from becoming Aleen Cust, MRCVS.

I wanted to blame my upbringing. After all, until I arrived in Edinburgh, I had relied on servants to toil on my behalf. This was different. There was no one doing difficult things for me behind the scenes. And why should they? Why should the suffragettes have paved the way for me when I had not raised my voice with theirs, publicized my ambitions, or even had the courage to ask them to take up my cause? I deserved nothing more than what

I received—a place at the back of the main hall as I watched Fred, Andrew, Toby, Piggers, and my other classmates stride to the podium, shake hands with the president of the Royal College, and receive their certificates.

When the ceremony was over, I stood outside on the lawn in the weak sun and congratulated my peers as they exited the hall. Except they were no longer my peers: they had swapped their bowlers for top hats, showing their advancement from trainees to qualified veterinary surgeons. Fred tried to rein in his smile when he saw me.

"Do not feel it necessary to be glum on my account, Mr. Taylor, MRCVS," I said, flicking his sturdy hat.

He pulled it straight. "Of course not, Miss Cust. I would not insult you so. It is just that—"

"Say no more, Fred. What else is there to say?"

"Other than that the person among us most qualified to be a veterinary surgeon is the only one who has *not* received her certificate today? Indeed, what is there to say?"

I held up my hands to stop him. It was bad enough listening to the voices in my head; I did not want to hear my problems discussed out loud.

Fred was not dissuaded. "What will you do? Where will you go?"

"I shall go back to where I come from."

"London? Leasowe Castle? Northumberland? But what—"

"No. I am going to Ireland."

"Ireland?"

"Yes. All is not entirely lost. Professor Williams has convinced the man he describes as a 'vanguard veterinary surgeon,' one Mr. William Byrne of Roscommon County, to provide me with work until, well, until who knows when…or what."

"William Byrne? Of Athleague, Roscommon? The man Andrew worked alongside in July?"

I nodded. "Yes. And what a vanguard he must be to have agreed to take me on."

Fred frowned. "Did you ask Andrew about him? About his time with Mr. Byrne?"

"No. Should I have?"

He stepped closer and opened his mouth to speak.

"No," I interrupted. "Do not answer, Fred. I do not want to know. It was a rhetorical question. Professor Williams has convinced a veterinary surgeon, a country veterinary surgeon at that, to take me on, to allow me to work alongside him. He is willing to take the risk of taking on an assistant who is not registered by the Royal College. Do you not see the significance of that?"

"Yes, but—"

"I was grateful when the principal convinced Andrew's father to allow me to work with him in Dundee in July. Now, whatever the RCVS believes, I am no longer a trainee. I am a professional who is forbidden from working. Yet, an Irish veterinary surgeon—a bona fide MRCVS himself—is prepared to give me work. Why would I question the motives, reasons, anything in fact, of a man who is prepared to do such a thing?"

"It is just that—"

"I thought you would be pleased for me, Fred. You know I cannot go back to England and pretend that the past four years did not happen."

"I am pleased for you. I mean, it is just that…" He threw his hands in the air and looked around. "Wait, there is Andrew. He can explain. Perhaps if you hear it from him…directly."

Andrew, also wearing a glossy top hat, walked toward us. He was carrying a book, which he held out to me. It was *The Management and Diseases of the Dog*.

"Miss Cust, my father asked me to give you this and offer his congratulations," he said.

"But—"

"Yes. He knows. I explained. He said you will make a fine veterinary surgeon no matter what the Royal College does or does not do."

I was touched by Mr. Spreull's kindness and confidence. As tempting as it was, at times, to think of all men as prejudiced against women, I thought again about how I had been supported by Major Fitz, Professor Williams, and, more recently, Mr. Spreull.

"Thank you," I said. "But the book?"

"He said to tell you that he has kept his copy but thought you might need your own, even in the country."

I laughed and tucked it under my arm. "I shall write to thank him."

"Andrew," said Fred, "did you know that Miss Cust is going to work with Mr. Byrne in Ireland. *Your* Mr. Byrne."

"That is excellent news."

"But…but…did you not say that Mr. Byrne was something of a… of a—"

Andrew and I looked at Fred. He was red and growing redder.

"What is it, Fred? What is Mr. Byrne? What have you heard that is twisting your stomach so?" I asked.

Andrew's mouth was twitching and his eyes twinkling, but he did not rescue our friend.

Fred wiped his brow and looked at us with the eyes of a trapped rabbit.

"He said… Andrew said that he—Mr. Byrne, that is—is something of a…of a…of a ladies' man."

I looked at Andrew.

He chuckled. "What I said, Fred, was that he is very popular in Roscommon, very well liked and respected, including by the ladies." He held my gaze for a moment. "The important thing, Miss Cust, is that he is a fine veterinary surgeon. I learned a great deal from him, and I believe you will too."

"That is all that matters. Thank you, Andrew."

I smiled at Fred, who had removed his hat to scratch his head.

"Come," I said. "I do believe you need a drink before you expire."

It was not as if I had no misgivings about going to Ireland. It had been more than twenty years since my father had died and we had fled Tipperary. I was now thirty-two years old. Gone were my sentimental notions, etched as they had been decades previously by images of Goliath, Taffy, and Ned, of being reconciled with the happy memories of my childhood. The century had turned. And with opinions on the Second Boer War fanning the flames of nationalism, more and more Irishmen turning their backs on imperialism, and Her Majesty's poorly disguised disregard for the island, the country was no more welcoming to an English Protestant than it had been in 1878. Indeed, even Dorothy was concerned about my taking up the offer to work there.

We rejoiced when we heard that Bertie would not go to South Africa. Now, instead, we must worry about your safety in Ireland. Edward says nationalism is on the rise, and although much of it is secreted, it is understood that dangerous political and cultural organizations exist all over the country. Can you not implore kind Principal Williams to find a safer alternative for you? I know you do not want to return to England, and most certainly, you will not work in the south, but there is surely somewhere else for you to go.

I wondered what she would say if she knew Mr. Willie Byrne was president of the Athleague branch of the United Irish League. I did not include that information when I wrote back, reassuring her that I would return from Ireland the moment I felt unsafe.

It amused me that my friends were more concerned about my well-being in Ireland—Fred, about the alleged reputation of Mr. Byrne, and Dorothy, about the rise of nationalism—than they were about the idea of me working as a veterinary surgeon without a professional certificate. It was what concerned me more than anything. Would the RCVS catch wind of the fact that Mr. Byrne had employed me? Would they take steps to prohibit me from working with him in Ireland? Reprove him?

Professor Williams dismissed my worries with a chuckle, and he handed me a testimonial confirming that I had completed my training and proved my competence.

"There is no need to worry about what the RCVS might or might not do to Mr. Byrne. Just as they did nothing to stop you from training here, they will not do anything to him. When you meet him, you will realize that he is not a man to be trifled with," he said.

"What about me? Am I to be trifled with? Will they try to prevent me from working?"

He sighed. "That, I cannot predict, Miss Cust. However, the choice is just as it was when we sat in this room years ago discussing whether you would continue to study or give up when the organization first refused to admit you to its examinations. Will you work as a veterinary surgeon because it is what you want or give up because the RCVS is still fixed in the past? The only thing that has changed, and which is to your great advantage, is that you are trained now and have a testimonial from me confirming your competence."

He was right. I told him so and rose to go.

"One minute, Miss Cust. I have something to show you."

He scrabbled among some papers and handed a page to me. It was headed "Presentation on Veterinary Ethics to the Irish Central Veterinary Society by William Augustine Byrne."

"Read the paragraph I have underlined," said Professor Williams.

Man's treatment of woman is one of the most absorbing and diffi-cult ethical questions of today, as it has been for all time. I cannot leave the question of veterinary ethics without adverting to the discussion which has arisen within our ranks as to the admission of women to the veterinary profession. George Meredith is the only novelist I know of whom women admit knows their sex. I never knew anyone else who knew them. But I think we can all admit this knowledge: that, though the difficulties may seem insuperable, lovely women "get there in the end." Women will, of course, be admitted to the veterinary profession. If there is a majority of misogynous old bachelors and henpecked husbands on the council, their admission may be delayed, but it will come. Why any woman who loves a horse or dog—or, as many of them do, all dumb things—will not be allowed to acquire a knowl-edge of their diseases is a thing I cannot understand. Nor can I comprehend the mental attitude of those who insist that there is no work for a woman veterinary surgeon except castration and obstetrics.

I looked at the name at the top of the page again and saw the date. It had been written three years previously, around the time that my case was reported on in the *Veterinary Record* for the first time.

"William Augustine Byrne is Mr. Willie Byrne? Of Athleague, County Roscommon? The man I am to work for?"

Professor Williams nodded. "That is the man. He is also, you might want to note, a lively and respected member of the RCVS council."

I read the paragraph again.

"He is quite the wordsmith," I said. "I particularly admire these lines: 'a majority of misogynous old bachelors and henpecked husbands' and 'Why any woman who loves a horse or dog—or, as many of them do, all dumb things…'"

We chuckled.

"Yes, as I understand it, Mr. Byrne is not only a fine veterinary surgeon and a passionate nationalist but also something of a poet. He is Irish, after all," said Professor Williams.

So it was that I bade him, Mrs. Logan, Fred, and my other classmates goodbye and left Edinburgh for Ireland, pastures green, and a future I could not predict.

CHAPTER 20

❦

1900
Athleague, Ireland

I ARRIVED IN IRELAND IN OCTOBER 1900 ON THE WETTEST DAY OF WHAT
locals assured me was typically the country's dampest month any year. It was
late afternoon when, as I approached Athleague, the rain cleared just long
enough for me to make out the River Suck as the carriage rattled across the
bridge. Other than that, I might as well have traveled from Dublin by night
or while wearing blinkers. I saw nothing beyond the window but a wall
of gray precipitation, and though lulled by the swish of the wheels rolling
through puddles and the splashing of water beneath the horses' hooves, I
was sorry not to be able to see if Roscommon resembled my memories of
Tipperary.

When the carriage stopped, I thought we had reached our destination
in the village.

Then, I heard the coachman call, "Do you need a hand there?"

"Aye. No. Thank you. I have sent for help. Though sure, I don't think
there's much that can be done," came the reply.

I stretched to look out of the window and saw a man in a waistcoat
standing, hands on his hips, on the roadside alongside an unhitched cart. It

had begun drizzling again, and I could just make out the mound of a pony's stomach as she lay on the verge. I opened the carriage door.

"It's okay, miss," said the coachman, who had climbed down and was hitching the horses. "I'll take a look."

I ignored him and nodded to the other man as I stepped over several puddles and crouched next to the pony. She was groaning and twisting her head, eyes darting left and right with pain and fear.

"What happened?" I asked, placing my hand firmly on her neck.

The men stared at me, silent.

"Well?"

"We were back from delivering spuds and on the way home. She took fright at something as we came around the corner and veered into the ditch," said the farmer.

"Did the cart tip?" I asked.

The men looked at one another.

I tried again. "Did it tip when she fell?"

"No."

That was not good news. If a cart or carriage did not turn over when the horse fell, the animal was at greater risk of spinal injury.

"What is her name?"

The men glanced at one another again.

"Pony," said the farmer.

"Hold Pony's head still and stroke her neck while I examine her legs."

He stared at me, motionless.

"Please," I said, trying not to sigh. "I can help. Believe me."

The farmer blinked, shrugged, and crouched to hold the animal's head still.

With Pony lying on her side in the mud, it was not easy to see where she was injured. When I lifted her hock and saw the jagged shape of the leg underneath, however, it was clear that the bone just above her fetlock was broken. It appeared that the horse had stumbled into the ditch, lost her balance, and fallen with one leg trapped in the mud. It was a severe break, and even if we could get her to her feet, she would be unable to put any weight on the leg.

"Her leg is broken," I told the farmer.

He stood up. "Oh? Well, I'll wait for the doctor."

"Doctor?" I asked, returning to Pony's head so that I could rub her ears.

"The veter…the horse doctor," he replied. "Your man Mr. Baker rode by shortly after she fell and went on to call him."

Pony wheezed and groaned. I did not waste time asking who Mr. Baker was and how long ago he'd ridden by.

"She should not have to suffer any longer. I need a rifle," I said.

"I beg your pardon, miss?" said the farmer.

"There is nothing else to be done. I am sorry."

"I will wait for the horse doctor," he muttered, turning from me and walking away.

"Miss, I think we should go on," said the coachman. "There is not much we can do here, and we are getting rather wet."

"We cannot leave her like this. Who knows how long it will be until the veterinary surgeon arrives? Where can I get a rifle from?" I asked, making a note never to travel without my own in the future.

"Sure, I don't know, but—"

The clatter of hooves announced the arrival of another horse. I turned toward the sound and, straining to see through the rain, made out the imposing form of a tall, upright man on a broad-chested bay as they pulled up alongside the carriage.

"Your honor!" called the farmer, as if from a sinking raft on the ocean. "She's over here."

Your honor?

Despite his size and lofty horse, the man dismounted in a smooth, single motion. He was as agile as a cat. Still crouching as I stroked Pony, I stared as he approached, the farmer at his side.

I had long admired and understood the perfect proportions of horses. Samuel had taught me about Thoroughbreds at Leasowe. He'd shown me how to evaluate the ideal measurements of a horse's head and told me why the distance between the eyes, nostrils, and poll mattered. I knew that hip angles and shoulder slope were important guidelines regarding bloodline and performance. I could distinguish a beautiful horse from a magnificent one.

Indeed, I had an educated eye for horses from a young age and the confidence to make public my judgments. I knew horses, but until that moment on the roadside to Athleague, as I watched the man I rightly assumed to be the "horse doctor," Willie Byrne, emerge through a veil of light rain and stride toward me, I had no idea that I might also appreciate the ideal standard of a man.

Among the things I noticed was that while, as an MRCVS, he qualified to wear a top hat, Mr. Byrne was bareheaded. A lock of damp, dark hair had collapsed onto his forehead where it curled like a sleeping kitten, content to be there. His eyes widened ever so slightly as he caught sight of me. They were kingfisher blue and unlike any I had seen before. I stood up, unable to look away. The words tumbled from my mouth.

"It is a complete fracture to the cannon bone with an extensive wound and compromised vascular supply to the skin. I suspect spinal injury too because she went down with the cart, which remained upright and offered no relief as she fell."

He gave a small nod. "Miss Cust? How do you do?"

I held out my hand. As he took it and gave it a firm shake, I imagined my mother's disapproval. I also noted how long and elegant his fingers were and that it was not just that he was tall but that he was significantly taller than me.

"Mr. Byrne," I said, my mouth papery.

On my way to Ireland, I had rehearsed what I would say to the man who had agreed to take me on despite my not having sat the RCVS's professional examinations. I had silently rehearsed how I would thank him when we met and immediately clarify that I expected him to treat me as he would any other veterinary surgeon—male and thus certified by the Royal College—he might employ. I had resolved to say he'd already done me a favor by agreeing to employ me. I did not expect any further special treatment. Indeed, I had lined up my words neatly. However, as I stood before Mr. Byrne, staring at the perfect cleft in his chin and the small smile on his lips that seemed to make his eyes sparkle and even more vivid, I was mute.

"I thought I would let you settle in this evening and only start work tomorrow," he said.

"I saw no reason to delay. You have a rifle with you, I assume?"

He nodded twice. "Show me what you see first."

About an hour later, my carriage pulled up in front of Mrs. Doyle's house in the village. Mr. Byrne had informed Professor Williams that he had secured lodgings for me with her and told me that I should wait there for him. We would have met there if not for Pony's accident.

The coachman shielded me from the rain with an umbrella as we walked to the door of the two-story stone house. For a while after he had knocked, I thought there was no one home and imagined becoming even more drenched as I waited on the step. The door was eventually opened by a statuesque woman, whose curly white hair was in stark contrast to her black outfit.

"Miss Eileen Cust?" she asked.

"Yes. Well, it is Aleen. With an *a* and no *i*. But yes, I am Miss Cust. Mrs. Doyle?"

She gave a curt nod and stepped aside so I could enter.

"Gracious. You are...wet." Mrs. Doyle glanced at my skirt, which I noticed was not only sodden but also coated in sand and mud.

"Yes. There was an incident on the roadside."

I caught sight of a slender girl with long dark hair in the hallway behind her. She slipped out of sight when I caught her eye.

Mrs. Doyle, I learned, was the widow of the headmaster of the local school. He had died two years previously, leaving his wife and their sixteen-year-old daughter, Cathleen.

"I have never had a lodger before, Miss Cust, and only agreed to take you in because Mr. Byrne was so kind after my husband died. He stables our horses at Castlestrange," said Mrs. Doyle as she led me up the stairs.

"Castlestrange?"

"Castlestrange House is where Mr. Byrne lives and has his veterinary practice," she said, stopping at a closed door and turning to look at me. "What, might I ask, is your business with Mr. Byrne, Miss Cust? Are you family?"

It seemed odd that Mr. Byrne had secured a place for me with Mrs. Doyle but had not told her why I had come to Athleague.

"No. We are not family. I have come to work for him. I am a veterinary surgeon," I said, feeling myself color with pleasure at my pronouncement. It was the first time I had described myself as such to anyone. I wanted to repeat the words. *I am a veterinary surgeon.*

She stared at me, as if seeing me for the first time.

"How is that possible?"

I shrugged. "A year at university followed by three at veterinary college in Edinburgh."

"University? College? A veterinary surgeon? But surely—"

I was weary and hungry and longed for a wash and something to eat. I glanced at the door handle. "Is this my room?"

She opened the door, and I followed her in. The room was significantly larger than the one I had become accustomed to at Mrs. Logan's home, and thank the Lord, there was a fireplace.

"Mr. Byrne said he would come by later. Would you like some hot water brought up before tea?" she asked, her tone now distinctly brusque.

I heard Mr. Byrne's voice, deep and low, when I went downstairs later. I followed the sound to the drawing room, where I recognized his broad back and head of dark hair, which coiled upward as if tickled by the collar of his jacket.

"There is nothing strange about it at all, Mrs. Doyle," he said. I distinguished a smile in his voice. "It's grand, really. You are an educated woman yourself. If women are becoming physicians, why would they not also become veterinary surgeons?"

"School education is one thing, and yes, women physicians might have their place—particularly where they attend to other women—but this? Working with animals? I am shocked, Mr. Byrne. It is…it is unnatural," she replied, her voice rising. "I wish you—"

Mrs. Doyle caught herself when she spotted me at the door. Mr. Byrne turned, held my eyes with his, and smiled. It was a look that suggested we shared a secret. I felt myself redden.

"Miss Cust! Dry and warm, I hope?" he asked.

"Yes. Thank you," I said, suddenly aware that I was leaning against the doorway as if my legs could not hold me upright. What was it about the man that affected me so?

"Did Miss Cust tell you that she attended to Mr. Flynn's pony on the roadside on her way to Athleague, Mrs. Doyle?"

She shook her head.

"Mr. Flynn believes the horse was around twenty-five years old. She had done well."

"The animal died then?" asked Mrs. Doyle, staring at me as if eager for Pony's demise to have been my fault.

"It was the only solution. Miss Cust and I agreed."

There was a moment of silence, perhaps for the horse or maybe for Mrs. Doyle to swallow her disappointment.

"Well, I hope you will settle in with Mrs. Doyle, Miss Cust." Mr. Byrne glanced at our host, who looked away. "I cannot think of anywhere in Athleague that you will be more comfortable or better cared for."

Mrs. Doyle looked at him, blinked several times, and surrendered to a smile.

"Shall we have tea?" she said. "I will call Cathleen."

Certainly, particularly given the spaciousness and warmth of my bedroom, my accommodation in Athleague was luxurious compared to what I had grown accustomed to in Edinburgh, but the Doyles, especially Cathleen, were not a fraction as friendly as Mrs. Logan had been.

Despite Mr. Byrne's best attempts at cheerful conversation around the table that evening, there was an awkwardness even he, with his easy smile and quick wit, could not shift. As far as Cathleen and her mother were concerned, I was as welcome as a fly in a milk jug.

While Mrs. Doyle might have agreed to take me in because she believed herself beholden to Mr. Byrne, her daughter clearly felt only repugnance. At first, I thought it was simply an aversion to having to share her home with a stranger, but as the girl stared across the table at my employer, her dark eyes glittering beneath thick eyelashes, I realized there was more to it. Cathleen was smitten with the man. And perhaps, I thought, as he complimented Mrs. Doyle on the quality of her colcannon—and certainly, the potato and cabbage dish was delicious—Mrs. Doyle was not only thankful for what the veterinary surgeon had done following her husband's death but also believed he was a good match for her daughter. Whatever the truth was, I resolved to find myself somewhere else to stay as soon as possible.

I was waiting on the doorstep when Mr. Byrne arrived in his gig to fetch me the next morning.

"Her name is Blaze," he said as I greeted his black mare, named, I assumed, for the wide white stripe on her face. "I was riding the all-powerful Zeus when we met yesterday."

I was pleased; it said a great deal to me about the character of a person that they introduced me to their animals.

Although the air was still cool, the skies had cleared, and I had already taken a stroll around the village, stopping to watch the wooden stream wheel at the mill and the horses as they were ridden or drew carts and carriages up the road. I had set aside some of the money Dorothy had sent me from Nugget and Honey's last litter of puppies and longed to buy a horse of my own. I had been horseless for too long. Ideally, I would acquire one suitable for riding to clients during the week and hunting on the weekends.

We were about to set off for Castlestrange when I saw the Catholic priest walking purposefully toward us. Mr. Byrne spotted him too, looked down, and whispered, "Oh dear."

"Mr. Byrne," called the priest. "A moment, if I might."

"Top of the morning to you, Father O'Flanagan. May I introduce my associate, Miss Cust."

He gave me a cursory nod.

"Can I have a word with you, Mr. Byrne? In private if I may."

I glanced at my employer. Did he want me to climb out of the gig? Instead, he handed me the reins and hopped out.

"Back in a minute, Miss Cust," he said, following the man in the cassock some distance down the road, presumably to where I would be unable to hear the conversation. I watched as Mr. Byrne nodded, smiled, and shrugged for several minutes during which Father O'Flanagan, mouth flapping, hands flying and occasionally pointing in my direction, seemed to be delivering an animated sermon. At last, the priest stopped talking and the veterinary surgeon began. His was a short response. I saw the priest's eyes widen and his brow crease. He tried to start up again, but Mr. Byrne cut him short with a small bow before walking back to the gig.

"Well?" I asked as we clattered out of the village.

"Well, what?" he asked.

"Forgive me, but it appeared Father O'Flanagan might be objecting to my presence in the village."

"Ah, Miss Cust, you should not jump to conclusions in this business. Did Professor Williams not teach you how dangerous that can be?"

"Yes, but—"

"You are right. Father O'Flanagan *is* upset about your presence in Athleague. You are a woman on her own, an English woman, not Catholic, and"—he glanced at my outfit—"aristocracy too."

"But—"

"To be sure, that is not the worst of it. You are a veterinary surgeon. He is not upset; he is appalled."

"What did you tell him?"

He lifted his shoulders and let them drop. "I said I did not realize that you were a woman."

"What?"

"I did not know until your arrival, did I now? I explained that all our prior correspondence was in writing and that no one mentioned your gender. How could I have known? I was duped."

"What? By me? But—"

"Not necessarily by you. By someone at the college perhaps. I don't think it was deliberate." He glanced at me, his eyes twinkling. "Do you?"

I shook my head, amused. It made him smile, and his smile was disarming. Again, I was silenced.

"You are not surprised, are you? You must have expected some resistance.

You knew it was not going to be any easier for you here than it was in Scotland. Or how it would be for you in England."

"No, I am not surprised. It is just that I had not yet experienced resistance from the Roman Catholic clergy."

"Ah, sure. Well, you're in Ireland now."

It was not the last I heard of Father O'Flanagan that day. That evening, when I returned to Mrs. Doyle's after my first day at the practice at Castlestrange, she met me at the door.

"Tea is ready when you are," she said, in an even voice.

Cathleen was silent throughout the meal, but her mother filled the air.

"Father O'Flanagan paid me a visit after you and Mr. Byrne left this morning," she said, eyeing me over the rim of her cup.

I was unsure of how to respond and settled on a small, ambiguous smile.

"He is not happy with Mr. Byrne," she continued.

"Oh?"

"It seems he—Mr. Byrne, that is—told Father O'Flanagan he believed he had hired a male veterinary surgeon from Scotland. He told the priest that he was as surprised as anyone when he found you to be a woman."

"I see."

"Well, I do not, Miss Cust. Mr. Byrne was quite clear on the fact that you were a woman when he asked if I would take you in. You do not think that he would expect me to take in an unmarried man, do you?" She glanced at Cathleen. "The thing he forgot to mention to *me* was that you are a veterinary surgeon."

"Yes."

She speared a small wedge of potato with her fork, placed it in her mouth, and chewed, giving me a moment to, perhaps, absorb the extent of Mr. Byrne's deceit. I continued eating.

Finally, Mrs. Doyle dropped her cutlery on her plate, producing a meaningful jangle. "Father O'Flanagan wants me to put you out," she said.

Cathleen froze, her eyes fixed on her mother.

"He said that?" I asked.

"Well, not exactly, but I know it is what he would like me to do."

"I see."

There was another pause.

"Do you not want to know what I said to Father O'Flanagan?"

"Of course, yes. What did you say, Mrs. Doyle?"

She smiled, which took me by surprise.

"I said I had no idea who to expect. After Mr. Byrne's kindness, I was simply doing the Christian thing and taking in someone who needed a place." She giggled. "I told Father O'Flanagan that I had prayed about how I might repay Mr. Byrne, and the very next day, he asked if I could help him by providing lodging for someone. I thought it was the Lord's answer to my prayer."

Mrs. Doyle's and my attention was drawn to our dinner companion when she emitted an unladylike grunt, pushed her chair back, and stood up.

"Cathleen? Where are you going?"

She glared at her mother and left the room.

Mrs. Doyle sighed.

"Thank you," I said.

Her brow creased.

"For defending me or, rather, Mr. Byrne. I will find somewhere else to stay as soon as possible." I glanced after Cathleen. "It is probably for the best."

"Don't judge her too harshly, Miss Cust. She's very young, and well, Mr. Byrne has turned her head. I do not think he realizes it, and of course, he... Please don't hurry to find another place on her account. That would not reflect well on us."

"Of course not. I would not want that. However, I want to find somewhere I can keep a horse or two and bring my dogs over as soon as I can afford it, so I will not be here long, regardless."

She sighed again.

"Do you think Father O'Flanagan will do anything more? I mean, to rally against my working here?"

"I am afraid so. He said he would call on his congregation not to allow you to work with their animals. That it is ungodly and unladylike. That you will be asking to castrate their horses and bullocks next."

"He is correct. I will. It is one of a veterinary surgeon's jobs. Oh, dear. This is not going to be good for Mr. Byrne's practice."

"What? Oh no, Miss Cust, make no mistake. Nothing Father O'Flanagan says will stop people from calling for Mr. Byrne's help. There is no one for miles around more revered than he is. Not even, Lord forgive me, God's man on earth himself. You will see that for yourself soon enough."

"Oh? Might that explain why Mr. Flynn addressed Mr. Byrne as *your honor* yesterday?"

"Indeed, but that is not an uncommon way of addressing a veterinary surgeon in Ireland. Mr. Byrne, though, is not just an animal doctor, you see. It is also because of his politics. He is…well, you know…"

She paused and changed tack, deciding, it seemed, not to discuss "his honor's" politics with me. Perhaps my Englishness prohibited it.

"My late husband, God rest his soul, put it this way: Give an Irishman a God-fearing horse doctor who, like Mr. Byrne, rides like the devil, hunts like a king, and smiles at everyone like they are the center of his universe, and you will have a man more popular in Ireland than our blessed Mother Mary."

She gazed into the distance, as if pondering her husband's words. Then, she looked at me. "He did not mean any blasphemy by it, but it was the only way he knew to describe how admired Mr. Byrne is around here."

"That is reassuring," I said, wondering if there was any hope that some of Mr. Byrne's popularity might eventually brush off on me. Of course, my gender, regardless of the fact that I was not the right kind of God-fearing person for Roscommon, did not help. Being English further diminished the likelihood that I would be highly regarded in Athleague. Might it make a difference though, I wondered, that I could ride as well as any man and, most importantly, that I was a "horse doctor" with the same education and training as Mr. Byrne?

"I do not know how it is in England, Miss Cust, but in this country, life revolves around the horse. If men are not talking hunting, racing, or horse fairs, they are discussing their own horses or those of their neighbors. That puts horse doctors up there with the saints. I would not worry about Father O'Flanagan ruining Mr. Byrne's business. But you…"

I nodded. She did not have to explain. I knew what she meant: that I should not worry about how my presence in the village might affect Mr. Byrne's practice, but rather whether the people of Athleague would listen to Father O'Flanagan or give me the opportunity to prove myself as a veterinary surgeon.

CHAPTER 21

1900
Athleague, Ireland

FATHER O'FLANAGAN MADE GOOD ON HIS THREAT. MRS. DOYLE WAS BREATH-less after walking home from church to relay the news. The priest, she said, had dedicated several passionate minutes of Sunday mass to reminding his congregation that although women were, like men, created in God's image, they "nevertheless symbolize the lower self, representing this in their physical and sexual nature." He warned his flock to beware the rise of women's suf-frage, which "shone a further light on the decadence of Protestantism" and was demonstrated by things like the unholy proposition of women "doctoring, perhaps even castrating, beasts. It is immoral and should not be tolerated."

"There was not a murmur or even a breath of surprise. Mr. Flynn slept as usual, and Mrs. Flynn did not even try to rouse him. It seems the con-gregation anticipated Father O'Flanagan's outburst. They all knew of you already, of course. There were, however, many an eye on Mr. Byrne, who held his chin high and his head still throughout, as if fixing his thoughts on every word," she said.

If Mr. Byrne had any new views on Father O'Flanagan's assessment of me, he did not speak to me of them; neither did I ask. My employer's relationship with God and the church was not offered for discussion in the surgery or anywhere else.

Whether or not the priest's sermon had any effect on the people of Athleague's attitude toward me I cannot say. Would they have been more welcoming if Father O'Flanagan had not warned them against my evil intentions of attending to the health of their animals? I cannot be certain, but I doubt it. As Mrs. Doyle explained, Mr. Byrne's clients were deeply in his thrall. Even so, it was fair to assume it was always going to take time for them to accept and acknowledge that a woman knew how to and was capable of handling their beasts.

That is not to say Mr. Byrne's clients were blatantly rude to me. I believe their affection for him prohibited that. During my first weeks in Athleague, most tolerated me as they would a lowly assistant to their trusted doctor. To others though, I was invisible.

"Will you hold up her tail so that she does not kick while I stitch the wound, please," I asked Mr. Gaffney when he called us to attend to a dairy cow who had injured herself on a jagged plank.

Mr. Gaffney looked at Mr. Byrne as he selected instruments for me on the other side of the animal.

"You're going to sew her up then, your honor?" he asked.

"Miss Cust will do so."

The farmer did not move.

"Hold her tail, Mr. Gaffney," I repeated.

He blinked, as if confused.

"The tail, Gaff. Lift the tail," said Mr. Byrne. "As Miss Cust, the veterinary surgeon, instructed."

I smiled at the farmer. He did not return the look but lifted the cow's tail so that I could get to work.

"We are going to have to keep a close eye on this," I said. "The skin is tight around here and there is danger it will rip before it heals. You need to examine it regularly, Mr. Gaffney, and let us know if you see any tearing, yellow seepage, or major swelling."

"I will call you immediately if it goes bad, your honor. She's my best milker," he said, his attention on my employer as if I had not uttered a word.

"Keep it clean by wiping it with a soft cloth and warm, salted water twice a day. Be very gentle so as not to agitate the wound or slow the healing," I said.

"How should I treat the wound then, your honor?" he asked.

"Exactly as Miss Cust instructed, Mr. Gaffney," Mr. Byrne replied, handing me the scissors.

"The water should contain one teaspoon of salt to a pint of warm water," I added, looking directly at Mr. Gaffney as I recalled Mr. Spreull's lesson about how I should compel respect from clients.

The farmer blinked and looked at Mr. Byrne.

"Any questions, Mr. Gaffney?" I asked, raising my voice to ensure he heard.

He shook his head, eyes still on the other man. "That's grand, your honor."

A day or two later, we were called to attend to a sheep, whose maggot-infested wool was not only discolored and damp but also foul-smelling. I took the clippers and cut away the wool around the infected area of the ewe's rump. She bleated but, wedged between Mr. Byrne's thighs, did not struggle.

"Is it common to see fly-strike in winter here?" I asked.

"It looks like it has been infected for some time. Does it smell like anything other than rotting flesh?" he replied.

I put my nose closer to the soiled area and breathed in. The smell was intense, but it was more than putrid tissue and filthy wool. It also smelled of herbaceous plant and smoke. Or was it ash? The farmer stood at the gate of the pen with his young son at his side.

"Have you been treating this with something?" I asked.

He looked at Mr. Byrne.

I tried again. "How long has she been like this, Mr. Sheehan?"

The boy looked up at his father. Mr. Sheehan shuffled his feet. Mr. Byrne glanced at me, his bright eyes narrowing slightly, which I had noticed occurred when he experienced any measure of frustration.

"Pat, how long has she been bad?" he said.

"Well, no, I won't be telling your honor a lie, but she's bad this week and more," he replied, ruffling his son's hair.

I stopped clipping and walked to him. "And what is it you treated her with?"

Mr. Sheehan looked at Mr. Byrne. "Ah, well, an old recipe me Da swore by for the worms. It's a plant you find in the ditch near the roadside, mixed with ash."

I stepped into his line of sight so that he could not look past me. "Did it ever work? Your father's mixture, I mean, for any other sheep with worms?"

"Ah, I dunno. He never said."

I sent him to fetch some water. His son trotted away at his side. I heard a snort and saw that Mr. Byrne was laughing.

"Well done, Miss Cust. You finally met the worms," he said, not bothering to hide his mirth. "The worms, you will find, cause many problems in these parts—even when we do not see evidence of them."

"I see evidence of them today," I replied. "What is the plant? Do you know? And why ash?"

"The plant is the first of many you will find in homemade remedies in Ireland. Some you might even discover worthwhile. Ash is useful to treat some skin conditions. Of course, it only works if you get rid of the worms first and clean up the area," he said.

The farmer returned with the water and placed it carefully at my feet.

"Stay here, Mr. Sheehan," I said. "I want to teach you how to cut away the wool and worms, and wash the area so that it will heal. That way you might not even need your father's remedy next time, and you will avoid the risk of more worms in your flock."

"That'll be grand," he said, stepping closer and crouching to get a better view. Then, he looked up at Mr. Byrne. "If only the beast can be saved, your honor."

Mr. Byrne and I worked together initially, with most of our callouts taking us to clients' stables, barns, and paddocks. We were also called into the village and to other towns nearby. Professor Williams and Young Andrew

Spreull had not exaggerated when they described how skillful a veterinary surgeon Mr. Byrne was. Almost every case taught me something unexpected and new. The gentle yet firm manner he had with his patients was unlike anything I had ever seen. It was possible he loved animals as much as I did, and the notion pleased me.

Moving between farms, homes, and businesses alongside Mr. Byrne either in the gig or on horseback—he rode Zeus and allowed me to ride Blaze—gave me the chance to get to know the countryside and its people and animals. It was often cold and wet, but the wind and rain on my face made me want to sing. I was in the country once more, doing the work I had dreamed of doing for as long as I could remember. It had been a while since I'd had the opportunity to ride so frequently, and keeping pace with Mr. Byrne, who was as fine a horseman as Mrs. Doyle had claimed, was exhilarating. What did it matter that I did not have a certificate from the Royal College or the admiration of my family?

Roscommon was as green as I recalled Tipperary having been, but with its mossy banks and marshy fields, much wetter. Even so, as I traveled the narrow lanes and looked across the fields and paddocks separated by hedges, trees, and babbling brooks, I felt at home. For the most part, the cool reception I received from the people did not overly concern me. It was, I told myself, winter. The season would change, and things would thaw—including attitudes.

On the days business did not take us elsewhere, I was content to be at Castlestrange, both in the rooms of the veterinary practice and in the stables, which were adjacent to Mr. Byrne's house. The large property—with its three-bay, three-story-plus-basement stone house, gate lodge, and spacious L-shaped coach house and stables—was much grander than I had anticipated. Mr. Byrne had noticed my surprise when he drove the gig through the gates toward the house on my first day there.

"Twenty rooms," he said, as if I had asked a question. "It is unexpected, I know, but I have been lucky. I was not born to it, like you."

I looked at him, wondering exactly what Professor Williams had told him about me. He ignored the glance and went on.

"My Uncle James did well in America. When he saw I was an eager student and had a way with animals, he paid for veterinary college and set me up at Castlestrange. I will have paid him back before I am forty-five—all going as planned."

"You are buying it from him?"

"Aye, that's the idea. Although the agreement is that he and my cousin Thomas will still be free to visit whenever they want in summer."

It was, by anyone's standards, an excessive home for a bachelor, and even though Mr. Byrne had converted a section of the stables to an infirmary and a portion of the coach house into rooms from which to practice, I wondered about his plans for filling the house. Did he hope for a family? Four years older than I was, he was already thirty-six.

Then, I saw the dogs.

At first, as they bounded up the drive toward us, I counted five. Two gray Wolfhounds, a black Collie, and two smooth-haired Terriers. Then, I saw a red Setter bolt out of the long grass in a paddock nearby and race to catch up with the others, the size of his paws and his ungainly gambol revealing his puppyhood. I laughed, surprised by the joy that welled up in me. I knew I had missed my dogs while living in Edinburgh, but I had not realized just how much.

"They are all embarrassingly friendly," said Mr. Byrne as I climbed out of the cart. The romping pack tumbled over one another at my feet as if I had returned after a long absence.

"No, Spencer! Down!" roared my employer.

It was too late. The Setter pup leapt into the air and onto my chest, flinging me backward into Mr. Byrne's arms. He was firm on his feet, and once he steadied me, his eyes met mine. I felt a little heady from the dogs' excited greeting and took a moment to get my balance.

"I am a little behind with his training, I'm afraid," he said, setting me squarely on my feet and patting Spencer.

I would have mentioned that by petting the dog at that moment, he was rewarding the pup's boisterous behavior, but I did not have the breath for it.

I had told Dorothy that as soon as I was settled in Ireland, I would send for Nugget and Honey. When I realized it was going to take longer than I thought to find myself and them somewhere suitable to live, I wrote and told her so. I received her reply in a letter addressed to me at Castlestrange, where I opened and read it late one afternoon.

That gives me the courage to suggest what I have been thinking for some time. Of course, they are your dogs and always will be, but Nugget and Honey have lived with me for so many years I believe they think that Fallodon and the cottage in Hampshire are their homes. More than that, my dear friend, they have become my loyal companions. I cannot bear to think of being without them. Do you not think that it will be a happier solution, particularly since you will be so busy in Athleague and they are accustomed to company all day, if you leave them with me permanently? There is another advantage to it for me: it will encourage you to visit more regularly.

Despite the many years I had lived away from them, I had always pictured the Pomeranians being with me again one day. However, Dorothy was right. They had been with her longer than they had lived with me. They knew her better than they knew me. My dogs—were they really still mine?— led good lives with the Greys, and while bringing them to Ireland would please me, it would unsettle them. I folded the letter and looked out of the surgery window onto the lawns of the property.

"Bad news?" asked Mr. Byrne, walking in from the infirmary.

"Not really. It is from Dorothy, the friend I mentioned who has been taking care of my dogs."

"The wife of Edward Grey, that is, Viscount Grey of Fallodon and Under-Secretary of State at the Foreign Office for the British Empire?"

"Yes." I stared at him. "Did I tell you that?"

"No, but I read the newspapers. We Irish are not as illiterate as you might think."

He teased but there was an edge to it. I knew, of course, about his involvement with the United Irish League, but as was the case with religion, he had not, up until the oblique reference to Edward, raised the subject of politics to me. Our language was of horses, cattle, sheep, dogs, and the occasional cat. We spoke of hunting, racing, and breeding the best animals.

"So she has bad news?" he asked.

"Bad news?"

"Your friend, Dorothy."

"No. Not really. She proposes that my breeding pair of Pomeranians stay with her in England. I thought I might bring them here, but since I have not yet found suitable lodgings for us..."

He pulled the chair away from his desk and sat down. "She'll keep them indefinitely?"

"Permanently. It makes sense. They have lived with her for the past four years," I replied.

"What about bringing them here?"

"Here?" I tried to picture Nugget and Honey with Castlestrange's hodge-podge of hounds but could not. They were accustomed to ruling the grounds at Fallodon and at Dorothy and Edward's cottage in Hampshire. Adjusting to life with the pack at Castlestrange would not be easy for them—or fair.

"No. Thank you, Mr. Byrne, but it would not work."

"Shall we dispense with the Mr. and Miss when we're alone? I'm Willie. And no, I did not mean in the house with, erm, me."

I felt myself redden. "Oh."

"Perhaps in the lodge at the gate."

"With Mr. and Mrs. Duffy?" I asked.

"No. They are moving back to the village to be with their daughter. Mr. Duffy is not well. I thought you might like to take the cottage. Send for your Pomeranians?"

My thoughts rushed ahead. "Could I stable a horse here?"

"Sure, what does it matter? I don't see why not."

The gate lodge was, as its name implied, located at the entrance to the grounds of Castlestrange. Built in the same style as the main house, it was a pretty cottage with a small garden enclosed by climbing roses. It would mean I was less than half a mile from the practice and stables. I could employ a cook and a maid, and escape the sullen glare of Cathleen Doyle.

"Could I have a look at the place before I agree to it?"

"Of course. I will send word to Mr. Duffy. We should do it soon. It would be ideal to have you there when I am away."

"Away?"

"Yes. I will be in Dublin for the National Veterinary Congress next month."

"Next month? You mean, in two weeks' time?"

"Yes. In a fortnight. I will be gone for three weeks or so. Will that be a problem, Aleen?"

"Not at all, Mr.... Willie."

CHAPTER 22

1900
Athleague, Ireland

MRS. DOYLE FROWNED WHEN I TOLD HER I HAD FOUND ALTERNATIVE accommodation. Cathleen's eyes lit up. When I added I would move into the lodge at Castlestrange, the daggers returned. It struck me that even her darkest expression did not detract from her beauty.

"But how will you manage a household alone, given that you work all day?" asked Mrs. Doyle.

"I have appointed a maid, young Bridget Duffy, and her aunt, Fiona Walsh, will cook."

"Well, that's all settled then," she said, her tone suggesting I should have sought her approval before making such plans.

"I hope you will visit, Mrs. Doyle. Perhaps over a weekend sometime?"

"Yes. We might, might we not, Cathleen?"

Cathleen grunted and left the room.

It would take me some time to properly furnish the two-bedroom cottage, and I could not help thinking how Mama would have disapproved of my mixed crockery—not to mention the idea of my living on the property of a bachelor. However, I was pleased with the lodge and the independence it afforded. I had decided, despite having my own lodgings and a garden that opened onto the fields of the estate, I would do as Dorothy suggested and leave Nugget and Honey with her. However, it was only when, after my second night in the lodge—the day after Willie left for Dublin—I found Spencer curled up on my doorstep that I felt certain I had done the right thing by agreeing that the Pomeranians would stay in England; the Setter had claimed me.

"Come inside, Spencer," I said, smiling as I pictured how surprised Willie would be to find the pup properly trained when he returned.

The timing of the annual National Veterinary Congress could not have been better. Up until then, Willie had accompanied me on most callouts. Even on the ones where I did all the work, he undertook the introductions and reassured people that I was making the right decisions and doing the right things. The few times I had worked alone, clients did little to disguise their suspicions that my employer had sent his lesser-experienced assistant. With him gone, their choice was me or no veterinary surgeon at all. I took the assertive, Mr. Spreull-endorsed approach and, when I arrived in our clients' yards, preempted the inevitable question.

"Mr. Byrne is in Dublin," I announced as I dismounted. "Who am I attending to today?"

It surprised me, as days turned to weeks, how questions about the date of Willie's return dwindled and eventually stopped altogether. Several clients asked me to come back for follow-up consultations weeks ahead with no regard for the fact that he would probably be back by then. It was good and reminded me how I felt the first time I rode Taffy off the lead at age four. My father, worried I would not be strong enough to rein her in, cautioned me not to gallop immediately. I nodded, leaned forward across her withers, and flapped my legs up and down as fast and vigorously as I could. The pony took off across the field. I was elated and had never experienced such satisfaction and freedom. I recognized the feeling in Roscommon, when, having visited clients alone and worked with their animals, I gradually won their trust and respect. As I loosened my hair in the wind and galloped home

to Castlestrange after a long day of veterinary work well done, I felt liberated
and buoyed by triumph.

"To blazes with the Royal College!" I shouted at a flock of startled sheep.
"I *am* a veterinary surgeon!"

Indeed, Willie's absence was an opportunity for our clients to get to
know me and to see that I was more than his assistant and entirely capable
of working alone. I also did not miss the resentful scowls typically bestowed
upon me by the daughters, aunts, mothers, and even wives of our clients
when they spotted me at "his honor's" side.

Certainly, at times during the weeks he was gone, my pulse raced with
uncertainty, but mostly, I enjoyed being able to independently assess cases
and make decisions. I spent my evenings poring over Willie's books and
notes to confirm I had not missed anything during the day. I made notes of
my own about cases I wanted to discuss with him. In addition to the independence his absence afforded me, working without him gave me and our
clients the opportunity to become acquainted without the notion of being in
the presence of a deity. As much as I enjoyed working with him, I welcomed
the chance to strike out alone for a while. What I did not anticipate was how
it might also change my relationship with Father O'Flanagan.

I had spent the morning on the other side of the River Suck attending
to a cow with milk fever. I planned to eat a quick lunch and then go to the
rooms to consult one of Willie's books to confirm that I had not overlooked
anything in my diagnosis and treatment of the animal. As I rode Blaze
through the gate at Castlestrange, I was taken aback at the sight of Willie's
groom with Zeus saddled and waiting near the garden path of the lodge.
Before I could ask why he was there, Bridget ran out of the door.

"My lady," she called. "Father O'Flanagan sent a boy to call you.
Urgently."

I sighed. It was inevitable, I assumed. The priest had not changed his
mind about me. More than one client had mentioned his ongoing sermons
against accepting my help with their animals. Now, since it was not having
the desired effect on them, it seemed he had decided to rebuke me directly.

"Thank you, Bridget, but I will have lunch first," I replied, dismounting
Blaze.

"My aunt has wrapped it for you so that you can eat on your way to the village. I'll get it for you," said the girl, gesturing to the boy to bring Zeus to me.

"No. Wait," I replied, pulling off my gloves. "I will not hurry to the parish to be chastised for my gender and for going about my work. There is no urgency for that. I will have my lunch and ride to see Father O'Flanagan when I am ready."

"But, my lady, he says his horse has stomach pain and looks to be dying."

I sent her to fetch my lunch, pulled my gloves back on, handed Blaze to the groom, mounted Zeus, and headed for the practice to gather what I might need to treat colic.

Father O'Flanagan was standing outside the parish stables when I arrived. I looked over the door. A boy stood alongside the horse, his hand on its halter. The animal hung his head, as if exhausted.

"Has he been rolling?" I asked.

The boy shook his head.

"I did not want to risk the beast getting violent," said the priest, a hand on his crucifix as if I might have forgotten who he was. "So I told Pádraig to get him up and hold his head still. He was lying down this morning, fretting, and has been nipping at his belly constantly."

"Did you change his food recently?"

There was a pause as Father O'Flanagan and Pádraig glanced at one another.

"Aye," said the priest eventually. "His hay was finished and will not be replaced until next week. We got him some rye. Fed him last night. Pádraig said the beast was pleased with it."

"Is he stabled all day during winter?"

"Yes. The paddock is small and bare, and it has been so wet."

I opened the door. "Take him to the gate and back, Pádraig."

The animal's stomach was distended. He walked slowly. I asked Father O'Flanagan to show me the rye. Sure enough, it was damp and sour smelling. The horse's bellyache had not only been caused by a sudden change in diet but also by feeding him fermented grain.

"Will you have to cut him?" asked the priest after I explained what had happened and how intense the pain from the gas probably was.

"Not if I can help it."

I did not want to have to operate. The boy was young and small and would not be of much use, and Father O'Flanagan had made it clear that he preferred to keep his distance from his distressed horse. I suspected the animal was suffering flatulent colic and that the pain was caused by a build-up of gas, which, without any complications to the bowels, was usually the easiest stomach pain to treat. I did not mention the latter fact.

"I will need to use your kitchen, please, Father."

He nodded and led the way. I called to Pádraig to keep walking the horse slowly.

The priest watched from the door as I created a mixture of spirit of nitrous ether, laudanum, and sulfuric ether. He trailed me back to the yard and stood by silently while I administered it to the horse.

"If he shows no sign of relief within two hours, I will have to try something else," I said. "Take him to the gate and back once more, Pádraig, and then to his stable."

"I shall go and pray," said Father O'Flanagan. "What will you do, Miss Cust?"

"I will wait with the horse, Father, and eat my lunch."

Pádraig stayed with me but refused my offer of food.

"Do you think Father O'Flanagan has gone to pray for the health of the horse or for forgiveness for allowing me to attend to the animal?" I asked.

The boy gave me a blank look and shrugged. "Sure, he thought you would not come, and the horse would die," he said quietly.

I chuckled. "What kind of veterinary surgeon would do such a thing?"

Pádraig shrugged once more.

Less than an hour passed before the gas departed the horse in a loud and lingering blast.

"*That* is what we were hoping for," I said, smiling at the animal.

The horse blinked and emitted another, almost as impressive gaseous discharge.

Pádraig ran to call the priest. I instructed them to do away with the rye and replace it with hay immediately, find somewhere for the horse to forage for a few hours every day, and exercise him lightly. Father O'Flanagan sent the boy to find the hay, and I prepared to leave.

"Miss Cust," said the priest, shuffling toward me without meeting my eye. "I owe you my thanks."

"It is my job, Father," I replied, wanting to suggest he owed me an apology too. "It is what I trained to do."

"And yet you have no certificate to confirm it."

His expression was smug. I felt slapped by it. Had Willie told him about the pigheadedness of the RCVS? I said nothing, but he provided an answer to the unasked question.

"One of my colleagues was in Edinburgh for a while and heard about your case at the college."

"Is that so, Father? I am pleased you have all the facts then. It means you also know I undertook all the training necessary and that I am thus as qualified a veterinary surgeon as Mr. Byrne is," I answered.

"I did not know that until I saw it today. Good afternoon, Miss Cust."

It was while Willie was in Dublin that I received word from Owen of Professor Williams's death. It was a shock, for while he was no longer a young man, the principal had seemed vital and in good health when I'd left Edinburgh. I regretted not having written to him after arriving in Athleague as I had meant to. I wanted to tell him how well things were going and how much I appreciated everything he had done. I had procrastinated, and now it was too late.

I sat in front of the fire that night, Spencer's chin on my knee, and thought about how greatly the man had influenced my life. I wrote to Owen, who had informed me in a note accompanying the death notice that he had taken over the role of principal at the New Veterinary College.

Dear Owen,

I would like to express my sincere condolences on the passing of your father. I shall always think of him with fondness and the deepest gratitude. He was, as you well know, a remarkable man who made a great difference to my life.

Remembering the many kindnesses which I have received from your father and you, and also the fact that to him I owe the present position which I occupy, I would like in some way to express my gratitude. Therefore, if you will kindly allow me, I will give a prize of £25 annually for the next four years, to be competed for by students of the New Veterinary College, Edinburgh. I would suggest that the prize be given to the student who obtains the highest aggregate number of marks in his or her A, B, C, and D examinations of the Royal College of Veterinary Surgeons; also that the student must have been regular in his or her attendance and of good behavior during the time he or she has attended the New Veterinary College.

And I may say that should I still be living in the land of prosperity at the expiration of the four years and the giving of the prizes prove to be a success, which I sincerely hope they will be, I shall do my best to consider giving the prize annually.

If there is any other scheme that you think would be more advantageous to the students or the welfare of the profession, I shall be very pleased to hear from you on the subject.

In giving these prizes, I wish to be anonymous.

With every good wish, believe me, ever yours faithfully,
An Old Student

That night, with Spencer snoring softly on the carpet by my bed, I dreamed that Professor Williams arrived at Castlestrange on a white pony. He called to me, and when I went to him, he held out a scroll.

"Your certificate, Miss Cust," he said. "I brought it from the other side."

I reached out, but before I could take hold of it, he, the horse, and the document disappeared. I awoke crying.

A day or two later, I received another letter. It was from Bertie. Finally, after years of assuring other members of the Widdrington family that we would do so, one of us had written. It was not, however, the sight of Bertie's handwriting on the envelope that surprised me but rather that I had thought so little of him since arriving in Ireland. I told myself it was because I had been so busy and that my thoughts were occupied by the many things a veterinary surgeon had to think about every day.

College might have filled my head with new information and skills, but working, particularly alone in Willie's absence, was the true coming-of-age as a veterinary surgeon for me. Although I had received a glimpse of how it might be while working with Mr. Spreull in Dundee, in Ireland, I learned that being a veterinary surgeon was made up of two halves. One involved attending to sick and injured animals, and the other required convincing their owners that whatever I did and the outcome thereof had the best results possible. And that *that* left me no time to think about Bertie was surely not surprising.

I left the letter unopened until I was in bed that night. Only a page long, it was more of a note, which told me, in his small, neat hand, that Bertie was soon to leave with the army for India. It was a farewell letter, which ended with the promise that he would write again when he had an address in Delhi. He hoped I would reply then and tell him about my life in Ireland.

What would I say if I wrote? I wondered, as I set the letter down and turned off the oil lamp. I thought about how easy I had found it to talk to Bertie previously. It had seemed to me, perhaps because he so often trailed behind us when we were children, he had been an extension of Dorothy. That changed when I saw him with Enid Ford at Christmas. He was suddenly different. Or perhaps, I was. Now, in Ireland, the distance between us was greater still. What was there we shared other than a childhood and our fondness for Dorothy, Major Fitz, and Lady Widdrington? I could not imagine what I would begin to tell him about Athleague, Castlestrange, and my life as a veterinary surgeon. My life was different. I was changed. What would I say about Willie? Willie, who I was now beginning to feel had been away too long and whose return filled me with the kind of excitement I once only experienced before a hunt.

CHAPTER 23

1901
Athleague, Ireland

"YOUR QUEEN IS DEAD," SAID WILLIE, BRANDISHING THE NEWSPAPER IN MY direction as I entered the practice one afternoon, brushing the snow from my shoulders and Spencer's coat.

"God save the King," I replied, feigning boredom. I knew better than to encourage conversation with him about the royal family. Although he and I did not discuss public affairs at length, I knew from conversations I had overheard between him and our clients how seriously he took his role as president of the Athleague branch of the United Irish League.

"What will happen now?"

I played ignorant. "What do you mean?"

"To your mother? Your brother?"

I shrugged and sat at the desk to make some notes in the diary about the two horses and one bull I had just attended to in the infirmary. The weather was closing in, and although it was early, we had finished work for the day. I hoped that nothing new would arise to demand that we head outdoors once more. I could have told Willie that with Charles having long been equerry to his friend George, the Duke of York, Queen Victoria's death meant my brother would be promoted. George's father's accession as King Edward VII meant Charles's friend would become Prince of Wales, and Charles, equerry to the heir apparent. My mother, I imagined, would finally retire.

"Perhaps your mother might visit in the spring," said Willie.

I looked at him, surprised. He knew about my family's aversion to my profession. Yet, there was no sign that he was teasing.

"She might enjoy seeing you at work and discover how the people of Roscommon have taken you into their hearts," he continued.

"There is little chance of my mother wanting to see me at work and even less chance of her ever coming to Ireland."

"Why?"

So it was that I imprudently recounted the story of my father's time as a land agent in Tipperary. I prattled on about his argument with the priest and how, challenged and angry, he had placed his boot on the nun's grave. I described how my father's death had soon followed and how we'd fled Tipperary.

As unwittingly as a wet dog shaking the mud from his fur on a clean rug, so I did not pause to think of the probable consequences before unburdening myself upon Willie. I was well into the tale when I looked up and noted his stony expression, the twitch along his jaw line, and slight flaring of his nostrils. Only then did I realize what a mistake it had been to speak to Willie of my father's final days. I rushed the ending, my voice growing quieter with each word.

"So as you can imagine, regardless of her opinion of me, my mother will not come to Ireland," I said, practically whispering by then.

He stared at me, silent. His jaw twitched again. The room was still, save for the wind rattling the windows. A chill settled upon me.

"My God," he said eventually, his voice low. "Have you no shame? If I had known *that*…if I'd had any idea what you truly came from, I would never have agreed to have you here."

"But I am… I was only—"

"No!" he roared, flinging a chair to the floor and striding across the room to the window. "Would you give over saying another word! My God, Aleen! Do you have any idea what… That you should mention this to me… to anyone! It is disgraceful. I cannot believe you do not see that."

"Of course, I do. However, I—"

"No, you do not. Sure, you have no idea at all."

"I do. Now. I was a child. I did not realize what it meant. I—"

But he would not hear me. "You are a spoiled, entitled Englishwoman with no notion of what it is like to be landless, oppressed, and abused by English landlords who have no place in our country. You are here because your own people will not have you…as if Ireland is your play place. You are just like—"

I stood up and slammed my hand on the table. Spencer leapt to his feet and scampered to the door.

"How dare you? You have no idea what it has taken me to get here. You have no idea what I have given up."

"What *you* have given up? Tell me, Aleen. I would like to know. Hmm? Oh, wait, you only have two servants now instead of ten? And no horse of your own—only two of mine to choose from. Sure, you are a poor, deprived woman, my lady."

"Oh, the irony!" I said, making for the door. "What about *you*? Living in a twenty-room house bought for you by your uncle? Have you counted how many servants you have at Castlestrange? Your carriages? Stylish suits? Pfft! Landless and oppressed, indeed."

"I have worked for everything I have."

"And what am I doing here then, Willie? Who is first in these rooms every morning? Who rides miles and miles every day to see clients when you have council meetings, paperwork to deal with, or political gatherings to arrange? Who has not had a holiday in months and works every Sunday so that you can attend mass? Oh, wait! That must be the spoiled, entitled Englishwoman!"

I opened the door.

"Where are you going? You cannot leave now."

"Come, Spencer," I said, ignoring him as I pulled my hat over my head and ran into the blizzard.

I had sent Bridget and Fiona home early so that they would avoid the snowstorm. They had left a fire burning in the drawing room, and once I'd thrown off my coat and dried Spencer, I added some more wood to it. My cheeks were stiff with cold and salty with the tears that had come as I ran through the snow.

The fire crackled as if providing a tune to the fury I felt. How dare Willie Byrne judge me? What did I know about my father's business when I was a girl? What gave Willie the right to admonish me? What had I done other than tell him about an incident that occurred during my childhood? How was I to know, at the age of ten, how cold-blooded my father must have seemed to others?

Spencer whimpered, uncertain for a few moments, before he lay on the rug and stretched his belly in front of the flames. I sat down, exhaustion and sadness snuffing my anger.

What a mess, I thought. I'd imagined that I had found happiness in a place I could call home, but Willie's outburst indicated otherwise. While Father O'Flanagan had stopped preaching against me and some clients even requested that I, rather than Willie, attend to their animals, I was still an outsider. I pictured the cold looks I received from Cathleen Doyle and a few other women. Perhaps they were not jealous of how much time I spent with the county's most prized bachelor and simply disliked me because I was an impostor. Just as my family believed I did not deserve the Cust name and the Royal College argued I had no place in the veterinary profession, I was not wanted in Ireland. I would have to leave, but where would I go?

Bertie's letter lay on the mantelpiece. I reached for it and held it to my heart. I would go to the only place I knew I would always be welcome, Northumberland.

I was crying again when I fell asleep on the settee in front of the fire. How long I slept before Spencer woke me as he whined and scratched at the door, I do not know. There was a light tap. He barked excitedly. I stood up, pushed my hair from my face, and opened the door. It was Willie. I wanted to hate him. He deserved my loathing, but I was even too weary for that.

"May I come in?" He held up a dark bottle. "I brought port. It was given to me at a congress. I have no idea if it is any good, but the gentleman who presented it to me was an English aristocrat. So, well, I hope it will do."

I tried not to smile and almost succeeded. The wind and snow swirled around behind him, and although this time Willie wore a hat, the kitten curl once more lay upon his forehead. I stepped back. Spencer pranced around Willie's legs as he closed the door behind him.

He placed the port on the table, removed his coat and hat, and, spotting the claret glasses on the sideboard, picked up two. "Test it, shall I?"

Moving closer to the fire and turning my back to him, I did not respond. I heard the light pop of a cork and pouring of liquid.

"It's not bad," he declared, moving to stand next to me and handing me a glass.

I took it but did not drink. "I do not—"

"Forgive me, Aleen. I was… I was… I did not mean what I said. Please forgive me."

I moved away and put the glass on the table.

"That is the trouble," I said. "I believe you did mean what you said. My telling you about my father gave you permission to say it out loud. To tell me how you really feel. What an entitled English impostor I am."

He put his glass down near mine and stepped closer, placing his hand on my shoulder and gently turning me to face him. His eyes searched mine.

"No. That is not true. I—"

"You denounced me so easily, Willie. The words were on your lips, waiting to be said. As if you have always believed me to be spoiled, insensitive, entirely lacking."

"No. Please, Aleen, listen for a moment."

I was quiet.

"Can you not see how impossible it is? You are everything I should detest."

My mouth was dry. He agreed with me after all. I might have convinced myself that I did not belong, but I did not want him to confirm it.

"Why did you agree with Professor Williams that I could come here then?" I asked, aware of the hot tears coursing down my face.

"Because I was…am in awe of you. I could not resist you, even when I did not know you."

In awe? Resist me? My head spun and for a moment it seemed that his hand on my shoulder was the only reason I remained upright.

"What?" I asked.

"My God, Aleen. Do you not see yourself?"

Willie lifted his hand and stepped back, his eyes sweeping the full length of me. I felt myself sway. He turned and took a few short, quick steps to the window, his back to me now.

"I do not understand," I said. I was aware of my pulse throbbing loudly. Could he hear it?

Willie turned to face me again, his arms at his sides. "No, you do not see what I see." He sighed. "A magnificent woman determined to become someone, do something that no other woman dares. You took on a college full of men, only one of whom wanted you there initially, and won them over. You fought an army of misogynous old bachelors and henpecked husbands who wanted you gone. Picture it, Aleen. How it was to imagine you there."

He paused, as if giving me time to see it. I gave my head a small shake. He continued. "And here? In Roscommon. The image of you crouching next to Pony on the side of the road in the mist will forever be painted in my thoughts. Then, I see you on Blaze, cutting across the countryside like a warrior, unbridled in the wind, set on winning the hearts of beasts and men. My God, not even the Roman Catholic clergy can resist you."

He put his hands on his head as if concerned it might roll from his shoulders. "How could anyone resist such a beautiful, determined soul? How could I not want you?"

Want me? I stared at him, flabbergasted.

"Want me?" I croaked eventually, knowing as I spoke exactly what he meant and that it was what I longed for too.

He nodded, stepped forward, placed his hands on my arms, and drew me toward his chest. Our eyes locked. It did not matter that I was dumbstruck. There was nothing more to say.

When Willie's lips touched mine, I experienced no surprise. On the contrary, it seemed I was finally home. All my doubts about belonging in Ireland, in Athleague and Castlestrange with Willie disappeared as if swirled away like snowflakes in the wind. What remained was the warmth of the fire and Willie's body against mine, and a deep sense of being in the place I had been searching for my entire life.

We broke apart momentarily.

"Do you want me, Aleen?" Willie's voice was hoarse.

I blinked, and though I said nothing, he heard me.

"Are you sure of it?"

I saw myself swimming in his eyes and could only nod.

Had I known what I discovered that night about passion and how much pleasure one person could give another when Dorothy told me about her and Edward's platonic relationship, I would have beseeched her to not shut down that part of their lives. Why would anyone punish themselves so? Perhaps, though, it would have taken a lover like Willie to convince her, and I did not want to think about where she might find such a person if Edward was not the one.

In the dark hours of the morning, after Willie had made me gasp in surprise at the delight of it once more, and finally, he slept, I thought about what Fred Taylor had said about Mr. Willie Byrne being a "ladies' man." It made me smile. In a sated, unworldly state of bliss and charity, I felt I should thank the women who had schooled him in the art of lovemaking. I could not compare his talent for it to that of anyone else, but my body assured me he was masterful.

It occurred to me then, for the first time, how remarkable it was for me to have found a man so skilled in the thing I most valued in life—that is, veterinary surgery—to be as expert a lover, and for him to share both skills with me. How incredible it was, after all the places I had lived, that I should again find happiness in the countryside in Ireland. I closed my eyes and pictured myself in Tipperary, with Ned's head on my lap as I watched the farrier at work and overheard him talk of his colleague who had gone to train as a veterinary surgeon. It dawned on me as I snuggled closer to Willie that I might have even exceeded my childhood dream of achieving professional fulfillment and happiness in my life as a veterinary surgeon.

It was only later, when I heard Willie dressing, that, as if accompanying the shard of daylight stealing through a crack between the curtains, reality began nosing its way back into my consciousness.

"I have to go," he said, sitting at my side and brushing a strand of hair from my face. I rested my hand on his forearm, thinking about how often I had admired his muscular arms, shirtsleeves rolled up, as he held the leg of a horse, pulled a calf from a cow, lifted a sheep, or undertook some other such action. Had I imagined what they might awaken in my body? How could I not have? We kissed slowly, and he stood to go.

"I shall see you at our rooms, Miss Cust. You will not be late, I trust?" said Willie, his eyes twinkling.

As he left, I rolled onto his side of the bed. It was already cold. The warmth and freedom, where only he and I mattered, seemed to follow him down the hallway. I sat up and placed my bare feet on the floor, hoping that the icy, hard surface would help clear my mind, but reason eluded me. Like muddy piglets evading the hands of a farmer, thoughts and images dashed through my head, colliding against one another, fleeing in opposite directions, and disappearing as fast as they had appeared. It was a heady sensation I could not control.

What now? What had we done? What had we unleashed? Was there a name for it? Where did we go from here? Where would it end? How was it possible that we had worked side by side for so long without acknowledging what so powerfully existed between us? Or was it simply that we had not, until now, handed ourselves over to it? My knees, I realized, were trembling.

Given that I was in my thirties, most would classify me as being well into spinsterhood, but indeed, although inexperienced in matters of love, I was not an ignorant woman. I understood the nature of relationships between men and women and how foolish love and lust could make people. That surely did not apply to me and Willie. We had worked together for months. We were friends. Kindred spirits, despite our different backgrounds, religions, and nationalities. We might only now have given in to lust, but affection and admiration, though never spoken, had surely been there all along. Why, then, was I shaking? Was it regret? Fear?

I walked to the window, opened the curtains, and looked across the garden. It was white with snow yet soft to the eye in the morning light. No. I felt no regret. Only a sense that, despite the intensity of my doubts the day before, I belonged in Ireland. I belonged with Willie in a place I loved, doing what I loved.

Months later, as we rode home after the Roscommon Hunt, which had been as exhilarating as it was exhausting, Willie moved Zeus closer to Blaze and placed his hand on my knee. His touch was light, but the effect powerful. I drew a deep breath, exhaled, and looked away, pretending to take in the view of the forests and hills in the distance but in fact trying to hide the smile that tugged my mouth.

"Are you sure you were not born on a horse?" he asked. "I could watch you ride all day, but when you galloped toward the wall near the river, I closed my eyes. Even riding astride, I hesitated before taking it on. What you persuade Blaze to do is remarkable. Are you never afraid?"

I covered his fingers with my gloved hand. There were few things that pleased me more than his praise and touch. "As long as you keep watching me, Mr. Byrne, I shall remain fearless."

"The problem is every man at every meet watches you too. I sometimes wonder if that is the only reason some of them are there."

It was unlike Willie to be jealous, which made me chuckle. "There is a way of putting a stop to that, you know."

He glanced at me, saying nothing.

"If we were married, they would not look."

"Really, Aleen? You think that would make a difference?"

"Yes. Married women quickly lose their appeal, do they not? Hopefully, not too quickly to their husbands, of course."

"No."

"They do not lose their appeal?"

"No. It is not possible."

"What is not possible?" I asked, although I knew the answer and regretted my teasing.

He removed his hand from my leg. I had ruined the moment.

"I believe you know," he said, looking down now. "It is one thing for me to work with a Protestant, but to marry one is quite another."

There was a pause, silent but for the slow clip-clop of the horses' hooves. Then, he went on. "It will not only ruin the practice but also my reputation as a nationalist. It would ruin us, Aleen. Please do not hope for it."

"Athleague would get over it," I replied, trying to keep my voice light. "Think about how they resisted me when I arrived and how that has changed."

"We cannot do it," he replied in the tone that I recognized as being his final word on the subject.

Willie was right, and I said no more. I thought briefly about the ruckus that had followed when the leader of the Irish Parliamentary Party, John Redmond, married English Protestant Ada Beesley a few years earlier. Despite assurances that she would convert to Catholicism, Irish sentiment was set against her and did not change. It was not good for his career.

In fact, I was not set on changing things anyway. While I would not have missed scampering to and fro between the gate lodge and Willie's house in the dark after our servants had retired for the night and before they awoke the next morning, I did not mind keeping my own house. A few times a week, we spent the night alone in our own homes, and it suited us. I never doubted that he wanted to be with me or that I enjoyed being with him, but that did not stop us from enjoying being apart at times—neither did it prevent Willie from surprising me.

A week or two after the hunt, he handed me an invitation to the National Veterinary Congress in Windermere, Cumbria.

"I am on the program as a speaker. We shall go together," he said, matter-of-factly. "I shall reply for both of us."

"Together? Really? Do you need my protection in England? From the Protestants or the royalists?" I teased.

He ignored me. "Separate rooms, of course, but, well, you are a veterinary surgeon, and you should be there."

I tried to disguise my delight with a curt nod.

Despite my name being on the visitors' list rather than among the names of the professional attendees, I enjoyed the event. Although the subject of Willie's speech was "The Significance of Bacteriology and Pathology to the Veterinary Surgeon," he managed to make a point about women and the profession, which, while it was not discussed publicly or reported on in any of the journals afterward, was explicit to all in the audience.

"As I have demonstrated," he said during his conclusion, "bacteriology and pathology are crucial to the future of this profession. Without improved understanding of the subjects, we cannot advance as experts, and our work will suffer. Greater emphasis on research and laboratory studies will not only broaden our knowledge but also expand the profession, introducing new areas of specialization and focus for men *and women* in veterinary science to the benefit of all."

I was not demure in my applause.

"Do you think I should go into politics? I mean, dedicate myself to it," Willie joked that night, when fortified by the success of his presentation and more than one nightcap, he stole into my room at the hotel.

"No," I replied, wrapping myself around him. "I suspect politicians make terrible lovers. Let us leave things the way they are."

Back at Castlestrange the following week, I returned from a calving case to an empty practice, and with the dogs at my heels, went to the infirmary to look for Willie. He was nowhere to be found, despite the diary indicating he should be in.

"He said he'd be back by dark, Miss Cust," said his groom when I inquired.

It was dusk when I closed the practice door and set off with Spencer toward the lodge. I heard horses approaching and peered down the road. Willie was riding Zeus while leading an elegant gray Arabian I did not recognize.

"Ah, Miss Cust. That's grand," he called. "Perfect timing. I have a delivery for you."

I took the stallion's reins and led him onto the lawn. He was tall for an Arabian but had all the grace of his breed. His neck was long and arched, and he carried his tail high. I placed my hand in the indent of his pretty, wedge-shaped head. He nudged me playfully and snorted.

"He is magnificent," I said.

Willie dismounted and walked to my side. "Bred from the best, say his papers. He has seven names but goes by Nasser."

"Hello, Nasser." I ran my hand down his sleek, sloping shoulder, imagining his floating gait. I had ridden one of Major Fitz's friend's Arabians years previously and had been delighted by how smoothly she moved. "Are you going to breed from him?"

"He is not mine. I bought him for you."

"What?"

"He is yours."

Still leading Nasser, I ran to Willie and threw myself into his arms. The horse balked and, tossing his head backward in fright, almost pulled us to the ground.

"Whoa! Calm down, the pair of you," laughed Willie, taking the lead from me and stroking the horse's neck. "It is all right, boy. She is just a little excited."

"Excited? I am…I am…" I looked at Willie. I looked at the horse. I could not remember being as happy. I kissed Willie without even looking around to ensure that we were out of sight. "Thank you. Thank you. I have never received such a beautiful gift. But why, Mr. Byrne?"

He smiled. "Why? Sure, you would ask. Well, Miss Cust, I cannot give you a ring, a wedding, or my name, but I hope you will accept a white horse as proof of my love for you."

CHAPTER 24

❦

1904
Athleague, Ireland

SEASONS CHANGED, YEARS PASSED, AND WILLIE AND I WORKED TOGETHER AT Castlestrange, traversing the county come rain, snow, and blue skies to attend to the animals of an ever-growing number of clients. It was not just that the farmers of Roscommon were increasingly forsaking their charms and potions in favor of our counsel, methods, and medicine, but also because the number of animals they kept was increasing that we were busier. Farmers were keeping more cows to increase milk yields, and particularly where pastures were not fertile, flocks of sheep were growing too.

By 1904, our practice had grown from a three-horse operation to six, including Nasser. As ever, we attended to cases individually—me seizing every opportunity to ride the Arabian to visit clients—but also together as was necessary. When we required equipment too cumbersome to carry on our horses, we took the gig.

If eyebrows were raised when we rode or drove together, I did not see them. In company, we were unswervingly discreet and professional. On the face of it, fewer and fewer people seemed to care that I was a woman and a veterinary surgeon, and that Willie and I, both unmarried, worked side by side. Indeed, that Mr. Byrne had appointed a female veterinary surgeon to help at his flourishing practice was no longer news. I had proven myself worthy. Even Father O'Flanagan waved and smiled when our paths crossed.

At Castlestrange, I suspected that our servants knew that we frequently shared a bed. They never, however, gave any indication of knowing. Did Willie cover the footprints he left in the snow when he returned to the main house on winter mornings? I certainly did not. What else might Bridget and Fiona have imagined when they regularly found pairs of claret glasses and teacups on the table when they arrived for work? Whether the servants guarded what they saw or talked to one another and their friends and family about it, I do not know. It was never mentioned or alluded to by anyone. What I was certain of was that I was happy.

I rose every morning with anticipation. Even though most days Willie would have only recently been beside me, I was eager to get to the practice to see him, curls calmed and face freshly shaven, finalizing the schedule for the day. During work hours, we focused on our clients and patients. Sometimes though, when we were alone, we stole a touch or a quick kiss. A few times, I glanced up from whatever it was I was doing and found his eyes on me, warm, proud, and full of desire. It made me want to burst into song.

One sweltering morning, as we drove the gig along the river after castrating several bullocks at Bluebell Farm, I pulled off my hat and wiped my brow.

"Can you swim?" I asked.

"Sure, of course, I can swim. What about you?"

"I will have you know that I am a most excellent swimmer."

"Really? Did you learn when you fell into a river while out riding as a girl? Not drowning is not necessarily the same as swimming, you know," said Willie.

I struck his arm with my hat. "I have an idea. Let us stop at the big pool before the lane and we shall have a swimming race. That will decide who is best."

"Miss Cust! Not everything in life is a competition, you know."

"You are not up to the challenge then, Mr. Byrne?"

He was, of course. We left Blaze and the gig in the shade and ran to the water. The race began as we threw off our clothing. Unsurprisingly, Willie was naked first, and I watched as he ran and dove neatly into the pool. There was no doubt that he was comfortable in the water. I took off my blouse and chemise, undid my corset and tossed it on the grass, stepped out of my skirt, petticoats, and drawers, and followed. I gasped as the water, cold against my hot flesh, surrounded me. It was shockingly delightful.

"Come on then," he called, treading water in the middle of the pool.

I swam toward him, and as I approached, he took off, calling over his shoulder, "The first to touch the willow is the winner."

Willie reached the tree well before me and, holding on to a low branch, caught me around the waist.

"Not bad, Miss Cust, but not quite up to college swimming team standards."

"You were on the college team?"

"I am a man of many talents," he said, his hand tracing the outline of my hip and his lips meeting mine.

We kissed, and as I wound my legs around his torso, Willie drew back to look at me. "I love you, you wild and wonderful woman. I cannot imagine life without you."

If we had drowned together in that moment, the smile on my face would have carried me to eternity.

Having used one of my petticoats to dry myself a little later, I was buttoning my blouse when I heard a voice coming from where we had left Blaze and the gig.

"Hello? Hello?" it called.

Willie glided through the water toward me. I held up my hand and pointed in the direction of the gig.

"Hello?" called the voice again.

He heard it this time, eyes widening.

"Just one moment," I called. "I will be with you shortly."

"Miss Cust? Is that you?" came the voice. "I thought I recognized the gig."

It was Father O'Flanagan. Willie slid below the surface of the water.

"Oh, Father! Hello, yes. It is I. If you would just wait there one minute, I am… I shall be with you shortly."

I dressed hastily, looking across the water for Willie. He had disappeared. Then I saw his curls peeping over the top of a log near the bank. He was lying low. I stifled a giggle and made my way to the gig, where Father O'Flanagan was sitting on his horse.

"I caught sight of the gig from the road and saw that it was unattended. I thought something might have happened," he said, eyeing my wet hair.

"No, everything is fine, Father. Thank you. I was overcome by heat and decided to splash some water on my face. I did not realize that my hair had come undone."

"Well, as long as you are all right. Where are you headed?"

"Back to Castlestrange."

"Come on then. I will accompany you to the turnoff."

Although Willie insisted that he was not amused by having had to walk home in the heat, we laughed about the incident later until my stomach ached. I could not remember laughing as much as I did with him during that time.

When Dorothy came to visit, after having promised to do so for years, during my fourth summer in Athleague, it pleased me to be able to talk to someone else about Willie and me, even if I did not initiate the discussion. Indeed, my friend knew me well.

"Will you marry him?" she asked as we walked back to the lodge after having an early dinner with Willie at Castlestrange shortly after she had arrived.

I was startled by the question. "What? Who?"

"Mr. Byrne, of course. Who else?"

"No. Of course not. He is my colleague. My employer, in fact. Why would you ask such a thing?"

My attempt at disbelief was not convincing.

"Oh, Aleen—" she said.

"But what makes you think—"

Dorothy chuckled. "I am not a fool. You forget I have known you since you were ten years old."

"But how…what gives you the impression that we? I—"

"I have seen how you are with men. Including my father, Edward, Bertie, your brothers, and the men who flock around you at hunts. I have seen how, even when you are fond of them, they do not stir you greatly. You are the same with them as you are with me: open, friendly. You are different with Mr. Byrne."

"He is my employer, so…well, I admire him as a veterinary surgeon. He is, as I have told you in my letters, one of the best."

She laughed again. "What are you saying? That you fell in love with him because he is an excellent veterinary surgeon? And he reciprocated because he believes you are good at the job too?"

I looked across the field to where the sun seemed to burst as it caught the top of the trees on the horizon and splashed across the grass. It was June, and the days were long and warm.

"It is not what you think," I said.

"You will not marry him?"

I shook my head.

"Why not?"

"It is not possible, Dorothy," I replied. "He is Irish, Catholic, a nationalist, the son of a farrier, and my employer."

"That does not—"

"The Royal College might not have granted me a certificate, but I am a professional. So is Mr. Byrne. We cannot cross that line."

She gave me a sideways glance. "Is it not too late?"

I swallowed but said nothing.

"Anyway, can a husband and wife not work together? That is not a rule I have ever heard of."

"It has been hard enough getting this far. I cannot ruin it now," I said.

We reached the garden gate of the lodge. She stopped and stood in front of the entrance.

"What is really going on?"

I shrugged and tried to step around her. She blocked me.

"No. Not until you tell me."

It was a relief to talk about Willie and tell Dorothy how much I loved him. I could not pretend that he did not reciprocate my feelings but did not admit that we were lovers. Did she realize that? Was it clear to her? I was not sure, for although Dorothy was emotionally intuitive—bar the time that she had told me about her and Edward's sexless relationship—she never spoke of carnal matters. Neither did she now.

"But you will not marry? Not ever?" she asked.

"No."

"It does not seem right. I understand that there are differences and perhaps some people will not approve but—"

"Willie is adamant."

Dorothy was quiet for a moment. "Is that fair? What about you?"

"Can you imagine what my family would say if I married an Irishman? A nationalist at that. My mother would finally die of shame just as she has threatened to for so long."

"You still care about what she thinks? After all this time?" Dorothy sighed.

"I cannot help it; I am a Cust even if I have tried to pretend otherwise."

"Do you ever hear from your mother? Charles? Any of your siblings?"

I shook my head.

Dorothy sighed again. "So Mr. Byrne is adamant he will not marry you, and you agree it is better that way? That you will continue as is?"

"Yes."

"What if he decides otherwise and finds a Catholic, an Irish woman, who meets the requirements of his faith, politics, and people? What will that do to you?"

"It will not happen. He would not do that to me."

Dorothy gave a small smile. "I hope not. It is just that complete love usually includes commitment—"

"He will not abandon me and marry someone else," I said, wondering what Dorothy might say if I said that complete love also included passion, something that she and Edward, though committed and otherwise intimate, had set aside.

"So you have everything you desire here, Aleen? Love and the work you have always dreamed of?"

"Yes. I have everything I want."

"Then I am happy for you."

We went into the lodge. Dorothy put her hat on the table and turned to me. "Bertie will be disappointed."

I smiled. "Of course, he will not be. And anyway, Dorothy, you cannot mention a word of this to anyone. Not to Bertie, Edward, or your parents. I cannot have Charles and my mother finding out. If there is any chance of my having any kind of relationship with my family in the future, they must never know about Mr. Byrne."

Dorothy had barely been gone a week when I finally accepted that I was pregnant. The signs could not be ignored. Not only had I not bled for a while, but my breasts were swollen. It was, however, the otherwise unexplained bouts of nausea that confirmed my state.

Had I thought about having children? Of course, I had. When I was a girl, I dreamed of raising a family like the Widdringtons. As Major and Lady Widdrington had done with Dorothy, Bertie, Ida, and Gerard, I would take my children riding, permit them as many animals as they wished, and speak openly to them about all manner of subjects. We would take our meals together and discuss world affairs. I would encourage them, girls and boys, to do what made them happy and to follow their dreams.

I stopped imagining becoming a mother when I began studying. It had never been a priority to me, and I no longer had time to indulge the whimsy. I conceded though, that when I fell in love with Willie, there were moments I fantasized about filling Castlestrange with our progeny. Mostly, since I knew we would never marry, I shut down the thoughts quickly and accepted it would not be possible.

Had Willie and I spoken of the risk of my falling pregnant? We had not. His faith insisted that using contraception was intrinsically evil. We did not discuss it, but I did wonder whether using contraception was considered by Catholics as sinful as intercourse without marriage. Or did they believe it was worse?

Certainly, while we did not speak of it, we knew how our bodies worked, and I especially understood mine. Or so I thought. I kept notes of my menses, noting ovulation and fertile days. During that time, I withheld myself from Willie, and I knew he understood why. I even sensed that he was grateful for my prudence. Alas, I was not as accurate in my monitoring as I imagined I was.

Hoping I was mistaken, I hesitated a few days to say anything to Willie. However, after he suggested I was becoming "strangely squeamish" when I dashed from the stall at Castlestrange to expel my breakfast while he was suturing the wound on a horse a client had left with us, I could not contain myself.

"I am *not* squeamish, have never been, and will never be," I said, hot and annoyed. "I regurgitated my food because I am pregnant."

He froze at the stable door. I saw something unfamiliar in his eyes. Was it fear?

"Pregnant?" It was as if the word required great effort to utter.

"Yes."

"Are you sure?"

"Why else would I throw up so frequently? And these?" I pointed to my chest, where my bosom strained against the fabric of my dress. "And the lack of blood."

He sat down heavily on a wooden stool. "My God. What will we do?"

I said nothing. The only option, I believed in that moment, was to get married. Our differences no longer mattered. Neither did what others might think. It was not about religion, class, or nationality. It was not about society. It was not only about Willie and me anymore. What mattered was the new life we had created.

It was not necessary to discuss how he would be judged for marrying out of his faith. It was a fact, but we would ride the storm of shock and scandal together. People would grow accustomed to us as a couple. Our work and the practice would outlast the wagging tongues. Athleague would not oust us. Willie was loved and admired for everything he was and did, and I, at least, was admired for my skills.

I said nothing but hoped he was thinking the same. We would be all right. We would get married. I would convert if necessary. We would have a child. And another if we wished. Our business would flourish. We could live the life we deserved. Together.

"What will we do?" he repeated, quieter now.

"What *can* we do?"

Willie shook his head, silent. He looked sad and defeated. It angered me to see him crushed. Where was the man who stood up for me against the Royal College? The man who dared to offer me a job when no one else would? Where was the person who every day filled me with pride when he came up with solutions to new problems in the animals we treated? Where was the man who looked at me with love and desire, and told me he could not imagine life without me?

"There is only one thing we can do, Willie. We need to get married."

He stood up, raked his fingers through his hair. Spencer slunk away.

"No," he said. "We cannot get married."

"But what—"

"We have been through this, Aleen. We cannot. You know that."

"I was not with child then. Your child. This changes everything."

"Yes. No. It changes nothing. Can you not see what it would do to us? To this?" He opened his arms, gesturing wildly around the yard.

I felt ill again. Not because of my hormones this time but because of his words. How could I have imagined that he loved me if he was too selfish to accept that we were going to have to make some sacrifices? Was our love not worth falling temporarily from grace? Did he not love me enough to defend my honor and support me and his child despite his religious and political beliefs? Was Dorothy right? Would Willie abandon me because of his stubborn principles and his inability to see how duplicitous he was? What a fool I had been.

"If we cannot get married, then I shall have to leave."

Willie said nothing. Perhaps it was what he wanted. He wanted me gone. That way the problem would be solved for him.

"I shall return to England and do what has to be done," I said, trying to stop my voice from trembling and willing him to take me in his arms. He did not.

"What do you mean?"

"What do you think I mean? If you do not want me, a child, a family, what am I supposed to do?"

His face turned red. "You would surely not do that? Abort a life."

"What?" I was appalled. It was not what I had meant. "I will—"

"My God, Aleen! Can you not see! That is why I cannot marry you. Your unholy, Protestant ways are repulsive."

"Repulsive? I will tell you what is repulsive, Willie: your pitiful excuses for not marrying me. Your cowardly way of hiding behind your God, your country, and your proud reputation every time things do not go your way. If I am repulsive, it is better than being the coward you are. How I ever imagined I loved you, I do not know."

"That is absurd. Be reasonable, Aleen. We—"

I could not listen and fled to the lodge, thinking about how poorly he understood me. Could Willie truly believe that I was so lacking in character and my love for him so insignificant that I would, in a heated discussion, make the rash decision to abort our child? How evil did he imagine me, my God, my people, and our beliefs to be? Was Catholic and Irish propaganda really that powerful?

Slamming the door behind me, I threw myself on the settee. Bridget came into the room, wide-eyed.

"My lady, I wasn't expecting you. Are you unwell?"

"Yes. Something I ate does not agree with me. Will you bring me some tea? No milk or sugar."

I sat there, sipping tea for a while. Spencer lay at my feet. I listened for Willie's footsteps, a tapping at the door. I imagined his eyes, full of regret. Asking for forgiveness. He did not come.

When I returned to the practice, Willie was no longer there. I went to the stables where the groom told me he had ridden away hours ago. There was no note on the schedule.

That afternoon, I hugged Nasser and Spencer goodbye, asked Bridget to take the Setter to the main house, and began my journey to England.

CHAPTER 25

❧

1904
Northumberland, England

DOROTHY WAS NOT AT FALLODON WHEN I ARRIVED IN NORTHUMBERLAND, so I went on to Newton Hall, where I spent two days with Major Fitz and Lady Widdrington. For the first time in my life, I found no sanctuary there. After I turned down the second invitation from the major to go riding, Lady Widdrington took my hand and led me into the garden.

"Can you not tell me what is ailing you, my dear?" she said.

"I am exhausted." I tried to smile. "I needed to get away. I will be myself again soon. I promise."

She looked at me, clearly unconvinced. "You should go to Dorothy."

There was nothing more I wanted than to be with Dorothy. She was the only one I felt ready to confide in, but it did not seem right to go to her in Hampshire. Edward had recently begun his service as British foreign secretary and was busier than ever. It was one thing to visit Dorothy at Fallodon, but their home near Itchen Abbas was the couple's private haven.

"The cottage is her and Edward's escape from everyone. I do not want to intrude."

"You could *never* intrude on Dorothy. Your friendship is one of her greatest joys, and I think you will find great pleasure in the birds, fish, and flowers along the stream. It is a most remarkable place. What is more, Edward is typically in London during the week."

So it was that I left for Hampshire the following day where I was warmly welcomed by Dorothy, and with full-body-wagging enthusiasm from Nugget and indifference from Honey. The Pomeranians were in good health and very much at home in Edward and Dorothy's cottage, which was much more than I had imagined it might be. It was, as Dorothy had described, a tiny place, which, surrounded by trees and plants that seemed to tumble toward it in green abandon, was all but hidden from sight until one reached the doorstep. But for the bird song, gentle swooshing of the breeze, and the burble of the river, it was quiet. I could see why it suited my friend. As Lady Widdrington had foretold, Edward was in London, and while I could tell by her puzzled expression that Dorothy was concerned by my unplanned visit, she did not press me to explain.

It was the next day, as we sat on a grassy verge alongside the river with the dogs, Dorothy making notes in the diary she and Edward kept about the birds they saw and heard, that I finally told her.

"You were right about Mr. Byrne," I said, rubbing Nugget's ears.

She put the book down. "What happened?"

"He has cast me aside."

"He has another woman?"

I shook my head and felt my throat constrict. "I am pregnant."

Dorothy stared at me. I wondered, as she blinked several times, if she was taken aback. Did she, despite having been at Castlestrange and having worked out that I was in love, imagine my relationship with Willie to be chaste? Or was she simply shocked by his behavior?

She adjusted her position as if the thick grass beneath her skirts was suddenly uncomfortable. "He cast you aside because you are pregnant?"

"Yes. Well, not in so many words. I said we must, despite everything, get married. He…he declined, said again it was impossible and left."

"Declined and left? Where did he go?"

I shrugged. What did it matter?

"That is why you came back to England?"

"Yes."

"Shall we walk?" she asked, rising without waiting for me to reply. The dogs trotted ahead of us along the path.

The River Itchen, in places as green as the grass on its banks due to the density of the watercress, flowed slow and clear. The shady path traced the waterway, meandering along the water's edge and then looping away to circle trees and thickets of bush. Butterflies, dragon flies, bees, and other insects I knew not how to name flittered about. Dorothy pointed out not one, but two kingfishers. I tried not to think about the blue of Willie's eyes.

"There is a family of otters who play on the banks near the cottage every morning and most evenings," said my friend. "I will introduce you to them tonight."

"I had no idea it was this beautiful," I said, "despite your poetic descriptions."

"There is no place more tranquil. Edward calls it his 'touch point with sanity,' particularly after the madness of parliament and busyness of the city. He stands knee-deep fishing for trout for hours at a time over the weekends. When I ask if he has had a bite, he says, 'I have no idea. Perhaps.' It does not matter; he is replete."

I felt a pang at the warmth in her voice as she spoke of Edward. How hasty I had been to pity her when I discovered passion with Willie. Now, I realized that, while their life together might be without the sensual pleasures I had experienced, their love would endure. Whatever it was Willie and I had felt would not.

"What will you do?" she asked.

"I do not know. I hoped being away would provide clarity, that I might wake up one morning and have the answer."

"Are you certain he will not change his mind about marrying you? Your condition was a shock, to him and you. Perhaps he simply needed time to get used to the idea?"

I shook my head. "He was very clear—as he has been all along—that getting married is out of the question."

Dorothy looked across the river. "I wish I knew the solution."

"So do I," I replied. "But I do not expect you to have the answers. Talking to you and sharing your peace help."

"Stay for as long as you like."

I did not find any answers at Itchen Abbas, but I did find tranquility. The quiet, undetermined nature of the days and the pace of life were very different from the busy, urgent years I had spent at Castlestrange. It took me a few days to learn to wake up slowly and remember that there were no appointments on the practice schedule to harry me. I tried not to think how busy Willie might be without me there.

Dorothy and I took our coffee onto the small veranda and watched the otters roll down the muddy banks and frolic in the water. We strolled to the village to replenish supplies, Honey and Nugget at our heels. We spent hours beneath the trees, pointing out birds to each other. Dorothy's knowledge of ornithology was remarkable. She recognized practically every bird by sight and sound and had interesting facts on each. Letters from Edward arrived every second day. I watched a little jealously as my friend read and reread each one, her eyes sparkling.

The weekend approached, and having been at cottage for almost a week, I knew it was time to go. I did not want to intrude on Edward's time with his wife. I would, I thought, go back to Newton Hall, go riding with Major Fitz, and tell Lady Widdrington about my condition. While Dorothy was my sanctuary, her mother, I had realized, was the best person to ask for practical advice. I was about to go and find Dorothy to ask if she would like to come to the village to examine the train timetable when she found me in the garden.

"I have news from Edward," she said, holding another letter. "He says your mother is very ill. He called on Ursula this week. She is very worried and has sent for Charles."

"They are in Kensington?"

"Yes." She looked at me, eyes narrowing slightly. "You do know that Charles sold Leasowe, do you not?"

"No. I did not know." It seemed odd that I would not visit the castle again, despite my long absence.

"Do you think I should go? To my mother, I mean?"

Dorothy nodded.

London was muggier and busier than I recalled, with more carriages, horses, and people on the streets than ever. There were even a few motorcars chugging about. I examined the horses who clip-clopped past my hansom cab as I was driven to my mother's house. What a magnificent spectacle of animals they were—glossy, proud, and strong—against the foggy backdrop of the city. A tall man rode by. The sight of his muscular thighs against the saddle made me think of Willie and how I loved to watch him, as nimble as a weasel, mount Zeus, settle into the saddle, and gallop away. I could not, however, picture Willie in London, even though he had lived there while at the Royal Veterinary College. What did he do when he was not studying? Surely the paved streets, throngs of people, and manicured parks stifled him as they did me?

So many people, so many horses. According to the *Veterinary Record*, there were more than a hundred veterinary surgeons in the city. Even with so many, they must have been busy. I wondered what it was like working in town. Did city veterinary surgeons often leave their rooms, or were most of their patients brought to them? How frequently did they tend to cattle and sheep? How many were turning their attentions to dogs with the increase in miniatures being bred as pets? I could not imagine working in London. I placed my hand on my belly and promised myself that, whatever it brought, my future would not lie in the city.

I did not recognize the butler who opened the door at the house in Kensington.

"Good morning, my lady. Are we expecting you?" he asked.

"No, you are not. I have come to see my sister, Miss Ursula Cust," I replied, pulling off my gloves.

He stared at me. Clearly, he had no idea I existed.

"Are either of my brothers here?"

"Sir Charles arrived yesterday. I shall announce your arrival, shall I, Miss...Cust?"

I nodded and followed the man into the hall as he disappeared into the drawing room. Charles came out of it almost immediately. Although it was unusual to see him dressed in a dark suit instead of his naval outfit, he was as meticulously preened and pressed as I recalled and perhaps, with a little less sun visible on his face, even more handsome. The life of a courtier suited him.

"Aleen. This is a surprise," he said, though his tone suggested no astonishment.

"I was with Dorothy and heard, via Edward, that Mother was unwell. How is she?"

"She is not well at all. The doctor is deeply concerned."

Ursula appeared behind him. Slender with glossy, dark hair, she was a replica of Mama as she was portrayed in a painting my grandparents had commissioned of her as a young woman.

"Hello, Ursula," I said, leaning to peer around Charles so that I could make eye contact with her.

"What are you doing here?" Her upper lip curved as if in a snarl. She shot a look at Charles. "She will only upset Mama."

Charles glanced at the butler, who stood at the door like a heron on the hunt. "Let us go into the drawing room. We will take our tea early, thank you, Dawson."

I had not expected to be warmly welcomed by my family, but I'd hoped they might be courteous. I'd imagined that perhaps with our mother ill, my siblings might put aside their disapproval so we could share a moment or two of mutual concern. Ursula's stiff carriage and condemning eyes indicated that I had hoped for too much. I wondered what advice Mr. Spreull might offer if she were a client. Should I be more forceful or pretend not to notice her stoniness? I took the middle ground.

"I do not want to upset Mama, Ursula, but I would like to see her. "

"I am quite certain she has no desire to see you. Have you any idea of the anxiety you have caused her?" asked my sister.

Charles frowned and gestured to me to sit, which I did. "You cannot be sure that she does not want to see her, Ursula. I shall ask her myself when she wakes up," he said.

"She is conscious then? Alert?" I asked.

My brother nodded. "She sleeps a great deal. The doctor thinks it is the best thing for her. But when she is awake, she is lucid."

"We cannot tire her," said Ursula.

"I understand. I will wait here until she is awake. And then, well, if she wants to see me, I will go to her. I shall do my utmost not to upset or tire her."

Ursula groaned and left the room. Dawson arrived with tea. Once he had served it and left, I tried to make conversation with Charles. He did not make it easy. My questions about his life at court were answered with monosyllables. He did not inquire about me or my life. I had not finished my tea, and we had already exhausted our graceless interaction. How was it possible we were siblings? We might as well have been different species. It was almost a relief when my sister appeared at the door.

"She is awake but far too uncomfortable to accept visitors," she said.

Charles stood. "You did not mention Aleen was here?"

She glanced at her feet. "She is not up to seeing anyone."

He sighed and left the room.

"I do not know what makes you and Charles think you can arrive here and take over the running of this house as if you have a right to it," said my sister in a low voice. "I have been at Mama's side my entire life. I have taken care of her and protected her from the disgrace and hurt you have brought upon us. I will not quietly stand by while you rub her nose in her shame, and I will *not* be ruled by Charles."

I folded my arms over my belly as if Ursula could see into my womb. Why had I come? How naive of me to have hoped for reconciliation and comfort.

"I do not want to argue with you or Mama or anyone else. I would simply like to see our mother. I thought if I—"

"Will you apologize to her? Let her meet her maker comforted by your penance?"

Perhaps I should have agreed to that. What did it matter if I lied and pretended to my family that I regretted having followed my dream because of the apparent pain it brought them? Would it make a difference if I allowed them to believe it, even for a moment? Perhaps I should have agreed to Ursula's request. I could not, however, bring myself to do so. I was not sorry. I was proud of being a veterinary surgeon and of having persevered at college despite the Royal College's efforts to stop me. I was proud of the work I had done in Athleague. With Willie.

I do not know whether it was the hopelessness I felt as my sister reprimanded me like a nursemaid would a naughty child or the instability of my hormones, but rather than agree with or even reject her terms, I began, to my dismay, to cry.

"Aleen?" Ursula shuffled her feet awkwardly, as if she wanted to flee but felt she should restrain herself. "Let me get you a handkerchief. Do not..."

Charles appeared. He stared at me and then at our sister.

"I am sorry," I said, wiping the tears with my fingers. "I do not mean to make a spectacle of myself."

My brother cleared his throat. "Mama says she will see you. But not today. She will see you tomorrow at ten o'clock and the day after that at the same time—if all goes well tomorrow."

I sighed. I could not remember when I had felt as exhausted. "Thank you."

"Where are you staying?" asked my brother, not pausing for a reply. "I will ask Dawson to call the carriage. See you tomorrow. At ten."

Even after all the years of being apart and the cold, awkward reception I received that morning, it dismayed me that my siblings would not invite me to stay in our family's home. The fresh dismissal provided the shock I needed to reinstate my usual ironclad approach to life. My tears disappeared as quickly as they had come.

"I shall be back tomorrow," I said, pulling on my gloves and walking to the door.

The coachman recommended the Royal Palace Hotel. It was an indulgence but conveniently close by, and I was grateful for the comfort.

The visit had left me shaken. I had forgotten how cold and distant the Cust family could be. The time I had spent with the Widdringtons and Greys, as well as Willie's wit and love, had lulled me into a place where it seemed normal. I longed to be back there again. As I stood in my hotel room and looked over the autumn leaves of Kensington Gardens, I knew without a doubt I wanted nothing more than to be back in Ireland with Willie. Athleague was home, where I belonged. I had to return. There had to be a way for Willie and me to reconcile. I wanted a life with him as much as I wanted a life as a veterinary surgeon. I had fought for the latter and now it was time to fight for the former.

I wrote to him that night.

Dear Mr. Byrne,

I apologize for my abrupt departure and any inconvenience it might have caused. I was not myself but have now fully recovered. I am, at present, in London, where I am to visit my mother, who is critically ill. I expect to be here for a week, perhaps two. After which, I will return to Athleague, where I hope we can talk about recent events and the future of the practice, which I look forward to continuing to be a part of.

Please respond forthwith to this letter at the address above, acknowledging receipt and understanding of it.

With every good wish, believe me, ever yours faithfully,
Aleen Cust

I was prompt the next morning. Dawson opened the door to me, and Charles left the drawing room to escort me to our mother. Ursula was nowhere to be seen.

"The doctor is pleased with her improvement today but cautions against her doing too much," said my brother as we reached her door. I nodded, wondering what he imagined I might do with Mama. Did he think I would whip her outdoors for a brisk walk around Hyde Park?

The tiny woman who looked like she might at any moment be swallowed by her bedclothes did not resemble the strong, elegant person I remembered. The room was dark and stuffy with the scent of menthol and eucalyptus. I wished I could open the curtains and windows. Her eyes followed me as I made my way to her side.

"Hello, Mama."

She lifted a bony finger and pointed at a chair beside the bed. "Sit."

I did. Charles hovered at the door.

"Do you want me stay, Mama?" he asked.

She gave her head a small shake, and he left, closing the door quietly behind him.

"It takes news of my imminent death to bring you to me?" She might have diminished in size, but her voice was the same commanding one of my youth.

"The doctor is pleased with you today, I hear."

"What does he know?" Her eyes flicked up and down the length of my torso. "You are larger than I remember."

I felt hot. Was my pregnancy showing? Surely, it could not be. No. It was, as ever, simply my mother pointing out what she saw as my feminine flaws.

"Of course," she continued, "you have always seemed large compared to dainty Ursula. She is looking well, is she not?"

"Yes. She is. Very well."

"What brings you to London?"

"You, of course. I was visiting Dorothy and—"

"I am not going to die, you know. Not now, anyway. So it was unnecessary for you to come. After ignoring us for so long."

"Mama, I wrote. I sent cards every birthday and Christmas. I have let you know my every movement, made sure you know my exact whereabouts at all times."

"I did not want letters, birthday greetings, cheery Christmas cards."

"What did you want?"

"You know what I want. I want you to stop embarrassing yourself. Us. Come home. Distinguish yourself as a Cust. Like Charles has."

I swallowed. "I am here now."

"Yes. But now I am tired. Come tomorrow. No. The following day. At the same time."

"Can we not—"

"No. We cannot. I will see you in two days."

She closed her eyes and I left.

There was no letter from Willie the following day or the next. I wrote again, repeating my news, keeping my tone light, hopeful. I dared not say all I felt in my letters in case someone else read them. I was convinced Willie would understand when he read them that I was willing to do whatever it would take to keep us together. But he did not respond.

I continued to visit my mother at her bidding. Even though it seemed her health was improving—and indeed, the doctor confirmed as much—she tolerated me for only a few minutes every second day. Our conversations were limited to the quality of her sleep, the incompetence of her doctor, and how boring she found life outside court. I did not see Ursula again, and after a few visits, Charles stopped escorting me to her room.

Between visits, I occupied myself with walks through the city's parks. I watched the horses in Hyde Park and longed to ride.

One afternoon, I found myself outside the rooms of Mr. Henry Gray, the veterinary surgeon Mr. Spreull had told me about years ago. I approached the large window that advertised the business as an "Infirmary for Horses, Dogs & C," the signwriter apparently having run out of space to complete the final word. It looked more like a drapery shop than a veterinary surgery, I thought as I tried to peer in.

"Can I help you, Miss?"

A slight man with a drooping mustache, a cane, and a glossy top hat stood in the entrance.

"Mr. Gray?"

"Yes," he said, peering up and down the street as if my horse or dog might have escaped. "Do you require my services?"

"No, thank you. I was simply curious about your business. Do you have stalls at the back?"

He frowned. "No, across the street. Why do you ask?"

"You treat dogs too, I see. Would you mind if I looked at your equipment?"

"I beg your pardon?"

"I would like to see if a city veterinary practice is much different from one in the country. I have been told you are the preferred veterinary surgeon among the dog fanciers of London. So if it is not inconvenient—"

"How do you know so much about me?"

"Mr. Andrew Spreull of Dundee, Scotland, and the *Veterinary Record*," I replied.

"Mr. Spreull? You're not... Are you, by any chance, Miss Custance?"

It pleased me that a veterinary surgeon in London had heard of me, even if only by the pseudonym I had used as a student. I smiled.

"Well," he said, looking up and down the street furtively, "I do not suppose it could hurt to show you around for a moment. I do not have much time, however, so...well, follow me."

The inside of Mr. Gray's practice was not that different from the rooms at Castlestrange. I spotted two or three implements I had not seen before, but none of them impressed me as that novel. He explained how his work with dogs was increasing but said his real interest lay with caged birds.

"I think that is going to be the next pet fashion that will demand veterinary expertise. Yes, indeed, exotic birds. Public fascination with them has grown over the years, fed, I believe, by the appetite for their feathers in fashion," he said. "Would you be interested in treating birds, Miss Custance?"

"I have not given it much thought, but I do not think so, Mr. Gray. I like birds in the wild. The idea of them in cages does not please me."

"Well, it might be an area that women, should you ever be permitted to practice, might manage. You should think about it."

What an impertinent idiot. I wanted to punch him and tell him about the work I did with horses and cattle in Roscommon. Instead, I laughed.

"No thank you, Mr. Gray. I do not think I will settle for birds, but I am sure you will do a fine job smoothing their feathers in London."

I returned to the hotel, hoping to find a letter from Willie. Still there was nothing.

A week went by. I wrote four letters, each one with rising despair. What if something had happened to him? Was he injured or ill? Did he need me? Unsure of what else to do, I wrote to Mrs. Doyle.

Two days later, I found my mother sitting up in bed.

"You look well, Mama," I said, taking my designated seat. "You slept soundly? Without pain?"

She gave a small, reluctant nod.

"Shall I open the curtains? The sun is almost shining today."

"No. Leave them be." She might have felt better, but her mood had not improved. "Ursula said you are staying at the Palace Hotel?"

"Yes."

"Is our house not to your liking?"

"Of course, it is, Mama. Charles and Ursula… It seemed too much to have me here while you are ill."

"That is absurd."

"Yes."

"You should move in here. It will do you and Ursula good to get to know each other. She can introduce you to her friends. Get you back in circulation."

"Thank you, Mama. I shall speak to her about it," I said.

"Good. Perhaps you might like to buy yourself a horse. I know you will miss riding."

It dawned on me then. My mother thought that I planned to stay in London indefinitely. She believed that I had given up my work and returned to the family, tail between my legs.

"Mama, I do not expect to be in London for, well, for very much longer."

She stared at me. "What are you doing here then?"

"I took a…a holiday, heard you were unwell, and came to visit you. And I am glad I did, Mama. It has made me happy to see you again."

"You are here on holiday? You have no intention of giving up that so-called profession of yours, which by the way, I am aware you practice illegally. Is that what you are saying?"

"Mama, I wish—"

She raised her voice and repeated the question, "Is that what you are saying?"

"Yes."

Her arm trembled as she pointed to the door. "Get out. Get out and do not return."

I walked back to the hotel. Strangely, I did not cry. Perhaps my body had adjusted to its new state, or maybe I had anticipated my mother's rejection ever since arriving in London. I felt lighter somehow. As if I was on the final leg of a journey and could at last leave some luggage behind. I would pack my bags and return to Ireland that day. There was nothing left for me to do in London.

The concierge looked up with a smile as I walked to the front desk.

"A letter for you today, Miss Cust," he said, handing me an envelope with my key.

My heart skipped a beat and I took them from him.

"Thank you," I said, holding up the envelope to examine it.

It was postmarked Athleague, but the handwriting was not familiar. I felt a tug of disappointment and, impatient to read it, took a nearby seat and tore the envelope open.

Dear Miss Cust,

Indeed, we were surprised to hear of your sudden departure from Athleague. I am pleased to read of your mother's improved health. I hope that it hastens your return.

Thank you for remembering my preference for gloves from Peter Robinson's of London. I do not believe there are finer gloves to be found anywhere else and would be indebted to you if you would bring me a dove-gray, elbow-length pair.

Indeed, it seems Mr. Byrne is extremely busy in your absence. It has, however, not prevented him from stopping by several times during the past week. I do believe he has finally noticed that Cathleen is no longer a sulky girl.

Yours faithfully and with gratitude,
Mrs. Margaret Doyle

CHAPTER 26

1904
Northumberland, England

WITH MY LONGING TO RETURN TO IRELAND EXTINGUISHED, I CAUGHT THE
train to Northumberland and returned to Newton Hall, where I discovered
the Widdringtons were away for a few days. That meant I could not immediately seek Lady Widdrington's advice about the pregnancy. Neither could I
ride with Major Fitz. I could wait for the major's return, but knowing that I
would not be able to ride in my condition for much longer, I did not want to
delay it. I sent word to the stables, asking Watts to saddle one of the major's
horses for me. He arrived with Hector, the young hunter that he had trained
that summer.

"A youngster?" I said. "I am a little out of practice, Watts. Do you think
he is the best choice?"

The groom chuckled. He thought I was joking. "He is a wonderful ride,
Miss Cust. Will do anything you ask. Let me know when you return if there
is anything I have missed and should work on before the new season."

"What is he?" I asked, walking around the horse, who was much heavier
than the horses Major Fitz typically used for hunting.

"We are not sure. He has a bit of draft in him, I believe. He arrived at

Newton Hall out of the blue as a one-year-old. We have no idea where he came from, and no one claimed him, despite us putting out word."

Hector was a solid black bay with dark eyes and a faint star above his eyeline. He had two peculiar light brown patches on either side of his upper lip, which made it seem that the bit had rubbed the color off in that area. I placed a hand on his nose. Perhaps we were kindred spirits. Like me, Hector had nowhere else to go but Newton Hall.

Watts had not exaggerated. The horse was a perfect combination of brave and calm. I took him on a rough country route to the beach. He was agile and fleet footed as he scrambled over banks, leapt over ditches, and popped over hedges and logs. Hector moved cleverly and stood quietly while I opened gates that, had I not been pregnant, I would have asked him to jump.

"Sorry, boy," I said. "I know it is boring, but I have to be cautious."

What was remarkable about the horse was how, despite being so young, he paid careful attention to where he was going, as if anticipating what lay ahead and what I might ask of him. When we reached the beach and I gave him his head, he galloped across the sand like a racehorse. It was as if Hector knew how badly I needed to feel the wind in my hair and how I hoped it might blast thoughts of Willie from my mind and shake the pieces of my heart back together.

"I do not think I have ever ridden a more intelligent horse," I said as Watts met me at the stables afterward. "It seemed that he anticipated my every command."

"That's his magic, I believe," Watts said, smiling broadly. "He is going to be the best hunter this estate has ever seen. I hope you will ride him regularly while you are here, Miss Cust. He will benefit from it."

"Almost as much as I will," I replied, feeling happier than I had for weeks. "I shall ride until—well, every day I can. Thank you."

I took the long route back to the house. It was early autumn, and the leaves were beginning to turn. The garden was ablaze with budding dahlias and a few beds of late chrysanthemums, which seemed to revel in the cooling conditions. The season and flowers reminded me of Dorothy and Edward's wedding, when Newton Hall was abuzz with activity and excitement. It was a pity I had not appreciated how easy life was back then.

The exhilaration of the ride waned, and my restlessness resumed. I felt anxious that I was hoping for too much from Lady Widdrington. What would she suggest that I did not know myself? I would have to go away to give birth. The child would be raised by someone else. He or she would never know Willie or me. There was nothing else to do.

What about my work? It would be difficult to find another veterinary practice to take me on without certification from the Royal College. Perhaps I could establish a country practice in another remote part of the world. Work quietly and re-establish myself as a skilled professional by simply doing what I was trained to do. There was no other way. I wandered toward the house, dreading another night with only my misery for company.

"Are you ever going to look up?" came a voice.

It was Bertie. He was sitting on the stairs to the front door. I did not know that he was in England, let alone at Newton Hall.

"Good gracious, Aleen! Say something."

"What are you doing here?"

He stood, smiling. "This is my home. I am Bertie Widdrington. Major and Lady Widdrington are my parents."

"But—"

"Soldiers take leave, even in India."

"But no one said anything. I was with Dorothy just a few weeks ago. She did not—"

"I know. I came from there yesterday."

His smile did not change, but there was something about the expression on his face that gave away the fact that he knew. Dorothy had told him. I caught my breath.

"Come," he said. "I need to stretch my legs before lunch. Will you walk with me?"

Bertie was a skilled conversationalist. Unlike the stilted exchange I had endured with Charles in the drawing room in Kensington a fortnight earlier, Dorothy's brother and I communicated easily. With Coal, chubby as Labradors are inclined to become with age, trotting ahead of us down the lane, Bertie spoke about India and how he loved living in the warm, colorful country. He enjoyed the spicy food, the lively people, and the pace of living there.

"I think it is the contrast between the country's spirit and my life of a soldier that makes it so fulfilling," he said. "Everything is organized and disciplined in the army, but India, with her vast, disheveled jungles and cities, tempestuous weather, and animated people, is the opposite. I live in perfect balance. I love the place."

We had walked for some miles before I realized I had not thought of Willie or the baby since I had looked up and found Bertie on the stairs.

"If it were not for my family, I do not believe I would ever return to England," he said as we made our way back toward the house. "Of course, I would have to leave the army since I would not have the freedom to decide where I wanted to settle, but if that were an option, I would pursue it."

"Really? What would you do, Bertie?"

He chuckled. "You are right. I am a soldier. I have no idea what else I could do. I am certainly not ready to settle here."

"That is not what I meant. What might your other options be in India?"

He stepped in front of me. There was an urgency to his voice. "Come with me. Perhaps you can help me find something."

"What?"

"Come to India. You will love it. It is unrestrained, like you," he said, his tone light, but his eyes serious.

I laughed. "Do not be silly, Bertie. I cannot go to India. You are a soldier, and I have no reason to be there."

"You would…if you were my wife."

I felt my jaw drop, but I said nothing.

"Wait," he said. "That is not how I meant to say…to propose."

He bent his leg and knelt in the dusty track.

"Bertie—"

"Aleen Cust, I have loved you since I met you. My earliest regret is that your father died before I knew him so I could not ask him for your hand. I am asking you for it now. Will you marry me?"

"Bertie, you do not… This is not what you want. I know—"

He smiled, though his eyes reflected concern. "Am I doing something wrong? Is it not clear that this is *exactly* what I want? To marry you and take you to India."

"Dorothy told you, did she not?"

"It does not make any difference."

"Please stand up," I said.

"Not without—"

"Please, Bertie."

He slowly rose to his feet and took my hands in his. "Will you go back to him?" he asked.

"No. I cannot."

"Then, am I so unappealing a man that you cannot imagine a life with me?"

I looked at him. Bertie's kindness and loyalty never faltered. He was, next to his father, the most uncomplicated and sincere man I knew. Bertie would never let me down. He deserved love.

"You are not unappealing at all," I said. "I am sure Enid would agree."

"I have not seen Enid for…for some time."

"That is beside the point. You are kind and caring. I am more grateful for that today than I have ever been, but you should not ask me to marry you out of pity."

"Pity? Nobody pities you. Did you not hear what I said earlier? I have loved you ever since I saw you standing in the gazebo with Dorothy twenty-six years ago. I love you, and I want to be your husband."

"Does Dorothy know that you planned this?"

"Of course. She has known that I would ask for years."

"Really? But now? Did she know that you would ask now?"

He nodded.

"What about the child?"

"Raised as ours. Of course. Can you not see, Aleen? This is the perfect solution for all of us."

"Are you serious? Really? Have you thought about this carefully?"

He nodded and sank to his knee again.

"Will you marry me, Miss Aleen Cust?"

It was implausible, but I said yes.

I lay awake for many hours that night. Major and Lady Widdrington were due home the next day. Bertie and I had agreed that he would speak to them alone first. We should not, he said, mention my pregnancy. It would be better for everyone if only he, Dorothy, and I knew the truth about the paternity. I wished it was not necessary to expect them to keep my secret, but I agreed that it was in everyone's best interest and easier for all not to disclose the truth.

Praying was not something I had done a great deal of in recent years, but that night, I prayed. I asked God to forgive me my negligence and my sins, to help make me a wife worthy of Bertie, and to grant us a child who resembled me and not Willie. I prayed that the Lord would give me the strength to forget the Irishman and learn to love Bertie the way I had loved Willie.

In retrospect, I should have anticipated Lady Widdrington's objections to the news of our engagement. She always saw things as they were.

"I wish I could be overjoyed by this news, Aleen, but I am not," she said when she called me to the drawing room after Bertie had spoken to his parents. "It is not that I do not love you. Good gracious, no. You know that. You are already a daughter to me, but Aleen, you? A soldier's wife in India? You would give up working as a veterinary surgeon for that after all you have been through?"

I looked at the carpet and said nothing.

"Major Fitz is overjoyed, as I am sure he will tell you himself in a few minutes, but I am too much of a realist not to ask you to reconsider."

"Reconsider?"

"To reconsider your haste. Bertie says you will marry as soon as possible so that you can join him in India once arrangements have been made. Why not wait until he is re-assigned or finds something else to do. Somewhere else to live. Wait until he comes back to Newton Hall."

"We do not want to wait."

"So he says. But Aleen, look at me. Can you imagine yourself an army wife in Delhi? Can you imagine drinking tea all day and listening to the other soldiers' wives complaining about the heat? You have a career. You work. Can you see yourself giving it all up? What would you do all day?"

It occurred to me to say that I would raise a child, but I thought better of it.

"Perhaps I could work with the army's horses?"

She stared at me. We were silent for a moment.

"When you came here from Ireland, before you went to Dorothy in Hampshire, you were upset. What happened? Does this sudden decision— yes, I know Bertie insists he has loved you since you were children, and I believe that—but does it have something to do with why you returned so suddenly? What happened in Ireland? Why did you leave?"

"My working relationship with Mr. Byrne became intolerable. We could not agree on matters…on things pertaining to the treatment of our clients' animals or the running of the business. I could not stay."

"But Dorothy said it was going so well just a month or so ago. When she visited."

"Things changed."

"I see," she said, not trying to disguise the doubt in her voice. "Well, let us go and see Fitz then." She ushered me out the door.

"Ah, ladies," Major Fitz said as we entered his study.

Lady Widdrington was right; Major Fitz was pleased about the engagement. For a moment, I thought he might hug me, but he settled for a gentle squeeze of the elbow.

"This is excellent news, Aleen. Excellent."

"Thank you, Major Fitz," I said, catching his wife's anxious glance.

"You have some urgent organizing to do. Bertie says you will marry before he returns so that he can go back to Delhi and apply for married quarters. Will you stay here with us until then?"

"If that is in order, yes, thank you," I said, feeling a little teary at his enthusiasm. "I, well, I have not yet told my family, so I had better write some letters."

"How is your mother?" asked Lady Widdrington. "Dorothy said she was unwell and that you left Hampshire to visit her."

"Yes, I did. She was much better when I left."

"How did she receive you? After all this time? Was it a good visit?" she asked.

"Well, we spoke. She will be pleased, I think, with the news of Bertie and me. And that I will go to India as an army officer's wife."

"I am sure she will be," said Lady Widdrington quietly.

"Would you like to join me for a ride this morning, before you begin writing your letters?" asked the major. "Watts told me you were pleased with Hector. You might take him out again."

"I would like that. Give me a moment to change into my habit," I said, delighted by the idea.

Bertie met me at the bottom of stairs on my way to meet the major.

"You are going riding?" he asked, taking in my outfit.

"Yes. With your father. Will you join us?"

"No, thank you. I have some things to attend to. Do you..." he glanced around. "Aleen, should you ride? I mean, is it not—"

"No. It is not. Not at this stage and not if I am careful."

"Careful? Of course, you will be careful. Nobody goes out hoping to fall off a horse, not even fearless riders like you, but it is risky nonetheless."

"There is nothing to worry about," I said, patting his arm as I brushed past him and hurried to catch up to Major Fitz.

Once mounted, the major and I took advantage of the cool weather and followed the long, gentle route along the river. Hector was as confident and serene with another horse as he had been the day before on his own. The major agreed that given the horse's youth and inexperience, we should avoid taking him over major obstacles and not gallop too much. Another year of calm outings would, we concurred, reinforce his self-assurance before he would be ready to hunt.

As we chatted amicably about impersonal matters like horses, our surroundings, the weather, and what the Northumberland hunting season had been like, I marveled at how easy life seemed once more. It would have been foolish to think that Major Fitz was not curious about my unexpected and clearly unhappy return to England followed by the unforeseen announcement that Bertie and I were to be married. He and Professor Williams were the two people who had best understood my unappeasable desire to become a veterinary surgeon. They had risked their reputations to help me realize my dream. The notion of me giving it up to be an army wife in India must have been perplexing for the major. If anyone deserved to interrogate me, it was him, but he did not, and I was grateful for it. I did not want to think about the future. Whenever my mind wandered ahead, I repeated silently to myself, "Everything will work out. Everything will work out."

We watered the horses in the village and turned for home. As we trotted up a tree-lined lane, I admired the soft, green hills that framed the horizon. I wondered what it would be like to ride in India. It would almost certainly be too hot to be out in the middle of the day as we were now. Hector flicked his ears and arched his neck. He had seen the head of a cow poking out behind a tree. We pulled up and approached slowly to find a farmer standing by the animal, who had wedged her head between the wooden slats of the gate and was firmly trapped.

"You need some help, I think," said the major.

"Good morning, sir, my lady," he said, removing his cap. "Aye, she's stuck solid."

We dismounted, and I walked to the cow.

"Careful miss," he said. "She is very agitated."

I could see that. The cow was rolling her eyes, and the top of her neck was bleeding where she had scraped it raw against the wood.

"How long has she been like this?" I asked.

The farmer looked at Major Fitz as he spoke. "I do not know. I found her twenty minutes ago or so. I have tried twisting her head and pushing her back, but she simply thrashes around, doing more damage."

"Miss Cust is a veterinary surgeon," said the major.

The man blinked and looked at me.

I ran my hand along the top of the gate, thinking that the job was more suited to a carpenter than a veterinary surgeon.

"We should remove the rail," I said. "Repairing the gate will be much less trouble than having to deal with an injured cow. Do you have a saw?"

"Aye. At the house."

The cow bellowed and threw her head back and forth. "Go and fetch it. We will try to restrain her in the interim."

The farmer put his cap back on and ran across the field. I asked the major to remove the stirrup leathers from our saddles and created a makeshift halter, which I strapped around the cow's head. The harness meant I could restrain her, and although she continued breathing heavily, the animal was standing still by the time the farmer returned with the saw and began severing the rail. The wood was dense and wide, making slicing through it slow and difficult. I held on to the straps, keeping the cow still. The major took over whenever the farmer tired. Finally, as I saw that the blade was almost through the wood, I leaned forward to examine the injury to the cow's neck more closely. A large section of her skin was wounded, but it had stopped bleeding.

"You will need to keep an eye on that. Clean it with salt water as regularly as you can so that it does not get infected," I said.

The farmer stopped sawing and moved his head closer to mine to look at the raw spot. "Thank you, miss. I will. Do you—"

At that moment, with the weight of the farmer's arm on it, the rail snapped, falling onto the cow, who jerked and pulled the leather straps from my hand. She thrashed her head left and right, walloping my abdomen, which sent me flying backward onto the ground. I lay there, winded and stunned, as the cow, free of the gate, shook off the leather straps and thundered toward the rest of the herd with a low bellow of victory.

"Are you all right?" said the major, leaning over me. "Good gracious, that was a blow."

"Miss! I'm sorry! I did not realize it was already through!"

I took a deep breath and sat up. "That was a surprise. I will be fine. I just need a moment."

My vision was blurry. I leaned forward and brought my head to my knees. I *was* fine. Once I had recovered from the shock, life could go on.

"Should I ride to the village? Call the doctor?" said the farmer to Major Fitz.

"Give me a moment," I repeated. "I will be fine."

The men were quiet. I sat up. The earth had stopped spinning.

"Shall we reassemble our stirrups?" I asked.

Major Fitz and the farmer looked at one another and went to gather the leather straps the cow had tossed off. I stayed seated while they threaded the stirrups and put them back on the saddles.

"Can you stand?" said the major, as the farmer led Hector to us.

"Of course," I said, holding my hand out to him. He took it, and as he pulled me to my feet, I felt a searing pain shoot through my abdomen. My knees gave way.

I could not remember the journey to the village, being seen by the doctor there, or the trip back to Newton Hall. Later, I learned the farmer and Major Fitz had arranged a carriage and somehow gotten Hector home. I awoke that evening in my bed to find Pattison sitting at the window, sewing. She came to me.

"How are you feeling?"

My mouth was dry and my head thick, but it was the dull ache in my belly that reminded me what had happened. It hurt to breathe. I wondered if the cow had broken one or more of my ribs.

"How did I get here?" I asked.

She explained and left to call Lady Widdrington. Bertie appeared instead, his eyes wide with worry and his face drawn.

"I am sorry," I said, trying to smile as I recalled his concern about me riding in my condition. "But the horse is blameless. Hector had nothing to do with the accident. The cow—"

He took my hand. "I know. My God, you scared me, Aleen."

"I am all right," I said, patting his hand. My abdomen throbbed and there was a burning sensation around my lower back. "I am all right, am I not?"

"I do not know. I did not see the doctor. My father reported that Dr. Bain examined you in the village, declared nothing broken, and said there are no obvious signs of bleeding. But if… Well, they do not know that you—"

I put my fingers on his lips. "I know."

"Are you in pain?"

"It is probably just bruising. That was an incredibly hard-headed cow with a strong neck."

Bertie nodded.

It was more than bruising. I stayed in bed for two days, and on the second night, when I felt the warm, stickiness of blood between my legs, I realized that the force of the cow's head and possibly also the way I smacked onto the ground afterward had caused a miscarriage. I wrapped my arms around my stomach and wept. For the baby. For Willie. For me. And for what the loss would mean for Bertie.

The next morning, I pointed to the bundle of soiled sheets and apologized to Pattison for not anticipating the arrival of my menses. I was not, I said, feeling better and would stay in bed a little longer. Dr. Bain was summoned. He looked me over and asked several questions. I did not tell him about the baby. He diagnosed shock and trauma and prescribed more rest. Finally, I asked Pattison to call Bertie. I saw, as he walked into the room, stooped and pale, that he had guessed what had happened. He sat on the edge of the bed but did not touch me. I could not meet his eyes, and we sat without saying anything for several minutes.

"Will you be okay?" he asked eventually.

I nodded, unable to talk.

"You know that this changes nothing for me, don't you?"

I swallowed.

"You do not want to marry me, do you?" he said.

I felt the tears spill onto my cheeks. "Bertie—"

"No. I do not want to hear you say it. I cannot bear it."

I took his hand. "You deserve better."

He shook his head. "Please don't, Aleen," he said, pulling his hand from mine.

"You have to listen to me, Bertie. This is not how a relationship should begin. It is not a reason to get married. You—"

"I love you. That is the only reason I need."

I took his hand again and held it this time. "I believe you, and I wish it were that simple, but Bertie, your mother is right. I cannot live the life of an army wife in India. It would drive me mad. I would drive you mad."

"We will find something else. Live somewhere else."

"It is not only that. I do not know how much Dorothy told you about my life in Ireland, but I was happy there. I want to go back."

"But he—"

"I know, but there is more to it than that."

"You want to go back to work there?"

"Yes."

"Will you go back to him? Now that…"

I shook my head but could not look him in the eye.

CHAPTER 27

❧

1904
Athleague, Ireland

I HAD BEEN GONE FROM CASTLESTRANGE FOR LITTLE MORE THAN SIX WEEKS, but as the carriage crossed the River Suck and the familiar fields flashed by, it seemed that a lifetime had passed. So much had happened during that time. So much had changed. So much had been lost. I was a different woman.

Bertie had left Newton Hall for India shortly after we told his parents that we had reconsidered and decided that we would not marry after all. Lady Widdrington was right, I'd said; I would not make a good army wife. I needed to work. I wanted to work.

"Does that not simply require delaying rather than calling it off?" Major Fitz had asked, his eyes darting from Bertie to me. "Perhaps Bertie will relocate to somewhere that will allow you to work. Why do you not remain engaged?"

Bertie had looked at me as he spoke. "We thought it better to call it off entirely because…because there are too many unknowns, Father," he'd said. "We will know if…when the time is right."

I'd rested my hand on his forearm. Lady Widdrington had nodded, holding my gaze. I sensed that she recognized her son's anguish. She might not have been able to picture me an army wife, but she had not meant for me to hurt her son by accepting as much. I wondered whether my place in her heart was secure. It saddened me, and I hoped that I would one day find a way of winning back her trust.

Before he stepped into the carriage to leave, Bertie had leaned toward me and whispered in my ear. "Be strong, Aleen. Do not go down a path too narrow that you cannot turn back."

Now, as the naked trees and low clouds at Castlestrange confirmed that my absence had not slowed time, the carriage drew up at the gate lodge. Tangled rose vines, bare and thorny, seemed to bear witness to my treachery. I had written to Bridget, telling her she should prepare for my return. I did not want to think about how Willie might receive me but had, of course, prepared my reasons for returning.

I would say I had come to fetch Nasser. I would also offer to buy Spencer from him. "No," I would say, "do not worry that I might linger where I'm not wanted or where I might embarrass anyone." I would not add that I could not guarantee my good mood would prevail should I encounter Cathleen Doyle.

I would tell him it was my intention, since I had established a reputation as a skilled veterinary surgeon in Athleague, to set up my own practice elsewhere in Roscommon. If the RCVS had not bothered me in the years I'd worked in Ireland with him, why would they complain if I worked somewhere else in the county? And why should the animals of Ireland and their owners not benefit from my expertise simply because he and I could not work together? Yes, of course, our paths might cross at hunts and race meetings, but I was a professional and, as he had regularly pointed out over the years, a noble lady. I would be gracious. What about him? Could he be civil? Indeed, I had worked out everything I would say to him.

Where Spencer came from as I walked to the door, I did not know. I saw a flash of red as he threw himself at me with the same vigor the first time we met. This time, though, my footing held. I knelt on the path and put my arms around him. Oh God, grant me the forgiveness of a dog, I thought as his torso wiggled in my arms and he plunged his cold nose into my neck.

"I have missed you too, you beautiful brute," I said, running my hands up and down his spine.

"So you are back."

I looked up to see Willie in the doorway, in his vest and shirt sleeves as if he had hurried from the surgery or infirmary. How was it possible that I had forgotten the intensity of his eyes and the way he stood, solid on the earth, like a bull contemplating charging even when there was no sign of conflict ahead?

I got to my feet and pulled myself to my full height. "Hello, Willie."

He did not smile. Instead, I saw his jaw twitch.

"I thought Bridget would be—"

"I sent her home when she was done," he said.

It was worse than I imagined. He was not even going to let me into the lodge. I turned to see the carriage disappear out of the gate. What had I done? Why had I come?

I spoke quickly. "I came to sort out my things. To fetch Nasser."

"I see. You asked the servants to prepare the lodge for a fleeting visit?"

"I was not sure how long it might take."

"Of course."

"Can I come...go inside?"

He stepped aside and I walked in. Nothing had changed. A fire crackled in the hearth, and the settee that I had fallen asleep on the night Willie came through the snow to me was in the same position it had always been. Someone had picked some white yarrow and arranged it in a posy on the table. As I looked around, Spencer tapped my hand with his nose.

"I would like to take Spencer with me too," I said, not looking at Willie. "I will pay whatever you ask."

"No."

I turned. "No? But—"

"Spencer is not for sale. You cannot have everything your way, Aleen."

"Why would you be so cruel? He attached himself to me the moment we met. You cannot argue with that. What pleasure could it bring you to keep us apart?"

I glared at him. He was thinner than I recalled, and as he ran a hand through his curls, he seemed weary. Perhaps that was what happened when a hardworking, forty-year-old veterinary surgeon fell in love with an eighteen-year-old.

"I did not say he could not go with you. I said he was not for sale. Not everything or everyone has a price."

"Oh...well then, thank you."

There was an awkward silence. The fire hissed and Spencer groaned as he stretched out at my feet. Willie and I spoke simultaneously.

"How long do you think you will stay?"

"How have things been at the practice?"

Another uneasy pause.

"I do not know," I said.

"It has been enormously busy. Gaffney's brother has joined him on the farm, and they have almost doubled the size of their herd. Unfortunately, they bought cows from all over the county, and they are not all as healthy as they should be. I had to pass some of my council responsibilities on to other members."

"I am sorry," I said.

"Are you?"

I stepped over Spencer to get closer to the fire and turned to warm my back. It was not a particularly cold day, but I imagined the warmth might fortify me, give me the strength to resist begging him to give up Cathleen Doyle and forgive me for not staying and fighting for us.

"What are you sorry for, Aleen?"

"For..." I opened my arms. "For this, for—"

His jaw twitched again. "You cannot ask me for forgiveness for...for that. That is between you and God."

"What?"

"Pfft. Of course, *your* God probably condones it."

"What are you talking about?"

He narrowed his eyes and glanced at my stomach.

"No. God no, Willie. I did not harm the baby. That is not what happened. How could you think that?"

"Think? It is what you said you would do. Why you went to England."

"No!"

"You did not?"

"No. That was—"

"But what happened? You are not still—"

"No. I am not. There was an incident…with a cow."

He took a step toward me. "A cow?"

"I…yes. She was caught in a gate. I was helping free her. She swung her head. Hit me."

"Hit you?"

"Yes. Hard. I fell, miscarried."

He placed both hands on his head and stared at me, trying to make sense of what I had told him. I closed my eyes, trying to recall my exact words when we argued before I left. What had I said? "I shall return to England and do what has to be done." He thought I meant I would terminate the pregnancy, but I had told him that that was not what I would do. Had he not listened? Heard me?

"You decided against it then?" he asked.

"No. It was never what I—"

"When you left you said you would 'do what you had to do.' Those were your exact words."

"No. Yes. But I never meant I would harm the baby. I would never—"

Willie collapsed onto the settee as if his legs would no longer support him and put his head in his hands. I wanted to console him. To sit next to him and take him in my arms, but I did not.

"Why did we not talk more that day? Why did you run away without explaining what you meant?" he asked at last.

"I *told* you that was not what I meant. You did not listen. I came back to the surgery to talk to you later, but you were gone. I wrote to you from London, but you did not reply."

He shook his head. "I was mad. I confessed to Father O'Flanagan. Explained what had happened."

"Father O'Flanagan? Why would you—"

"And I threw your letters in the fire without opening them."

And, I thought, found comfort with Cathleen Doyle, though I said

nothing. What was there to say? It did not matter that I was no longer pregnant to throw Athleague into a frenzy of gossip. As if Father O'Flanagan's
initial horror that I, a woman, would castrate animals had not been mountain enough to scale, the priest now had proof of my immorality. I might
have to find work well beyond the borders of Roscommon.

"What did Father O'Flanagan say when you confessed?"

"Father O'Flanagan?" he repeated dully.

"Yes. The man who knows our sins."

"I did not name you."

I wondered what Willie might have confessed to. Did it matter though?
Whatever it was, it seemed probable that the priest would blame me—the
English Protestant castrator of horses, cattle, and sheep—for leading his
faithful Catholic servant to sin. It seemed to me that Willie had not only cast
me aside because I was an unsuitable woman and that Cathleen Doyle would
fill a place in his life that I would not, but also betrayed me to the priest, the
church. Perhaps it was indicative of my tenuous relationship with God, but
I could not imagine what would make a man cast aside love that existed as
flesh and bone in favor of heavenly obedience. The only reason could be that
the love Willie once professed to feel for me was not true. I thought about
Bertie and the sacrifices he was willing to make for me. Part of me wanted
to tell Willie about him and our fleeting engagement. Another part felt that
none of it mattered.

"I would like to see Nasser before nightfall," I said, pulling my shawl
over my shoulders and walking to the door. Spencer scrambled to his feet
and followed.

"Of course. I will accompany you," he said.

"I would rather go alone."

I did not expect Willie to wait for me at the lodge while I went to the stables
to see Nasser, but there he was, in the same place on the settee when I came
back at nightfall. Spencer ran to him and put his chin on his knees.

"You found him well? Nasser?"

"He is rounder," I said. "Was he not exercised?"

"Not as much as he is accustomed." Willie stood. "Fiona left a meal for you in the kitchen. She and Bridget will be back tomorrow. Will you…do you plan to leave soon?"

"As soon as I have found somewhere else to live and work."

"If you do not know where you are going to go, why do you not stay? Continue working here, I mean."

I felt my anger flare like a fanned flame.

"Continue working here? With Father O'Flanagan preparing to burn me at the stake? Ha!"

"That is not how it is."

"Is that so? Will he pray for my forgiveness and let me continue as if nothing happened? Even if he did, how could I work with you? Knowing how little you think of me."

"I was unreasonable, in shock."

Still, he did not apologize.

"Does that explain Cathleen Doyle too?"

"What?"

"I know about you and Cathleen Doyle."

"What are you talking about?"

"You have been courting her."

"What gives you the idea that Cathleen and I—"

"I wrote to her mother, about some gloves she wanted from London. Mrs. Doyle replied and said…indicated that you and Cathleen—"

"I had a few meals with Mrs. Doyle, and Cathleen was there. I have been friends with the family ever since I arrived in Athleague. Arthur Doyle was my first client. He introduced me to the parish and encouraged locals who had never given their animals anything more than a touch of rosehip to call me. Cathleen Doyle's late father helped establish the practice here. I am beholden to the family for that but no more."

"You and Cathleen—"

"No. Never. Not then and not now. She is but a girl. Is that what this is about? Is that why you will not stay?"

If it had been that simple, I would have thrown myself into his arms, but even if what I—and Mrs. Doyle and probably Cathleen—believed was not true, it did not change the fact that Willie and I could not be together. Willie would not put me ahead of his faith or country. That he did not realize *that* made the idea of me staying at Castlestrange even more absurd. Even so, I could not leave.

"I will stay until I find somewhere else to go," I said.

CHAPTER 28

_1904_
Athleague, Ireland

A FEW MONTHS LATER, I FOUND ANOTHER PLACE TO LIVE, AND IN FACT, I bought it. Fort Lyster was built in 1837, and while nowhere near as grand as Castlestrange, it was large enough for Spencer, Nasser, Bridget, Fiona, and me to settle in to immediately. Fiona's husband, Ronan, moved into the groundkeeper's cottage with her and took on the role of groundsman. I appointed his nephew Kevin as the groom to Nasser and Molly, the gentle, bay mare I bought from a client near Roscommon town to keep the Arabian company and to pull my gig. I also added two dairy cows and a pair of goats.

Despite our altered living arrangements, I quickly fell back into a working routine at Athleague. Willie had not exaggerated about how busy the practice had become in my absence. Between moving to Fort Lyster and visiting clients, I thought of little but work and my new home. Even when, on a visit to the village a few weeks after my return to attend to a horse at the mill, I had come across Father O'Flanagan talking to Mrs. Sheehan in the street, I was so preoccupied I had forgotten that it might have been wise to hide my face from the priest.

"Good afternoon, Father, Mrs. Sheehan," I said, when I saw them looking at me.

Mrs. Sheehan bobbed her head. The priest raised a hand and, to my surprise, smiled.

"Miss Cust," he said, "good day. It has been a while since I saw you. It is good to have you home. I was glad to hear that, by God's grace, your mother has recovered."

The only person in Athleague who knew that I had visited my mother was Mrs. Doyle. She must have told the priest. Was it possible, then, that Father O'Flanagan believed the reason I left the village was to visit my ill mother and that it had nothing to do with Willie's confession? Well, in that case, thank goodness for gossip, I thought, smiling to myself as Nasser broke into a canter on the way back to the surgery. I never mentioned the exchange to Willie.

To try to keep Spencer from paying Willie random visits at Castlestrange—which, just a few miles away from my new home, was well within the limits of his daily exercise—I also bought a pretty pair of Springer Spaniels called Gunner and Lacey. They were not yet four months old when, one morning, the Setter brought them to visit us in the surgery.

Willie greeted the trio in the yard, unaware that I was within earshot in a nearby stable.

"New friends then, Spencer? Hello, you two. Aye, lad, you would rather everyone lived here too, would you not? Well, it could be worse," he said.

Indeed, while I no longer lived at the estate, I continued to work with Willie. I told myself that it was simply because there was never time for me to find other work or establish another practice. The truth, though, was that I did not want to work elsewhere. That is not to say that matters between Willie and me went back to the way they had been.

Where we once conversed easily and laughed often at work, we were now guarded and worked quietly, limiting our conversation to professional matters. There were no spontaneous races across the fields when we rode to see clients together, and we never swam again. We took lunch separately and kept strict work hours. Months became years and the practice flourished as we worked side by side, as efficient as a steamer and as polite as a pair of courtiers within earshot of the throne.

One day, I returned to our rooms from a call to find Willie standing at the window, his back to the door, a folded newspaper in his hands.

"We will need to change the dressing on Gaffney's bull in two days' time," I said, sitting down to make a note on the schedule.

He turned and handed me the newspaper. "Page two," he said, his jaw twitching.

Bad news, I could see, but just how bad, I could not even begin to imagine. I unfolded the paper, turned the page, and ran my eyes over it.

The headline read, *"The Foreign Minister's Bereavement."*

An accident which happened to Lady Grey, wife of Sir Edward Grey, Minister for Foreign Affairs, last Thursday afternoon, terminated fatally. Lady Grey was flung out of a trap while driving and was carried unconscious into the School House at Ellingham, Northumberland, situated in the valley between Preston Main and the village.

Lady Grey never recovered consciousness, the middle fosse of her skull being fractured, together with a severe contusion of the brain substance, and her death occurred at twenty-five minutes past three the next day, in the presence of Sir Edward Grey, Miss Herbert, the Rev. W.A. Mc Gonigle, and Dr. Waterson, her medical attendant.

Sir Edward Grey, who was devotedly attached to his wife, never left her bedside after his arrival from London late at night on the day of the accident, and his grief over her unfortunate and terrible death is extremely deep and painful. The very sad event has cast a great gloom not only over the people of North Northumberland, to whom she was well known and greatly endeared, but also in many circles throughout the kingdom.

The Deceased Lady Frances Dorothy Grey, who was forty-one years of age, was the eldest daughter of Major Shallcross Fitzherbert Widdrington, of Newton Hall, and Cecilia his wife, eldest daughter of Edward John Gregge Hopwood, Lancaster. Lady Grey was devotedly attached to her husband, and whenever she could, was always by his side, in his angling excursions and in pastimes in which he indulged. Her Ladyship leaves no children.

Willie knelt at my feet and took me in his arms. I laid my head on his shoulder. I did not know how long I sobbed, but he held me until I could cry no longer.

"I sent word to Bridget to pack and go with you," he said, brushing the sodden strands of hair from my face. "Your carriage is on the way. I will ride Nasser back to Fort Lyster."

It was on the way back from Dorothy's funeral that I made the decision. I would love Willie no matter the consequences. I would love him even if he could not return my love. The death of my dearest friend and the grief that it unleashed in Edward, Major Fitz, Lady Widdrington, Bertie, me, and others who filled the pews showed me how transient life was. It was pointless, I realized, to allow days, weeks, and months to go by, passively hoping that something magical would happen to make my life whole again. That was not the way things worked. After all, it was only because of my own stubborn determination that I had become a veterinary surgeon. It would never have happened if I had simply waited for something or someone to remove the obstacles from my path. Distracted by loving Willie and its consequences, I had forgotten that I held the reins to my life. Dorothy's death was a heart-breaking reminder that I needed to take them back.

"Will you walk to the river with me before dinner?" I asked as Willie and I finished up in the surgery the day after I returned from the funeral.

"The river? Yes. It will be good for the dogs. They have been restless this week without an outing."

Spencer—visiting without the Spaniels this time—led the pack out of the gates and across the field toward the river. We laughed as he tucked his tail between his back legs and the Terriers chased him through the grass.

"I have never known so playful a dog," I said.

"Are you thinking of going back?" asked Willie.

"To England? Northumberland? No. Gosh. I have just settled at Fort Lyster. Why do you ask?"

"You did not bring the Pomeranians back with you as I thought you might."

"Edward asked me to leave them with him. He is, it seems, as devoted to Nugget and Honey as Dorothy was. It would be unkind to all of them to bring them here. They are Edward's now."

Willie nodded. "I see, but that is not all that makes me wonder. You barely said a word all day and then you suggested a walk. I am anticipating an important announcement. I imagine Dorothy's death has made you want to be closer to your family."

"My family?"

"I mean the Widdringtons, of course."

"No. I do not want to go back, but there is something that involves them that I want to tell you."

"All right."

We walked quietly for a moment as I chose my words.

"When I was pregnant and you did not respond to my letters, I left London and went to Newton Hall in search of answers. I thought that Lady Widdrington would tell me what to do, where to have the baby, and who might take care of him or her. However, she and Major Fitz were not there when I arrived. To my surprise, Bertie appeared. He was on leave from India and had been to see Dorothy before coming north. She told him about me."

We stopped and he turned to face me. "Go on."

"Bertie proposed and I accepted."

"Marriage?"

I nodded.

"But—"

"We told his parents when they returned. Major Fitz was pleased, but Lady Widdrington was doubtful. I was due to write to my family and tell them the news but agreed to go riding with the major first. That is when we stopped to help the farmer with his cow. The rest you know."

"You are engaged? To Bertie Widdrington? But why—"

"No. No. We called it off."

Willie looked toward the river, where the dogs were ferreting in the reeds. "Do you love him?"

"I love you."

He stared at me, blinking. "But you agreed to marry him?"

"Yes. It was the best option. I could have the baby. Keep the baby. We would—"

"Bertie loves you."

A gust of wind blew a few strands of hair across my face. I tucked them behind my ears. "No. He thinks…thought he did. He is an honorable man. A kind, caring friend. He was doing what he thought—"

Willie nodded, impatient. "Why are you telling me this now?"

"Because you should know everything about me. There is no reason for me to hide anything from you. I am not ashamed of anything I have done. I am not ashamed of you, my love for you, for agreeing to marry Bertie, or for coming back to you. Dorothy's death reminded me I must be brave to get what I want. It is how it has always been for me. I had forgotten."

"But Aleen—"

"If you are going to say that we cannot get married or be together as husband and wife in any way because of who you are and who I am, and what Athleague, Ireland, the church and its people think and believe, then say nothing. I know it all."

"I was not going to say that."

"What then?"

"Is it enough for you?"

"If you say I have your love and you mean it, it is enough for me."

Willie took my hands in his and said, as I had to Bertie years earlier, "I do not deserve you."

CHAPTER 29

1906
Athleague, Ireland

My living at Fort Lyster made it more difficult for me and Willie to slip to and fro between our residences than it had been when I resided across the lawn at the lodge. It was not, however, impossible, and given that we were together during the day at the surgery most days, the arrangement was, we agreed, satisfactory. He lived at Castlestrange, and I, at Fort Lyster. It was not just that we had lived independently for most of our lives but also that even if it were possible, living together permanently was not what we wanted. We discussed it in bed late one night.

"I believe it works because my desire to be with you is buttressed by my need to be alone," I said. "One does not take away from the other. Does that make sense?"

"Yes. It does. I have thought about it too. Just as being apart too long risks unraveling that which holds us together, too much togetherness blurs the things that make us separate."

"Our independence. The things that attract us to one another."

He nodded. "That too, but the danger, I think, is that too much togetherness leaves no room for that which is between us that draws us together and urges us forward. If we were fused, there would be nowhere to go. We would be stuck with nothing more to hope for."

"Indeed," I said, impressed by his philosophy and the fact that he had clearly given the matter considerable thought.

"Love, I think, longs for togetherness, but desire flourishes with distance. We have the ideal situation," said Willie.

"And yet the church, both mine and yours, would be horrified by our rationale."

He grimaced and rolled toward me. "Let us keep it strictly between us."

Indeed, the setup worked well for us. The only one who was dissatisfied with it was Spencer, who did not truly relax when we were apart.

Although I had thought about working elsewhere in Ireland when I was unsure about how things would be for me and Willie, I never investigated the possibility and do not regret it. Working together at the Castlestrange practice benefited us both.

When Professor John McFadyean, by then principal of the Royal Veterinary College in London, offered a six-month post-graduate course on bacteriology and pathology, Willie was able to attend, leaving me to take care of the practice. He returned with a gift: an elegant hunting whip covered in mahogany-colored braided leather with an ivory handle and a raised gate pusher. Engraved on its silver collar was "Aleen I. Cust, MRCVS." Next to Nasser, I had never received so wonderful a present.

"It is now official," said Willie as I laughed at his audacity. "Who needs a diploma to frame and hang upon the wall when they have their qualifications engraved upon a whip?"

A year later, an opportunity arose for me to visit the imperial horse-breeding studs and large herds of Austria-Hungary and Serbia with, among others, Major Sir Frederick Hobday, whose novel services as a general consultant veterinary surgeon were widely sought after. Willie urged me to go. It was during this trip that Frederick and I became friends.

Some months on, when I arrived at the surgery one morning, Willie pushed the newspaper toward me.

"The Galway County Council is advertising a vacancy for a veterinary inspector to administer the official acts and orders concerning the diseases of animals," he said, pointing to an article.

It was, I read, a part-time post for a local practitioner who could combine the duties with "his" private practice.

"You should apply," said Willie. "The salary is attractive, and it would be good for business."

I stared at him. "Why me? The matter of my certification is bound to come up. You could do it."

"I have too many other responsibilities for the RCVS. Moreover, after all these years as a successful practitioner, I believe the argument about whether or not the RCVS ratified your training is null and void. This will be a good time to put the matter to rest."

"Ha! That is easy to say when you are not the one who will have to defend herself against the insults and small-minded bigotry—again," I replied.

"You have all the ammunition. Why not use it? Put the idea that you are not a qualified professional to bed once and for all."

"How so? If I am given the job, will the Royal College open the profession to women and finally give me my certificate?"

"Probably not, but it will make it harder for them to resist in the future."

"So I should do this to pave the way for future women veterinary surgeons?"

"That is one way of looking at it."

Incredibly, my application for the position was successful. Despite competing with two men, both of whom were included on the Register of Veterinary Surgeons, I was appointed on the grounds of being "the most suitable candidate and well known in the area." I was astounded.

"You see," said Willie as we celebrated with a glass of port that evening, "change is afoot."

We should have known better, particularly Willie. He had been a member of the RCVS council for long enough to know that there were too many men determined to keep women out of the profession to allow my appointment to happen quietly, as was noted in the following edition of the *Veterinary Record*.

The County Council has appointed a person who is not an MRCVS but a lady. This sort of action against the Government could take place nowhere except in Ireland, but even there must be sharply looked after by the Corporate Body, who are threatened with a breach of their privileges. We do not dispute Miss Cust's intelligence or acquirements for the post, but as she does not possess the license to practice granted by the diploma of the RCVS, her appointment is obviously a trespass upon their domain.

I had never seen Willie so angry. Not even the image of my father's boot on the nun's grave had provoked such fury.

"How dare they?" he said. "'Nowhere except in Ireland'? Who do they think they are? One might have understood the debate when you were a student and there was uncertainty about what the law required, but times have changed. Not only that, you are now an established and prosperous practitioner, recognized by imminent veterinary surgeons, including Major Hobday, and indeed, some of us are Irish and proud of it. You are equal in training, competence, and integrity to the best of them. How dare they? Who are they? The RCVS is a failing body on a slippery slope to bankruptcy because of its stubborn discord. I have reached the end of my patience."

He sat down at his desk, snatched a sheet of letter paper, and began writing.

"What are you doing?" I asked.

"I am putting it on record—once more, I might add—that the RCVS should do the sensible thing, pass a resolution to grant you your diploma honoris causa, put your name on the register forthwith, and accept this appointment. I am also resigning from the council. I want nothing more to do with it."

"Do not do that on my account," I said. "It will cause unnecessary trouble for you."

"No, it will not. It will benefit my health and humor."

I never learned exactly what Willie wrote, but whatever it was, it spread panic in the RCVS council. Perhaps he pointed out that women were training as veterinary surgeons in America, Australia, France, and Russia, proving that Britain was regressive. Or maybe he showed how the case for admitting women to the profession was backed by more and more members, including several professors, and that the RCVS was not only becoming increasingly powerless but also that it could not afford to finance the lawsuits for the alleged trespasses against it. Although I was not granted my diploma or included on the register, whatever Willie wrote in that letter convinced the RCVS to withdraw its objection, and my appointment as an inspector stood. The *Veterinary Record*, of course, could not resist a final dig:

> The County Council has made an appointment in the horse and brute kingdom which appears to us at least disgusting, if not absolutely indecent! Of the many callings embraced by women, that of judging and doctoring horses appears to us the most unsuitable and repulsive. We can understand women educating themselves to tend women—but horses! Heavens!

"It is as if they do not know how long you have been doctoring horses and other brutes. Poor simple creatures," said Willie as we laughed at the report.

He was right. Years had passed since I'd looked up from where I knelt next to Pony near Athleague and saw him hop off Zeus and walk toward me with Mr. Flynn. For years, I had worked as a veterinary surgeon, and now, I was also an inspector.

The RCVS might have withheld my diploma and tried to keep me from putting the letters MRCVS after my name, but Willie had helped me become a veterinary surgeon. He had put me to work and helped me prove my worth. I had chosen the best profession in the world, and after Major Fitz and Professor Williams had opened the door to me, Willie had allowed me to prove that I was as skilled a veterinary surgeon as anyone else.

"Years," I said, putting my arms around his neck. "Years of tending to horses and the brute kingdom with you at my side. Heavens! I would not have it any other way."

CHAPTER 30

⌐∾⌐

1910
Athleague, Ireland

"WILL YOU ACCOMPANY ME TO THE IRISH CENTRAL VETERINARY SOCIETY meeting in Dublin next month? I will present my proposal on amending legislation on tuberculosis in cattle."

I opened my mouth to ask if it would be prudent for us both to attend. What about the practice? Willie did not give me a chance to speak.

"I would like you to be there. I think it will be important."

So we went together, and I sat in the audience and listened to him. It was not the clinical matter he proposed or the adjustments to law he thought necessary that held my attention but rather the poignancy of the opening of his speech. I realized later that he knew then what was to come.

"I have a vivid recollection of standing before a similar group of colleagues in comparable surroundings," he began. "It seems recent, except on that day I opened my speech by apologizing for my youth and inexperience. Today, I look around and see faces among you that I have seen for more than twenty years, during which time we have worked hard. But I see many more fresh, youthful faces, and I realize that I am a patriarch among you. It is age, not vigorous youth or naive confidence, that imposes upon me the duty of opening today's discussion. Indeed, the years have whitened the flowers of the grave upon my head." He touched the side of his head, where truly, there was some gray in his curls.

"But I will not dwell on the sad passing of years, but rather on how it gives me the privilege of delegating tasks to the new recruits among our ranks who I am pleased to notice are present here today. As such, I will present my findings and ask that you will take the baton from me and cross the finishing line."

All of us present were accustomed to Willie's wit and his poetic way with words, and his presentation was no less well received than any other he had made over the years. However, the introduction stuck with me, and I could not help mentioning it on the train on our way home.

"You have every right to be vain, Mr. Byrne," I said, daring to place my hand on his thigh given that we were alone in the carriage. "But I have never thought of you as such."

He put his hand over mine and glanced at me. "Vain? What do you mean?"

"The reference to the gray in your hair. You are only forty-six, after all."

"Ah, sure. It was just a means to flatter the youngsters into taking on some of the work."

"Is that all it was?"

"Of course. Although if it got you to look at me with fresh eyes and find me worthy of vanity, then I am pleased that it had dual purpose," he teased.

A few weeks later I realized that as a pathologist, Willie had known that his speech at the Irish Central Veterinary Society meeting would be his last one. It was his farewell speech. I also understood then why Spencer had suddenly moved back to Castlestrange with Willie, ignoring me every evening when I tried to lure him home to Fort Lyster. Willie knew, and so did the dog: Willie was dying.

"It is an early sarcoma," he insisted, touching the spot on his neck, when he finally had to tell me that he was going to hospital. "The doctor in Roscommon assures me the operation will be uncomfortable but of small consequence. I shall be home within days."

"Will you not seek another opinion from someone in Dublin? It would surely be wise if—"

"No. It is arranged. The carriage is waiting."

He lifted my chin, kissed me gently, and said with a wink, "If you were registered by the Royal College, I might ask you to perform the operation yourself."

It was the last time we spoke.

I had thought of nothing but Willie for days, but it was only when I recognized the white snip on the muzzle of the bay outside the church on the day of his funeral that I truly felt the significance of his death.

"Will you look at that? Conor McCarthy has finally schooled the filly we pulled three Easters ago," I said.

Of course, he was not with me to offer a sniff of acknowledgment or, if the mood took him, a line of wit. It struck me then that he would not respond, neither on that April day in 1910 from his velvet-lined casket nor ever again from his dark nest in the earth. It hit me squarely in the breastbone, as solidly as the hoof of a cow upset by cold hands upon her udder might. It took the air from my lungs. I rested my forehead against the horse's neck for a moment, breathing in the familiar scent of sweat, stable, and oiled leather before I climbed the stairs into the church.

Inside, I tried to ignore that Father O'Flanagan avoided meeting my Protestant eyes—despite my height placing them at least a head above almost everyone else's in the crowded pews. Instead, I listened closely to his words. I wanted to believe the priest's assurance that Willie's soul, purified by the clergyman himself, had already entered the joy of heaven. It worried me, though, when Father O'Flanagan recited the shepherd's parable about the herdsman placing the sheep at his right hand and the goats at the left. What if God, weary from the endless troubles that the world placed before him, was distracted, and confused his sheep with his goats? It could happen. I recalled a story Professor Williams had told about the farmer who confused his Jacob sheep with piebald goats. Where might similar confusion place Willie in the holy kingdom? Moreover, my experience of God was that His actions could be as irrational as those of some of His most absurd subjects. The deaths of my beloved Willie and

Dorothy were surely cases in point. No, I was not comforted by Father O'Flanagan's words.

Willie's cousin Thomas offered me his arm as we walked the short distance to the cemetery. I wondered why he was not among the pallbearers. It was possible he was too short for the task, and certainly his skinny legs were already greatly burdened by his bulbous belly. Or perhaps his journey had coincided with the planning, and Willie's friends had been unaware that he would be present. He'd arrived in Athleague only hours before the wake. We'd spoken there but only briefly. I did not stay long. The Irish tradition of holding a final party to honor the deceased was not one I understood.

"Did you see how long the procession was?" asked Thomas, steering me around the graves as if he feared I might step upon them. I wondered if Willie had told him the story of my father.

"I did," I replied.

"I was a little late in leaving Castlestrange, and by the time I joined the cortege, it was, I would estimate, more than two miles long."

Thomas was not exaggerating. I could not remember seeing as many horses and carriages on the roads of Roscommon outside of race day. It was as if Willie's friends had been joined by both our clients and patients to bid him farewell. The animals were resplendent in the sunshine. It pleased me, as it would have Willie, to see so many in good health and at work. I resolved there and then to include instructions in my will that, regardless of how popular motorcars might become in the future, only horse-drawn carriages should be included in my funeral procession.

Standing two or three rows back at the graveside, Cathleen Doyle caught my eye. She glanced down quickly and then looked up more slowly, holding my gaze momentarily with her gunmetal blue eyes. It may be the only time I had seen no malice in her expression. She might even have given me a short nod. Or perhaps I imagined it. She was flanked by her mother and her beau from Creggs. I tried not to let it vex me that she was so beautiful. I failed. Life would go on for Cathleen Doyle.

Thomas invited me to drive back to Castlestrange and take lunch with him, but I was not ready to be in the house without Willie. I hoped I was gracious when I told him I had things to attend to at Fort Lyster and that I might visit him in a week or two. I meant to ask him not to feed Spencer, so the Setter would stop visiting Castlestrange in the hope of finding his master there. Would Thomas even know who Spencer was?

The road from Roscommon to Athleague was empty. I had imagined the business of the day was over, but it seemed Willie gave others reason to dally in town. I could not imagine what more they had to say about his passing. Only grief remained, and it was surely silent.

I had planned to ride Nasser to the funeral, thinking I would follow the route Willie and I'd ridden on the Roscommon Hunt the previous year. I pictured the stallion and me soaring over the wall near Castlecoote, the one he'd balked at and where he'd unseated me that day. It was possible Willie's hoots of laughter were still ringing through the valley. I had thought the ride would clear my head. However, when Bridget had laid out the black paramatta silk dress I'd purchased in haste and with a heavy heart in Northumberland for Dorothy's funeral, I told Kevin to harness the gig instead. I'd overheard him asking Ronan if he might suggest to me that he drive the carriage for me. Ronan had the good sense to say no.

Now, as I made my way home with the sun on my back and the rhythmic sound of Molly's hooves and the rolling of the wheels in my ears, I found the drive and the easy nature of the mare soothed me. She was the ideal mourning companion, discreet and serene. If Molly had been human, she would not have lingered in town to blather about the wretchedness of death. She would have gone home, as I did, to work out how to live on.

If the weather held, I would take Nasser out tomorrow. It was a warm spring day. Even the finches were singing the sun's praises. I saw as I drove that the whitethorns were budding. Several hedges, presumably those that enjoyed the longest sun hours, were already dotted with the tiny white flowers. Sheehan's sheep, grazing in a pasture near the road, lifted their heads to watch me pass. Whitethorn blossoms and sheep would forever remind me of Willie and springtime in Roscommon County.

"Lambing begins twelve weeks before the whitethorns start budding," he'd explained, shortly after I had arrived ten years ago. "By the time they're weaned and it's warm enough for the wee ones to really enjoy being out and about, the blossoms will be almost as woolly as they are."

Indeed, Sheehan's lambs, tripping about in grass as green as leeks, were woolly and white, just as the hedges would be in a week or two. Willie had known the seasons of Roscommon almost as well as he knew the animals of the county.

Gaffney's geese, fat and squawking, waddled across the road, a fluffy squad of goslings in tow. Half a mile on, the woods were carpeted with bluebells, and the air, pungent with the smell of wild garlic.

The seasons were passing, new life beginning, and the promise of a warmer, more abundant tomorrow was in the air. Yet, my beloved had died. He had left although we had just arrived. He had left, despite the obstacles we had overcome to make the journey. The family we had created—Willie, the dogs, the horses, and me—no longer existed.

CHAPTER 31

⁓❧⁓

1914
Athleague, Ireland

THE YEARS THAT FOLLOWED WERE INTERCHANGEABLE. DAY FOLLOWED DAY; week came after week; month proceeded month; and months turned to years. Bridget, Fiona, Kevin, and Ronan took care of Fort Lyster. They cleaned the house, milked the cows, kept me and the animals fed, saddled Nasser when I rode to see patients, and harnessed Molly when I needed the cart. The grass was mown in spring, flowers bloomed in summer, Ronan raked the leaves in autumn, and in winter, Kevin kept the stables dry and full of hay.

Eventually, the playful light in Spencer's eyes returned. The Setter resumed his games with Gunner and Lacey and stopped visiting Castlestrange, which stood empty when Thomas went back to America. Our clients became my clients and grew in number. With their attitudes tempered by Willie's death and because there was no other veterinary surgeon for miles around, the people of Athleague and Roscommon finally took me to their hearts fully and without reserve, with many addressing me as *your honor* for the first time.

The volume of work warranted the practice's taking on another veterinary surgeon, and indeed, when I stopped to think about it, I believe I even planned to advertise the post. As ever, there was more than enough work for two of us, and I missed not only being with Willie but also having someone to discuss cases with, particularly unusual and tricky ones. However, having moved the surgery to Fort Lyster, I practiced alone, working long hours and tirelessly to ensure that I was too weary to lie awake and mourn at night.

In the few lulls between patients, I designed a horse hobble for the improved casting of horses—which, less complicated, lighter, and cheaper than others available, I had manufactured by the veterinary instrument company Arnold & Sons of London. If I could keep my hands and mind fully occupied, there would be no place for grief, I reasoned.

However, I was not always alone. There was an occasion I worked with another veterinary surgeon, if only for the one procedure. Frederick Hobday had, I read in professional journals, undertaken several operations on "roarers," that is, horses who make abnormal noises during exercise because the smooth passage of air is hindered in the larynx. By applying good anesthesia to the horses and stripping out the lining of the space between the vocal cord and the side of the larynx, Frederick opened the cord so that breathing was no longer obstructed. When Conor McCarthy called on me because his young hunter was roaring, I told him about the operation, saying it was new and not one that I could perform alone yet.

"I shall write to the professor," I said. "Perhaps he will be prepared to do the operation with me the next time he is in Ireland."

A few months later, Frederick and I undertook the procedure on Conor's horse using a set of my hobbles.

"It is quite an honor that a man of such esteem as you operated on one of my horses," said Conor as he bade Frederick goodbye, ignoring me completely.

Naturally, it occurred to me that it was more significant that Frederick had agreed to work with me during the operation. What would the men of the RCVS have said had they known? The true reward for me, though, was seeing the horse strong and roar-free at hunts thereafter.

Indeed, there were few other events worth noting during those years. For the most part, I steamed through the days as if mechanized.

When news of my mother's demise reached me in a letter from Major Fitz, I realized how impervious I had become to death. Once, when I was awake in the dark hours one morning, guilt washed over me. Where was the misery a daughter should surely feel when her mother died? I rolled over, annoyed with myself for allowing my sleep to be disturbed. Why should I mourn my mother? She had not communicated with me since I had sought reconciliation with her and my siblings at her sick bed in London ten years previously. Despite her final rejection, I had continued to send birthday and Christmas greetings to Kensington, even as I chastised myself while writing them. No matter how many times my family spurned me, I could not bring myself to cut ties completely.

When, however, my siblings left it to the Widdringtons to inform me of our mother's death, the bond was finally severed. I might as well have been dead to my brothers and sister, and if I was going to indulge myself in any mourning, it would be for Willie and Dorothy, not my mother.

Certainly, had they known my thoughts, people might have considered me indifferent. It was not just that I trained myself against brooding but also that when work was done for the day, I was too tired to contemplate that there might be other ways of living. Anyway, what else should I have done? I was doing what I loved as a veterinary surgeon, and with clients to visit and patients to attend to both away and at the practice, there was enough engagement with others to keep me from feeling lonely. Beyond my work, my animals and, whenever the opportunity arose, hunting, I felt no urge to do anything else.

It was only in August 1914, when in his speech in the British House of Commons on the eve of war, Edward said, "We are going to suffer, I am afraid, terribly in this war, whether we are in it or whether we stand aside," that I realized how deadened I had become to everything and everyone outside my work and my animals.

"What do you say, your honor, about us going to war then?" asked Mr. Gaffney the next day as I examined a coughing cow at his dairy.

"Our sons are talking of volunteering," said his brother.

"Really?" I asked, surprised that Irishmen were ready to go to battle alongside England "Why? I mean, do they feel that it is *their* war?"

"Oh, aye," said Mr. Gaffney. "They're after the justice of it for sure. Although it might be that some of the younger lads are spurred by the idea of enlisting to see what it is like—get a gun, you know, visit another country, pretend they're grown men."

"I see. Is that the general sentiment around here? Supporting England in the war?"

The men looked at one another as if they had not considered it from that angle. "Aye. I guess it is. I mean, both nationalist and unionist leaders are for it, are they not, Darragh?" asked Mr. Gaffney.

"Aye. That they are."

Irishmen were not conscripted, and yet hundreds of thousands joined the war over the next few months. It became increasingly difficult to talk of anything else but the war. Even when the state of the animals they called me to attend to were dire, my clients preferred to discuss what was or was not happening on the Continent and all else that might involve the war.

"Did you read about your man Bertrand Russell, your honor? He and some other lily-livered lads have formed an association to try to stop conscription. They're anti-war, they are. Who do they think will fight for them? They should be thrown in jail. Don't you agree, your honor?"

"What do you think about all those poor horses they're shipping over the sea? Will they come back the same, do you think, your honor? I mean people will understand, but the animals… What will they think?"

"Let us focus on the job at hand," I typically replied.

Despite Lord Kitchener's warning the cabinet that England should prepare for a three-year blood bath, I wanted to believe those who said the war would be over in months. However, when I received a letter from Lady Widdrington telling me that Bertie was on his way to France, I began paying more attention to news about it. It was then I read that the British army needed substantially more than the twenty-three thousand horses that it owned to fight the war. From then on, I found it impossible to ignore it.

I studied the papers and paid attention to talk. I learned that horses—essential to mount cavalry charges, pull and transport weapons and supplies, and carry the wounded and dying to hospital—were being requisitioned by the government for the army from across the kingdom. Before long, many of the finest animals in Ireland were taken.

One morning, Bridget showed a weary-looking officer into the house.

"The Army Act of 1881 entitles the military to seize horses and carriages for use in emergencies in strict terms laid down in the Act," he said, once we had greeted each other.

"Would you like a cup of tea?" I asked.

"Thank you, my lady, but we do not have time. Can I see your horses?"

"I cannot sell my horses, not to you or anyone else. I am a veterinary surgeon, you see. They are essential to my business."

"My men saw a motorcar in your coach house. Surely, that is adequate for your needs? I am sure I need not remind you that we are at war, my lady."

I pitied the man. The heaviness of his expression and posture showed that he took no pleasure in his task, but his troubles did not persuade me.

"Did you notice the state of the roads as you came here, Major?" I asked.

He nodded.

"So you can imagine how difficult it is, on a less moderate day than today, for me to reach my clients by car. I cannot rely on the machine to always deliver me safely. There are times that I am obliged to take equipment in the cart pulled by my mare, Molly. In other cases, I need to speed across the fields to attend to emergencies, in which case, I ride my Arabian, Nasser. My horses are integral to my work."

"As are the horses of hundreds of farmers across the land that have been commandeered by the army," he said, bored, it seemed, by how often he had had to repeat his argument.

"You are missing something important, Major. I am a veterinary surgeon. My work is essential to the health and breeding of more horses, which, should they be required, and by God, I hope they are not, could be called upon to reinforce the army's needs in months and years to come. If you take my horses, you will not fortify the forces at the front but rather put their future at risk."

So it was that Molly and Nasser remained at Fort Lyster. Still, the army left Roscommon with strings of beautiful horses of every description.

Hunters and hacks, both light and heavy, carriage horses, and draft horses. The animals lined the roads and were led away.

The few veterinary surgeons I knew who had not yet joined the war effort kept close watch from home. On the increasingly rare occasions we met, we discussed how, when the kingdom's supply of horses was exhausted, the army had turned to America, Canada, Australia, and New Zealand for animals. It was in a letter from Frederick that I learned thousands of horses were arriving at the channel ports where they were rested and examined. Any sick or injured animals were pulled aside before they were sent to the front. The unhealthy animals were treated, and when they recovered sufficiently, they were sent on after the others. Exactly what conditions the horses faced at the front were at that point unknown, but even at my most optimistic, I knew that the animals would require more attention than what was available.

It was as I rode Nasser home after a meeting with colleagues in Roscommon town, during which we had discussed an outbreak of ringworm among war horses, that I realized I could not stay in Ireland and take care of my practice while so many animals were suffering on the front lines. I had to go where I could provide the most assistance.

That night, I wrote to the director of veterinary services with the British Expeditionary Force in France, Major General Sir John Moore, whom I had met at meetings of the Irish Central Veterinary Society during the years he had been in Ireland, offering my services with immediate effect. The reply I received from his office was curt.

> Volunteers for the Army Veterinary Services should be in possession of full MRCVS qualifications. As such, your application is denied.

The letter was still lying on the mantelpiece when Bridget told me that Kevin was in the kitchen asking to see me.

"Miss Cust," said the skinny young man, shuffling his feet, "I have come to tell you that I will be going to the front on Friday."

"You are? How is that possible, Kevin? Have your eyes miraculously recovered? I understood the army would not have you under any condition."

"No, my lady. The army has not changed its mind about me. I have joined the Young Men's Christian Association."

"Ah. The YMCA? You will be catering to the spiritual needs of the soldiers then? At the front?"

"Aye, and doing a great deal more asides, I'm told. I will do whatever it takes to help win the fight, Miss Cust. I have to do something."

"Yes, Kevin, you do. Well done then. I will be sorry to see you go and hope you will come back when all this is over."

"Aye, Miss Cust. Thank you. I will say my formal goodbyes on Thursday."

"All right. Good."

Then something occurred to me.

"Kevin, do you know if the YMCA also accepts women volunteers?"

CHAPTER 32

❦

1914
Abbeville, France

So it was that I joined the YMCA, shipped my motorcar across the channel, and reported to the Royal College's office near Abbeville on the River Somme, which was where the Army Veterinary Corps headquarters and the Advanced Remount Depot were also located.

I did not waste time settling in. Within hours of my arrival, I saw the most effective approach to making oneself useful during a war was no different from doing so in other circumstances. One simply had to have intent and get on with it. There was much to be done and no room for indecisive dallying or waiting for permission to act.

While most of the YMCA workers concentrated on providing whatever levels of comfort they could for the soldiers, be that practical, emotional, or spiritual, my focus was on the animals. In some cases, this involved the health of the few cattle, sheep, dogs, and cats that had survived the chaos around them. I was there, however, for the horses who unwittingly bore the brunt of the war as they carried soldiers, supplies, and machinery into the belly of death.

A few days after arriving in France, I navigated the muddy road to the

Remount Depot quarters and requested a meeting with Major General Sir John Moore. I said I wanted to talk about the horse services offered by the YMCA. If the major was surprised to hear that such a service existed—it had not until I established it—or shocked to see that I had come to France despite his office rejecting me, he hid it well.

"Good morning, Major General," I said. "Thank you for seeing me. I will not keep you from your work but thought I should advise you that at the YMCA, we have taken it upon ourselves to exercise and rehabilitate the semi-recovered horses that are capable of light work at Remount."

He raised his eyebrows ever so slightly.

"Your men told us that there is a surplus of animals in this category and that the veterinary corps are stretched too thin to adequately work with them. We will assist."

"Exercise and rehabilitate? Here?"

"Yes."

"That is all very well, but—"

"Excellent. Thank you, Major General. I shall show myself out."

There was, of course, a great deal more to it than exercise and rehabilitation. Indeed, I was right about my services being desperately required at the front. Never had so many horses required this much expert care with such limited access to medicine and equipment. It was not just the animals who were injured on the battlefield who needed suturing, rest, and recovery but also those who suffered saddle and harness sores, and skin diseases. They also experienced colic, lameness, and respiratory diseases, which were difficult to overcome in the dreadfully muddy conditions of the winter months and during the dusty days of summer. Feed shortages made taking care of the animals even more difficult. The dullness of the horses' coats was matched only by that of their eyes, except for those so traumatized that they quivered incessantly and showed more sclera of the eye than any other horse I had known. For many, no amount of soothing was enough.

The days were long, the work unending, and there was little time for rest. It was difficult to find enough to eat to sustain one's energy, and like everyone around me, I grew thin.

When I collapsed on my bunk at night, I thought briefly about the years I had run the practice at Fort Lyster alone and marveled at how I had imagined that I was busy then. Working on the front lines, with the endless stream of horses who were led, hobbling, bleeding, groaning, and sometimes screaming in pain, could not compare to anything else I had done. It was difficult, heart-breaking work. For the first time ever, there were moments I wished I had chosen to do something else with my life, something that would have prevented me from having to see what war did to man and, consequently, what man demanded of beast.

I had been in Abbeville for more than two years, officially as a YMCA volunteer but working exclusively with the horses at the Remount quarters, when Major General Moore sent for me. I anticipated a dressing down. Perhaps he would even demand I remove myself from the facility. On the other hand, given how short-staffed and relentlessly busy they were, none of the officers and men I worked alongside, most of whom were qualified veterinary surgeons, ever questioned my presence among the horses. In fact, they regularly called for my opinion and handed over cases that they were unable to resolve. Even so, it was not impossible that someone objected about my working there. Or perhaps it was just that the division anticipated a visit by a senior official. Regardless, I could not have been more surprised by Major General Moore's proposal.

"As you are aware, we are in dire need of developing and preparing vaccines. The War Office has given me the go-ahead to establish a new laboratory. I need someone who…who has the right kind of experience to work there as a bacteriologist," he said, pacing his small office, which was once the storeroom of a café. "I, erm, well, I have applied to the office for you to be given a suitable grading in the Women's Army Auxiliary Corps and so that when all is in place, you take up the position."

For a moment, I could think of nothing to say.

"If you are in agreement, of course," he added.

It occurred to me afterward that it would have been an excellent time to insist that he ask the RCVS to issue my diploma honoris causa and finally put my name on the register. Instead, I said, "Yes. That sounds useful. I accept and shall give the YMCA my notice."

Shortly thereafter, I received a letter confirming that I was a member of Queen Mary's Army Auxiliary Corps and that my role was that of unit administrator in Abbeville.

In fact, my new status as official in France was not as advantageous as it had promised to be. My work in the laboratory under Captain Watson of the Canadian Army Veterinary Corps was frustrating. Much younger than me and unaccustomed, it seemed, to working with anyone with the ability to think independently, let alone a woman, Captain Watson took an immediate and unshakable dislike to me. I concede that I did little to try to dissuade him otherwise. His attitude galled me, and I could not find it in myself to submit to his demands. I had worked independently for too long to adapt to taking orders. We disagreed on most matters, and even when I drew on my years of experience to demonstrate my point, he responded with disdain.

It was during this time that I learned of Major Fitz's death. Despite the fact I was constantly trapped in a mire of trauma and death, the news hit me hard. No one else had been more of a father figure to me than Major Fitz, and the hollowness of a world without him seemed too much to bear. As I took in the news, the cold silence of the laboratory did nothing to soothe me. I wanted to be outdoors; rain or sun, it would not matter. I needed to be outside to think about the major. If I could not be in Northumberland, I should be among the horses in Abbeville. I longed to be back with the animals, providing comfort where I could and receiving it too. I found no solace in peering into a microscope and arguing with the captain. I wanted to be somewhere where I could provide immediate and practical help, even if that meant swapping my membership to Queen Mary's Army Auxiliary Corps for a YMCA badge once more.

Some weeks later, before I had a chance to request a transfer out of the laboratory, I received another letter from Lady Widdrington. Thinking that it was her response to my condolences about Major Fitz, I did not immediately open it but tucked it into my pocket to read when I was alone in my room. I anticipated feeling sad again as she described her life without the major. That, however, was not the reason for her letter. Instead, she wrote that in recent months, Bertie's letters had been returned to her unread, and when she inquired via her friends in the upper ranks of the army, it emerged that his whereabouts were unknown. Could things get any worse?

Bertie and I had barely spoken since I broke off our engagement and returned to Ireland. The last time I'd seen him was at Dorothy's funeral, where shock froze our tongues and we said little more than hello and goodbye. However, I often fantasized about how he and I would one day reconcile. I did not expect him to ever love me the way he once imagined he had. But that did not stop me from hoping we might again be friends. I wanted his affection once more, as he would always have mine. Now, he was missing. I curled up on my narrow bunk and tried to convince myself that his disappearance was simply due to the chaos of war and nothing more tragic. The thought of life with neither Major Fitz nor Bertie was inconceivable. I cried myself to sleep.

I could barely haul myself out of bed to go to the laboratory the next morning, even though I had risen with purpose and energy every morning since arriving in Abbeville. It seemed so pointless. Whatever I did or suggested was dismissed as inconsequential by Captain Watson, and I felt worthless. The day dragged by, and for the most part, I gazed into the distance. In my mind's eye, I was riding Nasser across the fields of Roscommon or galloping on the beaches of Northumberland.

That night, I resolved to ask Major General Moore if I could be released from the laboratory. I made a list of all the things I had done under the auspices of the YMCA previously to buoy my argument. I would convince him I was of more use among the horses than in the laboratory. When the list ran onto a fourth page, I set down my pencil, convinced that he would agree, and went to bed.

The next day, I was too ill to go anywhere or visit anyone.

CHAPTER 33

❧

1919
Northumberland, England

It was months later, while I convalesced at Newton Hall, that Lady Widdrington explained how I was shipped from France the very day before the Allies and Germany signed the armistice and hostilities on the Western Front ceased. I had no recollection of even being aware that the war might be ending. Neither did I recall the weeks I spent in hospital in London before having recovered enough to be put on a train bound for Northumberland.

"Of course, you do not remember," Lady Widdrington said, opening the curtains to flood the room with light. I was in the very room in which I had told Bertie I would not marry him. "When you were not delirious, you were medicated to the eyeballs and asleep. Edward believes the influenza pandemic will kill more people than the war did, but it will not take you."

She smiled at me, her bright eyes and smooth skin belying her age and the heartache of recent years. I had not forgotten the major's death or Bertie's disappearance. I asked if there was news.

"Bertie is not dead," she said. "I am certain of that. I knew of Dorothy's death before we even heard about her accident. I saw a dove on the windowsill that morning. There was something about it being there and how it moved that told me by the end of the day my daughter would no longer be of this world."

I stared at her, silent. She had always been forthright and extraordinary. It was unlike Lady Widdrington to be fanciful.

"The morning Fitz died, I watched a pair of doves strut about on the drive. They did not flee when I approached, flying off only when the dogs pursued them. I have not seen a dove since. Bertie is alive."

"I hope so," I said, averting my eyes from the window to avoid spotting any doves.

"Every day, one reads another story about a missing soldier returning home," she said. "Keeping track of everyone during the war and establishing where they are now is impossible. People made mistakes. Records got mixed up. Perhaps Bertie is recuperating from the influenza, suffering amnesia, or recovering from another injury somewhere. I do not know why he is unaccounted for, but I know he is alive."

It *was* possible that Bertie was alive. I wanted to believe it, but my spirits were low, and I kept my hopes tightly harnessed. Where once I would have unreservedly joined his mother and held on to the idea of Bertie's sudden reappearance, I now kept myself in check. I had witnessed too much to believe in miracles. Too worn and tired to fantasize and too weak to withstand having my hopes dashed, I silently grieved Willie, Dorothy, Major Fitz, and his son.

There was no news of Bertie by the time I had recovered enough to begin planning my return to Ireland. I was eager to get back to the work and the place that had brought me such joy. Doing the work I loved would distract me from the pain of the recent past and give me purpose and pleasure once more.

I wrote to Mrs. Doyle, telling her of my imminent return. She replied:

The war notwithstanding, things have not been the same here since 1916, and I am not sure you will feel at home in Athleague again, Miss Cust. Indeed, Fiona and Ronan might have stayed on at Fort Lyster, but while I have no doubt that they will be pleased to see you, I worry that they will not be able to guarantee your safety there. That said, many will no doubt be glad of your services again.

While the muted tone of her reply surprised me, I remained eager to return to Fort Lyster and get my practice back up and running. Despite memories of my early days in Athleague when I was seen as little more than a bothersome attachment to Willie, it was hard to imagine that I would not be welcomed back. I might be an English Protestant, but it was where I had settled and worked. I had built my career there. Roscommon was my home, and its people, my people. Surely, I reasoned, the Irish loved their animals too much to allow their anti-English sentiments to get in the way of the health of their beasts.

"If things do not work out as you hope, you will always have a place here," said Lady Widdrington as I bade her farewell. I hugged her, grateful again for her love and support, which bore no trace of the misgivings I'd believed she had experienced when Bertie and I were engaged.

As I drove through the gates of Fort Lyster, I saw that Fiona and Ronan had done well to maintain the land in my absence. However, the buildings—familiar and welcoming as they were against an unusually blue sky and framed by trees that were taller than I recalled—needed repair. I would, I assured myself, work hard and make the necessary improvements as soon as I could afford them.

Bridget, I discovered, had married a farmer and was expecting her second child. The whereabouts of Kevin were uncertain. Fiona said his mother was sure he had married a beautiful French girl but could not afford to return to Ireland with her.

"She is convinced there are grandchildren too," Fiona said. "I have no doubt she'll ask you if you bumped into him while you were in France."

I walked to the rose garden where Spencer was buried. Although, for a while after I left, the Setter had run between Castlestrange and Fort Lyster searching for me, Ronan told me he'd eventually settled and lived happily to the end. He'd been almost fifteen years old when he died. Gunner and Lacey wagged their tails when I greeted them, but I realized as they followed Ronan to the stables, the Spaniels had fully transferred their loyalty to the groundsman.

To my surprise, Nasser and Molly had been spared the army even after I left for France. The horses had led a quiet life at Fort Lyster and wore their years well. The Arabian was eager and responsive when I asked Ronan to saddle him the next day so I could ride to Castlestrange.

It was odd, even after all the time that had passed, to follow the cross-country route from Fort Lyster to Castlestrange without Spencer galloping ahead, and as Nasser settled into a gentle canter on the sandy path near the river, I imagined I saw the Setter turn the corner ahead of us. Would I, I wondered, see Willie at the window of the surgery at Castlestrange?

The ornate metal gates, rusty and stained with age and neglect, were chained and locked. Ronan had told me that Thomas had sold Castlestrange during the war. Clearly, although the new owners were yet to disclose their identity and take occupation, they were intent on keeping interlopers at bay. Before, I would have urged Nasser over the hedge, onto the property. Now, though, I was not sure whether either of us was up to such athletic endeavors. Instead, I held him at the gate, peering through it and picturing Willie and me there as we had been a decade previously. How dedicated we had been to our work. We had allowed our passion for what we did, our life together, and our love to consume us. We had taken it all for granted with no inkling of how short our time together would be.

That night, once Fiona and Ronan had retired with Gunner and Lacey following them to their cottage, and I prepared for bed, there was a loud knock at the door. I smiled to myself, thinking that the people of Athleague must have heard of my return and were calling on me for an emergency.

Expecting to find a farmer or one of his family members on my doorstep, I pulled on my coat and opened the door. Instead, an angry-looking young man with arms as thick as a prize boar's hock shoved me backward into the hallway and stomped inside. He was followed by three similarly aggrieved-looking men, two of whom were brandishing pistols. They were, the front man declared in a booming voice, members of the Irish Republican

Army and demanded the keys to my motorcar. I glared at them, furious at their cheek and uncertain how to respond. With Ronan and Fiona in the cottage some distance away and the wind blowing hard, no one would hear me call for help.

"You wish to confiscate my motorcar in the name of the Republican Army?" I asked. "That is preposterous! I am a veterinary surgeon. You cannot have it. It is crucial to my business."

The men looked at one another. Was it possible they had not anticipated that I might refuse their demand?

"Off you go then," I said, pointing to the door. "Let us consider the matter closed."

Hock Arms emitted what sounded like a growl, leaped forward, and grabbed my arm, twisting it behind my back.

"Don't be doing anything you'll regret now, lady sassenach," he said, his hot breath ruffling the hair around my ears. "You must know you're hated here. No one will miss you if you're gone tomorrow."

"Oh, stop it!" I said, twisting around to face him. "Unhand me! There is no need for that threatening propaganda. What if tomorrow your horse comes down with something, and I am unable to get to you because you have stolen my car?"

The men stared at me, Hock Arms still holding my arm.

"That made you think, did it not?"

The leader shoved my arm further up my back. The pain was agonizing, and I feared he would break it.

"Let me go," I said, pleading now. "I cannot think like this."

He did not release me. Instead, he pushed me toward the door and, with his free hand, reached out and snatched up the hunting whip Willie had bought for me in London fourteen years earlier.

"Let's see how long we'll have to whip you before you stop being a silly woman," he said.

There was nothing to do but to give them the key to the motorcar.

"Give me my whip!" I shouted as the brute shoved me backward into a chair and sauntered toward the door.

He turned, glanced at the rod in his hand, swished it through the air in my direction, and left, still holding it. The blood rushed to my head. I ran to my room, pulled the shotgun from the cupboard, and fired at the motorcar as it disappeared down the road.

Less than a month later, Fiona and Ronan were threatened as turncoats in the village by members of the same party, possibly the same men. The couple hung their heads when they told me they would be leaving. Mrs. Doyle, I realized, was right: Ireland was not the place it was before the war, and I was no longer welcomed there.

"You need to keep your curtains drawn, Miss Cust," said Ronan as he and Fiona loaded the last of their belongings into their cart. "They fancy themselves snipers, and they'll be watching you."

I stood on the stairs and watched them go, Gunner and Lacey trotting beside the wheels of the cart. The idea of being at Fort Lyster without dogs was unimaginable, but as I looked over the empty yard toward Nasser's and Molly's stables, I knew if I was going to bring any new animals home, this was not the place to do it.

That night, I wrote to Lady Widdrington, telling her that I would sell Fort Lyster and return to England.

I would be grateful if I could stay with you at Newton Hall until I find somewhere to settle. I shall try not to disrupt your life and will come only with two aging horses and my own restless soul.

Her reply, inviting me to come as soon as I wanted to and assuring me that I could bring Nasser and Molly, was welcoming, kind, and anticipated. It was the letter from my old friend Frederick Hobday, which was delivered to Fort Lyster the same day, that surprised me.

After the war, where he had served as a major in Abbeville, Frederick had established a small animal practice in the West End of London where he tended the needs of a burgeoning population of beloved urban pets. He was also official veterinary surgeon to Her Majesty Queen Alexandra and arguably the best-informed vet in Britain. Frederick wrote:

You should, if you are not already, be aware that the circumstances of the RCVS are much changed in light of the Sex Disqualification Act of 1919. I have been following the case of a young woman, Miss Edith Knight, who recently made an application to the RCVS to train as a veterinary surgeon. In terms of the 1919 Act, Miss Knight's application has been approved by the council, who has finally accepted that it can no longer prohibit women from entering the profession. Forgive me if you are aware of this and have already taken steps to make things right, but given that you are far removed from the news, I want to be sure you were advised of the developments. They do, I believe, open the way for you to apply to present yourself for the final RCVS exam and finally be officially named, Aleen I. Cust, MRCVS. I hope you will notify the council of your intent forthwith, and I look forward to, once and for all, officially welcoming you to the profession.

I sat in the drawing room, which seemed lifeless without my canine companions, and read Frederick's letter three times before the significance of what he had written sank in. If it was to be and the RCVS would process my application in a timely fashion, I would finally be acknowledged as Great Britain's and Ireland's first woman veterinary surgeon. More than two decades after I had finished my training, I could finally brandish a diploma. I would be Aleen I. Cust, MRCVS.

If the thieving thugs had not taken my whip along with my car, I would have held it and run my fingers over the engraving. Willie might not have pictured the circumstances when he gave it to me, but he never doubted that I would one day officially be a veterinary surgeon. I would, I resolved, follow up on Frederick's letter as soon as I arrived in Northumberland.

CHAPTER 34

1922
Athleague, Ireland

As I prepared to leave Fort Lyster for the last time, I recalled the depth of my misery when, forty-four years earlier, I'd said goodbye to Taffy and Ned at Cordangan. Life could have been repeating itself. Although this time my horses would accompany me to England, the anguish was just as keen. I was now even more tethered to Ireland than I had been as a girl. It had been on Irish soil that I had finally fulfilled my dream of working as a veterinary surgeon. The country, its animals, and its people had confirmed to me that I had chosen the best profession in the world. If I lost anything in the process, the things I had gained had made it all worthwhile. I had lived and worked among the Irish, whose love for their animals was as profound as mine. I had once again lost my heart—no, I had given it freely—to the hills, vales, rivers, forests, and fields I had come to know in Ireland as I'd ridden Nasser or steered Molly from farm to farm and village to village. It was in Ireland that I had loved and been loved in return. Indeed, it was another sad goodbye.

By the time I arrived at Newton Hall, my spirits had lifted somewhat. I had spent the journey setting out my plans to approach the Royal College to sit my final examination and receive my diploma. After decades of pushing the thought to the back of my mind and getting on with the business of being a veterinary surgeon, it was time for the RCVS to finally recognize and certify me as a professional.

It gave me a new sense of purpose and took my mind off what I had left behind in Roscommon. In fact, so distracted was I that it took me several moments to notice the tall figure standing next to Lady Widdrington on the stairs of Newton Hall when I pulled up at the house and climbed out the motorcar I had bought to replace the stolen one.

Freshly shaven and much thinner but rosy-cheeked as ever, it was Bertie. I looked from him to Lady Widdrington. She nodded and smiled.

"You doubted me," she called, smiling widely.

"My God, Bertie!" I said finally.

He laughed, shaking his head. "I am sorry I was late from the war, but I am glad I am here to welcome you home," he said, bounding down the stairs and taking me in his arms.

Days later, the RCVS council agreed that given my years of work and war record, I should undertake a single oral examination, which proved no trouble at all. My results were published in the *Veterinary Record* on December 23, 1922, along with those of seven other candidates—all men. At last, at a small ceremony at the college in London, I received my long-coveted diploma. Twenty-two years had passed since I had watched Fred Taylor, Andrew Spreull, and my other classmates receive their certificates, and now, among strange, very young men, I finally got mine.

When I returned to my hotel room and unrolled and inspected the certificate, I emitted an unladylike snort. The pre-printed *Mr.* on the form had been struck out in ink and replaced by an inelegantly scrawled *Miss*; the RCVS had not even bothered to get a new certificate printed. Even that did not diminish my satisfaction.

Later that evening, I attended a celebration hosted at the home of Frederick and his wife, Mary, for a small group of friends and colleagues from London.

"At last," said Frederick as I walked into the room. "A long-delayed and greatly deserved celebration."

"Thank you," I said, aware once more of the important role that absent others had played in helping me to realize my dream. I would raise a glass tonight to Orlando, Major Fitz, Dorothy, Professor Williams, and Willie, I thought.

I glanced around the room and saw that, although I had given my host my siblings' addresses, none of them were present.

Frederick was perceptive. "I am afraid I received no reply from either of your brothers or your sister. There are, however, others here you will be pleased to see."

He took my arm and propelled me into the dining room, where I was surprised to see that Lady Widdrington and Bertie had traveled from Northumberland to be there. They beamed as if my success was theirs, and indeed, in part, it was. The Widdringtons had been more of a family to me than my own. Lady Widdrington had consistently encouraged me not to let my skirts stand in the way of my ambitions.

"How do you feel?" she asked.

Bertie and Frederick looked on, waiting for my response.

I had given it some thought since receiving my diploma earlier in the day. Did the document make a difference to me? Not really. I had been a veterinary surgeon ever since Professor Williams had handed me the testimonial confirming I had completed my training and proven my competence in Edinburgh twenty-two years previously. I had been a veterinary surgeon when I worked with Willie at Castlestrange and later, alone, at Fort Lyster. I had been a veterinary surgeon when I had stroked the necks and sutured the wounds of hundreds of warhorses. The diploma did not make a difference to me, but I had made a difference to the profession. From now on, the RCVS would admit women into its ranks. Women were free to join the best profession in the world.

I smiled and gave a small bow. "I feel like Miss Aleen Cust, MRCVS."

AUTHOR'S NOTE

As I understand it, the purpose of writing historical fiction is to tell the stories of fascinating people and interesting times in a more entertaining manner than the information on public record might otherwise insist. The joy in creating such work comes from imagining and describing related thoughts, conversations, emotions, and relationships, the accuracy of which only the people involved could verify. Writing historical fiction is like reading between the lines of historical records and filling in the gaps with speculative delight. It also comes with the privilege of retrospection.

The most exciting historical fiction, in my opinion, is that which so seamlessly blends fact and imagination that readers do not distinguish between the two—and feel no compulsion to do so. Writing about Aleen Cust made this easy. Her story is so remarkable that it does not call for large-scale embellishment. In fact, it would be more expedient to describe the parts that *are* fictional than those that are fact. However, because, even after working on it for so long, I remain thrilled by how remarkable the true story of Aleen Cust is, I cannot resist emphasizing the facts here.

Aleen was born in Tipperary, Ireland, to the aristocratic English Cust family, and indeed, when she was ten, her father, a land agent, died shortly after placing his boot on a nun's grave. The locals did not disguise their satisfaction with what they believed to be holy retribution. The rest of the family left for England under something of a cloud.

Lady Mary Anne Cust—Aleen's paternal grandmother—was well known for her "way with animals" and, among other biological endeavors, wrote a book about cats and studied chameleons. Aleen believed she inherited her grandmother's love and understanding of animals, and she decided at a very young age that she wanted to be a veterinary surgeon.

Aleen's family was appalled by her ambitions. Her mother was a woman of the bedchamber for Queen Victoria, and her brother Charles was equerry to King George. They were ashamed of the notion of Aleen's working. It was her brother Orlando's untimely death that provided the financial means for her to study. Aleen's guardian, Major Widdrington, and his family provided the support Aleen did not receive from her own family. Lady Widdrington was a well-read and forthright woman who encouraged Aleen to fight for her independence and pursue a profession. Her daughter Dorothy Widdrington, who married British statesman Sir Edward Grey, was one of Aleen's closest friends until Dorothy's death after a cart accident in 1906.

The chaste nature of Dorothy and Edward's marriage has been written about elsewhere, with most speculation concluding that despite Dorothy's aversion to sex, their relationship was strong. Biographers have also noted that because many upper-class marriages were matches of convenience, it was not uncommon for sex to be found elsewhere at the time. It is possible Dorothy might have been diagnosed as autistic and hyper-sensitive to touch had she lived in another era. Biographers have also noted that Dorothy was taken care of by a particularly stern and aloof nursemaid when Cecilia Widdrington was ill for some time after giving birth. It is possible the lack of physical touch in her early development affected Dorothy for life. Despite Dorothy's untimely death, Aleen and Edward remained lifelong friends.

Aleen was briefly engaged to Dorothy's youngest brother, Bertie. The actual circumstances around their engagement and why it was broken off were known only to them, and as such, my version is imagined.

That Aleen used the surname *Custance* when she began her studies is historically accurate, as is the matter of her being penniless during her student days in Edinburgh. She did indeed go running to warm up before climbing into bed each night. The "meat fight" described in this book is based on actuality, as is Aleen's internship with Mr. Spreull in Dundee.

It is fact, too, that Professor William Williams was among her preeminent supporters. He not only stood up for Aleen against the Royal College of Veterinary Surgeons (RCVS) but also found her a place to work alongside Willie Byrne in Roscommon, Ireland.

Unfortunately, the resistance and relentless efforts of the RCVS to prevent Aleen from joining the profession are factual. These details were researched over several years by Connie M. Ford, MBE, MRCVS, and recounted in detail in 1990 in her book, *Aleen Cust, Veterinary Surgeon: Britain's First Woman Vet*. I am deeply indebted to Connie's fascination with Aleen and her meticulous attention to detail about the series of hurdles that Aleen faced in her endeavors to be admitted to the veterinary profession.

The outrage led by the Roman Catholic clergy that ensued when Aleen arrived in Athleague to work with Willie is also based on fact. There is evidence that the priest was more accepting of her after she saved his horse.

What is not on public record is the exact nature of the relationship between Willie and Aleen. While there were rumors that the couple lived as husband and wife—though they never married nor resided in the same house—and that they even had children together, the precise details of their relationship were known only to them. The version offered in this book is largely the product of my imagination.

However, it is fact that Willie was widely admired as a friend, nationalist, philosopher, poet, and veterinary surgeon and that Aleen was one of several hundred people who attended his funeral when he died suddenly in 1910. There is to this day in Roscommon town a monument that was erected in Willie's memory. Engraved alongside his name and dates of birth and death is the line "Erected by a few friends in affectionate remembrance."

Aleen's self-funded expedition to France during the war under the auspices of the YMCA is also factual, as is the account of her work on the Western Front and her return to England due to her ill health at the end of the war. The matter of Bertie's disappearance at the end of the war is not historically recorded. What is fact is that while he and Aleen remained friends for life, Bertie eventually married Enid Ford. Aleen never married—nor did she ever reconcile with her family.

By 1924, Aleen had sold her property in Ireland and settled in Hampshire, England. Although she was only fifty-six, her health, possibly due to the influenza she contracted during the war, was poor. She continued to work here and there and attended association meetings, but Aleen did not set up another veterinary practice after leaving Ireland. She resumed breeding Pomeranians and added Cocker Spaniels to her kennels. She kept two horses and eventually, after decades of extreme riding and hunting side-saddle, swapped her skirts for jodhpurs and rode astride.

Aleen died of a heart attack shortly after attending to a bleeding dog while visiting friends in Jamaica in 1937. She was sixty-eight. Despite the years of bigotry she had endured from the RCVS, she left the professional body £5,000, which she stipulated should be invested, and the income used for a scholarship for veterinary research.

The year 2022 marks the centenary of Aleen's finally receiving her diploma—pre-printed with *Mr.* struck out and *Miss* added by hand—from the RCVS. In 2020, the RCVS was rated by Great Place to Work as one of the top five medium-size organizations for women to work for in the United Kingdom.

In an article addressed to other women veterinary surgeons, written for the *Veterinary Record* of April 7, 1934, Aleen concluded, "I take great interest in all of you and in your careers and successes, and my wish for you is that you, my Women Colleagues, may all feel as I do after a lifetime—that the profession you have chosen is *the* Best Profession in the World."

READING GROUP
GUIDE

❧

1. How did the time Aleen spent at Newton Hall in the company of Lady and Major Widdrington and Dorothy influence the woman she would grow up to become?

2. Aleen's landlady in Edinburgh, Mrs. Logan, at one point says, "It is possible to outgrow family, you know." Do you agree or disagree with this statement?

3. One of the reasons the RCVS gave for wanting to prohibit women from becoming veterinarian surgeons was that they lacked the physical strength to do the job, the same excuse used by the U.S. military to prevent women from enlisting in certain areas. Do you think this is a valid reason women should be excluded from some professional endeavors?

4. Even though Aleen's family tried with all their might to keep Aleen from pursuing her dreams and didn't support her at all, she was still concerned with drawing attention to her case and further humiliating her family. To the very end, she still hoped for reconciliation with them. If you were in her position, what would you have done?

5. Aleen scored the highest marks of her class at New Veterinary College. But rather than that accomplishment being a cause for celebration, her classmate and the principal recommended adjusting her scores so as not to call attention to her proficiency from the

RCVS. Do you agree with the decision to do so? Do you think it was necessary? Do you think the outcome would have been any different had she submitted her actual scores?

6. Aleen had many advocates along the way who supported and encouraged her to pursue her dream despite the obstacles set before her—Professor Williams and the New Veterinary College, Mr. Andrew Spreull, the Widdringtons, and Willie Byrne. Do you think she would have accomplished her goal of becoming a veterinary surgeon without their backing?

7. Even today, when children are asked what they want to be when they grow up, one of the most cited careers is veterinarian. Has that ever been a dream job for you? What did you want to be when you grew up, and how did your answer then differ from what you do today?

8. Discuss how Aleen was able to win over and earn the respect of her peers and clients. How would this have been different had she been a man?

9. Aleen and Willie kept their relationship a secret, mostly because of their differences in religion and the social statuses of their upbringing. Do you still see people facing these kinds of barriers today?

10. Dorothy Widdrington expressed to Aleen that she was not sure she wanted to marry, that she wanted to do something else with her life. Ultimately, she did marry though. Why do you think she decided to do so? Do you think it was a personal choice? Pressure from her family or from society? Or some other reason?

11. Bertie offered to marry Aleen when he discovered she was pregnant with Willie's child. She initially accepted but then reneged after she lost the child. Do you agree with Aleen's decisions? Or do you think

Aleen should have committed to Bertie? If she had married Bertie, how would her life and career have been affected?

12. Were you surprised that none of Aleen's family—her brothers or sister—were willing to reconcile with Aleen and that they didn't show up to the celebration when she received her official RCVS certificate?

13. The word *ambitious* is often used as a negative trait when applied to women but a positive one when referring to men. What other attributes or descriptive words can you think of that connote something different for women than for men?

A CONVERSATION
WITH THE AUTHOR

❧

How did you first encounter Aleen's story? What made you decide to write about her?

Like countless other animal lovers, I fantasized about becoming a veterinary surgeon when I was a child. Instead, I became a writer. However, my fascination with the profession endured. I wanted to write about it from a female perspective and began researching the history of women veterinary surgeons, which led me to Aleen. Her story gripped me immediately. I understood her love of animals, and I was fascinated by her determination and appalled by what she had to endure to realize her ambition. Hers was unlike any other story I had encountered, and once I knew it, I could not imagine *not* writing about it. It had all the ingredients I relate to and love: animals, a strong, driven woman, a rural life, and a positive outcome. How could I not write it?

Tell us about your research process when writing this book.

Among the first things I did was contact my Irish veterinary surgeon friend, Richard Lyons, who practiced in Britain for most of his career. He helped me access information that would have been difficult to find otherwise. I tracked down a copy of Connie M. Ford's out-of-print biography on Aleen and read it and everything else I could find about her and veterinary surgery in the late 1800s and early 1900s. In addition, I read everything I could about Aleen's family, the Widdringtons, Queen Victoria, and Edward Grey. Although I have been to Ireland, Scotland, and England, my research also took me on in-depth virtual trips to Tipperary, Shropshire, Cheshire, Northumberland (Newton Hall is now a wedding venue, and the gardens of Fallodon Hall can be visited at certain times), Edinburgh, London, and Roscommon.

What was the most surprising thing you learned about Aleen while doing research for this book?

I was struck by how loyal Aleen was to her family, despite the fact that they were ashamed of her desire to be educated and to work. They repeatedly spurned her efforts to reconcile. She chose not to pursue her case against the RCVS in London to protect her mother and siblings. Despite their heartlessness, Aleen longed for her family's approval and admiration. It reminded me that even the most single-minded individuals want love and acceptance.

At a time when familial loyalty and adherence to societal and gender standards were of utmost importance, why do you think Aleen chose the path she did?

She was motivated by her love of animals and by her desire to do something that would give her life purpose. Although it was extraordinary for aristocratic women of that era to do so, she wanted to work. Aleen could not imagine finding fulfillment in being a wife and mother. It is possible too that having competed with her brothers as a child and having enjoyed schooling that most girls would not have received at that time, she was driven to prove that women were as capable as men.

In both *The Invincible Miss Cust* and in your contemporary novel *The Wilderness Between Us*, it's evident you have a great love of animals and nature. Where does this love of the natural world stem from?

I grew up on a farm and was raised to love animals and nature. I enjoy the quiet of the countryside where the nights are dark and the seasons are distinctive. I am at peace among animals, who have always been central to my life. My maternal grandmother, in particular, taught me how to understand and respect them, and showed me how wonderful it is to befriend animals.

What was your path to becoming a writer? Did you always know you wanted to be a novelist?

I've dreamed about writing fiction for as long as I can remember, but I worked as a journalist and columnist for almost thirty years before mustering up the courage to do so. Somehow, the idea of writing a book terrified me. In 2017, I wrote a children's chapter book based on the story of my grandmother's friendship with a vervet monkey called Nicko. It was a tale I had grown up with and was easy to write. I think of it as my "gateway book" because it took away the fear and showed me that writing books was not only possible but also most enjoyable.

What do your writing space and process look like? Do you outline before you write? Or do you let the story progress organically as you write?

I am lucky to have a spacious office with large windows that look onto the mountains in Cape Town and, if you peer through the trees, the Atlantic Ocean. It is my favorite place in the house. Since I've worked as a journalist all my life, my approach to writing is businesslike. I keep work hours and am driven by deadlines, even when they are self-imposed. I am a planner and typically outline my stories by sketching messy mind maps. I also write a synopsis before I begin. However, I do not feel compelled to stick to the plans. Part of the pleasure of writing fiction is going where the story and the characters take you wherever possible. Unlike with most journalism, there's a playfulness to it, which is wonderful.

What books are you reading these days?

I have been reading a great deal of historical fiction recently, including books by Marie Benedict, Audrey Blake, and Tracey Enerson Wood. I have also enjoyed literary fiction by Sarah Winman (*Still Life*), Elizabeth Strout (*Oh William!*), Rachel Joyce (*Miss Benson's Beetle*) and Anne Griffin (*Listening Still*). Reading gives me great joy, and I am forever grateful for the diversity and immense and bottomless creativity of the world's authors.

BIBLIOGRAPHY

Chance, Cecilia. *The Widdrington Women and Their Eminent Men.* Phillimore & Co., 2010.

Cust, Lady Mary Anne. *The Cat: Its History, Diseases and Management.* Dranes, 1880.

Ford, Connie M. *Aleen Cust, Veterinary Surgeon: Britain's First Woman Vet.* Biopress, 1990.

Grey, Sir Edward. *The Cottage Book: The Undiscovered Country Diary of an Edwardian Statesman.* Edited by Michael Waterhouse. Orion Publishing, 2001.

Ross, Ian. "Aleen Cust: Forebears." Sutori.com. November 29, 2018. https://www.sutori.com/en/story/aleen-cust-forebears—NNa7LHjAbfJyGoWwii4fDwcv.

Vivash Jones, Bruce. "Against All Odds: The Story of Aleen Cust." *Veterinary Record.* September 29, 2018.

Warwick, C. M. and A. A. Macdonald. "The New Veterinary College Edinburgh, 1873 to 1904." *Veterinary Record.* September 27, 2003.

Waterhouse, Michael. *Edwardian Requiem: A Life of Sir Edward Grey.* Biteback Publishing, 2013.

ACKNOWLEDGMENTS

I came across Aleen Cust after a chat with the brainstormer extraordinaire in my family, Claudia Hitzeroth. As I girl, I dreamed of becoming a veterinary surgeon, and as an adult, I was intrigued by how lionized veterinary surgeons are by animal lovers, myself included. I wanted to write a book with a veterinary surgeon as the central character. Claudia and I chatted about how the challenges of being a woman veterinary surgeon could make an interesting story. Her ideas prompted me to research the history of women veterinary surgeons.

The moment I discovered Aleen Cust, I knew that I wanted to tell *her* story. I've been a writer all my life, and no story excited me more. Thank you, Claudia, for nudging me in the right direction and for your and Sebastiaan's unwavering support at every juncture in the journey.

In addition to my family, my friends have been superbly supportive. I thank them all and dare to name a few. To Marianne Marsh, thank you for listening and encouraging my writing endeavors for more than two decades of dog walks in the mountain. To my writing group friends, Gail Gilbride, Peter Horszowski, and Paul Morris, who shared my interest in Aleen's story, urged me to write it, and offered their critique, an enormous thank-you. Thank you, too, to my most energetic cheerleader, Karen Stark, for always knowing what to say to quell my doubts and propel me onwards.

Certainly, many have supported and encouraged me with this book. No friend, though, has been more helpful than Richard Lyons, MVB, MRCVS. Not only is he a recently retired—but as passionate as ever—veterinary surgeon with more than forty years of experience, but Richard is also Irish. He helped me access information I would not have known existed without him.

Richard also helped me treat dogs, hoist horses, save cows, and deworm sheep. He guided me through the technical aspects of the story and on all things Irish. He reminded me to check on the Pomeranians and tried to convince me to allow Aleen to deck one of her detractors. Richard's love of animals, his knowledge, and enthusiasm for Aleen's story and the project were constant and invaluable. Add to that his love of reading and his natural aptitude for literature, and I cannot imagine having a better adviser. Thank you, Rich, for sharing my excitement, answering my many questions, going through the drafts with such a keen and involved eye, and championing the book at every turn.

Another person who shared my excitement for Aleen's story and without whom *The Invincible Miss Cust* would not have become what it has is my editor, Erin McClary. I will never forget waking up to an email from her saying Sourcebooks was interested in making an offer on the manuscript. Her enthusiasm for the story was palpable across oceans and continents. The rest of the day passed in a blur. As I got to know Erin, I not only appreciated her expertise and energy as an editor, as well as her kind yet firm approach, but also learned that she too had imagined herself becoming a veterinary surgeon when she was a girl. I knew I could not have wished for a finer editor. Thank you, Erin and Sourcebooks, for providing the perfect home for Aleen's extraordinary story.

I also thank my agent, Jill Marsal, whom I knew I would like when I read in her Twitter biography that she loves animals. Thank you, Jill, for reading the manuscript over a weekend, believing in it, teaching me how to write a convincing pitch, holding my hand, and concluding a deal that would see another day pass in a happy blur for me.

A special thanks to Jan-Lucas de Vos, who not only kept me fed and exercised as I wrote but endured (and continues to endure) endless conversations about Aleen Cust. Thank you for your love and support.

Finally, a posthumous thanks to Aleen Cust for never giving up on her dream despite the sacrifices and for paving the way for other women veterinary surgeons. Thank you, too, for living such a remarkable life, which will not only continue to inspire others for hundreds of years but also motivated me to write this book.

ABOUT THE AUTHOR

© J-L de Vos

Penny Haw worked as a journalist and columnist for more than three decades, writing for many leading South African newspapers and magazines before yielding to a lifelong yearning to create fiction. Her stories feature remarkable women, illustrate her love for nature, and explore the interconnectedness of all living things. *The Invincible Miss Cust* is Penny's debut historical fiction. She lives near Cape Town with her husband and three dogs, all of whom are well walked.